... mes bestselling author of the Otherworld series, as well as the young adult trilogy Darkest Powers, the Darkness Rising trilogy, and the Nadia Stafford series. She lives in rural Ontario, Canada.

Praise for Kelley Armstrong and the Nadia Stafford series

"Armstrong is a talented and evocative writer who knows well how to balance the elements of good, suspenseful fiction, and her stories evoke poignancy, action, humour, and suspense." —*The Globe and Mail*

"Taking a break from her Otherworld series, the hugely talented Armstrong delves into a truly shadowy world where honor and morals are set to a different frequency. In Nadia Stafford, she's created an anti-heroine whose motivations are convoluted, yet utterly gripping. Take a walk on the dark side—where contract killers become both the bait and the hunter of a vicious serial killer." —*Romantic Times Book Reviews*

"[*Exit Strategy* is] original, dark and gritty, with enough humanity to keep you caring about its antiheroes and enough suspense to keep you turning the pages." —Cody McFadyen, author of *Shadow Man*

"Armstrong has a definite talent for sensual descriptions." —*National Post*

"*Exit Strategy* is a perfect suspense novel for the summer. It is fast paced and high in action with a colorful cast of characters that will leave you wondering who you can trust. There is a wisp of romance, but that takes a backseat to the main events in the novel. . . . It is one adventure not to be passed up for fans of suspense thrillers." —*Curled Up with a Good Book*

BOOKS BY KELLEY ARMSTRONG

The Otherworld Series

Bitten
Stolen
Dime Store Magic
Industrial Magic
Haunted
Broken
No Humans Involved
Personal Demon
Living with the Dead
Frostbitten
Waking the Witch
Spell Bound
13

The Nadia Stafford Series

Exit Strategy
Made to Be Broken
Wild Justice

The Cainsville Series

Omens

Collections

Men of the Otherworld
Tales of the Otherworld
Werewolves
Spellcasters

KELLEY
ARMSTRONG

WILD
JUSTICE

A PLUME BOOK

PLUME

Published by the Penguin Group
Penguin Group (USA) LLC
375 Hudson Street
New York, New York 10014

USA | Canada | UK | Ireland | Australia
New Zealand | India | South Africa | China
penguin.com
A Penguin Random House Company

First published by Vintage Canada, a division of Random House
Canada Limited, Toronto, 2013.
Published by Plume, a member of Penguin Group (USA) LLC,
2013

P REGISTERED TRADEMARK—MARCA REGISTRADA

CIP data is available.
ISBN 978-0-452-29881-1

Printed in the United States of America
10 9 8 7 6 5 4 3 2 1

Original design by Terri Nimmo

For Jeff

CHAPTER 1

Alan Wilde was supposed to die at 8 p.m. on October 17, 2007. It was right there, on my agenda, and I am nothing if not precise about my schedule, even if it only exists in my head.

I was lying on a cliff overlooking docks. The sign called it a marina. Having seen actual marinas, I'd disagree. It was a collection of battered and rotted wharfs mooring a collection of battered and rusted boats. The boats might not have been yachts, but they were all someone's pride and joy, with names like *Buoys & Gulls* and *Seas the Day*. Owned by folks who'd dreamed of retiring "up north" and spending lazy days pretending to fish.

Wilde's boat was not meant for fishing. Or relaxing. From what I'd seen in my two days of surveillance, it was meant for racing up and down the coastline, setting canoeists and kayakers cursing as they struggled against the boat's wake. Tonight he was due to arrive at eight with his girlfriend, having told his wife he was going for a moonlight ride alone.

So at 7:50 I was settled in, lying on my stomach, sniper rifle at the ready. The docks were quiet. This was Michigan cottage country, and it was too late in the year for tourists, too late in the day for locals. When a car pulled in, I expected Wilde's Mustang. Instead it was his winter beater—an ancient Corolla. The Mustang must have been out of commission. Not surprising given that I'd seen him fussing with it yesterday.

Then a second set of headlights turned into the tiny parking lot. Alan Wilde's bright yellow Mustang. The Corolla driver's door opened and out climbed Mrs. Wilde.

The Mustang paused at the edge of the lot. Mrs. Wilde didn't notice the hesitation. She was pulling her seat forward to get their three-year-old daughter, Hannah, out of her booster.

Wilde had time for a getaway. *Whoops, I didn't see you there, honey. I realized I'd left something at the shop and went back.*

He wouldn't even need to worry about his wife phoning and telling him she was there. Rose Wilde no longer had a cell phone. He'd taken it away after their last fight, when he'd dragged her out of the car, ten miles from town, and left her there. She had used her phone to call her father to come get her, which completely defeated the purpose of the lesson. So Wilde confiscated it.

That meant he could get away. But after a moment's pause, he continued into the lot. Through my binoculars, I could see his girlfriend in the passenger seat. He knew his wife would, too. He just didn't care. He roared up beside the Corolla and threw open the car door.

"What the hell are you doing here with the baby?" he shouted. I could hear him even without my earpiece amplifier. "Do you know what time it is?"

"Sh-she's sick," Rose said, still standing by her back door. "She's running a fever, and I wanted to know if I can take her to the doctor."

"Bullshit! You snuck out here—"

"She's burning up, Alan. I don't give a damn about you and your whores—"

The girlfriend got out. "Who you calling a whore, bitch?"

Rose ignored her and tried talking to her husband. The girl kept yelling at her. Wilde did, too.

I watched through the scope. Wilde hadn't moved since he got out of the car. I had a perfect line on him. A clean shot, with no chance of hitting the girlfriend or Rose. Just a squeeze of the trigger and . . .

And I'd shoot a man in front of his wife and child.

I could argue that Rose would be happy to see her husband dead. It was her only way out of this marriage. She'd tried to leave twice. The first time, he kidnapped their daughter. The second time, she'd been pregnant and when he found her, he'd punched her in the stomach and she'd lost the baby. Going to the police hadn't helped. When he was released from custody, he beat her so badly she needed painkillers for weeks, which he soon replaced with higher octane ones. He got her hooked, then convinced her that her addiction would mean she'd never get custody of Hannah.

Yes, when it came to abusive husbands, you couldn't get much worse than Alan Wilde. Which is why I agreed to the job. Rose wasn't the one who'd hired me—her father had—but I'd seen nothing to suggest that Alan's death wouldn't be the best thing that ever happened to her. That did not mean she'd actually want to witness it. And she sure as hell wouldn't want their daughter to.

So I waited. Finally, Rose strapped Hannah back into her booster and got into the driver's seat. "I'm taking her to the doctor," she said.

"The hell you are!" Wilde stormed toward her car.

"How the fuck are you going to pay for it? Call your daddy? If you do, I swear—"

The car leapt back, tires squealing. Wilde barely got out of the way in time.

"You bitch!" he yelled. "Don't you dare . . ."

I didn't catch the rest of the threat. I was busy lining up my shot, waiting for the moment when Rose's car was out of sight. Just another few seconds . . .

The girlfriend walked over to Wilde, trying to calm him—and stepped right into my line of fire. Wilde pushed her aside and headed for the driver's door. She followed, staying between me and him.

I could make the shot, but there was a chance I'd hit her instead. I remained in position, hoping she'd move. But she kept pace until he got to the driver's door. He climbed inside and peeled away, leaving her in the parking lot.

CHAPTER 2

I'd missed my hit. It happened. Not often, thankfully, but no amount of planning can cover every contingency. I'd need to stay in Michigan to finish the job, so as I walked the two miles to my rental car, I called home.

Home for me is a wilderness lodge northeast of Toronto. I'm the owner, operator, backcountry guide, shooting-range instructor, and entertainment director. Hell, some days I'm even the busboy and chambermaid. It's that kind of business.

In October, we rarely have guests off-weekend, which is why I'd picked midweek for the job. Ostensibly, I'm taking a little personal R&R. Do my caretakers, the Waldens, believe that? They've been with me long enough to know I don't do R&R, as much as they would like me to, but they just wish me a good trip and assure me everything will be fine in my absence.

Now I called to say that I'd be gone a little longer. Emma answered the phone. Her husband, Owen, never does—telephones require talking, and the only man I know who talks less is my mentor, Jack.

"I'm thinking of taking a couple of extra days," I said. "How are the bookings?"

"Same as they were when you called last night, Nadia. Three rooms, seven guests. Not one has requested range access or shooting lessons or rock climbing or white-water canoeing, probably because they're all over sixty and have learned common sense. It's past Thanksgiving. Everyone who wanted a fall-colors getaway did it on the long weekend. Also, they're forecasting snow."

"Already?"

"I'm sure it'll just be a sprinkling, but I wouldn't be surprised if we have cancellations. You know what idiots drivers are in a first snow. Go enjoy your vacation."

"I will. And don't spoil Scout too much. Last time I came back, I thought she'd swallowed a beach ball."

"That's Owen," she said. "Damned fool's a sucker for sad puppy-dog eyes."

"Maybe you should try it on him."

She laughed, and we ran over a few business items, then I reached the car and signed off.

One call down. One to go. I took a different phone from the glove box. It was a toy from a hitman friend, Felix—the same guy who gave me the amplifier. The phone is a sweet piece of tech and probably damned expensive. It was untraceable, of course, but also came with built-in voice modulation, GPS blocking, interception alert, and a number randomizer. In short, it was perfect for calling to report a failed hit.

I wasn't phoning the client. I had no contact with him. I work exclusively for Paul Tomassini, nephew to the don of a New York Mafia family. This wasn't their job, but one that came to Paul himself, as a special request from a connected friend whom Rose Wilde's father had contacted. Paul knew it was my kind of work, so he'd put me on it.

"It's Dee," I said when he answered.

That's my professional name. Jack's idea, proving that the guy has not an iota of imagination. His own nom de guerre? Jack.

Paul did know my real name. He'd been a regular at the lodge when he invited me into my side business, knowing I was good with a gun and, at the time, I'd really needed cash.

"It was a bust," I said, phrasing it carefully. "His better half showed up, with the little one."

"Shit." A brief pause. "You trying again?"

"Of course."

"Good. I'll let him know."

"Can you tell him he should check in on her, too? There was a bit of a scene." I explained what had happened.

"What the fuck? Wife needs permission to take the kid to the doctor?"

"She needs permission for everything. She doesn't have her own cell phone, car, credit cards, access to the bank account . . ."

He let out a string of profanity. "And he waved his side dish in her face? Fucking bastard."

"You'll let your friend know? If hubby is pissed off with her . . ."

"He might beat the shit outta her again. Yeah, I'll call now. Make sure he knows what's up."

In any job, it's nice to have colleagues you can call for a postmortem when things go wrong. A shoulder to whine on doesn't hurt, either. That's one thing I'd loved about my former career as a cop. There were always guys I could talk to.

There's no support group for hitmen.

I was lucky. I had a network. Very small, of course— this is a career that caters to loners. There's Jack, of course . . . who'd be the last person I'd call for a pick-me-up. In person, yes. On the phone, I might as well talk to myself.

Then there's Jack's mentor, Evelyn. I could imagine her response. *Why the hell didn't you take the damned shot?* My reluctance to traumatize the wife and child would be silly sentimentality to her. I was paid to kill, so I should have killed.

There was only one person I could talk this out with. Quinn. A U.S. marshal who moonlights as a vigilante hitman. Quinn understands the ex-cop part of me that Jack doesn't really get, just as Jack understands the part of me that isn't like Quinn, the part still bleeding from my cousin's murder twenty years ago.

If this happened a month ago Quinn would expect me to call. He'd be pissed if I didn't. Now I'd probably get as far as "hello" before he hung up.

After a year of flirting and circling each other, Quinn and I started dating six months ago. It had been good. Better than good. It made me wonder why the hell I'd put him off so long. It was a long-distance relationship—he lived in Virginia—but we got together at least one weekend a month.

Six weeks ago, he'd asked me to his cousin's wedding. I shouldn't have been surprised. For months, he'd been joking about dragging me to this family dinner or that family party. I realized now it'd been the kind of fake joking where you're hoping for an encouraging response. Anyway, I missed the signals so I'd said no to the wedding. It escalated to a fight. He wanted more; I wasn't ready to give more and wasn't sure I ever would be. He hung up.

A week later, he came to the lodge. He'd done that once before, and Jack tore a strip out of him. Quinn knew better than to show up there when I hadn't introduced him to that part of my world. Obviously waylaying me at home had not smoothed things over. We fought. He accused me of wanting nothing more than friendship with sex. It got ugly. He said we were through and stormed out.

The hard truth? He wasn't wrong. I did want friendship. I did want sex. That's it. We led separate lives, and as happy as I was with him, I didn't see that ever changing for me. I didn't want to meet his family, because I knew how close he was to them and I knew that was the first step onto a road I wasn't willing to travel.

It wasn't really the hackneyed "friends with benefits." There was more. It just wasn't what he wanted.

After that, he'd gone silent. No calls, no e-mail, not even a text. I phoned a couple of times. He didn't answer. It was over. So there was no calling him tonight. There was no calling anyone.

Normally, I'm up by dawn and out for my jog, but after a rough night, I needed my rest, so I turned off my alarm and dozed fitfully until nine. I ran fifteen kilometers after that, working off excess job frustration. Then I brought breakfast back to my motel room and waited to start tracking Wilde again. By midafternoon he'd leave work for the day, and I'd be waiting to follow him, figure out when and how to finish this.

When my "business" phone rang just past noon, it was Paul Tomassini, which was odd. That's one advantage of working for the mob. They don't panic and pester you for updates. I wondered if the client was having second thoughts. Damn I hoped not. As a cop, I'd seen enough domestic violence to know it was only a matter of time before Rose was lying on a morgue slab. I'd much rather see him there.

"It's me," Paul said when I answered. "Thought I'd hear from you."

Ah, so, the client was just getting antsy. "Tell him it's under control. I can't promise it today, but it'll get done this week."

Silence. Then, "Have you read the paper this morning, Dee?"

My hand clenched the phone. "No. Why?"

"Go read it. Call me back."

The story made the front page of the regional paper: "Local Businessman Kills Wife, Self." The subheading: "Preschool Daughter in Intensive Care."

Alan Wilde had caught up with Rose and Hannah. He'd cornered them in the hospital parking garage. People had heard them fighting. They heard it and hurried on their way, not wanting to get involved.

Wilde had tried to stop Rose from taking Hannah inside. He'd threatened her. Then there'd been a gun. Rose's gun—that's what the paper claimed, quoting an anonymous source who said her father bought it for her after the last incident. No one knew exactly what happened, but I could figure it out. She'd pulled the gun and told Wilde she was taking their daughter to see a doctor. He'd wrested the gun away and used it on her. According to the article, he'd shot Rose point-blank. In front of their daughter. That's when, according to some who heard the shot, the little girl started to scream. Another shot. Hannah stopped crying.

The person who heard called 911, then ran to notify a security guard. By the time help arrived, Wilde had turned the gun on himself.

Rose Wilde was dead. Her daughter was clinging to life. It was my fault.

When Paul Tomassini called back, I let it ring. He

hung up and tried again. I continued ignoring it until someone pounded on my motel door, telling me to answer my goddamned phone. I turned it off and tucked it into my bag. Then I walked out the door, turned toward the highway, and kept going.

CHAPTER 3

I walked for hours. Dusk came as a shock, and I snapped out of my stupor to stare, disbelieving, at the sunset. But it was like rousing from sleep just long enough to check the clock before falling under again.

During the day, a few cars had slowed to offer me a lift. I'd waved them off. After sunset, when another one rumbled along the gravel behind me, I stepped onto the grassy shoulder. It pulled up alongside me, passenger window rolling down.

"Get in the car."

My hand instinctively slid under my jacket to my gun.

"Get in the fucking car."

I heard the faint brogue and stopped walking.

The car was a nondescript economy model, the cheapest kind you can rent. Through the lowered passenger window, I caught the smell of cigarette smoke, a familiar brand, and I thought . . . *You're not supposed to smoke in a rental car.* Quite possibly the stupidest, most irrelevant thing I could worry about at the moment.

"Nadia?" The door slammed. "Get the fuck in the car."

I glanced over, my mind still swimming upward toward full consciousness. I saw a man. A couple inches under six feet. Average build. Angular features. Wavy black hair threaded with silver.

"Jack?"

I stepped backward.

"Nadia . . ." His voice was low. Telling me not to bolt. Warning me he sure as hell didn't want to have to run after me, not after he'd come from god-knows-where to find me.

You're not real, I thought. *You can't be. I'm hallucinating.*

His hand caught my elbow, holding me still, dark eyes boring into mine, the faint smell of cigarette smoke riding a soft sigh.

"Fuck." Another sigh. "Nadia? Can you hear me?"

He took me by the shoulders and steered me to the car. The next thing I knew, I was in the passenger seat and he was pulling the car back onto the road.

"I'm sorry," I said.

The tires chirped as the car lurched off the shoulder. "Things went south last night? Should have called."

"I didn't want to bother you." I looked out at the passing scenery and hiccuped a short laugh. "Which I suppose would have been a lot less bother than this. I'm sorry." I paused. "Was it Paul?"

"Paul called Evelyn. She called me."

"I'm sorry."

"Stop saying that." A hard look my way. "What the fuck were you thinking? Didn't even tell Quinn."

"Evelyn called Quinn?"

"I did."

"I'm sor—"

He cut me off with another look. I *was* sorry, for this, of course, and especially for him having to call Quinn. I'll be generous and just say they don't get along.

"Why didn't *you* call Quinn?" Jack said. "Thought you and him—"

"Not anymore."

He looked over sharply. "Since when?"

I shrugged. "About a month ago."

"Fuck." He gripped the steering wheel tighter. "Didn't know about that. Don't know about this. Never even knew you had a hit. Why?"

"Didn't think—" I stopped myself and started again, trying not to copy his speech pattern. "I'd have told you about Quinn the next time you called. As for the hit, it seemed straightforward."

"And last night? After it went south. You didn't think to call?"

Yes, I did think to call. You're the first person I thought to call. But getting in touch with you isn't like just picking up the phone and dialing. It's a process. Call, leave a message, wait—sometimes days—for you to get your damned messages. And even then, I might as well be talking to voice mail. I'd tell you the hit went bad and you'd say, "Not your fault." Three words. That would be the entirety of the conversation, and I'd hang up feeling foolish, like I'd bothered you.

A half hour later, the car turned and I looked up to see we were pulling into a roadside motel.

"Oh," I said. "This isn't my—"

"Yeah. Found yours. Twenty fucking miles back. Brought your stuff."

"I hid my passport—"

"Got it." He nodded at the motel. "Gonna check in. You need rest. I come back, you'll be here?"

"I wasn't trying to run away from you before, Jack. I was confused." I rubbed my face. "I don't need to rest.

I should head home. If you can just take me back to my
rental car—"

"Car's gone. Phoned it in."

"Then I'll rent another and—"

"You'll stay here while I check in. You bolt . . . ?"

Normally, I'd joke, "You'll shoot me?" and he'd
make some wry retort. He glanced at me, as if waiting.
When I said nothing, he reached over and opened the
glove box, then tossed a pack of cigarettes onto my
lap.

"Have one. Won't be long." He opened the door,
then glanced back. "Can smoke in here. Already did."

I fingered the package of cigarettes. Jack's brand.
Irish imports. I used to wonder if it really was his
brand, or an affectation, like the slight brogue, present-
ing a fake background. He really is Irish, originally, at
least. The brogue only comes out with those he trusts.
Same as the cigarettes.

He's also usually careful about doing things like
smoking in rental cars. It makes him memorable, like
the cigarette brand. If Jack had a hitman motto, it
would be "stay invisible." With fewer syllables, and
maybe a "fuck" thrown in for good measure.

So smoking in the car meant something. So did the
plastic drink cup lid overflowing with butts—he's been
down to a cigarette or so a day since I've known him.
Jack was stressed. Worried I'd gone off the rails and
now I'd do something stupid and put him at risk. He'd
been driving around for hours, looking for me and
working his way through a pack of cigarettes.

I emptied the makeshift ashtray. I'm not good with
messes. When I'm already anxious, I'm really not good
with them. As I returned from the garbage, he was
coming back.

"I really should go home," I said as he approached. "I'm fine. Crisis averted. If you'll just take me to—"

"Room twelve. Go."

I leaned on the car roof, looking at him. "I'm serious, Jack. I know you have better things to—"

"Nope. Got nothing. Room twelve. Go."

Once inside I took off my jacket. Jack noticed my gun with a grunt of satisfaction.

"Yes, even during a meltdown, I don't wander empty roads unarmed." I sat on the end of the bed. "I know you don't want me to keep telling you I'm sorry, but I don't know what else to say. You shouldn't have had to do this."

"Didn't have to. Chose to. Owed you anyway. You did it for me."

"At least you had the sense to stay in your motel room."

"No choice. Wouldn't have gotten far."

Last May, I'd been the one getting a call from Evelyn. Jack had broken his ankle on a job and was holed up in a motel outside Buffalo. He was too stubborn to ask for help, so she wanted me to fetch him back to my lodge to recuperate. I'd walked into a room full of cigarette smoke, and thought something had gone wrong on a hit. It hadn't. Jack only hurt his ankle in the escape.

The problem was what it meant: that this was a job for young men and he was almost fifty. Retirement was coming. That was tough. A contact of his had retired too late, his reputation shot to shit by the time he went. Jack didn't want that. Yet he understood the impulse to keep working. This was his life. There wasn't a retirement plan.

"So we're even." He pulled a chair toward the bed. "Wanna talk about it?"

I shook my head.

"Too bad." He settled in. "You didn't do anything wrong. What happened to his wife and little girl? His fault. Wilde's. Not yours."

"I could have taken the shot. It was a failure of nerve—"

"Not in front of the kid. Even at my worst, I wouldn't have done that."

"I could have shot him after they left. If I hit the girlfriend, well, that's her own fault for hooking up with a guy like Wilde."

He gave me a hard look that said he wouldn't dignify that with a response. I would never have taken that shot.

"I didn't even call Paul until I was back to the car," I said. "I phoned Emma first, and chatted away about the lodge while Wilde was going after his wife and child. Her father could have gotten there and saved her—"

"Never left the house."

I frowned at him.

"Paul called the father," he said. "Told him what happened. Father phoned his daughter's house. Left a message. That's it. Wouldn't have mattered *when* you called. Never left his goddamned house."

"Which means I didn't explain the situation clearly enough."

"What situation? Same shit Wilde's been pulling for years. Father knew that. You want to blame someone? Blame the idiot who gave her the weapon. *Here's a fucking gun.* No lessons. No instructions." He shook his head.

"I still feel—"

"Like you could have saved her. You couldn't."

I pulled up my legs and sat cross-legged. After a few minutes of silence, he walked to the door.

I took a deep breath. "Okay, get my shit together or I can mope alone, right?"

He glanced at me, frowning slightly. "No. Not that. Just getting something. Be back."

CHAPTER 4

Jack was gone about twenty minutes. When he returned, he was carrying two steaming cardboard cups.

"Coffee," I said. "You're a mind reader."

"Not coffee. Not for you."

He handed me a cup. The smell of chocolate wafted out. I smiled.

"You need sleep," he said. "Figured you wouldn't take pills."

My dad used to make me hot chocolate when I couldn't fall asleep. I'd mentioned it once to Jack and he'd never forgotten. I wonder sometimes if that's how he sees me. His student, his protégée, his surrogate daughter.

How *do* I see Jack? Definitely not as a father figure, no matter how many times he brings me hot chocolate. I see him as a mentor. As a friend. And, as I realized this spring, as someone I'd like to be more than a friend. But there's never been a hint of reciprocation, and it's for the best. Jack is not dating material in any way, shape, or form. That's one of the reasons I'd stopped circling Quinn and given it a shot. Which had gone so well . . .

Except it *had* gone well with Quinn. I'd screwed

that up, too. I'd been a disappointment to someone I really hadn't wanted to disappoint.

"Nadia?"

"Thank you, for this." I managed a smile for him as I lifted the cup, then took a deep drink. "Mmm."

"Still warm?"

I nodded and scooted back on the bed and motioned for him to sit on the edge, which he did.

"How's Scout?" he asked.

I smiled, genuine now. Jack had given me Scout last spring, as a thank-you for his stay at the lodge. Also because he'd been wanting me to have a dog for years for protection. He knew I wasn't opposed to the idea. I'd taken in a stray when I was a kid, only to come home and find my mother had made it disappear. I'd wanted a dog; I just didn't feel my life was stable enough for one. It was and he knew that.

I told Jack a few Scout stories, including her encounter with a "black-and-white kitty" last month. That relaxed me, along with the hot chocolate. Soon I was crawling under the covers. He kept me talking, about the dog, the lodge, anything not related to Wilde and last night, until I finally drifted off.

I dreamed of Rose and Alan Wilde. And of my cousin Amy and her killer, Drew Aldrich. I dreamed that Amy and Drew *were* Rose and Alan, a version of them, the two stories merging. I was at the marina, arguing with Amy, telling her Aldrich was dangerous. She laughed and said I was being silly, I was always being silly.

Then Drew came with another girl and they fought and Amy drove off. Drew went after her. I didn't try to stop him. I just headed to my car, telling myself it was nothing, they always fought, no big deal. Then Paul

Tomassini called and told me Amy was dead. And I knew it was my fault.

It had always been my fault.

I half woke and heard Jack's distant voice, telling me it was okay, everything was okay, go back to sleep.

When I did, I fell into a memory. I was thirteen, walking home from the train station with Amy. We'd spent the day at the Canadian National Exhibition in Toronto, and Amy's dad was supposed to pick us up at the station, but he wasn't there. I'd wanted to wait. She'd started walking, so I had to walk, too, had to stay with her, keep her safe. That was my job.

Amy was a year older than me, but reckless, impetuous. Her dad had told me to keep an eye on her that day, knowing I would.

We were still walking when Drew Aldrich offered us a ride. I said no. He was twenty-four, and I didn't like the way he looked at Amy. Didn't like the way she looked back, either.

Drew wanted to take us to his cabin for "some fun." I was sure—absolutely sure—that Amy would refuse. As wild and impulsive as she was, she was still a cop's daughter, like me. She knew better.

When she said yes, I freaked out. She begged. She really liked him and if I was there, it would be fine. We could talk. Maybe smoke a joint. I didn't have to, of course, but she wanted to try it. Just once. We'd go for an hour. That was it. One joint. One hour.

I was furious. Yet I didn't feel that I had a choice. If I refused, she'd go alone. So I had to go and keep her safe. Later, I'd make sure she never did anything this stupid again.

There was no later. Not for Amy.

I dreamed I was back in that cabin. That horrible cabin, stinking of rotten wood and mildew and dirt. I could hear Amy in the next room. Crying. Telling Aldrich no, please no, please stop.

He'd left me tied up, but I got free. I should have gone in there and saved her. Instead, I did what my father had taught me from the time I was old enough to walk to school alone. If there's trouble, don't try to handle it yourself. Just run. Get help.

So I ran.

In real life, I'd raced to the station, where my dad was on duty. He'd jumped into his car and taken off to that cabin. I stayed with the dispatcher.

That wasn't what happened in the dream. When I got to the station and told my dad, we both ran back to the cabin on foot, tearing through the forest, me in the lead, running so fast I thought my chest would explode. I could hear Amy. Screaming. The faster I ran, the farther away the cabin got. I shouted for her to wait, just wait, we were coming. She just kept screaming, horrible, terrible screams.

And then she stopped.

She stopped screaming and the cabin was suddenly right in front of me. I looked back for my father, but he was still in the woods, so far away I could barely see him.

I threw open the door. The smell hit me. The stink of rotten wood and mildew and something else, something sharp and acrid that I didn't recognize. And when I smelled that, I froze. I felt a cord around my wrists, a cold blade at my throat, hot breath on my neck, fingers digging into my thighs, rough clothing rasping against my bare skin, Drew Aldrich's voice in my ear.

"Nadia. Pretty, sweet little Nadia."

I could hear Amy whimpering and crying in the next room and I knew I had to get to her, but I was frozen there, Aldrich whispering in my ear.

Except none of that happened. Not to me. It was Amy he'd raped. I needed to snap out of it, save her.

Finally, I forced my feet to move. One step, then another, leaving those false memories behind as I walked into the next room where—

Amy was there. Naked. Sprawled on the floor. Covered in stab wounds. Blood pooled around her. Dead eyes staring up at the ceiling. Then, slowly, her head turned my way, eyes still wide and unseeing.

"You did this, Nadia," her voice came out in a raspy whisper. "You ran away. You left me. You killed me."

I started to scream.

I was still screaming when someone began pounding on the cabin door.

"Shut the hell up!" a voice boomed.

"Nadia?" a second voice, closer. Hands gripping my elbows. Shaking me gently. "Nadia?"

I bolted out of sleep to find myself staring at Jack. I was sitting up, and he had me by the elbows, steadying me.

More pounding at the door. Jack strode over and opened it, chain still engaged.

"What the hell is going—?" a man's voice began.

"A nightmare. It's over."

"It better be or I'll have the goddamned manager . . ."

Jack didn't throw open the door. He didn't snarl at the man. He just unlatched the door and eased it open. Silence. Then the man backed off, mumbling, and stomped away.

Jack waited until he was gone. Then closed the door and shook his head.

"Woman's screaming. Not gonna call 911. Not even gonna make sure she's okay. Just complain about the fucking noise."

I sat there, clutching the sheets, throat raw, breath rasping. Jack walked to the bed and sat on the edge near me.

"Was it Amy?" He paused and shook his head. "Dumb fucking question. You think you got that woman killed? You're gonna dream about Amy."

"I froze up. I heard Amy in the cabin, still alive, and I was so close and . . ." I squeezed my eyes shut. "Which is not how it happened. Sorry. I'm confused." I rubbed my face.

"What happened? In the dream?"

I shook my head. "I get things confused. Nightmares aren't supposed to make sense."

"What happened this time?"

"I dreamed I was the one who found Amy. That she was still alive when I got there, but I froze up. I started thinking about Aldrich, that he'd attacked me, too, and . . ."

My heart thudded so hard I struggled for breath. I rubbed my throat, fingers touching the paper-thin scar there. Jack's gaze followed.

"How'd you get that scar again?" he asked.

I pulled my hand away. "Chain-link fence."

"Right."

I could feel his gaze on me, as if he expected more.

"You've dreamed Aldrich attacked you before," he said finally.

I shrugged. "I've also dreamed he killed me, which disproves that old saw about not being able to die in your dreams—"

"Don't."

"Don't what?"

"Divert. Digress. Make jokes." He twisted to face me. "We need to talk. About this. The dreams. You say Aldrich never—"

"He didn't."

A long pause. "You sure?"

"About what? Whether Drew Aldrich attacked me? Check the damned records, Jack. If you think I'd lie about it—"

"Course not."

"Drew Aldrich walked free. Do you know why? Because Amy was the kind of girl who wore short skirts and flirted with boys and drank at parties. People believed she had it coming. She went to his cabin and, while I waited in the next room, they had rough sex, and she died. Any evidence to the contrary was clearly planted by her father and uncle, who were first on the scene."

"I know the story. You don't need to—"

"Yes, I do, because you don't understand what you're saying. Sometimes I *wish* he'd attacked me. At least I wish I'd lied and said he did. Because then he'd have gone to jail. I was the good girl. If I was hurt, they'd have put him away. But I wasn't."

"Okay."

"The dreams are a fucked-up version of what happened. Look at tonight's—I didn't find Amy's body. She wasn't stabbed. *That* was Dawn Collins—the girl killed by Wayne Franco, the guy I shot. The shooting that got me kicked off the police force. A nightmare takes bits and pieces from different memories."

I got out of bed. "I appreciate what you did, but there's no reason for me to stay in Michigan, and certainly no reason for you to babysit me. I promise not to have a breakdown on the highway."

He handed me my jacket and gun. "In the car."

"I can call—"

"Get in the car."

CHAPTER 5

We'd been driving for an hour. I felt like an idiot, which is my usual postmeltdown reaction. Most times it's a minor and temporary derailment—a nightmare, an anxiety attack, a day where I'm just not my usual perky self. An actual meltdown, like tonight's, is very rare. Poor Jack has been there for the last three, which all happened when I felt like I failed to save someone. First, when a serial killer we were stalking took another victim. Then when the guy who killed my teenage employee did the same. Now this.

These breakdowns shamed me. Amy died twenty years ago. I killed Wayne Franco and lost my job seven years ago. My life has hit rock bottom twice and I'm still standing, and I'm damned proud of that. Then it all goes to hell and I'm wandering along highways and screaming in motel rooms.

"You'll need to take the next exit," I said when I saw the signs for Detroit. "I didn't fly—I drove. I'll rent a car and cross at the bridge."

He grunted and drove right past the exit.

"Um, Jack? I need to—"

"Not going home. Got something else."

"But I need to go—"

"You told Emma not to expect you, right?"

"Yes, but I really should—"

"Not yet." He glanced over. "You insist? I'll take you. Can't kidnap you." His tone said that was regrettable. "You trust me?"

"Yes, but—"

"No buts. You trust me? Want to take you someplace. Drive you home tomorrow."

I drifted off and woke in Ohio. I wondered if Jack was taking me to Evelyn's place in Fort Worth. I hoped not. She wouldn't understand my guilt over Rose Wilde's death. The concept of caring about a stranger is unfathomable to her. It's enough of a stretch for her to give a damn about people she actually knows. Yet while Evelyn wasn't good at empathy, she *was* very good at using situations to her advantage. She'd pounce on my guilt to entice me to check out the Contrapasso Fellowship again.

The fellowship was a legend among both cops and hitmen. An urban legend, most said. It derives its name from a region in Dante's *Inferno* where the punishment of souls fits their crimes in life. It's said to be a "club" composed of former judges, lawyers, and law-enforcement officers who hire assassins to right judicial wrongs. Organized vigilantism. Evelyn says it exists and tried to get me interested. I'd be perfect, she said, and it might help me get over Amy. Not that she gave a shit about my mental health, but if I joined she'd earn a tidy sum as my middleman. Ultimately, I'd said no.

I shifted forward in my seat, reading signs to get my bearings. We were headed east. Indiana—and Evelyn—were west.

"What's in Ohio?" I asked.

"Not much."

I gave him a look. He took a drag on a cigarette. I

glanced at the lid he was still using as an ashtray. There were two new butts in it. I resisted the urge to dump them.

"Lose the battle?" I said, gesturing at the makeshift ashtray.

"Nah." He stubbed out the cigarette. "Back-to-back jobs. Went a few weeks cold turkey. Never cures me. Just catches up later."

"Jobs go—" I cleared my throat and switched to full sentences, before we were reduced to exchanging grunts. "Did the jobs go all right?"

"Yeah. Routine."

That was all I was getting. If something was bothering him, he wasn't sharing. Nor was he telling me our destination.

Though Jack wasn't talking about anything he didn't wish to talk about, he was up for conversation. Or what usually passes for conversation when we're together on a long trip—me talking and him listening.

I talked about the lodge. It's not just a business; it's a never-ending project. I bought it after my professional disgrace, shooting Wayne Franco. A few years ago, I'd been about to lose the lodge through bankruptcy. That's when I started working for the Tomassinis. A few jobs a year for them doesn't just keep the lodge afloat; it gives me the money I need to turn it into my dream business. Of course, I can't just pull a hundred grand out of my stash and go crazy with the renovations. It has to be a slow, measured withdrawal, weighing cost against income potential. With the work I've done so far, the lodge is breaking even. One day, it might even make a profit.

Little things do make a difference. Extras, I call them. Amenities is the business term. I don't allow

hunting on my property—yes, hypocritical, I know—
which means I can't court the market that doesn't give
a shit about hot tubs and groomed hiking trails. I need
to appeal to everyone from wilderness sports enthusi-
asts to honeymooning couples to church ladies on retreat. The amenities are what draws them.

"So the ATVs are a big hit," I said. "Thanks to you."

Jack shrugged. He'd been the one who'd saved the
secondhand—or probably twelfth-hand—vehicles from
being a money pit, after my caretaker bought them and
discovered new spark plugs weren't quite enough to get
them running.

"No problems?" he said.

"Just wear and tear, and I've got a kid from town
who handles that. I'm not a fan of things with motors
racing around the forest, but with restrictions on where
and when they can be used, I'll admit they worked out
better than I expected. Which now has Owen eyeing a
few used snowmobiles that 'just need a little work.'"

"You want them? I'll fix 'em. Thinking about coming up this winter. Couple weeks maybe. If that's okay."

"It's always okay, and while you don't need the
snowmobiles as an excuse, I know that your idea of a
vacation doesn't mean sitting around ice fishing. I'll
take you up on that offer if you're serious."

"I am. Only tell Owen I'll find the machines. He
doesn't know shit about motors."

I grinned over at him. "I'll tell him the first part and
skip the last."

Jack took the exit for Cleveland.

"Is this our destination?" I asked.

"Yeah."

After a minute of silence, I said, "I'd love to ask
what we're doing here, but apparently, I'm not getting
that. Just as long as there isn't a surprise party at the

end." I paused. "Actually, I'd be okay with a party. Just no clowns. I hate clowns."

Jack didn't even acknowledge the lame joke. He kept his gaze fixed forward, his face tense. He drove down two more streets before pulling into a mall parking lot. I was about to get out when I realized he'd stopped to make a cell phone call. I motioned to ask if he wanted privacy, but he shook his head.

His voice took on a flat midwestern accent as he asked to speak to David Miller. His gaze slid my way, as if checking to see if I recognized the name. I didn't.

"Yeah, I figured he was on duty today," Jack said. "Can I leave a message? Tell him Ted called. He's got my number."

A pause. Then, "Thanks. Oh, and when does his shift end? It's kinda urgent."

He waited for a reply, then thanked the person on the other end again and hung up. When he did, he sat there a moment, staring out the windshield.

"Is that someone we need to talk to? A cop?"

"Yeah. Don't need to talk to him. Just making sure he's at work. Figure he knows a Ted." He paused. "Speaking of names. David? Most popular male name for a guy his age. Miller? Sixth most common surname in the U.S. Put them together? Fifteen thousand Americans named David Miller."

"That's . . . fascinating. Either you've taken up a new hobby or this is a roundabout way of telling me it's fake."

"Yeah."

"A fake name for a cop in Cleveland? That's not easy to pull off."

"Works in a small town nearby. He just lives here."

I nodded. "It's easier to get past background checks on a small force, but it's easier to live anonymously in a big city. Still, becoming a cop with a false identity is tough. I'm presuming there *are* cops named David Miller somewhere. Probably dozens of them, which would make it an easy identity to steal."

"Especially if you've done it a few times."

"So we have a serial identity thief posing as a small-town cop in Ohio. Intriguing." I glanced over at him. "You have a job for me, don't you? A mission to take my mind off Michigan."

He didn't turn from the windshield. "Something like that," he said and backed from the parking spot.

CHAPTER 6

Jack drove us to a section of townhouse complexes that looked like exactly the kind of place I'd find a single, middle-aged beat cop. Older, well-kept buildings with gardens and bikes in the front yards and five-year-old cars in the drives.

"Which place is Miller's?" I said.

Jack gave a vague wave down the road as he pulled over.

"Is this a break-in or just reconnaissance work?"

A shrug.

I turned to him. "Okay, Jack, I need more here. Presuming this is a job, is it something you want *me* to do or am I helping *you*?"

He tapped his fingers on the wheel. Then he reached under his seat, withdrew a folder, and held it out.

"It's your job, then," I said. "You wouldn't be this prepared if it was a spur-of-the-moment suggestion for me."

"Not mine," he said. "Just brought it. In case."

I set the folder on my lap. When I went to open it, he reached out, his fingers holding the file closed.

"If you don't want me to see this, Jack—"

"I do. You should. It's just . . ." He looked me in the

eye. "If I fucked up— I'm not trying—" He exhaled. "Fuck." He pulled his hand away.

"Let me interpret," I said. "You've brought me a file—a job, a case, something—and you aren't sure how I'll take it."

"Yeah."

"But you meant well."

"Yeah."

I looked at him. "I know that, Jack. You don't need to explain."

"I might." He waved at the folder. "Open it."

I did. There were photos on top. Surveillance shots of a guy in a patrol officer's uniform. Getting into his car, talking with a girl on the street, then walking into one of these townhouses. All I could make out was that he had dark hair, was of average height and hefty build.

I turned to the next photo. It was a full-face shot, taken with a telephoto lens. Bushy brows. Thin mouth. There were lines around his mouth and gray at his temples, but I looked at that photo and I didn't see a forty-five-year-old man. I saw one half that age. It didn't matter if I hadn't seen this face in nearly twenty years—my gut seized and I heaved for breath.

"Fuck," Jack said. "Hold on. Just hold on."

He slammed the car into drive.

"No!" I slapped my hand down on his, still holding the gear shift. "No. Don't. Just . . ." I struggled to breathe. "I'm okay."

"I'm sorry," he said. "Fuck. I'm sorry. I—"

"I know."

"I didn't—"

"Just . . . give me a minute."

I lifted my gaze to the road, staring at a yard with no flowers, no bikes, just an empty planter. The photo from the pictures, the house he'd been walking into. I thought of him sauntering up that drive and—

My stomach clenched.

"Let's go," Jack said.

"No, just . . . just wait. Please."

I took a few deep breaths, then lifted the photos, now scattered at my feet. I set them on my lap and stared down at the pile.

"David Miller is Drew Aldrich," I said.

Jack nodded. I clenched my fists and fought for calm. When I found enough of it, I said, "I looked for him. After I became a cop. I don't know what I planned to do." I paused. "No, I'm pretty sure I know what I planned to do, even if I told myself I just wanted to keep an eye on him, wanted to make sure he didn't hurt anyone else. But I couldn't find him."

"Wasn't easy. Took me—"

I cut him off. "You said this isn't his first alias. How many?"

"Four."

"After the trial, he moved to the States. That should have been enough. So why take on an alias? Something else happened, didn't it."

Jack was silent for a moment, then said, "Your uncle went after him. Tracked him down. Beat the shit out of him. Someone intervened. Saved his fucking life. Unfortunately."

"I never heard . . . They didn't talk . . ." After Aldrich walked, I hadn't heard another word about it. His name became taboo in our family. I thought they'd put it aside and moved on. I should have known better.

"So after Uncle Eddie went after Aldrich, he decided to change his name. But then he *kept* changing it. When did he become David Miller?"

"Not important. Point is, he's Miller."

I flipped through the file and found what I was looking for.

"David Miller joined the Newport police force four years ago," I said. "My uncle has been dead for ten years. My dad died eight years ago. He wasn't running from them."

Silence.

"Did they ever find him after the first time?" I asked.

Jack exhaled. "Don't see why—"

"You know why." Anger shot through me. "Do you think I'm too stupid to figure out why he had to keep changing his name? Amy was just the first. He got away with it, so he didn't stop. There were other girls."

"Investigations, yeah. Statutory rape. Unlawful restraint. Always took off before he got charged. Ran. Changed his name."

"Did any of those girls disappear?"

"No. Charges were filed by parents."

"Who found out he was sleeping with their under-age daughters, which doesn't mean he *wasn't* doing anything worse—just that he learned to hide it better."

Jack opened his mouth then shut it again. There was no way to know, without a doubt, that he'd never killed again.

I fingered the folder. "He wanted to become a cop. My dad said he'd come around the station, asking if they had any openings. He even volunteered, thinking you could do that, like with firefighters. No one at the station would have anything to do with him. So now he's fulfilled his dream."

"Seems so."

I felt a flash of anger. Aldrich should never have gotten a single thing he wanted from his life after he'd taken my cousin's. But that's not how it works.

"So he's a cop," I said. "That makes him even more dangerous. He can use his position to get close to teen-age girls. And he can use it to make them keep their mouths shut."

"Yeah."

"So you brought me here to investigate him."

He slanted a look my way. "You think so?"

I glanced at Aldrich's townhouse again and my heart started to pound. Jack restarted the car.

"No," I said. "Not yet."

"Nothing more to see. Just wanted to . . ." He seemed to struggle for words. "Ease you into it. Didn't know how to bring it up. Guess coming here . . ." He shrugged. "No point in it. Just . . ."

I lifted the folder. "What do you expect me to do with it, Jack?"

"What you want to do. What he deserves. Doesn't matter if he's a saint now. Still killed Amy."

"And now you expect me to kill him," I said, look-ing out the window.

"You can. I can. Whatever you want."

He said it so matter-of-factly, like deciding who was going to drive. It really was that simple for him.

I glanced down at the cup lid full of cigarette butts. This is what had been stressing him—bringing me here, telling me about Aldrich, not knowing how I'd react. The actual killing? That was easy.

How did I feel about Jack finding Aldrich for me? Confused. I suppose a firmer reaction would come later, but it wouldn't be anger. We'd been dealing with this issue for years. To Jack, Amy's death was a prob-lem, and a problem needed a solution.

Why did he feel the need to solve it? Was he worried that this was my one weakness and it had to be mended before I imploded and he got caught in the fallout? If that was his motive, did it sting? Not really. He could have just walked away. Instead he chose to stay and fix the problem.

"Should go," he said. "Start surveillance tonight. You want to do shifts?"

"Jack, I don't think—"

"Yeah, should take shifts. You need sleep. Could use some, too."

"I don't think I can—"

"Find a motel. No, a *hotel*. Nice place."

It's tough to babble when your sentences rarely exceed four words, but Jack was managing quite nicely.

"Jack, stop. I'm not killing Aldrich. That crosses a line—"

"Don't need to cross it. I will."

"You'll cross it for *me*, which is the same, if not worse—"

"Then tell me not to. Forbid me. He dies? Not your fault?"

I looked sharply at him. "I hope you're joking."

He shrugged. "Up to you."

"Then yes, you are joking. The only thing that would make me feel worse than asking you to kill Aldrich for me is pretending I don't want you to, while hoping you'll do it. I'm not a coward, Jack—"

"Not cowardice. Misguided morality. Misplaced ethics."

I fought a lick of anger. "That's my choice."

"Yeah? You know what's *not* your choice? How you'll feel when Aldrich goes after another girl. He will and now you'll know it. You'll be watching. Something will happen. You'll blame yourself."

"I'm not walking away from this, Jack. I'm going to investigate and when I find something, I'll turn him over— No, I don't even need to do that. I can turn him in now. I'll contact the police departments that were looking for him under other names, and I'll tell them where to find him." I leaned back in my seat. "That's what I'll do."

"That'll be enough?"

"It'll have to be. I can't justify killing him."

Jack drummed the steering wheel. Then he put the car in gear, tires chirping as he swerved from the curb.

Jack was pissed. And I felt terrible, because I'd refused his gift. Yes, that sounds fucked up, calling it a gift. But it was. He'd given me Drew Aldrich on a platter. I couldn't imagine how much work he'd done to find him and now I was going to turn Aldrich over to the police, as if he was just some random guy seducing underage girls. Jack had given me a chance for real justice, and I'd rejected it.

We drove around a bit after that. I asked Jack to take me to a car rental so he could go home. He didn't answer. When the silence got awkward, I checked my phone and immediately wished I hadn't. There were two voice messages and three texts from Quinn. I jammed the phone into my pocket, messages unplayed, texts unopened.

"Problem?" Jack said.

"No."

"Lodge?"

"No."

"Quinn?"

I said no again, but this time, there was enough hesitation to give me away.

"Fuck," Jack muttered, and I wished I'd been faster denying it. Even at the best of times, Quinn wasn't a subject Jack liked to discuss.

Professionally, Jack was fine with Quinn. He'd even

brought him in on the job where we'd met. Personally, though, the less time they spent together, the happier they both were. For Jack's part, I think it could have been a simple case of "he's not someone I'd choose to hang out with." Quinn was too volatile, too brash, too sure of himself. Jack didn't "get" Quinn's vigilantism, but it didn't affect him, so it didn't bother him. To each his own. Except Quinn didn't see things like that. To him, Jack was a murdering thug. Quinn could grit his teeth and work with him, but he made no secret of the fact that he was gritting his teeth. And like anyone with an ounce of self-respect, Jack didn't take kindly to that. Quinn treated Jack with contempt, so Jack returned the favor.

Now Jack rubbed his hand over his mouth, then looked at me. "Didn't mean to call him. Figured he was in the loop. Didn't know . . . You two . . ."

"If I'd foreseen any chance you'd call him for anything, I would have told you, but under normal circumstances, you'd rather cut off a limb than talk about me and Quinn."

"Yeah. Still . . . Would have liked to know. So . . . everything okay?"

I nodded. "He's just checking up on me, a little freaked out by your call and wanting to know what's going on. I'll send him a text."

"Not what I meant."

I paused, then said, "He hasn't sworn vengeance and vowed to expose either of us. So there's no potential security breach."

"Fuck. You think that's what I'm worried about?"

"It *was* what you were worried about six months ago. You said I shouldn't get involved with Quinn because mixing my job and my personal life was a security risk."

He gave something like a sigh. "Yeah. Then. Not now. I just . . . Want to make sure you're okay. With the . . . ending."

I forced a wry smile. "You mean, did he break my heart? No. I'm . . . I'm hurt and bewildered but—"

"What'd he do?"

"Nothing. We just—"

"You said you're hurt. He did something. Fuck, if he—"

"Jack, I'm fine. It was just normal relationship issues. You start seeing someone and realize you have different expectations, and it doesn't work out. It hurts, but there's nothing that can be done about that. Part of life." I met his gaze. "A part that I don't need you to fix for me."

Silence. Another five minutes of driving with no apparent destination in mind.

"Jack, just drop me off and I'll—"

"Gotta talk," he said.

I sighed. "If your plan was drive until I'm ready to talk about Aldrich again—"

"Won't say a word about Aldrich. Or Amy. Or even Quinn. Just me."

"You?"

"Yeah. Gonna talk about me." He glanced over. "That a problem?"

"Of course not. If there's something I can help you with, you know you only need to ask."

He grunted something unintelligible and kept driving.

CHAPTER 7

When Jack said he wanted to talk to me, I figured we'd have a conversation in the car. Or, if he expected it might take a while, we'd pull off somewhere or check into a motel. I did not expect to end up twenty miles outside of Cleveland, pulled over on a dirt road, then hiking into the forest by that road with cigarettes and a bottle of whiskey.

"Is this a conversation or a body dump?" I asked as we climbed over a fence.

"Wouldn't need this for a dump," he said, lifting the smokes and booze.

"Sure, you would . . . if you planned to shoot me, dowse me with alcohol, and light me on fire."

"Not today."

"So we really are heading into the forest for a chat?"

He shrugged. "Don't feel like talking and driving. This?" He waved. "Like the lodge."

Almost all our early conversations had taken place in my forest. We even had a particular fallen tree we'd sit on. That was back in the days before our first case together, when Jack was still sussing me out under the guise of mentoring. He would come at night and we'd sit in the forest and talk. Which didn't make the present circumstances any less odd, really, but that was Jack.

He let the professional nature guide lead the way. I picked a route through until I found a suitable fallen tree in a clearing. Night was falling slowly, but I could already see the bright moon through the cloudless sky so I knew we wouldn't be sitting in the pitch black when the sun disappeared.

"Here?" I asked.

He nodded. We sat. Two minutes later, we were still sitting. Then Jack lit a cigarette. He took a drag and passed it to me. I accepted it. We'd smoked half the cigarette in silence before he said, "Don't know how to do this."

"You don't need to tell me anything you don't want to."

"Want to. Just . . ." Another drag. "You know that saying? About riding a bike? Remember this spring? At the lodge? You took me for a bike ride."

I sputtered a laugh at the memory.

"Yeah," he said. "Maybe people don't forget how to do it. But it's not as easy as it sounds. Not when it's been so long." He let the smoke swirl away before continuing. "Never told anyone this. Not even Evelyn. Sure she knows some. Dug until she found it. But knows better than to mention it. I don't talk about this. Don't talk about anything. Except to you."

He slanted a look my way. "Yeah, I know. You don't feel like I tell you anything, either. Like I just let stuff slip. Don't slip. It's a choice. Want to say more. But . . ." He shrugged. "Not easy. Presumes you want to know. Seems . . ." He struggled for the right word. "Forward."

"I'd never—"

He continued as if I hadn't spoken, "This part's important. Relevant. You should know."

He paused and eyed the whiskey bottle, left at our feet.

"Do you want—?" I reached for it.

"Later. Get through this." He finished the cigarette, then ground it out. "Told you some stuff. About me. When it's relevant. Grew up in Ireland. Three older brothers. Not much money. Thing is . . . At the time? Circumstances? Poor and Irish. Easy to blame the English. Doesn't mean they're not responsible. But still . . ." He trailed off.

He lit another cigarette. "My brothers joined a group. Not IRA. Smaller. Regional. Less organized." He paused. "Worse." Another pause. "Brothers felt the IRA didn't have what it took. The balls. These guys did. You're young? Action is important. Don't think it through."

He shifted, getting more comfortable. "So my brothers signed up. Our father was all for it. Our mother? Not so much. But they were adults. She only made them promise one thing. Don't get me involved. I was furious. Felt left behind, like always. The baby. Came up with a plan. I was good mechanically, apprenticed to a mechanic. Good with a gun, too. Not distance, like you. But I hit what I aimed at. Hunted for my family. Brothers left? Hunted more, practiced more. One day? My brothers bring guys to dinner. Leaders in this organization. They drive up? I'm shooting. Planned it, of course. Got their attention. Took me aside. Said when I turned eighteen, come to them. They'd train me. Wouldn't be a grunt like my brothers. I'd be an assassin."

A long drag on his cigarette. "So that's what I did. Fuck my family. My da was dead by then. Heart attack. He's the only one I would have listened to. Rest could yell all they wanted. I was an adult. I signed up. Got trained. Started missions. Pretty soon? Best fucking hitman they got. Which wasn't saying much. But I was full of myself. Comes a day, I don't agree with a mission. Too risky. My brothers would be there in the line of fire. Didn't think it was safe. Told the guys in charge. Got my ass kicked. Mission comes, I'm outta commission. Mission goes to hell. Two of my brothers? Dead. Other one? Nearly got his fucking leg shot off."

He said it matter-of-factly, but he didn't look at me when he did. He just stared into the forest, his gaze empty, his whole face empty. I wanted to say something, but words seemed meaningless, so I just shifted closer. He glanced my way, then squeezed my knee briefly, surprising me. Then he lit another cigarette before continuing.

"Got out after that," he continued. "Took my brother and told those guys to go to hell. They didn't like that. Thought I owed them. They didn't care about my brother. A cripple now. But I was valuable. They'd let him go; I had to stay. Told them to fuck off. Told them, if they came after me, I'd put a bullet between their eyes. Tough guy." He gave a harsh, humorless laugh. "Fucking stupid kid."

He passed me the cigarette. I tried to refuse, but he seemed to want me to take it—or want the pause it afforded. Only after I passed it back did he continue.

"Never came after me. Never said one more word. Week later? I come home from the mechanic's. House is on fire. Find my mother. My brother. Dead. They'd tied them up. Couldn't escape." He stubbed out the cigarette. "My fault."

"You—"

His hard look silenced me. "Know what I mean. Better than anyone. Yeah, I was young. Didn't see it coming. Didn't kill them myself. But I fucked up. Over and over I fucked up. Joined when my mother begged me not to. Didn't warn my brothers about the mission.

Wasn't on the mission because I shot my mouth off. Didn't haul my ass out anyway and make goddamned sure I was there, no matter what shape I was in. Could have saved my brothers. Protected them. I failed. Then what did I do? Told off the bosses again. Fuck 'em. Don't owe them nothing and if they think I do, they can fucking come and take it from me. Which they did. Whole family's dead. My fault. No one can ever convince me otherwise." He looked at me. "Can they?"

He was right. He'd made youthful mistakes, as I had with Amy, and he'd feel the full weight of responsibility.

"I went after the guys in charge," Jack continued. "Fucking useless. Gave up. Knocked around Ireland. Then England. Hired myself out. Didn't give a fuck. Didn't feel anything. Made the job easy. After a couple years? Cross the ocean and Evelyn finds me. Trains me. Turns me into a pro. Not a two-bit thug with a gun. But deep down? That's still what I was. Didn't give a shit. To her? Made me a better hitman. Cold. Ambitious. But I never forgot." He glanced at me. "You know why I go by Jack? That's what they called me. My family. My father was John. Came from a line of Johns. Didn't want it for his sons. Gets his way with three boys. Then I came along. My mother insisted. Thought the tradition was important. They compromised. Named me John. Called me Jack."

I stared at him. The possibility that Jack was his real name—or even a version of it—had never occurred to me. Given how security conscious he was, he'd never do that. Unless it was too important to give up.

Jack finished the cigarette, tossed the butt. "Told you once you wouldn't have wanted to know me then. Meant it. Did shit I won't ever forget. You ever find out? Might understand I'm not that guy anymore. Or maybe it wouldn't matter because I *was* that guy. Cold and empty. Sooner or later?" He shrugged. "Something's gotta give. Realized that's not what I wanted. Only one way to fix it. Go back. Get revenge. Get justice. Or something like it."

"So you did?"

"Yeah." He picked up the bottle. He didn't uncap it, just held it, staring out into the forest. "Did it make me a good person?" He snorted. "Obviously not. Still in the game. Don't want out. But I'm not that guy anymore. Not dead anymore." He met my gaze. "Needed to be done."

"I know what you're saying—"

"Not asking you to change your mind now. Don't even want to discuss it. Just think about it. You're not me. Same kind of guilt. Different kind of damage. But I think I know you well enough to say it's not going to get any better until Drew Aldrich has paid for what he did. Until you know he's not a danger. To anyone."

I twisted to look at him and I wanted to say . . . There were a lot of things I wanted to say, and none of them seemed quite right. Tell him I was sorry for what happened to him? He didn't want that. Tell him I understood? No one can understand another person's experience—they can only sympathize and, sometimes, empathize. He didn't tell me the story for that. He told me his deepest secret because he wanted to convince me to kill Aldrich, and I couldn't even give him that.

He glanced over and when I looked at him, I didn't see my mentor, my sometimes partner, sometimes friend. I saw Jack, a real person, with a past, with a name.

"Thank you," I said.

He turned toward me, and I saw his face in the dim moonlight, the familiar angles of it, the familiar dark eyes filled with something that wasn't familiar. Haunted eyes, looking backward, but also a wariness, an uncertainty. I wanted to reassure him. I wanted to . . . Oh, hell, I knew what I wanted to do. Lean over and kiss him and make everything else go away.

I dropped my gaze before he saw that. I looked away and when I did, I felt his touch against my jaw, his fingers rubbing along it, gently turning my face back to his. My heart hammered. His fingers hesitated, then pushed my hair back behind my ear. I looked at him then. His gaze was lowered. Then he straightened, uncapped the whiskey, and took a hit. A long hit, before passing it to me.

"I really do appreciate—" I began.

"Drink." He stood. "Got your gun?"

"Always. But—"

"Get it out. You start."

I could have asked what he meant, but I knew. We were going to shoot stuff. And drink. Two things that don't normally go together, but we'd done it once before, when I'd been upset over not saving a victim. Jack said it was good practice at shooting under less-than-ideal conditions. Which was bullshit. It was stress relief. That's what he wanted right now, so that's what I was going to do. It was a whole lot safer than what I'd had in mind anyway.

As he walked away to find targets, I took a slug of the whiskey, feeling it burn off a lingering feeling that I'd missed out on something I wanted very much. Wanted and didn't want. Hoped for and feared. Drink and burn it away and go back to where we should be, where I looked at Jack and saw a mentor and a partner and maybe a friend. Nothing more.

Another shot of whiskey.

"You gonna shoot?" he called. "Or get drunk first?"

"I'm leveling the playing field for you," I called back.

He snorted. "Seem to recall I won last time."

"No, you were just so drunk you *thought* you won."

He shook his head and waggled a rusted pop can. I took out my gun. He threw it. I fired.

CHAPTER 8

Jack won. Again. In the early stages, it was close, but the more we drank, the more it became obvious that I wasn't in his league for short-range shooting. With every hit from the whiskey bottle, my aim got worse. Jack had to get almost halfway through it to even affect his aim. And that's about all the effect it had. When he drinks, he doesn't get any louder, any more talkative, any more open, and his aim stays good. He just gets a little unsteady. Which is how we ended up on the ground.

We abandoned the bottle and ran out of bullets around the same time. I'd used up my ammo first, so I was stumbling around the forest, finding our shot-up cans to throw for him, drunk enough that even that was a chore.

"Passed one," Jack called.

I looked back, squinting at the ground. Or it looked like the ground. When it comes to drinking, I'm a lightweight. I was plastered, and I was not seeing the can, even with his directions.

Finally, he made his way out to me. Then I caught the glint of metal and bent to pick it up. Just as he came up behind me, I stood, smacked into him, and down we went, with me on his lap. Which would have been a whole lot sexier if I wasn't dead drunk.

"Damn," I said, craning my neck. "It's a long way up."

"Then don't get up. Not sure I could."

I laughed and leaned back against him for a moment before pulling away. "If we're going to pass out in the forest, at least let me find my own spot to do it before I crush you."

"Nah." He put his arms loosely around me. "You're light. Also, warm. Getting cold."

It was, and he was warm, too, warm and solid, propped against a tree. If he wasn't going to argue, then this was a perfectly comfortable place to pass out. Which I promptly did.

When we woke, it was morning and we were still sitting on the forest floor. And I was still mostly on Jack's lap. I felt him stirring and I tensed, ready to jump up, mumbling apologies. But he only yawned and patted my leg. "You awake?" he asked.

"Yes, and I'm getting up before you notice the damp spot on your shirt, which, by the way, is dew, not drool."

A chuckle and another leg pat as I rose. He then groaned softly as he pushed up.

"Too old for that shit," he muttered, rubbing his lower back.

"The boozing or the sleeping on cold ground?"

"Both." A faint shiver. "Fucking freezing."

I walked back to the log and retrieved his jacket, which he'd taken off after a few hits from the bottle. As he shrugged it on, he looked over, studying me, and I tensed. He was going to ask what I'd decided, and I braced for the question.

"You remember where we left the car?"

I smiled. "Follow me."

As we walked back, I realized he wasn't going to mention Aldrich. Not now. Maybe not ever. He'd found him. He'd told me what he thought I should do. He'd related his own experience. The ball was now in my court, and if I chose to quietly slip off the field, he wouldn't comment.

"I'm going to do it," I said.

He looked back at me.

"Aldrich," I said. "You're right. If I don't, I'll be constantly scouring the news, worrying that he'll go after another girl."

He stopped walking. "You rather I never found him?"

I shook my head. "If Amy was here, she wouldn't tell me to turn the other cheek. She'd want him to pay. He's had twenty years of freedom. Time to end this."

One would think that having made the decision, we should have proceeded amicably into planning and execution. Didn't happen. In fact, the first thing we did was argue.

"You doing it?" Jack asked as we pulled onto the highway. "Or you want me to?"

"I am. Thanks for the offer, but there's no way I can justify—"

"Don't need to justify. I'm offering."

I took a deep breath. "I don't feel any overwhelming need to pull the trigger myself. It isn't about killing him—it's about seeing him dead. But I don't have an aversion to doing it, so that's best."

A few minutes of quiet driving. Then, "If I disagree?"

"I'm not going to screw this up, Jack. I won't see his face and flip out and—"

"Never said that. But I presume you plan to look

him in the eye. Tell him why he's dying. Might bring shit up."

"Bring shit up?"

"Stuff you've forgotten."

I stiffened. "I know it's going to bring back memories, Jack."

"Do you?" He glanced over. "Really?"

I glared at him. "Yes, really."

He said nothing more until he turned off into the city. "I'm not a shrink. Never been to one. Shot a couple. Don't think that counts. Point is, I don't know how this works. Memories and shit. Better off confronted? Or buried?"

"Confronted," I said. "I'm sure there are things I've forgotten or repressed that might come back when I see him. But I choose to take that risk. I choose to deal with it."

"You gonna remember that?"

Another glare aimed his way. "If you're asking me to remember my choice if it all goes to hell, I will."

"Know that. Just . . ." He looked over now as we paused at a stoplight. "I want this to help you, Nadia. Make things better. If it makes them worse? Really do not want that."

"I know," I said, and we resumed driving in silence.

I called Emma to say I wouldn't be home for the weekend. It was Friday, and we couldn't pull this hit until Sunday at the earliest.

The next step was disguises. In Michigan I'd been wearing a variation on my usual hitman outfit. Not leather and stilettos, as much as I'm sure that would fulfill someone's idea of a female assassin. I go the polar opposite route. I wear no makeup and sweats with padding to add an extra thirty pounds. My own hairstyle doesn't exactly rock the fashion world—shoulder-length auburn curls—but the wig is worse, nondescript brown hair trimmed with scissors to give it that "I cut my own hair" look. Middle-aged nobody. The invisible woman.

It's a lot harder to be invisible when there's two of you. So Jack usually picks our disguises, which have two basic variations, depending on the locale. Aldrich's neighborhood was nice enough that the biker-and-bitch combo we sometimes use wasn't going to work, so we went with working-class guy and second wife.

I got straight, dark hair and dark contacts. Jack got gray-free hair and contacts that turned his dark eyes hazel. He also got dark beard stubble, which he didn't need to fake, having not been near a razor in a few days. He added a small tattoo on the back of his hand, some youthful whim that I'm sure his character regretted now. I added bright red glasses. The tattoo and glasses were "distinguishing features." They're what people notice, often at the expense of more mundane but important things like face shape and body size.

We set out to Newport, where Aldrich worked. To pull a good hit, you need to know the target's routine. That's not how every pro operates. In fact, contrary to what Hollywood shows, your average hitman isn't a skilled assassin, slipping up on his target in some clever disguise, killing him in some endlessly creative fashion before vanishing into the night. The average hitman is just a thug who doesn't mind killing people. He finds his target alone, walks up, and pulls the trigger.

I located a vacant apartment over a shop across from the police station. Judging by the dust, the apartment had been empty for months, maybe years, and the owners had given up trying to rent it.

We took turns using binoculars. It was nearly noon when I spotted Aldrich coming out of the station.

Jack worried that seeing Aldrich might be too much for me. But as I watched him coming down the steps, I didn't see the man who'd raped and killed my cousin. I saw a target. Any emotional reaction had come when I'd seen his photo in Jack's folder.

I watched Aldrich walk down the stairs and I thought *He's gotten old*. And, *He's put on weight*. And, *He's favoring his left leg*. The observations of a predator sizing up prey.

"That him?" Jack said, squinting out the window.

"It is."

I handed him the binoculars, but he didn't take them, just studied my expression.

"I'm fine, Jack. I had my freak-out yesterday. Now all I'm thinking is that he's gotten old and slow."

"Yeah. Know what that's like."

"Believe me, it'll be a long time before you're that *old*."

CHAPTER 9

We followed Aldrich for the rest of the day. We established that he had a partner, but I wouldn't have shot him on the job anyway. I had too much respect for the police institution to kill a cop in uniform, even a fake cop.

We'd already decided our basic plan. Kill Aldrich and hide his body well enough that it wouldn't be found. Then I'd leak his real identity, and it would be presumed that he'd bolted, which would avoid the shit storm that comes with a murdered police officer.

When his shift ended, Aldrich went drinking with the guys. Jack decided that the bar was busy enough for a middle-aged couple to slip in undetected. We'd only stand out if we made ourselves stand out, which we had no intention of doing. The more we watched Aldrich, the better we'd get to know him—his personality and habits. Jack thought it was safe. As for whether Aldrich might recognize me . . .

Have I ever fantasized about that? Meeting him someplace and he recognizes me, and sees that I'm not a helpless little girl anymore? Hope that he'd seen me in the papers after I shot Wayne Franco. That he'd know what I'm capable of, and so when I look into his eyes, I'll see fear? Of course I've thought of it, and I've savored those thoughts. But realistically, I wasn't sure he'd recognize me even *without* the disguise.

I'd only been Amy's little cousin. An obstacle to be tied up and left. That was the last time he'd seen me. I never faced him in court. My family didn't want me to testify, and my dad had persuaded the prosecutor to agree. Aldrich probably didn't even remember my name. I just hope he remembered Amy's. And if he didn't, I sure as hell planned to remind him . . . right before I put a bullet between his eyes.

Jack was still careful. He chose a table off to the side, at least twenty feet from Aldrich and the other cops at the bar. He ordered a beer. I got a Coke. We settled in to observe our target.

When Aldrich used to come around the station, my dad and the other cops wanted nothing to do with him. They said it was because they suspected him of dealing marijuana, but in small-town Ontario, that's like running moonshine in the Ozarks. The truth was that they just didn't like Aldrich. As I listened to him with his colleagues here, I could tell nothing had changed. He was welcome to hang out with them and join in general conversation, but that was it.

Jack was facing Aldrich. I had my back to him. I was regaling Jack with the story of a honeymooning couple who had equated "wilderness lodge" with "nudist camp," and taken to hiking, swimming, and even picnicking naked. Which gave them quite an appetite, and not for Emma's home-cooked meals. All of which wouldn't have been so bad if the lodge hadn't been hosting some kind of teen purity group from the U.S. I'd tried to point out to the group leaders that the couple *was* married, but it hadn't really helped.

I noticed Jack's attention shift and stopped talking.

"On the move," Jack said, as he tracked his prey.

"Piss break. Fuck. Coming this way. Keep looking at me. Keep talking."

I nodded and glued my gaze to his. "So I have a chat with the couple, and we establish a schedule of when and where they can have their clothing off—"

Aldrich stopped three feet past the table. He looked back over his shoulder—directly at me.

"Keep talking," Jack murmured.

I did. I have no idea what I said, just blather, my gaze still on Jack, sweat breaking out along my hairline as I could feel Aldrich staring right at me. Then he continued walking.

"He looked right at me," I whispered when he was out of sight.

Jack shrugged. "Checking you out."

"I'm well above his age range for that and this outfit is definitely not bar bait."

Another shrug. "Doesn't matter. Still gonna look."

I doubted that. Even on my best days, I'm not bar bait. When I hit puberty, guys started telling me I was cute, and twenty years later, the description hasn't changed. Looking like the quintessential girl next door is helpful for a hitman, but it doesn't make guys stare in bars.

"I think he recognized me," I said. "It was as if he was trying to place me."

Jack shook his head. "Too many years. Good disguise. He was checking you out."

"He's standing at the back by the restroom, looking straight at me."

Jack turned.

"Don't—" I began.

Too late. Jack turned right around in his seat and stared at Aldrich. This wasn't his usual don't-fuck-with-me stare, like he'd given the motel guy who'd complained about the noise. This look was ice-cold. I-want-to-blow-your-fucking-head-off cold. I shivered in spite of myself.

"Jack?" I whispered.

He snapped out of it, swung back to me, and took a gulp of his beer, as if to wash that look away.

"Could be," he said as he finished.

"Could be what?"

"Might recognize you."

My stomach clenched. "Goddamn it, if he knows who am I—"

"He'll do what? Call the cops?"

I glowered at him.

"I mean it," he said. "What's he gonna do? He's using fake ID. Impersonating a cop. On the run from rape charges. Got nowhere to turn. No one to tell. And what would he say?"

"I don't want to take that chance. Can we leave now?"

"Makes it worse. Confirms it's you. There a rear exit?"

I shook my head. The first thing I'd done when we came in was casually scout exits.

"Good. He can't slip out."

Aldrich returned by a route that didn't take him past our seats. After a few minutes, Jack pulled a ten from his pocket and slapped it on the bill. "Let's go."

We left out the front door. As we passed a car, Jack glanced in the side-view mirror.

"Followed us out," he said.

"Okay." I struggled to keep calm. "How do you want to play this? Avoid the car, I presume, or he'll run the plates."

"Wild-goose chase. Let him have it." Jack meant the

plates wouldn't lead anywhere and it would be more suspicious if we wandered aimlessly.

For someone who hates attention, I'm actually a good actor. Jack is, too. So as we headed for the car, I raised my voice to normal volume.

"I have a bunch of errands to run in the city before the wedding tomorrow afternoon," I said. "That means an early morning, so I don't want to be out too late tonight. Should we check into the hotel first or go straight to dinner?"

"We have one night without the kids," Jack said. "Definitely to the hotel first." He put his arm against my back, his fingers sneaking down to my ass. "That's what room service is for, babe."

I chuckled. "How many beers did you have?"

"A couple."

"I believe the definition of a couple is two."

He shrugged. "It was a multiple of two."

I laughed and put out my hand. "Car keys, please."

He started handing them over, then dangled them just out of reach. "Where are we going?"

"To the hotel. For rest, relaxation, and room service. Or something like that."

He patted my ass while handing me the keys. "That's my girl."

As we got into the car, I said, "Okay, he'll notice the rental stickers on the plate, which will make it tricky for him. The easiest thing to do is call the station and report he saw us heading for the highway driving erratically after leaving a bar. We'll get stopped and carded. Which means I'm not taking the highway."

CHAPTER 10

We returned to Cleveland on the back roads. Jack dropped me off a half mile from Aldrich's place as he went to switch cars, renting another from a different agency, under a different name.

Aldrich was already home, his truck under the carport. It was past eight, getting dark, and I was able to slip into another carport across the road, where a few days worth of flyers in the mailbox told me the owners weren't home. I had my tactical earpiece, but mostly what I picked up was conversations from the surrounding houses. I had binoculars, too, but I saw Aldrich pass a window only once.

An hour later a whispered, "Going okay?" had me scattering Skittles on the drive.

"Could you please warn me before you do that? Particularly when I'm wearing this?" I took the amplifier out and winced.

"Don't need that shit. Dangerous." He motioned at the bag of candy. "Found those?"

"Yes, and thank you." They'd been in his equipment rucksack. "Although you might regret buying them for me now." I bent to pick them up. "I can just see the headlines: 'Professional Killer Leaves Behind Nothing but Skittles.'"

He chuckled and took a few from the bag.

"You don't want these?" I held out the dirty ones. "Destroy the evidence?"

"You dropped them. You eat them."

I pocketed the Skittles, wiped my hand on my jeans, and gave Jack an update.

He checked his watch. "Still early. You wanna come back? Break in later? Take a look around?"

That might seem risky, but searching for evidence of other crimes *after* we made Aldrich disappear would be riskier.

"Works for me."

"Got a few hours then. Come on. Parked over—"

He stopped as a car drove past slowly.

"That same one went by a minute ago," I said.

The car—a nondescript silver sedan—reached Aldrich's drive and the brake lights flashed solid, as if the driver just found the place. He turned in, parked, and got out.

He was around Aldrich's age. Average build. Dark haired with a beard and mustache, and dressed in jeans, a light jacket, and a ball cap. I could make out the Cleveland Indians emblem on the back of his coat, and when I looked through the binoculars, I could see it on his hat, too.

I didn't manage to get the camera up before he turned away, but I snapped a few shots of him from the rear. I got a couple of his car, too, and the plate.

He was carrying a six-pack of beer and a bag of pretzels. A buddy coming over to knock back a few on a Friday night. I lowered the camera, but I put my earpiece back in. I left it out slightly, motioning for Jack to listen. He nodded and leaned in, his hip brushing mine, his hand resting lightly against the small of my back.

The man reached the door and rapped. Aldrich answered.

"Hey, bud," the visitor said. "Got your call. Sounded like you could use a little company. I brought friends." He lifted the six-pack.

A chuckle from Aldrich. "Come on in."

The door closed behind them, taking the conversation with it.

"Can you get around back?" Jack whispered.

I nodded.

"Do that. I'll cover you. Follow if I can."

It took me a while to get around to Aldrich's small rear yard. It took Jack even longer to join me.

"Nothing," I whispered when he found me, crouched between the garden shed and the back deck. "They went downstairs." I gestured to a dimly lit basement window. "Wherever they are, there isn't a window, and they've shut the door. All I can pick up is the TV. Baseball, I think. So now what?"

"Your call."

"I'd like to wait. See if he starts talking about his day."

Jack nodded and we settled in.

The game ended. The volume on the TV dropped enough for me to hear what sounded like preparations to leave. We decided I'd slip around front and see if I could get any photos of the friend.

I got to a hiding place as the friend was coming out the front door. He held it for a second, calling back, "Give me a call tomorrow. No, wait— Sunday would be better. Got the kids coming by tomorrow." A short laugh. "Val would kill me if I forgot that."

A pause as Aldrich must have replied.

"Sure, I'll do that. Call me Sunday then. Have a good night."

I took my photos as he headed to his car. When he drove off, I returned to Jack.

"The TV is still on," I said as I picked up the sound from the house. "Can you tell where Aldrich is?"

"Downstairs again, seems like."

"Okay, so . . . should we come back later or wait it out?"

"No need to wait."

"Break in while he's watching TV?"

Jack shrugged. "Room doesn't have windows. Door seems closed."

There are gadgets for detecting typical home security systems and even Jack uses one. Aldrich's townhouse wasn't armed. We had lock picks, too, but the rear door was unlocked, the faint smell of burgers suggesting he'd cooked dinner on the grill, then gone inside forgetting to relock the patio door.

I'd argue that the biggest security challenge isn't alarms or locks—it's pets. Even cats can be a pain in the ass. Once during recon a cat yowled for my attention so loudly that I'd taken off before the neighbors decided someone was being murdered. Neither Jack nor I picked up the scent of pets, but we scanned the kitchen for bowls, just in case. There were none.

Aldrich was the kind of housekeeper that gives bachelors a bad name, with a kitchen counter piled with dishes and takeout boxes, and clothing draped everywhere. Even surveying the mess made me twitch, the urge to tidy almost overwhelming.

While Jack was prowling, I headed upstairs. I wanted to look for souvenirs of past crimes. Many sex offenders keep them, and the most obvious place to find them is in the bedroom, which was the advantage to breaking in before Aldrich retired for the night.

At the top of the stairs, I found an office. Compared to the rest of the place, it was surprisingly tidy. Drawers were closed, paper stacked neatly—

A stair creaked. I was backing farther into the office when Jack whispered, "It's me."

He crested the steps. "Just thinking. Someone should watch Aldrich. You want it?"

I nodded and went down to the main level. The basement door was cracked open, the light on. The stairs came out in the laundry room where there was, unsurprisingly, no laundry—it was draped over everything upstairs. The area extended across the back of the house. Along the inside wall were three doors. The middle one was open an inch, and through it, I could see the faint blue glow of the television.

The earpiece meant I could pick up any sound from inside that room, but all I heard was the TV. Aldrich was settled in, maybe even asleep. If I could be sure he was sleeping, I could go back upstairs and help Jack search.

I moved as close to the door as I dared, then strained to listen when the TV chatter paused. But even with the earpiece, I heard only silence. That meant he was probably awake—his breathing too shallow for me to catch.

I could make out the TV screen now. There seemed to be a pinkish blob on it. I pulled out my binoculars. It took some adjusting, trying to magnify something less than ten feet away, but after a moment, the nickel-size blob came into view. It looked like . . .

It couldn't be. I started to retreat. Then I stopped. I took a deep breath . . . and crept right to the opening, so close that I could see that blob and the tiny spots spattered over the beige carpet.

I pulled out my gun, put my gloved fingertips against the door, and pushed, braced for a cry of alarm. None came. I reached into my rucksack and took out a small mirror. Fingers trembling, I held it to the gap, adjusted the angle, and then . . .

Drew Aldrich sat in a worn recliner opposite the door. He was looking straight at me, eyes open. But he didn't see me. He didn't see anything. He slumped to one side, slack-jawed and empty-eyed, his arm hanging down, blood on the carpet, brains spattered on the TV screen.

He's dead.

Drew Aldrich is dead.

That's all I thought as I pushed open the door. There wasn't any spark of disappointment, of rage, of anger that I hadn't pulled the trigger myself. As I stared into Drew Aldrich's dead eyes, my knees wobbled and I wanted to drop to them and weep. Cry with relief.

It wasn't until now that I realized how badly I'd wanted this. How badly I needed it. And I didn't give a damn if that made me a terrible person. I'd wanted this since I was thirteen years old, and now I had it, and it didn't matter who had pulled the trigger.

Drew Aldrich was dead.

"Nadia?"

I wheeled to see Jack. He winced as he realized he'd startled me again and then came forward, gun lowered, gaze on me.

"I— I didn't—" I began.

"I know."

"He was already—"

"I know."

"I don't care," I whispered. "I'm just glad— I'm so glad—"

"I know."

He put his arms around me, and I fell into them.

CHAPTER 11

It looked as if Aldrich had shot himself in the left temple with his service revolver. The gun lay on the floor beneath his dangling left hand. In front of him, on the ottoman, was a website printout. I could read the headline even upside down.

"Local Teen Murdered, Local Man in Custody."

Below was Amy's school photo. Beside it was a picture of Drew Aldrich.

I remembered the first time I'd seen this article, digging it up because I had to know, had to see it. I remembered thinking how much Amy would have hated that photo, with her hair pulled back in little-girl barrettes, her Peter Pan collar buttoned tight, no trace of makeup. Amy's annual "good girl" picture, a performance piece to please her mother, because she knew how much it meant to have a nice photo to send around at Christmas.

I remember, too, seeing the picture of Aldrich and wanting to take that article down to the paper, find the reporter, shove it in his face and say "How dare you?" How dare you put his picture beside hers. How dare you make his picture as big as hers. This was about her, about Amy, her life and her murder. Drew Aldrich shouldn't rate more than a footnote, just enough to say "Drew Aldrich has been arrested for the crime."

I reached down to touch the paper, then stopped myself. Even if I was wearing gloves, there was faint blood spray on its edge, and I couldn't risk smearing that. I settled for crouching to get a better look at the page. It was hard to see, with only the glow of the TV for illumination. When I bent, though, I noticed a marker that had rolled partly under the page. And there was something written across the article.

I'm sorry.

This was Aldrich's suicide note. He'd printed it out, scrawled his guilt and his remorse across it, and shot himself. I looked at that, and I looked at Aldrich, and then I turned to Jack.

"It's staged," I said. "He was murdered by the guy who came to visit."

"Yeah."

"You'd already figured that out?"

He shrugged. "Look at his hand."

"If you mean because he shot himself in the left temple, that's not a mistake. Aldrich was left-handed. Whoever killed him knew that."

"Look closer. Hand. Sleeve."

Now I saw what he meant. The white sleeve of Aldrich's pullover was clean.

"No back spatter," I said. "That's a pretty good indication. It's not foolproof, but it's better than my explanation, which is just that there's not a chance in hell he wrote that." I pointed at the note. "Even if he's changed, he's not going to collapse with guilt after seeing me, kill himself, and admit to a crime he was acquitted of. When the friend left, he was talking, but I never heard Aldrich's reply. The guy was faking a conversation in case a neighbor was listening in."

I stepped back from the body and surveyed the scene. "Aldrich knew the guy. He'd called him after he saw me. He must know what Aldrich did and has a damn good reason to shut Aldrich up, fast. But why?"

"Not important. Gotta—"

I turned sharply. "Yes, it is important, Jack. If you're in hiding, you don't go telling new friends about your old identities, and you sure as hell don't tell them about your past crimes. If this guy knew, then he—"

"Probably committed some crimes himself. Besides this." Jack waved at the body. "Saying it's not important *now*. Gotta finish searching. Then get out."

"Place was already searched," Jack said as we climbed to the second story. "I was coming to tell you that."

"You mean because it's a mess?" I shook my head. "I've met plenty of guys whose apartments always look like they were ransacked."

"Not that." He waved into the office. "What's wrong?"

"Nothing," I said, peering in again. "I was here earlier. This room is actually the cleanest—" I stopped. "Right. That's the problem people make when they break in. They tidy up after themselves. The trick is to leave it how you found it."

"Yeah. Searched here. Bedroom, too."

I followed him in. While the bedroom certainly couldn't be called tidy—it looked like a laundry hamper exploded and dirty dishes were stacked on various surfaces—every drawer was closed, every book stacked neatly. Even the porn magazines had been straightened.

We still searched, but found nothing.

"Maybe after being caught a few times, Aldrich got rid of whatever souvenirs he had."

Jack shook his head. "Guys like that? Take shit. Write it down. Something."

Which was true, though I hardly expected it to be

an area of expertise for Jack. I was the one who wanted to understand how criminals thought. When I commented, though, he just shrugged and said, "Read stuff."

We messed up the areas that had been tidied, so when Aldrich's body was found, there'd be nothing out of the ordinary. We took one last look around. I stopped in the middle of the hall.

"Do we know where he took his victims?" I asked.

"Hmmm?"

"He wouldn't bring teen girls back here, even if they were with him consensually. So he must have had places. Was there anything about that in the other investigations?"

"Yeah. Never changed his MO. Liked cabins." He looked back at the office. "Bet he has one. Maybe paperwork for it here?"

I shook my head. "If he's following his old pattern, he's not buying. He's finding an abandoned or unused cabin. Which is probably where he kept any mementos. But if he didn't own the place, we'll never locate it."

"Check the truck," Jack said. "Maps. Gas receipts."

I nodded and left.

Luckily, Aldrich had left his keys on the kitchen counter. I snuck out the rear door and around the side of the house then made an easy dash to Aldrich's carport.

I crawled into the passenger seat, shut the door, and used a flashlight to illuminate the glove box. It was jam-packed with crap. I was adjusting my position when my foot got tangled in a cord. I looked down to find a portable GPS on the floor, hidden by fast food wrappers. It was connected to the lighter. I reeled it in and turned it on.

Aldrich didn't seem to use the GPS very often. Of

the four places in the memory, three were out of state and he hadn't visited any of them this month. But he had gone to the fourth address—twice. A rural location about an hour east of Cleveland.

Before we left I went back downstairs for another look at Aldrich—or at the scene of his death. Would the police realize it wasn't suicide? They wouldn't know about his visitor and wouldn't realize that Aldrich would never admit to Amy's murder. It looked like a perfectly plausible scenario. He was an exonerated killer turned fake cop. That alone would keep the local police hopping.

The most damning evidence was the lack of back spatter on Aldrich's gun hand, and presumably a corresponding lack of gunpowder residue. Yet despite what people see on *CSI*, there isn't the time or the budget to test everything. If it looked like a clear case of motivated suicide, that's what it would become.

The address in the GPS led us to a tidy farmhouse with a minivan in the drive and a barn around back. The house was surrounded by dense forest, with the nearest neighbor a mile away. We drove half that distance and found a rutted road leading into the woods. Another half mile down it and we had to stop as the road petered out. That's when we started walking.

There was exactly one trail leading from that road. It branched after a hundred feet. The better-groomed section led to a small waterfall and pond, with a makeshift platform for swimmers and anglers. The second branch ended at a cabin, nearly hidden in the overgrown woods.

When I saw that cabin, my feet stutter-stepped and Jack plowed into me.

"Sorry," I said. "It's just—"

"I know."

It looked like "the" cabin—the one Aldrich had taken us to. There was nothing meaningful in the similarity. Most simple cabins look like this—a wooden shack with no running water, no electricity, no amenities save a fireplace and an outhouse.

I steeled myself and started forward.

"Wait outside," Jack said. "No reason—"

I glanced at him.

"You can keep giving me that look," he said. "Won't stop me from offering."

"Which I appreciate—"

"Don't want appreciation. You want to repay me? Take me up on it. Why go in there? Who are you trying to impress? Only one here is me."

No, I was here, too, and I needed to follow this through because otherwise I'd feel like a coward.

"Jack, I've faced Aldrich. I've broken into his house. I've found his dead body. There's not going to be anything in that cabin that makes things any worse." I managed a wry smile. "Save the marker. I'm sure you'll find something else you really don't want me doing."

He considered that, peering at me in the darkness. Then a snort and a wave. "Stay behind. Could be booby-trapped."

CHAPTER 12

The cabin wasn't booby-trapped. It wasn't even locked. Like Bobby Mack's place, where Aldrich had taken Amy and me, this was just a shack in the woods, used by whoever wanted it.

It was a single empty room, simple cover for campers, maybe originally for Boy Scouts or the like, to keep the younger ones out of the rain. There were signs that people had been here. Marijuana butts. An empty cheese puffs bag. Crushed Coke cans. A tequila bottle, broken in a corner.

"He wouldn't keep his treasures where a hiking family could find them," I said. "If they're here, they'll be hidden. Maybe outside or—"

Jack was bending to examine a floorboard. When it didn't budge, he paced along the edge of the room, looking and testing for give with his feet. He found a loose one and checked under it, then shook his head.

I started on the other side. We'd nearly met in the middle when I found a board that was slightly loose, with a single nail on one end. Jack pried the nail up with a knife. The board came out. Below was a dirt floor . . . with a slight depression. I carefully pushed aside the dirt and saw a steel box.

I pulled the box up and put it on the floor. It was

locked. Useless really, when opening the box was a simple matter of unscrewing the hinges. Jack did that, again using his knife.

When I raised the lid, I saw only black and for a second I thought it was empty. Then I realized I was looking at a folded black silk scarf. I lifted it. Underneath . . .

I sucked in a breath, then Jack's hand darted out, as if he was ready to snatch it from me before I saw some grisly relic. Then he looked and stopped. I reached into the box and picked up a hair clip. It was bronze—a crossed pair of old-fashioned pistols.

"This was mine," I whispered. "When my dad took me shooting for the first time, he bought me this afterward. Annie Oakley guns, he called them. It was my favorite clip until it disappeared. It must have fallen out at the cabin. But—" I shook my head. "No, it can't be. I was sure my mom had taken it. She hated it. Said it wasn't ladylike. I figured she'd made it disappear. But obviously I left it . . ."

Jack shrugged. "Maybe not. Could have broken in. Stolen it."

"No, Aldrich was arrested that day. He never got out on bail and by the time he was acquitted, this was long gone." I rubbed the hair clip. "I wore it to the exhibition that day. I remember that . . ." I looked up at Jack. "How would I forget losing it?"

"Too much happening. Probably thought you still had it. Took a while to realize you didn't. Never put the two together."

"I—" My eyes widened. "Shit! I'm not wearing gloves."

"Doesn't matter. Your prints already on it."

My thirteen-year-old fingerprints. Drew Aldrich had taken it and he'd hidden it here and he'd . . .

And he'd what? How many times had he taken it out? Run his fingers over it? Remembered—

The clip fell from my hand, clinking back into the box as I struggled for breath.

No, he wouldn't have taken my piece out. The important memento would be Amy's.

I put on my gloves and sifted through the other items in the box. Necklaces. Bracelets. Earrings. Rings. Another hair clip. A watch. I vaguely registered that each piece represented a victim and the box was filled with trophies. So many trophies. So many victims.

I'd think of that later. Right now, I kept sifting through for something of Amy's, and the more I did, the tighter my chest got, panic setting in.

"I can't find it," I whispered. "Amy's piece. I can't find it."

"It's there."

"I know it's here. It must be, but I don't recognize it. All this stuff and I should know hers as well as I know mine and—"

My fingers touched the bottom of the box, leathery and flat. I felt around the edges. Then, being careful not to dump the jewelry, I tugged out a leather-bound book.

I flipped it open to a random page and started reading the handwritten entry, dated three years ago.

Leigh sent me photos today. Photos of her friends in the change-room, their shirts off. She'll get a special treat for that. She'll also get a spanking, because she knows she's only supposed to use my phone number for emergencies.

The book disappeared from my hands. I wheeled to see Jack snapping it shut.

"Not here," he said.

He was right. I turned back to the box and felt that worm of panic rising again.

"That can wait, too," Jack said.

I nodded and shut it. I looked in the hole under the floorboards, but there was clearly nothing else there.

"This is it," I said, lifting the box. "Are you okay with me taking it?"

He nodded. I reached for the book, but he pretended not to notice, shoved it into his jacket pocket, and headed for the trail.

"Taking you home," Jack said as we approached the car.

"Um, did I do something?"

"Yeah. Guy who killed your cousin? Dead. And you? Out and about."

"Right." I took a deep breath. "Even if it isn't ruled a suicide, no one's likely to accuse me. Still, it's better if I'm home when the news hits. If you want to just drop me at a car rental—"

"Taking you back. Sticking around a few days." He glanced at me as he opened the door. "That a problem?"

"Mi casa es tu casa." When he hesitated, I said, "You're always welcome at my place, Jack."

He grunted something and slid into the car as I put the box into the trunk. I got in the passenger's side. When he started up the car, I put my hand out.

"Can I do some reading on the drive?"

"Too dark."

"Jack . . ."

"Get some sleep. Long drive. Switch off at the border."

I sighed, shook my head, and ratcheted my seat back.

—∾—

Jack's not one for speeding—at least not too far over the limit. It calls attention to yourself. But when I woke up at the border in Buffalo, it wasn't yet three in the morning. I was ready to take over, but Jack said no, he was awake, just let him grab a coffee and he'd be fine.

I would have argued, but I was barely conscious. I drifted off under the blaring lights of a Tim Hortons drive-through as he was asking me if I wanted anything. I woke again to more lights, these ones on the 401 as we passed through Toronto. I drank my lukewarm coffee and ate my chocolate-dipped donut. Then I said I had to use the bathroom, but I was really just getting him to pull over so I could insist on switching out. He let me. We were only an hour from home.

Jack didn't sleep on the rest of the drive. He sat there, quietly gazing out the windshield, until we pulled off the regional highway and onto the back roads.

"Almost six," he said. "Think you can slip in?"

He meant we should try to make it look as if we'd gotten back hours ago. Like I said, it was unlikely anyone would compare the timelines of my arrival and Aldrich's suicide, but it was better to establish an alibi.

"I can certainly try. The problem will be Scout. She sleeps in my room and as soon as I get upstairs, she'll go nuts."

"I'll get her. Bring her down." He paused. "Think she remembers me?"

"You were up a few months ago. She's a little scatterbrained, but she's a smart dog. And she's not big enough to rip your face off yet." I pulled into the drive. "I'll park in the rear lot so— Shit! The rental car. Drew Aldrich is about to be found dead in Cleveland, and I come home in a rental with plates from—"

"New York. Got a car with New York plates."

"Which I never even noticed. Okay. If you can take my bag up and toss it in my room, I'll head off for a morning jog. You grab a room and some rest."

He started getting out of the car.

"Oh," I said. "Since you'll be resting, I'll have time to read. Why don't you give me that journal—"

"Later."

CHAPTER 13

I was waiting at the boathouse, changed into my jogging outfit, when Jack brought Scout out. I could hear her whining as she pranced about, being remarkably restrained for a six-month-old puppy. Then she caught a whiff of me on the breeze.

By the time Jack reached me, I was on my ass, gasping for breath as I struggled to get out from under sixty pounds of very excited German shepherd.

"Think she missed you," Jack said.

"No kid—" I made a face as I got an unexpected mouthful of puppy tongue. "Blech. Just a warning—don't attempt to talk when you're on her level unless you like French-kissing dogs."

A soft chuckle. I gave Scout a hug as she whined and danced, then I pushed to my feet.

"Also, if she jumps up, knee her back down. Please. I know it's cute, but in a few months, it won't be and we're really trying to break her of that."

"Yeah. Getting big."

"And she has barely begun to grow into her ears and paws, which means she's got a lot left to go. Apparently, white shepherds get even bigger than black-and-tans."

"Huh."

"You didn't know that when you bought her, did you?"

He shrugged. "Bigger dog. Better protection."

"No, bigger dog means my bedroom is getting smaller by the day."

"You talked about getting out of there. Building a proper cabin. Got lots of property. Shouldn't have the smallest room anyway." He looked at Scout, who was zooming back and forth now. "We'll talk about it. Go jog. Need the exercise. Work it off."

"Me or her?"

"Both," he said and waved us on our way before heading toward the lodge.

I went for a ten-kilometer jog, which took me through the town of White Rock. Usually, on a weekend, I'll bypass it. When the weather is still decent, everyone's up and about early—kids on bikes, folks walking their dogs, homeowners working on their yards. If you're a local who doesn't get into town more than once or twice a week, and you try jogging through, you're guaranteed to get stopped a half dozen times. Today, though, I wanted to be seen. Establishing my alibi a little more.

I didn't overdo it. For most who tried to stop me, I just waved and smiled. I did pause for a couple—Benny Durant from the real estate office, who had questions about land near the lodge, and Rick Hargrave from the liquor store, telling me he might close shop early in case I needed more beer for my nightly bonfire.

By the time we got back to the lodge, we'd worked up a lather, so we took a dip in the lake. In mid-October, it's nearly ready for a skin of ice. Refreshing, to say the least.

As I walked up to the lodge, I caught the familiar scents of cinnamon buns and wet grass and wetter dog, and I listened to a woodpecker in the treetops and a clatter in the boathouse, as Owen came out, fishing pole in hand. I waved. He waved back as if it was any other morning and I'd never left. I watched his slightly stooped, white-haired figure trudge down the path to the lake.

I was home. I was me again. Not Dee, part-time Mafia hitman. Not thirteen-year-old Nadia, the girl who'd lost her cousin. Now I was Nadia Stafford, lodge owner. I could say that's the real me, but no, it's just the most comfortable part. It doesn't exist without the others. Still, this is my favorite part of myself and every time I find it, waiting here, it's like rediscovering a forgotten treasure.

As I neared the porch, Emma came out, her dyed red hair nearly blinding in the morning sun. Scout took off with a happy yelp. Emma saw her coming and zipped behind the door faster than you'd think possible for anyone on a hip-replacement waiting list.

"Don't you two come in here like that," she called through the screen. "Wait right where you are. I'll grab towels."

I climbed onto the porch as she disappeared into the lodge. I tried the door but found it latched. As I slumped into a Muskoka chair, Scout seconded my sigh and took the one beside me. When Emma came out, she sighed herself as she looked at us.

"Are you trying to give me extra work?" she said. "Getting mud all over that chair?"

"Scout? Down."

"I didn't mean her." Emma tossed us towels. "What are you doing back? You better not have cut your vacation short. I told you we weren't busy. They changed the forecast, but we still had one cancellation."

I finished towel-drying my hair and started on

Scout. "I stopped by to see John yesterday." That was the name she knew Jack by—ironic now that I knew it was his real one. "We got to talking about those ATVs he fixed, and I mentioned the snowmobiles. He offered to come up for the weekend and check them out."

"Oh, he did, did he?"

"Is that a problem?"

She gave a small, self-satisfied smile. "Not at all. Your *cousin* is welcome here anytime he likes."

I'm pretty sure she knows Jack isn't my cousin. For one thing, there's the complete lack of a resemblance. More damning, I suppose, is the fact that I'd never mentioned him until he needed a place to stay last spring, and since then he's bought me a dog and has come up for several midweek visits.

So what do they think is going on? I suspect it's more than the obvious. Emma and Owen never question my unplanned "vacations." Nor do they question my ability to buy hot tubs and gazebos despite being intimately acquainted with the lodge's tight cash flow. When our teenage helper, Sammi, vanished last year, and I was suddenly taking off with my newly rediscovered cousin John, they didn't question that, either.

They don't suspect the truth. I'm sure of that. As understanding as they are, the truth goes beyond what I think they could comprehend or accept. They probably figure I'm another type of vigilante, like a detective, and that Jack is a private eye I met on my investigations. Whatever the case, they like him coming around. As Emma said the last time, "He makes you as happy as that damned dog does." Which, I suppose, is true, though I doubted Jack would appreciate the comparison.

As Emma and I talked business I saw a figure pass by the screen door and into the kitchen.

"I think a guest is awake," I said.

"Then they can help themselves to coffee and buns, which are all laid out." Emma pegged a dishcloth on the line. "They asked for breakfast at ten, and I'm not serving it earlier."

"Yes, ma'am."

The door opened a minute later. It was Jack, changed and shaven, balancing two plates with cinnamon buns on two mugs of coffee.

Emma didn't attempt to exchange more than the most basic pleasantries with him. A lifetime with Owen had taught her that some people don't go for that sort of thing. But Jack made the effort, asking about her hip and making sure she was okay with him staying.

"Well, I'd have appreciated it if *someone* called me last night to be sure I had a big enough breakfast planned. But that's not your fault. If there aren't enough eggs, *someone* can go without."

"She means you," I whispered to Scout.

"No, I do not."

As the dog jumped off the chair, Emma waved at Jack's plates. "Don't feed her any of those. It's not on her diet."

"Hope she means the dog," Jack said as he handed me a bun and coffee.

"She does. We're trying to stop Owen from feeding scraps to Scout. If he does it, she can't understand why guests won't. She's snatched a few buns, which lands her in the doghouse. Literally."

"Ah." He turned to sit in the chair Scout had vacated.

"Don't! It's wet," I said. "We went in for a swim."

He shook his head, clearly refraining from commenting on the sanity of October lake dips.

"Let's go down to the dock," I said. "The sun's better there and the chairs are clean."

—~~~—

We sat in silence, enjoying the view and the coffee.

Still gazing out at the water, I said, "I'd like that journal."

He sipped his coffee. "You're happy to be home. Enjoy it."

"Because I sure as hell won't enjoy what's in that journal. I know that, Jack. But it's research. There are other girls in there. Maybe other Amys. If I can give their families closure, I want that."

"I know. And we will. But earlier? Said I could hold a chit. Stop you from doing something."

"I didn't mean—"

"Too bad. Taking you up on it. I won't keep this from you, Nadia. But I want to read it first." He held my gaze. "You keep saying you owe me. This is what I want. The only thing I want."

What could I say to that?

CHAPTER 14

As we drank our coffee, my cell phone rang. I was still carrying around my work one, in case Paul needed to contact me for anything about the failed Wilde hit.

When I looked at the screen, I must have reacted, because Jack said, "Quinn?"

I nodded.

A pause. Then, "Gonna have to talk to him, Nadia."

I definitely tensed at that.

"You have to," he said. "He'll read about Aldrich. Have questions. Especially since you were away from the lodge when it happened."

"Shit. I wasn't even thinking about Aldrich. You're right. I should have . . ." I shook it off and checked the voice mail.

"It's me," Quinn's voice said. "There's something in the news. I'm sure you know, but . . . Call me." A pause. "Please. This is important."

Jack watched my face as I clicked off. "Do it now," he said. "Get it over with."

I nodded, and phoned Quinn back as Jack took his coffee mug and headed toward the house.

On the second ring, Quinn answered with, "Hey." Scrambled number or not, he knew who it was. The second I heard that familiar "hey," something in me jumped, and something in me cracked, and I wanted to hang up, because it was just too hard. I might blame him for not contacting me since the breakup, but the truth was that when I made those calls myself, a part of me—an increasingly big part—had been praying he wouldn't answer. If he did, I'd only have to hear his voice, and I'd say anything, do anything, to put things right, and yet I knew that even if I managed to piece us back together, we'd only end up here again.

"Dee?" he said when I didn't reply.

"I'm sorry."

A pause from his end now. I'm sure he was trying to figure out what I was sorry for. I squeezed my eyes shut and pushed on.

"When I heard who died," I said. "I should have called."

"Yeah, you should have."

"I wasn't thinking. I just found out and I'm still reeling. I didn't think about you seeing it until Jack mentioned it and—"

"You're with Jack?"

I winced. "Long story. A business thing. Anyway, you're right. I should have called and notified you about Aldrich, and I'm sorry about that."

"Notifying me, Dee? How about simply talking to me."

Now I bristled. I didn't mean to. I wanted to get through this call with my temper in check. Instead, I heard myself saying, "And why exactly would I do that? You've made it quite clear that any personal contact is not welcome."

I expected him to bristle back, to snarl and snap, as he had that last time. But he only sighed and said, "Not for something like this, obviously."

"Then I apologize," I said, with zero apology in my voice. "I wasn't aware there were exceptions."

I braced for a retort but got only silence. Then I waited for the hang-up click.

"I was an ass," he said after a long minute.

No, don't say that. Goddamn you, Quinn, don't say that. Snap at me. Snarl at me. Hang up on me. That makes it easier.

"We need to talk," he said, "and I know this isn't the time. Let's start over. I heard who died. How are you holding up?"

"I didn't do it."

"That wasn't what I asked."

"But it's what you have to know, right? I'm not being a bitch, Quinn. I'm just . . . I'd like to stick to that."

"Business."

"Right."

"Because you have Jack there for support."

I wanted to bristle at that, too, and part of me did, but the image it conjured up was so ridiculous that I couldn't help sputtering a laugh.

"Yes," I said. "Jack came running to let me cry on his shoulder, because that's so Jack."

"All right." A pause. "I'm sorry. That was uncalled for. I just . . . He pissed me off. He calls me because there's an issue with you, gets me worried, and then refuses to tell me what it is. Being an asshole. Typical."

"He couldn't tell you my problem without—"

"Yeah, yeah. Security concerns. Which conveniently left me hanging, while he swooped in to—" Quinn bit off the sentence and swore. "And that's not why I called, either. Let's start again."

"I didn't do it. I know it seems suspicious. You get a call about a problem with me, I'm on the road, and the next thing you hear, a certain someone is dead, but it's a coincidence." *Mostly.* "I was dealing with another job, a state away, and he committed suicide. I got my ass home, just in case there were questions. So far, nothing, but I suppose it's just hitting the wire."

"Yeah. He had some warrants out, under aliases. Not exactly on our most-wanted list, but . . . I had something set up. To ping me if his name popped on our system. It did about an hour ago. His body was just found."

"Good."

"But you already knew."

Shit.

"It's a long story," I said. "I can only tell you that I absolutely didn't do it. Jack, either. I'll tell you the rest when I can."

"And when will that be?"

Silence.

"I'd like to see you, Dee."

"I—"

"If you're in any trouble, I can help. You know that."

"I'm not in any trouble."

"I'd still like to see you."

Silence.

"All right," he said, and I could tell he was struggling to restrain himself. "When can I talk to you again?"

"I'm not sure we should—"

"Goddamn it, Dee. I fucked up. I know that. But I miss you. I miss talking to you. Hell, I miss e-mailing you. I know you tried to reach out. I know I ignored you. I was being an ass. I can be. You know that. I would like to see you, but I can tell that's out of the question, so I'd like to talk."

"I—"

"Monday morning. That's forty-eight hours from now. I'll call or you can call, and you can tell me what happened with that suicide, if you want to, but we'll talk then. Can you do that?"

"Yes."

He exhaled. "Good. Thank you. We'll talk Monday."

The conversation left me confused. Confused about what Quinn wanted and, even more, confused about what I wanted. I had only to hear his voice to know that I wasn't over him. But the relationship was over, for me, because I knew that was the right decision. I cared about him too much to selfishly hold on, if that meant holding him back from what he really wanted—a wife and kids and a house in the suburbs.

After breakfast, Jack left with Owen to check on those snowmobiles. I headed out to shoot and clear my head. The lodge has a gun range, which is actually what sold me on the property. And, if I was being honest, it's what nearly sent me into bankruptcy, bumping the price far higher than I could really afford. As amenities go, it's not exactly a basketball court. I paid to have it, I paid to stock it, and I paid to run it, all because I wanted it. It was the kind of thing I'd dreamed about the way others might dream of horses or a private golf course. It's probably the only time in my life that I'd treated myself to any kind of luxury, and I don't regret it.

Today I stuck to the indoor range. I have a strip of land for distance, but even though guests are warned to avoid that edge of the property, I get nervous when it's all first-timers, as we had today. And as my bout with Jack in the woods had showed, short-range practice is always helpful.

I left Scout with Emma. She prefers the outdoor range as well, being not so keen on the sound—or smell—of gunfire in enclosed quarters.

I stayed out there for two hours. By the last thirty minutes, admittedly, I was stalling as I waited for Jack. I'd asked Emma to tell him where I'd gone, and I expected he'd join me. But he didn't. So I finished up, cleaned up, and headed up.

I was halfway back to the lodge when the smell of Jack's cigarettes wafted over. I pinpointed the direction and smiled. He was sitting at our old place, the log where we'd talk when he'd first started coming around. That's also where he'd invited me to join the hunt for a hitman-turned-serial-killer.

It'd been so different then. Jack had been different. The mysterious mentor. The guy I'd only ever seen under cover of night. I remember when he picked me up at the airport for that job. He'd been in his biker disguise, and I'd commented on his aging techniques. And then I saw him later without any disguise, and realized it hadn't been makeup. Ouch. But that says a lot about how little I'd known of him—I couldn't even have guessed at his age from our conversations. They'd all been about me. With each passing conversation since then, I'd learned a little more about him. Now I'd learned a lot about him, and while it was hardly his whole life story, it felt monumental.

Some things don't change, though. Jack was back at our log, smoking a cigarette. Doing it there, not from nostalgia, but because it was a secluded place and I didn't allow smoking on the property.

I drew close enough to see him through the trees and slowed for a better read on the situation. He was on our log, feet planted apart, elbows on his knees, leaning forward, cigarette dangling from one hand. It'd been dangling there awhile, the ash ready to drop, but he didn't seem to notice as he stared into the forest. When the ash finally did fall, it hit his shoe, sparks flying. He kicked it off and almost scowled, as if annoyed by the interruption. He ground out the cigarette on the stump. Then he paused, holding the butt. He put it aside and pulled out a fresh one, lit it, and took a long draw.

This wasn't just a smoke break in the woods. Something was wrong.

Jack went back to his forearms-on-knees pose, gazing into the forest. Then he straightened, legs stretching as he raked his hair back. He almost did it with the hand holding the cigarette, and I heard his muttered curse. He sighed, shifted again, and picked up something lying beside him.

The book. Aldrich's journal.

CHAPTER 15

He didn't open the journal. He just drummed his fingers on the cover, then resumed his position, leaning forward, smoking. I started to retreat, but he must have caught the flicker of movement.

He squinted over, cigarette lowering. "Nadia?"

"Sorry," I called, staying where I was. "I smelled the smoke. I'll leave you—"

"Come here."

As I approached, he scooped up the book and whisked it to his other side. Then he stubbed out the cigarette and motioned to the spot beside him.

"A little not-so-light reading?" I said.

"Yeah."

We sat there in silence. He was the one who finally broke it.

"Yesterday," he began. "Talked about you seeing Aldrich. Worried it'd bring shit back. You said whatever it was, you'd want to remember. Confront it. Face it." He glanced over. "That still hold?"

"Of course."

His gaze locked onto mine. "I mean it, Nadia. Don't answer lightly. Is there a limit?"

"A limit?"

"Stuff you wouldn't want to remember?"

"Um, that is a little hard to answer when I have no idea what we're talking about."

He sighed. "Yeah." He paused. "What if I'm not sure?"

"About what?"

"Whether you should remember. If you've forgotten? There's a reason. A damn good reason. I don't want to fuck with that." He met my gaze again. "I really don't."

"Okay," I said slowly. "So you've found something in that book that I seem to have forgotten. If I forgot it, you figure maybe I'm blocking it, because I couldn't handle it the first time around. But now I know there's something in there, and I'm going to imagine the worst."

"What's the worst?"

I hesitated and shook my head. "How can I even answer that, Jack?"

"Try."

"I guess . . . I don't know. The worst? Maybe that I killed Amy. That Aldrich's cigarettes weren't just weed, and I didn't refuse, like I remember. I took it and I went crazy and I murdered Amy."

He peered at me. "Do you ever even *think* that?"

"No, because even at my most messed up, I know that's not possible. But you asked for the worst. If it was something as horrible as that, I'd still want to know. Whatever it is, I must know it, deep down, and it's going to keep gnawing at me until I figure it out."

Jack dipped his chin in a nod. "It is there. Not going away. Giving you nightmares."

I took a deep breath. "It's about Amy, isn't it? He describes what he did to her, and there are parts I've forgotten. Or maybe something I failed to do. Something I let happen. Worse than running away."

"Amy's not in here."

I looked up sharply. "What?"

"There's no mention of Amy. Not that I can find."

"And you think that means something. That Aldrich didn't—"

"No. Think it means he left shit out. This?" He lifted the book. "It's about what else he did to girls. Raping them. Seducing them." He paused. "Seducing's not right. They were kids. Still rape. I just mean . . ."

"You mean that sometimes the girls were willing partners and sometimes they weren't. Considering that the allegations against Aldrich were all statutory rape, I'm guessing it was more of the former?"

"Yeah. He was good at that. Not sure how. Or why."

"Teen girls are vulnerable and sexually curious. Same as teen boys. An adult comes along and knows what to do and say, and it doesn't matter if he—or she—doesn't strike us as someone a teen would find attractive. Looks have very little to do with it. And when Aldrich was younger . . ." I shrugged. "Amy thought he was cute. A lot of girls did. Even now, I can't see it because all I see is the monster who murdered my cousin, but at the time, I wasn't into boys yet. A late bloomer."

"Yeah." He stared out into the forest.

"So the journal is rape and so-called conquests, and presumably he left Amy out because describing her murder crossed a line."

"Didn't leave her out."

"What?" I straightened. "I thought you said—"

"He doesn't talk about killing her. Doesn't talk about raping her. Skips that. Doesn't even give her a name."

I frowned. "What does he call her?"

Jack went quiet, and I was about to ask again when he said, "*The cousin*. Her cousin." His gaze finally lifted to mine. "*Your* cousin. He wrote about you."

I stared at him. Then I slowly shook my head. "No, that entry must be about another girl and her cousin, because there's no reason he'd write about me. It was all about Amy."

"He calls you by name, Nadia."

I didn't even think he knew my name.

"I . . . I don't understand. Why would he write about . . ." I trailed off. I looked at the book and I heard Jack's words again. Not murder. Rape. It was about the girls Drew Aldrich raped.

I shook my head. "No. There's a mistake. You're misinterpreting or he's lying or . . . or something. He never—" I swallowed. "He didn't . . ." I couldn't get the rest out.

"Do you want to stop, Nadia?" Jack said. "We can stop right here."

His words were soft, his voice low. Meant to calm me, to offer an escape.

"No, I do not want to stop," I snapped. "I'm not saying I can't handle this, Jack. I'm saying it did not happen."

A pause, then, just as softly. "Okay."

I looked at him. "It did not happen."

He picked up the journal and stuffed it under his jacket. "Okay." He got to his feet. "Come on. Let's go back. Forget this."

I sat there, my gaze fixed on his chest, not daring to raise it. After a second, he started moving away. I reached out and caught the edge of his jacket.

"Jack . . ."

"Hmmm?"

"If . . ." I took a deep breath. "I don't see how . . . I

couldn't forget—" I swallowed. "What else is there? About . . . that day. Can I read it?"

He slowly lowered himself to the log again. Then he found a page near the beginning and turned it to face me.

"Start here," he said. "I'll show you passages. There's no reason to read the whole thing. It's not ever going to help. But if you decide you have to, I won't stop you. I'd just . . ." His gaze locked on mine. "I'd really rather you didn't."

I nodded and looked down. The entry started at the top.

Nadia came by with her cousin today. As usual, it was the cousin's idea. I play along because I know it's the only way to get within twenty feet of Nadia. But I'm not interested in the cousin. She's a little tease who pretends to be a slut and probably hasn't even let a boy feel her tits yet. Plenty of those around. Nadia's different. She's a good girl. The police chief's daughter. So sweet and shy she won't even look me in the eye. Never had a girl like that. But I bet I could.

I heaved breaths and it was a minute before I could speak. "All right. So he thought about it, but that doesn't mean . . ."

Jack turned the page to another entry.

It went just like we planned it. The cousin told her dad the wrong time to pick them up at the train station, so he was late, and I just happened to be driving by to offer the girls a ride. It almost didn't work, though. Nadia's cousin really had to talk her into the truck and for a minute, I thought she wouldn't do it. But she did. Anything to protect her cousin. If she only knew that

her cousin set the whole thing up. Not for Nadia, of
course. She thought she was getting me all to herself.
Nadia was just along for the ride. Which was kinda
true.

The page ended there. I reread it. "I don't . . . I can't
believe . . ."

I didn't finish the sentence. I *could* believe Amy had
set that up. Blinded by Aldrich's attention. Not setting
me up—as he said, she hadn't known that was his plan.

Still it made no sense. I knew what happened. He'd
taken Amy to the cabin to get her high and maybe to
seduce her, and things went wrong, horribly wrong,
and he raped and strangled her while I was tied up in
the next room.

"What if it's fake?" I whispered, my gaze still on the
page. "Maybe he wrote it later. Because I escaped and
turned him in. Even if I couldn't get him convicted, I
ruined his life. So he fantasized about . . ." Again, I
couldn't finish.

"You can stop reading," Jack said.

I put my hand on the book, touching the words, as
if making sure they were real. My fingers brushed
Jack's. The sudden touch startled me and I flinched. But
I didn't pull my hand back. I could feel the warmth of
his hand against my fingertips, feel the weight of his
gaze on me. Wishing he didn't have to show this to me.
Wishing I'd say, "Okay, take it away." Knowing I
wouldn't.

I curled my fingers under, pressing my hand up
against his. His fingers wrapped around mine.

"I need . . ." I began. "Whatever part is . . . easiest."

He lifted our hands off the book, tilted the journal
his way, skimming and flipping two pages, and then he
stopped. He covered part of the page. I read the rest.

Nadia wouldn't smoke the dope. Her cousin did. The stupid twit tried to pretend it wasn't her first time, even as she coughed and gagged. When I tried to push it on Nadia, the cousin got mad at me. She had no problem bringing Nadia to a secluded cabin with a guy she barely knew, but she wasn't going to make her smoke up. Stupid twit. At first, I kept pushing. If Nadia smoked it, she'd relax and maybe I could talk her into it. But that's when I realized I didn't want to talk her into it.

The page ended there.

"Enough?" Jack said. I could tell he didn't expect me to say yes and when I didn't, he turned two pages. This page began midline.

left the cousin, after making sure she couldn't interfere. I went back to Nadia. I put the knife to her throat and I told her what I was going to do to her cousin. But Nadia could protect her. Just be a good girl and give me what I wanted and I'd leave her cousin alone. She was crying, big tears rolling down her cheeks, but she didn't make a sound. I'd warned her not to make a sound and she didn't. She was a good girl, who did as she was told, and if I said she could save her cousin by giving me what I wanted, she'd do it. So I made her take off her jeans and her panties and lie on the floor, and I put the knife at her throat and

I pushed back and scrambled to my feet. The forest seemed to pulse, growing dark and hazy, the ground beneath my feet uneven, unsteady.

"I—" I forced the words through my tight throat. "I need to walk. I—I won't run away. I just— I'm going to walk."

"Okay."

I started down the path walking as best I could on ground that seemed to rise and dip under my feet. Dimly, I could hear Jack behind me, staying his distance but keeping his eye on me.

I kept walking, seeing those words again, all those words, replaying in my head.

It didn't happen. Couldn't have happened. I wasn't the one he hurt. It was Amy. All Amy.

In the distance, I saw a shape through the trees. My neighbor's run-down cabins that he'd planned to fix up to rent and never did. This spring, I'd sleepwalked into one, thinking it was *the* cabin, that I was back with Amy and Drew Aldrich. I'd dreamed I was on the cabin floor, free from my bonds, blood on my thighs, trying to get my panties back on, to dress and run for help.

I'd told myself I was confusing my story with Amy's. But how many times had I had that dream? A nightmare where Aldrich told me to be quiet, told me to get undressed, made me lie on the floor, and held a knife at my throat.

Just like he'd described.

Nightmares where I tried to be still, tried to be so still and quiet, but I couldn't, because the terror and the pain and the horror and the humiliation . . .

I fingered the paper-thin scar on my throat.

I told you to lie still.

I doubled over and threw up whatever was in my stomach. Then I stayed there, on all fours, head pounding, fingers digging into the earth. A shadow passed over me, and I looked to see Jack hunkered down beside me.

"Tell me what you need," he said.

I shook my head.

"Tell me what I can do."

Another shake.

"Can I stay here? With you?"

I nodded.

After a minute, he said, "I'm sorry."

I backed up and sat down on the cold earth. "You knew. Even before you read it, you figured out what happened to me."

Silence. Then, "Suspected."

"No. You knew."

He had. The pieces were all there. The nightmares. The guilt. And the scar. How the hell do you cut your neck on a fence? That's what I've always said, and it's what I believed, not because I remembered doing it, but because I remembered saying it, over and over, all my life, whenever someone noticed. I'd scaled so many fences that the exact instance seemed irrelevant. I said I cut it on a fence and my parents said I cut it on a fence, so I must have cut it on a fence.

Jack could tell the difference between a metal scrape and a knife slice.

I wanted to say, "Why didn't you tell me?" But that was ridiculous. He'd tried. Over and over he'd suggested that my dreams meant something, and I'd flipped out every time.

This is what he thought I'd remember when I saw Aldrich. This is what he'd thought I might be better off forgetting. This is what he'd thought was in that journal.

I lurched forward and threw up again.

A minute later, he asked, "You want to talk?" I rocked back on my heels and caught my breath. I shook my head.

"Walk?"

Another shake.

"Want me to get Scout?"

Another shake, and in some deep part of me that wasn't completely numb, I felt bad. He was fumbling to help and there was nothing he could do.

Yes, there was. He could let me collapse against him. Hold me. Offer comfort—warm, quiet comfort. But he stayed a few feet away. Giving me space. Being careful, so careful. I'd just found out I'd been raped. He wasn't going to presume to offer any physical comfort, and I couldn't bring myself to cross that gap and take it.

"I . . . I want to go inside," I said. "To my room. Just be alone for a while."

He nodded and led me back.

CHAPTER 16

I sat cross-legged on my bed and tried to process what happened twenty years ago. I couldn't. I just couldn't.

Buried memories? How the hell did that happen? No, really. How the fuck do you forget you were raped at thirteen? That the first time you had intercourse, it was rape. That the first time a guy touched you, it was rape.

You cannot forget that. You just can't.

But I had, and right now, I couldn't process how or the why. Simple acceptance was difficult enough.

Drew Aldrich had raped me.

He raped me and he hadn't been charged with it, and I hadn't testified to it, which meant . . .

I sucked in breath.

Just days ago, I'd told Jack that I'd almost wished I'd been hurt because then Aldrich would have gone to jail. But I had and he didn't, because I'd told nobody.

Had I really told nobody?

I remembered the "dream"—the torn panties, the blood, the pain. Then running through the forest, never running fast enough because I couldn't run. Because every step felt like knives ramming through me.

That part I hadn't forgotten. I'd twisted it into something else in my memories—the pain of running too hard, of being too frightened. But it wasn't. I'd run to town, and I'd hobbled into the station, and—

And I couldn't remember exactly what happened next. I never could. I remembered my father's face, his horror. I remembered yelling about Amy, get Amy, help Amy. The rest was the blur. Wiped from memory.

Given my condition when I ran inside, my father must have known I'd been raped. Maybe they'd all known, every cop who'd been there that day—my uncle, two older cousins, the other officers I'd grown up with. They'd known what had happened to me and they made a decision to bury it. To pretend it never happened.

My uncle, my cousins . . . men I'd loved. Men I'd trusted. And my father. My wonderful, perfect father.

They'd known what had happened and they'd denied it. They'd denied me the chance to deal with it and, most important, they'd denied Amy the chance for justice.

I sat on my bed for at least an hour. Then I had a bath, as hot as I could stand it. I scrubbed and I lathered and I scrubbed some more, until the water was cold and when I tried to add more hot, it blasted my raw skin like molten lava. I got out, pulled on my robe, and went to my window. I stood there, staring into the forest, until I caught a flicker of white. I looked down to see Scout about a hundred feet in. Jack was with her, sitting on a stump, the dog at his feet.

Did I think he'd go amuse himself while I suffered in private? No. Like me, he'd spent most of his life feeling guilty for things he'd done, things he hadn't done, decisions he'd made, decisions he hadn't made. It didn't take much to tap into that well. He'd wrestled with this, and even if I'd forced his hand, he was going to feel guilty. Now he'd sit out there, making sure I didn't slip out my window and hurt myself somehow.

I did sneak out—through the front door, to avoid the guests enjoying dinner.

"Hey," I said as Scout jumped up to greet me. I walked to Jack. "How about we do something? Get me out of my head for a while."

"Talk?"

I shook my head. "Not yet. I want a distraction, and I don't care if that's not the responsible or the mature way to handle this. Is there something you'd like to do?" I waved around me. "We have a world of choices."

He studied my expression, as if trying to figure out if I was serious or playing hostess. After a minute he said, "You've got white-water rafting, right?"

"White-water canoeing actually. But it comes with the risk of hypothermia at this time of year."

"That's a no?"

"It would be a yes, if I thought you meant it. I'm well versed in your opinion of my extreme sports, Jack. Seriously, what do you want to do?"

"What I said. Take me out. Show me how it's done."

It was exactly what I needed right now, as crazy as that sounded. A distraction that would consume all my attention.

"Really?" I said.

He gave me a look. "You want it in writing?"

"I might. Okay, then, let's hit the rapids."

"F-f-fuck!" Jack said as he stumbled from the canoe, soaked and shivering uncontrollably.

"Did I mention the risk of hypothermia?" I climbed out and tied the canoe to the dock.

"Thought you m-m-meant if we fell in."

"When you run the rapids, the water comes to you."

"No fucking shit."

I bustled him into the gazebo. "Which is why I turned on the heater in here before we left. And brought hot cocoa and these." I lifted a pile of towels onto the table. "And even these." A second pile of dry clothing joined it. "You can change in the boathouse if you like, but I'm only going to turn my back. Scout will warn us if anyone comes."

He turned his back. We'd stayed in the same motel room—this wasn't any closer changing quarters.

I was in a weird mood—that almost giddy, stubbornly defiant, willfully oblivious one that comes with saying "screw you" to everything else. The nonstop adrenaline had drowned the confusion and the hurt and the guilt. Jack had been a trooper. Clearly, running rapids was not going to become his go-to entertainment anytime soon, but he'd stuck to it for my sake. And maybe that was the most important part of all. For those few minutes, he was just as determined to make me happy as I was to let myself be happy. While there are people in my life who care for me, there's no one who'd do *this* for me, with such a complete absence of expectation.

When we'd changed into dry clothing, I poured him a cup of steaming cocoa. Then I set out a container and pulled off the lid, revealing a wedge of fresh-baked pie.

He settled at the table and looked around. "You got a plate? Or another fork?"

"Neither. It's all yours."

He hesitated then seemed to realize I wasn't quite up to stomaching food yet. He leaned over to dig in, then brushed back his wet hair and dried his fingers on his jeans.

"I should put up one of those signs," I said. "*You will get wet on this ride.*"

He arched his brows.

"You know, like at amusement parks? The signs at the log and flume rides?"

"Last time I was at an amusement park?" He finished chewing a mouthful. "Fuck. You were probably in training pants."

I smiled. "So you've never pulled a hit in one? Shot a guy in the house of horrors? I saw that in a movie once. The audience loved it. All I could think of was the kids in line, about to be permanently scarred when a guy rolls out with his head blown off."

"Shotgun? In public?" Jack shook his head. "Can't hide that. Not the gun. Not the noise. Fucking Hollywood."

"Which was the second thing I thought. You'd want a small-caliber gun with a suppressor. A CNS shot from behind, so he dies quickly, with a minimum of mess. If he's wearing a jacket and you aim it through the collar right, it might not even be obvious he was dead when he rolled out."

"Or you could pull a switch. Wait on the ride. Shoot. Pull him out. Leave him there. Take his spot. No one would notice until he started to smell. They'd just figure he was a prop."

"That could work. Now I've just got to find a situation where I can pull a hit in an amusement park."

"I'll put feelers out. See what I can do." He stretched his legs. "Did have an odd one last year. Wanna hear?"

I eased back with my cocoa. "I do."

When it was dark enough, we moved to the fire pit. No one joined us except Scout, who lay between my chair and Jack's, head on her outstretched paws, watching the fire.

When Jack's cell phone blipped, he pulled it out and frowned down at a text message.

"Everything okay?" I asked.

"Just Evelyn." He upended his beer bottle, his gaze distant, as if contemplating something. "So how'd it go with Quinn?"

"All right. He was annoyed I hadn't called about Aldrich, but backed off when I reminded him he's been ignoring my calls."

Jack snorted. "Licking his wounds."

"That would be a great excuse, if he was the one who got dumped."

Jack looked over sharply. "What?"

"He . . ." I took a deep breath. "I'm not going to bore you with that."

When I handed him a second beer, he said, "None of my business. But I'd like to know."

I took a sip of my beer, then said, "He invited me to a family wedding."

"What?"

I gave a small laugh. "The nerve, huh? I mean, it's not like we were dating or anything . . . Oh, wait. We were."

"Doesn't matter. Under the circumstances? Had no right to ask."

"Yes, Jack. He did. He just . . . He didn't take my answer well, and it became obvious that the problem wasn't just the wedding. He was heading in a direction I wasn't ready to follow."

"Moved too fast."

I fingered my beer bottle. "It's not that I wasn't ready to follow; it's that I had no intention of following. I wanted a relationship. A solid, exclusive relationship. He was heading down the track that ends with wedding rings and babies."

"You don't want that?"

I gave him a look. "Seriously?"

"Yeah, seriously. You're thirty-three. No reason you can't."

"Except that I don't want to. I thought I'd made that clear to Quinn. Hell, I thought he wanted the same thing. He's been married—it didn't work and it never seemed as if he wanted that again. He loves being an uncle, but he told me once that he didn't want kids of his own. So I don't think— Fuck it, I *know* I didn't mislead him."

"He changed his mind. You two got together. Started thinking it might work."

"But it *did* work—as exactly what I signed up for—a relationship." I lowered my voice as my temper flared. "I thought it was going great, and I thought he was happy. Then this happens. One invitation to one wedding, and the next thing I know, he's telling me he wants this to end in our own wedding."

"Asshole."

I sputtered a laugh, "No kidding, huh? And that's why I feel like shit—because Quinn's not an asshole, and he was telling me something wonderful. He gave me a gift, and I threw it back in his face."

"Gave you something you didn't want. He didn't care. *He* wanted it. Makes him an asshole in my books." He paused. "Nothing new."

"You can say that, but you know he's not a bad guy. You just don't like him very much."

Jack shrugged. "Don't like him personally. Still, was good to you. Made you happy. Now?" He glanced over. "Think you could lure him into a fun house?"

I laughed.

Chapter 17

When we reached the porch, Jack said, "Got a room with two beds, right? Vacant?"

"Sure."

"Gonna suggest we take it. Just for tonight."

I glanced over before opening the door. "So I don't wake up screaming? Or sleepwalking into the lake?"

I said it lightly, but he just looked at me.

I nodded. "You're right. Both are a distinct possibility, as much as I hate to admit it. We'll both sleep better if someone can shut me down before I terrify the guests."

"Not worried about the guests."

"I am." I waved him inside.

None of the rooms at the lodge are as big as most modern tourists expect. I'm very clear about the size on the website and in the brochures, both giving square footage and using adjectives like *cozy*, but I still field complaints.

The rooms with two beds have just enough room to walk around those beds—and nothing more. Close quarters, especially when you add a big dog. This time, we had to get changed in the bathroom, if only for logistics' sake. I went first. Then I climbed into bed.

Jack came out a moment later. He was dressed in

sweatpants—the same pair he's worn since our first case, which still look new enough that I suspect he only brings them on "visit Nadia" trips.

As he got into his bed, I turned off the light and said, "I've kept you up talking long enough, but I want you to know I really apprec—"

"Don't."

"I just want—"

"You want to thank me, Nadia? Remove two words from your vocabulary. *Sorry* and *appreciate*. All right?"

I went quiet.

"Fuck. Came out wrong." He propped his head on his arm, his face shadowed in the dim light. "Nadia?"

"It's okay."

More silence. Another soft exhale. "No, it's not. Came out pissy. Wasn't supposed to. I just mean . . ."

"That you're tired of me apologizing, and you're tired of me thanking you. But I don't know what else to do, Jack. You came for me in Michigan. You got me through that. You gave me Aldrich. You got me through that. Now you're here to help me through . . . the rest, with the journal, and I know it's not enough to just say thank you, but I don't know what else to do."

"You don't need to do anything. I don't expect it. Don't want it. I'm not keeping a tab, Nadia."

"I know, but—"

"Me being here? Me finding Aldrich? Think that's an inconvenience? Taking me from something else? Fuck, no. Schedule's clear. Wasn't here? Be waiting for work I don't need. Coming here? Finding Aldrich?" He looked over. "Happy to do it."

"Okay. I'm—" I sucked in air. "I—" I stopped myself again with a laugh. "First, I almost apologized. Then I almost apologized for almost apologizing. It's a sickness, you know."

A short laugh. "Yeah."

Silence. I waited a moment, then lowered my head back to the pillow and tugged the blankets up.

"I care about you, Nadia. You know that, right?"

I felt my cheeks heat and was glad for the darkness. "I—"

"Just making sure you know. I don't come around because I have to. Don't help out because I have to. I want to. You need to thank me? Repay me? Let me help. Don't make a big deal. Okay?"

"Okay."

"Now go to sleep. You can't? Want to talk? Wake me up."

"Thanks." I paused. "Am I allowed to say that?"

"For now. Just don't overdo it."

I smiled and curled up under the covers.

I slept so soundly that if I hadn't been in possession of the beer all night, I'd have thought Jack dosed my bottle. Maybe part of my bad dreams had been my brain poking me to remember what happened, and now that I did, it could rest. It wouldn't last. It wasn't as if I'd just remembered where I left my wallet. This was huge, with major ramifications that eventually would pound louder than those forgotten memories. For now, though, I slept.

When the sun seeping through the curtains woke me, I slipped out of bed and dressed quietly, with Scout waiting at the door. I was padding toward her when Jack's sleep-thick voice said, "Heading out?"

He was propped up in bed, covers around his waist. He was bare-chested, lean, with muscled arms. Wavy, silver-threaded black hair tumbled over his forehead. His free hand scratched his stubbled cheeks as he struggled to wake. It was not a bad sight to start my day.

"I'm going jogging," I said. "Not fleeing into the night."

"I know." He stretched. "Hold up a sec."

He swung his legs out and stretched some more. Then he walked to the window and opened the drapes, blinking.

"Fuck. That's bright."

"Yes, we call it dawn. Also? Cold."

He shivered. "Yeah." He glanced over. "How far you going?"

"About five miles. Why? Are you thinking of coming with me?"

There was a moment where it almost seemed as if he was going to say yes. Then he glanced at the frost-laced window and shivered again.

"Fuck, no."

I laughed. "Go back to bed, Jack. When you smell cinnamon rolls, you know it's time to get up."

I reached for the door.

"Got your gun?" he said.

"I'll be grabbing it before I leave. I'll have my gun and I'll have my guard dog, so I'll be perfectly safe in the crime-infested streets of White Rock."

He grunted.

Before I could leave, he stopped me again. "I'll make the beds. Tidy up."

"Emma will still notice, so I wouldn't bother hiding the fact we slept in here unless it bothers you. She's not going to say anything—she'll be too busy trying to figure out why we used two beds."

A short laugh. "Yeah. I'll leave it then. Go on. Enjoy."

I grinned back. "I will."

Jack didn't know what he was missing. The cold air and bright sun that sent him back under the covers were exactly what made it perfect jogging weather, the sunlight dappling the road as the chill air woke me up and kept me comfortable. I stuck to the back roads, empty and clear and silent.

As I ran, I thought about the journal. Not about what Aldrich did to me. Not now. This was morning, time for moving on—or at least for faking it. What I thought of instead was the rest of the journal.

I'd ask Jack to remove the page detailing my rape. Yes, the cop in me balked at tampering with evidence like that and maybe the rest of me balked, too, as if I should read all the details and tough it out. But there was no point, nothing to be gained. I accepted that I'd been raped; I didn't need to read an account from my rapist's point of view. Here I'd draw the line. Take the page out so I could read the rest.

Scout stayed at my side, happily panting, not even distracted by the squirrels that sped across the road or birds that shot up from the shoulders. Then I noticed her glancing into the forest.

At first it was just a couple of quizzical looks, as if to say, "Huh? What's that?" On a run, it took more than a bunny or a raccoon to snag her interest. We don't get a lot of coyotes and black bears, but they are out there, and I really didn't want her tangling with them. Whatever was in those woods, though, clearly she considered it a potential threat, because every time I moved between her and the woods, she'd scoot back over, shielding me.

I touched the butt of the gun holstered under my jacket. If a bear lumbered out, I'd happily send it off with a warning shot. The forest remained quiet, though, so I kept the gun holstered and stayed alert.

The thing about predators up here? None of them are really a match for a human and a dog. And they know it. They'll watch you pass and breathe a sigh of relief when you do. They will not attempt to follow.

Yet as we continued along, Scout kept glancing into the forest; whatever was in there was tracking us. That could only mean one thing: this predator walked on two legs.

Jack might be in full protective mode, but he'd never stalk me. The chance it was a stranger was almost as low. Random assault and random murder, like stranger rape, are practically unheard of out here. We have our crime problems but they don't include guys lurking in the forest.

It had to be Quinn. He wanted to talk to me, and he'd been to the lodge twice before for that. He wouldn't stalk me, but he might follow me, gauging my mood.

To be safe, I waited until I reached an open portion of the road, near a house I knew was occupied year-round. Then I tugged the water bottle from my waist-band and took a long drink from it. When a twig crackled underfoot, Scout stiffened and growled, her gaze swinging to the forest. No one hailed me. Meaning it wasn't Quinn.

I snapped on Scout's lead as I tracked the noises in the woods. A twig crackle here, a dead-leaf scuffle there; my stalker was moving to the edge of the forest. I turned my gaze enough that I could see the forest but still seemed focused on the dog.

Finally, a figure appeared, dark against the sunlit trees. I turned and the figure seemed ready to duck back into the forest, but it was obvious he'd been spotted, so he stepped out.

"Hullo there," he called.

"Morning."

I sized him up. Late thirties. Average height. Stocky. Hard to tell if it was muscle or fat, given his bulky windbreaker, but he had the bulldog face and rolling, confident gait of a man in good physical condition. Also? He had a gun. I could see the butt taking form against the fabric of his jacket.

"Sorry if I startled you," he said. "I'm, uh . . ." A sheepish look. "I'm kinda hoping you can direct me back to my cabin. I got myself turned around in there."

Scout growled as the man approached.

"Ignore her," I said, patting her head. "She's not keen on strangers, but the worst she'll do is knock me over trying to hide between my legs."

He chuckled. "Beautiful dog."

"Thanks." I flashed him a friendly, small-town-girl smile. "Let's see about getting you back to where you're staying. Are you renting a cottage?"

"Yep. Over near town. Came out with the kids to see the fall colors. I'm out seeing them and they're sleeping in."

I laughed. "Typical."

He was less than five feet away now. Sizing me up. My gun was well hidden, and his gaze passed over it without hesitation.

"Actually," he said. "I've got another problem. I was out with our dog and he took off. Chasing a rabbit or something. If I go back without him, the kids will flip. They're always telling me to keep him on a leash."

"That's a good idea out here."

"I know." A deep sigh. "I hate to ask, but maybe if my dog saw yours, he'd come back. I wasn't far from here when he took off." He turned and pointed into the forest. "It was right over there."

Seriously? He expected me to follow him into the

woods? Apparently, my small-town act made me look dumber than I thought.

I flashed another bright smile. "That's a great idea. My girl here loves making friends. I'm sure she'll find him in no time."

As we started into the woods, Scout growled louder.

"She smells your dog," I said. "That's what's making her nervous."

"Well, hopefully, she'll see him soon."

"Oh, I'm sure she will. Just lead the way."

CHAPTER 18

The guy led me ever deeper into the forest, stumbling on the unfamiliar terrain. A city boy.

As we walked, he kept saying, "I last saw him just over here." Then, "Wait, over there." And, "Just a little farther now."

"What does he look like?" I asked.

"He's brown."

"Big? Small?"

"In between." The guy turned. "Why don't you take your dog off-lead? She might find mine that way."

"I don't do that in the forest. Much too dangerous." I paused. "But why don't I go ahead? I know the lay of the land better than you do."

He struggled not to smile. "That's an excellent idea."

"Great! Come on, girl. Let's find us a missing puppy."

I passed the guy and got ten paces before I heard the whir of his jacket being unzipped. I turned so quickly he jumped.

"Oooh," I said. "You might want to leave that zipped up. The deer ticks are bad this time of year, and we've had a few cases of Lyme disease."

He looked at my undone jacket.

"I'm wearing spray."

"So am I."

There is no such thing as anti-tick spray, but I grinned and said, "Carry on, then."

I turned back and tugged out my gun. I waited for the telltale whisper of him starting to unholster his weapon then wheeled.

He stared at the Glock pointing at his chest.

When his hand moved under his jacket, I barked, "Stop!" but he kept drawing his weapon. As soon as I saw the butt, I fired.

The shot hit him in the right shoulder and he staggered back, releasing his grip on the gun. I lunged, dropping Scout's lead as I grabbed his right arm and twisted it. I threw him down. I kicked his gun aside.

"On your stomach!" I said. "Hands behind your back!"

"You shot me," he said, gasping in pain. "You fucking—"

"On your stomach!"

I rammed my foot into the small of his back, knocking him into position. Scout jumped on his back, growling. I ordered her off, which she did, seemingly with reluctance.

"Hands behind your back!" I said.

"What are you? A fucking cop?"

I grabbed his right arm and pinned it against his back. He yowled but stopped struggling. I patted him down. There was a switchblade in his pocket. I pulled that out. Then I found a zip tie in his jacket pocket.

"You bring your own handcuffs?" I said. "Now that is convenient."

He resisted having his hands cuffed behind his back, but a slam to his injured shoulder stopped that. I got the zip tie on his wrists and then used Scout's leash to bind his legs. Once he was secured, I did another pat-down search, making sure I hadn't missed any weapons. Finally I removed his wallet.

He had a New York State driver's license. A decent fake. He had a credit card in the same name—Douglas Leeds—but the cash-stuffed wallet told me he preferred to pay that way.

"Why were you following me?" I asked.

Silence.

I did another pat down, as thorough as possible now. When something crinkled in his windbreaker, I realized he had an extra pocket sewn in the liner. Inside was a folded sheet of paper.

I pulled the paper out and opened it. It was a computer printout with two photos on it. One was a slightly blurry photo of me in disguise at the bar in Newport. The other was an equally crappy photo of me leading a group of rock climbers near the lodge—likely something he found online. Below that was my name, address, date of birth, and information about the lodge.

"Are we going to talk about this?" I said, shoving the paper down beside his face.

He turned his stony gaze to mine. "No."

"All right then."

I took off my shoe and then my sock, and I stuffed the sock into his mouth. He fought then, teeth gritted against the pain in his shoulder. But I managed to get it in without being bitten.

When I started to walk away, he decided he was feeling chatty. At least, that seemed to be what he was trying to tell me, grunting and wriggling madly as I abandoned him to the bunnies and squirrels.

As I turned the last corner near the lodge, I was confronted by yet another armed killer on a mission to track me down.

"Hey," I said to Jack. "Did you start worrying that a hired gun had attacked me in the forest?"

He rolled his eyes and jerked his chin back toward the lodge. "Emma's baking. Should be ready."

"Great, but I'm going to suggest you get your cinnamon roll to go. I shouldn't leave that guy bleeding in the forest."

"Guy?"

"The hired gun."

Jack stared at me. "You serious?"

"Also, I'd like my sock back." I gestured down at my bare leg. "I just hope he hasn't chewed any holes in it."

"Fuck."

"Agreed. All these times when I mocked you for telling me to take extra precautions on my jog and now you get to say 'I told you so' forever."

I handed him the page I'd taken from my would-be assassin. As he read it, his expression changed. If I was the guy in the woods, I'd start gnawing my arm off.

Jack folded the paper, carefully and deliberately, running his nails along the edges before he looked up.

"If I'd had any idea—" he began.

"—that Drew Aldrich's killer would presumably send someone here after me? It's a completely unforeseeable turn of events, Jack."

His grim look said it should have been foreseeable. He jerked his chin toward the road. "Let's go."

"You aren't wearing a disguise," I said.

"Don't need it."

I could have gotten my would-be attacker to talk without Jack's help. No matter how inclined a guy might be to discredit a woman's potential threat, it's possible to beat the sexism out of him. But I didn't need to do that when I had a partner who was a lot better at getting re-luctant people to talk.

Bringing back male reinforcements did not bolster my attacker's opinion of me. He lifted his head as we approached, saw Jack, and managed a snort, as if to say "Figures."

Jack walked over, gun at his side. With his free hand, he grabbed the guy by the hair and lifted him as he crouched to study his face. Then he dropped him and shot him in the other shoulder. The guy let out a stran-gled squeal through the sock gag and the stink of urine wafted over.

"He didn't piss himself when I shot him," I said.

"Saw yours coming. Gotta be faster."

The guy writhed on the ground. When Jack bent again, he tried shimmying backward.

"Stop moving or I shoot you *between* the shoulders."

The man stopped. Jack hunkered down in front of him, gun dangling so casually it might have been a half-empty beer bottle.

"I need to talk to you. I'm going to take that sock out. You yell, scream, holler? I shoot you. You don't answer my questions, I shoot you. Basically? You piss me off, I shoot you. Understood?"

The guy nodded.

Jack pulled out the sock gag, tossed it aside, and looked up at me. "What're we calling him?"

"His fake ID says Douglas. Dougie works for me."

Dougie followed our exchange, gaze slightly nar-rowed, as if not sure whether to be offended by my casual tone or take it as a sign that the situation wasn't as dire as it seemed. He opted for number two. He asked Jack, "You a cop, too?"

Jack looked at me.

"My throw-down tipped him off," I said. "Apparently, he didn't know his assigned target was a former law-enforcement officer."

"Fucking idiot," Jack muttered.

"He's not too bright," I said. "Did I tell you how he got me into the woods? He convinced me to help him find his lost dog."

Jack snorted. "How old does she look to you? Twelve?"

Dougie's eyes narrowed as he looked up at me. "She tricked me. Fucking bitch—"

Jack shot him in the leg. When he screeched, Jack grabbed his hair and slammed his face into the ground.

"Shut the fuck up." He lifted Dougie's head as blood surged from the man's broken nose. "Didn't I warn you not to piss me off? Calling her names is going to piss me off."

"You crazy . . ."

Dougie trailed off, watching Jack's emotionless face. He seemed to decide that *crazy* wasn't quite the word he wanted. He swallowed hard and dropped his gaze.

"What's the job?" Jack asked.

Dougie was having trouble focusing. "Wh-what?"

"The job. This." He shook open the page with my information. "What were you supposed to do?"

"Just . . . uh, find her. Get a look and see if she was the woman in the other photo. Which, obviously she's not, so I'll say there was a mistake and—"

"Stop babbling."

His teeth clicked shut.

"And if she was this woman in the photo?" Jack said. "What were you supposed to do?"

"Tell the guy who hired me. That's it."

"So you were only supposed to confirm whether Nadia Stafford was the woman in the photo. Which required a gun, handcuffs, and fake ID."

The man decided not to answer, instead shifting and wincing, trying to find a less painful position.

"Who hired you to check her out?"

"I don't know. That's not how I work. I have this other guy, like an agent, who takes the, uh, job requests."

"A middleman? Who?"

"He's just a guy. It's not like you can look him up in the Yellow Pages. Hell, even I don't know his—"

"—his real name. Yeah, I know. I'm asking what he goes by."

Dougie eyed Jack. I could see the wheels turning, hoping this was just idle curiosity. Knowing if it wasn't, that meant Jack might recognize the middleman's nom de guerre, which would mean Jack wasn't just some petty criminal I'd brought along for backup. One should hope the guy had figured that out by now.

"He goes by Roland. All I have is a phone number and even that changes—"

"Roland? Out of Pittsburgh?"

Sweat rolled down Dougie's cheek. "Maybe. I only know it's a Pennsylvania area code."

Jack turned to me. "I know him. Runs a pack of lowlifes and losers. Third-rate pros. Like this dumb fuck. Ask Evelyn. She'll know more."

Jack wasn't explaining this for me—this was for Dougie. It took him a minute to piece together that Jack knew his middleman, and he knew Evelyn. Pretty much everyone in the business knows Evelyn's name. She makes sure of that. All that added up to one conclusion—Dougie was dealing with a fellow hitman. And not some "third-rate pro." He looked at Jack as he tried to figure out who *he* was. Jack might be a legend in the business, but he wasn't nearly as interested in getting his name out as Evelyn.

"Let's back up," Jack said. "I asked what the job was. I already know, but I want to hear you say it. And if you don't?" Jack didn't raise the gun or threaten. He just shrugged.

"It was a hit," Dougie said. "The job was to hunt down this Nadia Stafford chick, and if she was the woman in the other picture, then I was supposed to kill her."

"Why?"

"It's complicated."

"We have time. And it'll make me happy."

Dougie wanted to make Jack happy. His life depended on it. He told his story—or as much of it as he knew.

Aldrich thought he'd recognized me in Newport. Yet he'd been uncertain so he'd snapped a shot with his cell phone, then called "this guy." That was all Dougie knew—Aldrich called "this guy." Aldrich was freaked out because he thought the woman in the pictures was from his past. Someone who could ruin his present. "This guy" then contacted Roland to hire a hitman to kill Nadia Stafford, if she was the same woman.

"Kill me and then what?" I asked. "Make me disappear?"

"The client offered extra if I could make it seem like a suicide. Otherwise you had to disappear." He looked around the woods. "Which would have been easy out here. I could have done the suicide part, too, if I'd known you had a gun."

"Real fucking tragedy," Jack muttered.

The guy didn't have the sense to look abashed. He just shifted again, struggling against the pain.

"Look, we're on the same team," Dougie said. "Clearly Roland had no idea the target was your girl. But now it's all been straightened out and the job is over. I'll drop it. As a professional courtesy."

"Big of you."

Jack hunkered down again, meeting Dougie's gaze. Sweat streamed down the man's face now as he audibly swallowed.

"What else you got?" Jack asked.

Dougie told him everything else. It wasn't much, but his life was on the line. He gave his name as Mark Lewiston, from Cleveland, along with some other personal information that may or may not have been true. When he was done, Jack turned to me.

"Nadia? Take the dog. Start heading back."

Scout had been sitting beside me, growing impatient, and was happy now to be moving again. As we walked away, I glanced back. Jack noticed me looking. He tensed, a muscle in his cheek twitching. He didn't want me watching him kill a man. It didn't matter if that was his job, or if we both knew it had to be done.

I turned away. The shot fired. I kept walking.

CHAPTER 19

A minute later, I heard Jack behind me. He didn't
catch up, even when I slowed. Finally, I glanced
over my shoulder. He was maybe twenty feet away. He
picked up his pace and was beside me in a few seconds.

"I'll clean it up," he said.

"I'll help—"

"Don't need to. My mess."

"I'm going to help you, Jack."

He gave me a sidelong glance. Seeing if I was okay
with what just happened. I could say I was, but then it
would seem as if his actions were indeed in question.
They weren't. When you kill people for a living, you
accept the risk that this is how it will turn out.

"I'll load tools into the truck while you go in for
breakfast," I said. "We should join the guests, too. It'll
look strange if we take off again too soon."

"Yeah."

More quiet walking. I glanced over. Jack was facing
forward, muscles tight, gaze distant.

"Hey," I said.

I brushed my hand against his. When he didn't tense
or pull away, I hooked my index finger around his and
gave a gentle squeeze. I started to let go, but he held my

hand there, fingers locked. We walked like that for another minute before he said, "I fucked up."

"I hope you don't mean about shooting that asshole. There's no way we could take the chance he'd
come back—after both of us this time."

"Mean him coming after you. My mess."

As his anger surged, his hand clenched mine, reflex-
ively. When he realized, he loosened his hold, but didn't
let go.

He looked over at me. "You don't care, do you?"

"About what?"

"That I almost got you killed. Biggest fucking error
in judgment since—" He inhaled and shook his head. "I
took you to that bar. My idea. We thought he made you.
You were worried. I said it didn't matter. I fucked up."

"There was no way to expect Aldrich would recognize me—in disguise—after twenty years. No reason to
panic when it seemed as if he did. Neither of us could
have foreseen that he'd deal with it by hiring someone
to kill me. We know, better than anyone, that it's entirely possible to hire someone to fix problems that
way. Yet we never saw it coming because it makes absolutely no sense."

"Could have killed you."

"And that's never been a risk before?"

He made a noise in his throat.

"It's a chance I take every time I accept a job. I
didn't get killed today, Jack. I didn't come close. That
wasn't dumb luck. I'm careful. Damned careful."

"I know."

"Then you know that however bad you feel about
this, I was never in any real danger."

He had nothing to say to that.

~∞~

Jack still had my hand when we got to the lodge. I don't think either of us realized, until Emma came off the porch to greet us and stopped in her tracks.

We broke contact fast.

"Did we miss breakfast?" I called.

She shook her head and looked from me to Jack. He murmured, "Fuck," under his breath.

"You've got time to wash up before you eat," she said. "Not much, though, so you'd better step to it."

She stayed at the bottom of the steps, drying her hands on a dish towel. As we reached her, she said, "John?"

"Hmmm?" Jack said.

"Can I have a word?"

"Sure."

"I'll be in the kitchen," Emma said. She glanced at me, too quickly for me to read her expression, and then she headed up and inside.

"Fuck," Jack muttered as the door closed behind her. "Feel like I'm sixteen. Got caught sneaking you out for the night."

"Which isn't like Emma at all. Hell, she practically shoves me at every guy who looks my way."

He shrugged. "Different."

"I'm sure she's long past believing we're actually related."

"Not that. Age difference."

"I doubt it," I said. "But I'll talk to her."

"Nah. I will."

"You don't have to—"

"Got it," he said and went into the house before I could argue.

Jack came out as I finished loading body-dump supplies into my old pickup. He was carrying a picnic basket and a thermos.

"Either you totally charmed her," I said, "or we aren't allowed to dine with civilized folks."

"Wasn't about that."

"No?"

He waited for me to accompany him down to the dock. I turned on the heater in the gazebo as he set up breakfast inside.

"Emma heard the news about Aldrich."

"His suicide?"

"Yeah. Said she was going to tell you and I offered to do it."

"That saves me from finding the right look of shock. Thank you." I poured coffee as he put out the plates.

"Emma said the papers are reporting that the suicide note was a confession. About Amy."

"Which is good on all counts. He's dead and she gets justice."

"And you? Your justice? How're you doing with that?"

"I think it still hasn't entirely sunk in. It feels like it happened to someone else." I lifted my hands. "*Not* that I'm claiming it did. I know what happened to me. It's just not . . . sinking in."

"You gonna talk to someone?"

"A therapist, you mean?" I shrugged. "Probably not. I had that after Amy died and after I shot Wayne Franco. I know it works for people, but I can't talk to strangers. Which sounds utterly ridiculous to anyone who knows me."

"It's different. Personal." He snagged my gaze. "You don't do personal."

I'm sure that if I did talk to a shrink, she'd tell me that my hyper-friendliness was a defense mechanism. If I'm open and extroverted, no one will notice that I don't really say anything about myself. In my own way,

I carry a Do Not Trespass sign as big as Jack's. I'm just better at disguising it.

"Speaking of dealing with it, I still want to read that journal and see if I can give other families closure. But the first order of business is to track down this Roland guy before he realizes his pro is dead and sends a backup." I paused. "I believe we've been in this situation before. Pretty soon middlemen are going to stop sending their guys here. Eastern Ontario: the Bermuda Triangle for professional killers."

Jack snorted.

"So we need to find Roland and get a lead on the client, preferably without telling Roland he's lost a hitman. As much as I hate to cut out on the Waldens again, I think we're off to Pennsylvania."

Jack asked if he could talk to Evelyn. I had photos of Aldrich's killer's license plate and that might help her find who'd hired that hitman. Normally, I'd hand the plate number over to Quinn, but that wasn't happening.

While I did have other resources—and so did Jack—Evelyn was a convenient choice. There's always the worry that she's a little too convenient, kind of like a little store in the middle of nowhere, where you can get what you need easily, but you know you're going to pay through the nose for it. I knew the cost for this—she'd insist on talking to me about the Contrapasso Fellowship again. She wouldn't do it overtly, but she'd ask if I'd heard about some case or other of delayed justice, a victim finally vindicated, and then say, "I heard the Contrapasso did that," and the minute she saw my resolve wavering, as I thought "Maybe I was too hasty," she'd pounce. I didn't need that. I already saw such cases in the paper and wondered if it was them, and sometimes felt the pangs of regret, of thinking maybe they were what I needed . . . No, I didn't need that.

But Jack knew it and he wouldn't put me in a position where I'd need to hear it. He'd talk to her. He'd say he wanted her help, and he was the one person she couldn't refuse, even if she'd be gnashing her dentures, knowing he was asking on my behalf.

I told Emma I was taking off again. Then we dealt with the body and went back to the lodge to pack. By the time I came down the stairs, half an hour later, Jack was waiting in the car. I flew out the lodge door, flung my bag into the trunk, and settled into the passenger seat with a sigh.

Jack said, "Look like you ran a marathon."

"I got a call just as I went to pack."

"Wasn't reporters, was it?" he asked as he pulled from the lodge lane.

"Believe me, I wouldn't have held you up for that. It was one of my cousins."

"You guys keep in touch?"

I fastened my seat belt. "We do. I'm still in contact with most of my extended family. It's the immediate family that doesn't want anything to do with me."

Jack made a noise in his throat. I'd barely spoken to my mother since she remarried and moved to the States. Same with my brother. There was no precipitating fight, no ongoing feud. We just drifted apart, and the greater the physical distance, the less need for contact. I think we all embraced that excuse. My mother had never made any effort to know me, even as a child. Nor had Brad. Dad had been my real family, and he'd died before the Wayne Franco incident.

I continued, "I still see Neil a few times a year for dinner, and since his divorce, he's been coming up to the lodge with friends. He lives in Burlington, so it isn't too far."

"Between Toronto and Buffalo. Right?"

I nodded. "Which is a segue to a question. Would you mind if we stopped in? He was at the station when I escaped from Aldrich, and he stayed with me while my dad and uncle went back for Amy. He was young, but he was family, which means he'd know . . . whatever there is to know."

"About you. The rape."

I flinched at the word. I tried to avoid it myself. I talked about "what happened" or "what Aldrich did." I didn't say the word. That was, I think, part of the problem. Use euphemisms and not only did it avoid the ugly reality of what happened, but it diminished Aldrich's culpability. He hadn't raped me. He'd just . . . done something.

"I want to understand what happened," I said. "Did Neil know? Did I tell *anyone*? Why wasn't Aldrich charged? How did I get raped and spend twenty years not knowing? Maybe he can fill in some of the blanks, because there are a whole lot of blanks."

"Just tell me where to go."

CHAPTER 20

I called Neil to warn him I was coming. It was past one when I rang his doorbell. It was the same bungalow I'd visited for the past fifteen years. He'd gotten it in the divorce. His ex had a McMansion in the suburbs with their two kids and her new husband. Fifteen years married to a vice cop had added up to too many nights when she knew he was out on a case and didn't know a damned thing about it except that it almost certainly involved drugs and guns and all kinds of shit that ate away at him and left her jumping every time the phone or the doorbell rang. My cousin loved his career, and his career made her fall out of love with him. It happens. Too often.

The last time I'd seen him he'd been carrying some divorce-stress weight, but that was gone now. Maybe a sign he'd met someone. Or maybe just a sign he was trying. It was good to see.

"Hey," I said.

"Hey yourself." He swung open the door. When I stepped in, he gave me a hug. Then he glanced over my shoulder. "You brought company?"

"A friend. We're driving down to Buffalo for the weekend."

"Would your friend like to come in?"

"He's fine."

I waved to Jack—for Neil's sake, so he didn't think I was being rude. Then Neil led me past the living room and into the kitchen. Stafford tradition. The living room is for guests; the kitchen is for family.

We chatted for a while. That, too, was tradition. A Stafford had to be polite and friendly, even with family. So we drank coffee and ate Oreos and chatted until talk turned to Aldrich.

"I don't want to give that son of a bitch any due," Neil said. "But I'm glad he confessed before he went. It makes it easier."

"It does."

"Have you heard from your mom?"

"Nope."

He swore under his breath.

"Last I knew she was in Arizona," I said. "And Brad was in New York doing some off-Broadway play."

"Off-off-off Broadway, you mean."

I quirked a smile. "Yeah."

"You're doing well, though. The lodge is getting bigger and fancier every time I'm there. You've got a dog. Got a *friend*." He nodded in the direction of the driveway.

I laughed. "He's not that kind of friend."

"But you *were* seeing someone, weren't you? Last time we spoke."

"Yep. Last time we spoke."

"Damn. I'm sorry."

I shrugged. "I'm fine. And you? Anyone special?"

"Working on it."

"Good." I cleared my throat. "As I said on the phone, I want to ask you a few things about Aldrich. About the case. His death is bringing it back and I just . . . I have some questions."

"About all the ways we monumentally fucked up?"

"Of course not." I met his gaze. "You know I wouldn't do that."

"Yeah, sorry. It still stings, obviously, and this vindication helps, but it's not enough." He reached for another cookie. "What do you want to know?"

"What happened to me."

His hand stopped. It was just a momentary pause before he picked up the cookie, but it was enough.

"You did know," I said.

He set the cookie, untouched, on his plate. Waiting to be sure we were talking about the same thing.

"I've had suspicions for a while," I said. "Bad dreams. Confusing memories. Then this news hit and I saw his face online and it . . . I remembered. Amy wasn't the only one Drew Aldrich raped."

Silence. Slowly, his gaze lifted to mine. "I'm sorry."

"Do you have something to be sorry for?"

"Yeah. We all do, don't we?" He rubbed his hand over his face. "It's so easy to screw up. To make a choice that seems right. Then time passes and you look back and you say, 'How the hell did I do that?' Attitudes change. Insights change. Eventually things that you were so damned sure were right become . . . incomprehensible."

"I know."

"I remember you coming into the station that day. I remember what it was like, seeing you staggering in, barely able to walk, the blood." He rubbed his mouth and shook his head. "It was like one of those nightmares. Where you're on a case, a terrible case, and you start dreaming that it wasn't a stranger who got hurt—it was someone you care about. Except this was real. Uncle Eddie had just come back from the station, panicked because you and Amy weren't on the train.

Before anyone could even react to that, you came in screaming for your dad. He tried to take you into the back, but you wouldn't go. Amy was in trouble—we had to get to her. Your dad wanted to send everyone else. He'd stay with you. You were hurt. You said you weren't, that it was Amy's blood and you only cut your throat getting away. You said no one touched you, that your dad had to go, he had to help Amy."

"I was blocking the rape."

He shook his head. "I don't think so. It was like . . . I had this call once. Years ago. Car accident. The wife was trapped inside, passed out. The car was on fire. The husband had been thrown clear—no seat belt. We tried to help him, but he kept saying he was fine. Save his wife. Wouldn't even let the paramedics check him. Everyone had to help his wife. We saved her. He died from internal injuries. You would have told us anything to convince us you were fine so we'd concentrate on Amy. Your dad still didn't want to leave, but you started screaming and fighting when he wouldn't. So he told me to stay with you and call Doc Foster."

"Which you did."

"The doc came and he took you into the back for an examination. When he came out, he confirmed . . . what we suspected . . . that Aldrich hurt you."

"Raped me."

He tensed as if he, too, would rather avoid that word. Then his face mottled as red as his hair, and he clenched the coffee cup in his hand. "You were a child. You were just a goddamn child and that—"

"Go on," I said. "Please. Tell me what happened. So Dr. Foster confirmed it . . ."

Neil nodded. "He did, but you wouldn't. You insisted you were okay. You wanted him to go to the cabin to help Amy. He said you couldn't process the experience . . . I don't agree. I think you were confused and embarrassed, and you didn't want to talk about it to an old man. All you could think about was Amy. You hadn't forgotten what happened. You were just putting it aside. And then your dad called and . . ." He inhaled sharply, gaze emptying, as if lost in those memories.

"Amy was dead."

He nodded. "We didn't tell you. As terrible as that news was, your dad's main concern was still you. When he came back, that's what he wanted to deal with, before he told you. Except you wouldn't talk about the rape. You knew something had happened to Amy, and you were hysterical, and you insisted nothing happened to you. Doc Foster said if you wanted to block it out, we should let you."

"If I wanted to forget it, then it seemed best forgotten."

"It wasn't like that. It just . . . got like that. Your dad feared if we covered it up and you remembered later, you'd think you'd done something wrong. He talked to Father Myers, which didn't help. It really wasn't the good Father's area of expertise, and he was more than happy to agree with the doctor. Clearly God was granting you the boon of forgetfulness, and we shouldn't interfere. Your mother was right onside with them. Strongly and strenuously onside."

Because she hadn't wanted the shame of admitting her daughter had been raped.

Neil continued, "It wasn't swept under the rug, Nadia. It was hashed over and over and over. It was a family matter, and it was a police matter, too. You know what rape trials are like for the victims. This was the eighties. It was so much worse."

"And Dad didn't want that for me."

"Would any father?" Neil looked me in the eye. "He

was still never comfortable with that decision. He made us all swear that if you said anything—*anything*—to suggest you remembered being raped, we had to tell him. He even made your mother swear. I heard him yelling at her next door. It was the first time I ever heard him raise his voice to her. He said that if you ever remembered anything, and she didn't tell him, he'd leave her. Take you and leave."

There are times when I think my father and I would have both been better off if he'd done exactly as he threatened. But divorce wasn't a real option at the time, not when you lived in a small town and had children. Dad had buckled down and made the best of it. That's what he'd done here, too. Everyone told him that if I'd "forgotten" the rape, then it was better for me to go with that. I'd forget it. Which I had.

I told Neil that I understood. That wasn't entirely true, but it's what he needed to hear. He'd been barely more than a kid himself, doing as he was told by his family and his superiors. He couldn't be faulted for that.

"The real problem," I said, "isn't how the cover-up affected me. It's how it affected the case. If I admitted I'd been raped, that would have changed everything. They couldn't blame the victim nearly as easily with me."

"Is that what you think? Shit." Neil shook his head and leaned over the table, braced on his forearms. "We made mistakes, but refusing to let you testify was not one of them. Sure, the defense argued that Amy went there willingly, hoping for more than a kiss on the cheek. They played the bad-girl card, but she was fourteen—there's only so far that goes." He paused. "How much do you know about the case? I seemed to remember you were there for part of the trial."

"I was, mostly at the beginning. Dad said he wanted me to see justice done." *Justice for me, I realized now. In case I did remember what happened, he wanted me to see my rapist go to jail.* "As the trial wore on, I guess he realized justice wasn't coming, so he kept me home. As for the details? I've only seen a summary of the case notes. The full file would have been . . . too much."

"So what you know is based mostly on what you heard. Gossip. A cautionary tale about the bad girl who got raped and murdered, and a killer who walked free because of it." Neil shook his head. "That's not what happened, Nadia."

"But if he could have gone to jail for raping *me*, it would have got him off the streets—"

"He wouldn't have. Your mother got rid of your clothing, which was the only forensic evidence. Your dad flipped out when he heard that, but it was too late. There was . . . physical evidence, I'm sure, but by the time we realized the case against Aldrich wasn't airtight, it was long gone. It would have been the worst kind of rape trial—the victim's word versus the accused. You'd have been put through hell for no reason. Aldrich still would have walked."

I stayed quiet after he'd finished.

"I mean it, Nadia. I'm not saying that to make you feel better. There is no way your dad would have let your rapist walk if he could have stopped that. Hell, when Aldrich did walk, they had to whisk him away, under protective custody, for fear we'd retaliate."

And my uncle still tracked him down. No one had forgotten.

"There's a lot you didn't know, Nadia. If you want the case files, I can get them. But Amy did get her justice, even if it came twenty years late."

CHAPTER 21

I climbed into the passenger seat and put an old travel mug in the holder and cookies on the armrest. "Neil insisted on feeding and caffeinating you."

"Huh. Relative of yours?"

"Apparently."

Jack lifted a hand to Neil, still on the porch, and then backed the car out. When we reached a four-way stop, he glanced over.

"Everything okay?"

I nodded. "It helped. I'm glad I went."

"Good." He eased the car forward. "Wanna talk?"

"I will. Right now, I'm just going to process."

We went over a pothole and the travel mug jumped. I reached to steady it, but Jack, seeing it from the corner of his eye, must have only noticed my hand move toward him. He gave it a squeeze. When I laid my hand on the armrest, he kept his hand there on top of it.

I looked down at that. This morning, I'd thought he was offering simple comfort. Was it? Or was something changing?

Did I want something to change?

There was no question there. No matter how much I tried to convince myself it was a bad idea, that didn't change how I felt or what I wanted.

And Jack? Well, he never seemed to want anything. Food, sleep, rest, a drink, a cigarette. He'd accept all of them, with gusto even, but there was never any sense of . . . I don't know. Wanting. Desiring. The same went for sex. I didn't catch him looking at women. Not men, either, so that wasn't the answer.

When I was a cop, there'd be times I'd need to change with the guys, and even if they were happily married, most would sneak a look. Jack never did.

I glanced down at our hands again, then up at Jack. I had no goddamned idea what this meant, and I could stare at him all day without getting a clue. I shifted in my seat, closed my eyes, appreciating the warmth of his hand, and relaxed.

On the leg from Buffalo to Pittsburgh, I told Jack what Neil had said. I told him, too, that I still struggled to understand how I'd blocked the rape. It seemed . . . Cowardly, I guess. As if I'd hidden from something I should have faced.

"The mind does shit like that," Jack said. "Defense mechanism. Protects itself. Subconscious."

"But to completely block out—"

"It happens. Post-traumatic stress." When he caught my look, he shrugged. "Done some reading. Trying to understand. Figure it out."

I wasn't sure what to say to that without seeming as if I couldn't imagine Jack poring over books on rape and post-traumatic stress. Which I couldn't, but that sounds like an insult to his intelligence. I know he dropped out of high school. That doesn't mean he's stupid. He's just not . . .

I didn't go to college after high school. Maintaining a B average took a lot of work, so I wasn't pressing my luck. In the last few years, I've taken courses to fill what I perceive as gaps in my education. While I don't regularly engage in debates on literature and psychology and economics, I *am* interested in them.

Jack? He's a problem solver. In thirty years as a professional killer, he's never even been arrested. That's not dumb luck. He's scary-smart at what he does. But if I'm with Evelyn or Felix and the conversation turns to something traditionally academic, Jack bows out.

So, yes, hearing him talk about defense mechanisms and PTSD was . . . unexpected. I wasn't quite sure what to make of that.

Jack's cell phone vibrated. Or that's what I presume happened, since he pulled it from his pocket, checked the screen, and grunted.

"Evelyn. Got us a hotel. Texting the address."

"Is she still meeting us there?" We'd discussed this earlier—she wanted to join the hunt for Roland and we didn't feel we could refuse.

"Yeah. Made her get her own room, though." Jack drove a few more miles and then said, "Could tell her to stay home for now. Do some legwork. Bring her in later."

"Will she squawk?"

He shrugged. "Don't really care." A sidelong look my way. "You want her along?"

"If you're okay with telling her to stay home, then I think we're doing just fine on our own." I paused and added, "I'd prefer that."

It was hardly an admission of anything, but I still tensed before I said it.

But he only nodded and said, "Sounds good." He passed over the phone. "Get her on the line." He rattled off the number as I punched it in.

"You could just set that up for speed dial."

"Why? Know the number."

I shook my head. The line rang a few times before voice mail picked up. Jack took it and said, "Call me."

"I could have done that," I said. "I might have even used more words."

"Don't need to. Clear enough."

If Evelyn did get the message, she didn't return it. I could say that meant she was on the road and didn't want to talk and drive, but that would hardly stop her. She suspected we were calling to tell her to turn around, so she wasn't answering. We were stuck with her.

Evelyn's taste in hotels was a big step up from our usual, but neither of us complained. Jack bought me candy in the gift shop, and I got bottles of pop before we headed up.

I blame the sugar, but by the time Evelyn arrived, I was a little giddy. Jack was in a good mood, too, relaxed and joking and even talking as we sprawled on the sofa in our suite. Or I sprawled. Jack sat at one end with my feet over his lap. When Evelyn rapped on the door, Jack was in the middle of a story. He got up and went over, still talking.

"So I refuse the job. Don't care if the client's been cleared. Too fucking squirrelly for me. Two days later? Hear this news story."

Jack checked the peephole. He undid the chain and tugged the door partly open before turning and heading back to me.

"Client took out a fucking want ad."

"In the paper?" I said.

"Yep."

A petite white-haired woman in an elegant blouse and slacks caught the door before it slammed shut on her fingers.

"Excuse me?" Evelyn said, pushing her way inside.

"Posted it under fucking 'contract positions,' " Jack said to me.

"What the hell kind of welcome is that?" she said.

I put my finger to my lips. "Shhh. He's telling me a story, and we've worked up to polysyllables and near-complete sentences."

He snatched the bag of sour candies from me and poured a handful before tossing it back. It hit my chest and a geyser of sugar sprayed.

"Hey, it's empty!" I said.

He lifted my feet and plunked down on the couch again. "Be nice to me. I'll get you more. Now where was I?"

"The fucking newspaper ad. Under fucking contract positions. Which, I might add, would seem the right place to hire a fucking contract killer."

"Fuck, yeah. Especially if you're so fucking stupid you actually advertise it as 'assassin wanted.' Guy figured cops wouldn't notice. Or would think it was a joke. He was wrong. Least he had the brains to skip town."

I laughed. Then I saw Evelyn still standing there, and I started to sit up. "Sorry. I'm hogging all the—"

Jack yanked my legs, pulling me down again. "Our sofa. We can hog it. There's a chair."

"And there was candy," I said. "But apparently this"—I shook the sugar from my shirt—"is all that's left."

"I don't think you need any more. Either of you." She peered down at the empty bag. "Are you sure that's sugar on those things?"

"Yes, sadly, it only takes sugar to make me this giddy."

"Apparently, you're not the only one." She shot a look at Jack.

"Giddy?" Jack snorted.

"For you, that's giddy. Either that or someone spiked your Coke with Quaaludes. If you looked any more relaxed, I'd be checking for a pulse."

He flipped her the finger.

"Oh, that's classy, Jacko. You really are in a good mood, aren't you?"

"We're relaxing," I said. "We had a busy morning followed by a long drive, so we've been chilling out waiting for you. Now we'll get down to business."

I started to get up again, but Jack pulled me back down.

I laughed and shook my head, then turned to Evelyn. "He's not letting me be polite and give you my spot, so pull up a chair and let's chat."

CHAPTER 22

Evelyn settled in. "The first order of business, apparently, is keeping someone from getting herself killed."

"Don't you love how she says that," I said. "Getting myself killed."

"You know there's a price on your head. Therefore, if someone manages to collect that bounty, it's through your own carelessness, isn't it?"

"*My* carelessness," Jack said. "I got her into this."

"You didn't—" I began.

"Enough," Evelyn said. "I was needling Dee, not provoking a blame war. I'm sure you're both equally responsible for what happened."

"Um, no," I said. "The guy who put out the hit is responsible. Now our job is finding out who that was."

"No," Evelyn said. "Your job is making sure Roland doesn't realize you killed his pro. You seem to be making a habit of that."

"We're narrowing the job field. It was getting crowded."

She snorted. "You know, I'd be impressed if I thought that's what you were really doing. If you develop a taste for weeding out idiots, I could give you a few names."

"Roland," Jack said.

"Back to business," Evelyn said. "Well, the last time you two got yourselves into this kind of mess, I managed to convince the middleman to hire Dee to replace the missing pro. That's not going to work here."

"Because Roland's not stupid enough to hire a mark to kill herself?"

"No, because Jack here pissed Roland off so badly that the man would probably send a pro after *me* if I so much as called him."

I glanced at Jack. "Something you forgot to mention?"

Jack frowned. "Roland?"

"Nineteen eighty-nine," Evelyn said. "He wanted to hire you for a job. You said no, and he came to me, pushing hard, and when that failed, he resorted to threats. So you killed his dog."

I turned on Jack. "You did what?"

Evelyn chuckled. "Oh, now you're in trouble, Jacko. That string of bodies in your wake doesn't bother our girl very much. But a dog?" She shook her head.

"Wasn't like that," Jack said. "Threatened me. Went to have a talk. There was a dog."

"And Jack murdered the poor beast as payback—" Evelyn began.

"Fuck off," Jack said, shooting her a glare. "Sicced the dog on me. Vicious brute. Didn't have a choice."

"You couldn't just wing him?" I said.

Now I was the one getting the look. I grinned and rubbed his leg with my foot. "I'm kidding. Under the circumstances, I'll accept the killing of the dog."

He looked at Evelyn. "That was Roland?"

"My God, you *are* getting old. Or course, admittedly, it does take work to keep track of everyone you've pissed off over the years."

"Memory's fine. Especially for enemies. I'm sure it wasn't Roland."

Evelyn turned to me. "So Jack killed his dog, and then he tied Roland to his bed and took away the phone."

"Huh," Jack said. "That's right. Wasn't Roland, though."

"What happened then?" I asked Evelyn.

"Nothing," Evelyn said. "Jack left him there. The poor guy lived alone, him and the dog, a mile from the nearest neighbor. It was three days before one of Roland's confederates came by and found him."

"Three days?"

"Left him water," Jack said.

Evelyn turned to me. "The dog's water dish was beside the bed."

"Food dish, too."

I laughed.

"Roland didn't think it was quite so amusing," Evelyn said.

"Reggie," Jack said. "That was the guy's name. I remember now. Reggie outta Miami. Left the business . . ." Jack glanced at Evelyn. "Ah, fuck."

"Fuck, indeed. The colleague who found him couldn't keep his mouth shut. He made Reggie a laughingstock in the business. Reggie was smart enough to not say who'd tied him up and left him eating dog food, but his career as a middleman was over. He retired. Then, ten years ago, he got tired of the regular life and came back as Roland."

"You never told me?" Jack said.

"You don't deal with middlemen. There was no chance you were going to accidentally bump into him. It seemed best for all if I let him keep his cover."

"But if you know who he really is, can't we use that?" I asked.

"It's been too long," Jack said. "Seventeen years. No one left to remember. Just us."

"And Roland," Evelyn said. "I bet if you paid him a visit, he'd be happy to give you the name of his client. In return for getting the hell out of his life and staying there." She paused. "I hear he has a new dog."

"Yeah," Jack said. "Great fucking plan. I show up. Demand to know who put out the hit on Dee. Who Roland knows by her real name. Linking her real life with me—a hitman."

"We could work it so he never realizes that you know her or—"

"No risk."

"Every plan has an element of risk and it's a matter of managing—"

"Not this. Won't risk tying Nadia to me. Or to you. Or to Dee."

Tying me to my hitman identity is what he meant. After a minute, Evelyn conceded his point. I had a real life, outside of this one, and even if she thought that was absolute foolishness, she knew Jack wouldn't do anything to ruin it.

We talked some more and settled on a reasonable plan.

"Dinner?" Jack said to me as the conversation ran down.

"We're going out?" Evelyn said. "Excellent. I've heard there's a wonderful—"

"Us," Jack said. "Not you."

"We just thought—" I began. "I mean, we know you don't like steakhouses, and I owe Jack for all of his help so I offered to take him out . . ."

"You're not invited," Jack said to Evelyn.

I shot him a look. "Of course she's welcome—"

"No, she's not. Stop being polite. We have plans."

"So I see," Evelyn murmured. "And, yes, Dee, you are correct that I have no interest in dining at anyplace that considers burnt hunks of meat haute cuisine."

"All right," I said. "Well, give me a few minutes to shower and change into something a little nicer than . . ." I plucked at my T-shirt.

"Should shower, too." Jack ran a hand over his face. "And shave. Forgot this morning."

"You go first," I said. "I'll find us a restaurant."

Jack patted my legs as I lifted them off his lap. I could feel Evelyn watching. Then her cell phone buzzed. She glanced down at it and went still.

"Everything okay?" I said.

"Of course. Just business. The usual idiots with the usual idiotic requests." She got to her feet. "Why don't I find that restaurant for you? And I wouldn't worry about showering and shaving. Just wash up and—"

"I want to shave," Jack said. "Not going someplace nice looking—"

"It's a steakhouse. Just because the bill hits triple digits does not mean it qualifies as 'someplace nice.' We have work to do tonight, and I don't have time to dawdle." She waggled her phone. "I do have other responsibilities. Just wash your face and—"

Someone rapped on the door.

"I'll get that," Evelyn said. "You two go—"

"And use the washroom together? You really are in a hurry to get us out of here, aren't you? Go shave, Jack. I'll get ready in the bedroom."

"Excellent," Evelyn said. "Go on, Dee, and I'll . . ."

She trailed off as I veered to the door and looked through the peephole. There a guy in the hall. About six foot two. Midthirties. A ball cap pulled tight over short, light brown hair. Pleasantly good-looking with a square jaw. His most arresting feature was his eyes, bright blue, and they were contacts.

I took a deep breath. Then I opened the door.

"Quinn," I said.

CHAPTER 23

Quinn caught the door. "Na—" he began, then he caught himself. "Dee."

"What the fuck?" Jack said as Quinn walked in.

"Jack. Good to see you, too. Always a pleasure."

Jack turned to Evelyn. "What the *fuck*?"

Quinn paused. Then, slowly, he turned to her, too. "I thought you told them I was coming."

"I didn't exactly say—"

"You told me about the attempt on Dee's life and—"

"You told him *what*?" Jack said.

Quinn turned to me. "There wasn't an attempt on your life at the lodge this morning?"

"Um, yes, but—"

"Didn't say she could go telling anyone," Jack cut in.

"I'm not *anyone*, Jack," Quinn said. "If there's a pro gunning for Dee, I sure as hell hope someone would tell me and ask for my help."

"Which is exactly what I did," Evelyn cut in quickly. "I cut through the bullshit and told Quinn because this is not the time for your personal crap. Dee's life is in danger, and his professional skills will be invaluable in tracking down whoever put out a contract on her. That is what's important now. Her life."

I'd be touched, really, if I bought Evelyn's excuse for a second. We all peered at her, trying to figure out her ulterior motive, knowing there had to be one.

"What?" she said. "Do you not agree that—"

"You wanted him in?" Jack said. "Figured I'd argue? You'd have told me you're bringing him in. Not asked. *Told*."

"You asked me to contact him, Jack."

"Yeah. To back him off."

"Back me off?" Quinn said. "Excuse me? I was concerned—"

"And she had enough to deal with," Jack said. "Without some ex-boyfriend bugging her—"

"*Some ex-boyfriend?* Oh, for fuck's sake." Quinn walked into the room and slumped onto the couch.

"Yes," Evelyn said. "I agreed to try to keep Quinn at bay, but he wasn't taking no for an answer. He was desperate to see her—"

"I never said—" Quinn began.

"Oh, please. You wanted to 'help out.' Anything you could do to help, but preferably a form of assistance that required your presence. Finally, I decided that was the best way to handle this. Dee could use your help in this matter and the sooner you two get over this angst-ridden relationship crap, the easier it'll be for everyone. Now, do we have work to do or are we going to bicker until someone tries to kill Dee again?"

We brought Quinn up to speed. I even told him about the journal. I just skipped the now-missing section on my rape. I wasn't ready to share that with anyone who didn't absolutely need to know. Quinn and Evelyn didn't.

Quinn had already been trying to track down the car used by Aldrich's killer. Quinn grouses that most people consider U.S. Marshals bounty hunters with badges, but tracking criminals *is* the main part of Quinn's job, so it made sense when Evelyn assigned him to hunt down our mystery man. The license plate turned out to be a dead end. It hadn't been renewed in years, likely taken from an old junker, and affixed with a fake renewal sticker. The car itself, though, had rental markings. Using the make, model, color, and some minor damage, he was trying to find the agency that owned it.

Our next move didn't require Quinn's help. His skills are extremely valuable, but he's a lousy actor. We could use him in an auxiliary role, though. We just needed to be careful, because . . . well, Quinn and I do have a lot in common. We share a background in law enforcement and a love for it. We share a belief in absolute justice. But while I may wish my motives for contract killing were as pure as Quinn's, they aren't. I do this because something compels me to do it, that deep rage and hurt over Amy's death—and, as I now realize, my own rape. I want justice for victims, but I also want justice for me and my lost cousin.

That rage and that pain means I will never be able to achieve Quinn's emotional distance. It also means I didn't flinch when Jack tortured and then killed that hitman at the lodge. I was fine with it. Quinn would not be. There was a reason his unofficial nom de guerre was "the Boy Scout." Professionally, he only took jobs that righted serious miscarriages of justice. He'd never been known to go after anyone who wasn't a contract, not even to beat information from a reluctant source. At his day job, he was so by-the-book that I think other marshals in his office would have a heart attack if they knew what he did for a sideline.

So we gave Quinn the job that suited him best. The

154 • KELLEY ARMSTRONG

starring role in our scenario went to me. It started with me dialing a number and leaving a message with a few cryptic key words.

By the time I got a call back, we were enjoying room service. Okay, *enjoying* might be the wrong word. It wasn't up to Evelyn's standards so she bitched. Quinn kept trying to make the whole situation less awkward by talking business, which only made things more awkward. Jack and I quietly ate as we mourned the private dinner we'd missed.

So when the call came, I snatched it up. Then I realized it had only rung once and let it buzz a second time so I wouldn't seem too eager.

I answered with a cautious, "Hello."

"It's Roland."

I exhaled in audible relief. "Oh, thank God. I wasn't sure I'd done that right. I mean, Marcos gave me the instructions, but I'd never done anything like this—"

"Are you alone?"

I said I was. He rapid-fired questions, making sure my reference was legit. Marcos was a high-ranking middleman, which meant he moved in circles that Roland didn't. He was also, according to Evelyn, in Europe for six months. Roland wouldn't exactly have a cell phone number for a guy like that, so he couldn't easily contact him to verify. He wouldn't dare anyway— he'd be thrilled that someone so high on the food chain knew his name.

Once Roland was satisfied, I said that I had a problem.

"It's my husband." Then I proceeded to tell him what an abusive dirtbag I'd married. Did he believe my life was in danger? Or did he think it was just an excuse for getting rid of an inconvenient husband? It wouldn't matter. Roland would be accustomed to dealing with laypeople who exaggerated their story in the mistaken belief that they actually needed a good reason to have someone killed.

Of course, in none of that conversation did I actually *say* I wanted my husband killed. He was just a problem I needed solved. Also, no personal details were divulged. That had to be done in person, so Roland could better assess me and be sure I wasn't a cop.

"We'll need to meet," Roland said. "What city do you live in?"

"Pittsburgh. That's why Marcos recommended you. He said you're in Pennsylvania and—"

"Right. So let's get together in two hours."

Now my hesitation wasn't faked. We hadn't expected to have so little notice.

"You want to meet tonight?" I said.

"Is that a problem?"

He was testing me. If I couldn't come quickly, that might suggest something was fishy. I agreed, and Roland gave me the address.

CHAPTER 24

I've never quite understood the allure of dive bars for underworld meetings. Oh, sure, places like that are made for shady folks and shadier deals. But if you're serious about keeping your criminal activities secret, you'd be better off in some overcrowded hipster joint, where the noise volume and sheer crush of people would guarantee privacy.

But no, it's almost always a dive bar or a place teetering on the edge of dive-bar-dom. This one fit better in the latter category, probably because Roland suspected Ms. Suburban Client wouldn't set foot anyplace worse.

In this case, Ms. Suburban Client had no intention of setting foot inside. The plan was for us to stake out the place until Roland realized he'd been stood up and headed home, where we could follow and perform a proper interrogation.

Evelyn didn't go with us. She's past the age where she cares to take any kind of unnecessary risk—of injury or exposure.

Jack was inside the bar, where he could keep an eye on Roland while enjoying a beer. A temporary dye had washed the silver out of his hair. He'd added a facial scar, green contacts, forearm tattoos, and a handlebar mustache. He could be a biker. He could be a trucker. Or he could just be a guy passing through town who thought the bar looked like a good place to grab a beer.

Quinn and I patrolled. We were watching for Roland, using Evelyn's general description—early sixties, dyed hair, my height, twice my weight. Quinn spotted him first, a block from the bar.

"Heading your way from the east," he said over the radio. "Dark jacket. Gloves. The street's empty, so you should spot him easily."

"Got him," I said as I picked up a distant figure trudging along the sidewalk. "Did you see where he parked?"

"In a lot farther down the block. I spotted him walking out. I'll go in, feel the hoods, find the warmest one."

"You're good."

A quiet laugh, as if surprised by the compliment. "Thanks."

I slipped into position in an alley across the road from the bar, where I could watch the front door. Roland was moving fast for his size, jacket pulled tight, looking anxious. Twice he glanced over his shoulder.

A first meeting is always dicey. Younger guys insist on handling everything by phone or e-mail, but the old-timers know that practice is actually more dangerous than a face-to-face meeting. Phones can be tapped. E-mail can be hacked. Yes, in person, someone can tape you, but you also have the advantage of being able to evaluate your client.

Still, an experienced middleman shouldn't be this nervous meeting a new client. How badly had Jack scared him all those years ago? We could joke about it—the killing of the dog, Roland tied up and left to eat and drink from the bowls. But if it had happened to an ordinary citizen we'd be horrified.

I know Jack wouldn't have left Roland there to die, but Roland hadn't realized that. Those three days would have been terrifying. Looking at him now, I wondered if he'd ever recovered.

Roland slowed as he approached the bar. He took out his cell phone and made a note or sent a text. There was no way to tell. I sent my own texts, though, to both Jack and Quinn, giving them a heads-up. Then Roland went inside and I got comfortable at my post.

After thirty minutes, the bar door opened and a single figure stepped out. I wasn't surprised it was Jack. He'd find it easier to convey a message in person than by text or radio. He lit a cigarette—an excuse for going outside—and strolled my way. I was in my alley behind a pile of recycling boxes. I stayed in position as he stubbed out the cigarette and swung in behind me.

"All good?" he whispered.

I nodded. "You?"

He shifted up against me, his leg against mine, tobacco-scented breath warm against my ear as I faced the bar. "Gonna be a while. He's settled in. Ordered nachos. Figures the client's just antsy. He'll wait."

"Okay."

"Need a break?"

I gave him a look. He smiled, as if he'd been teasing me. I was a sniper. I could hold position for hours.

He stayed behind me, leg against mine, chest brushing my back. I could feel his fingertips brushing, too, skimming my ass. I was sure he didn't know where his hand was, but my heart picked up speed. His hand moved and came to rest on my hip, as if bracing me. I was keenly aware of him there, right behind me. I figured he'd moved in to talk. Only he didn't say anything.

I leaned my head back, slowly, stretching at first, then rested it against his shoulder. He didn't budge. I could smell more than the cigarette smoke now, picking up shaving lotion and shampoo, too, which reminded me of *why* he'd showered and shaved.

"About dinner," I said. "I'm sor—"

"Uh-uh. Already apologized. Only one freebie."

I nodded. I wanted to just stay there, but while I was sure he wasn't distracted, I was. So I straightened.

"Should get back inside," he said.

"Have a beer for me?"

A soft chuckle. "You wouldn't want it. American beer."

A squeeze on my hip, and he was gone.

By the time Roland left the bar, he was pissed. By that, I mean he was angry, having wasted his time, but I suspect he was a little drunk, too. The combination of the two meant he wasn't paying any attention to his surroundings. I zipped ahead of him, climbed a fire escape, and took up position on a rooftop overlooking the parking lot, where I could watch for his silver luxury car.

There were two exits from the lot. One headed north, the other south. Quinn would wait in his rental along the north street, Jack along the south. My job was to see which exit Roland used and which direction he went. The closer of the guys would pursue while the other picked me up.

A perfect tactical plan. Except Roland didn't climb into the driver's seat. He walked to the passenger door, looked around, and then took out his phone.

Gravel crunched behind me. I whirled, gun up, finger on the trigger. I didn't fire. I couldn't because all I could see was a male figure, and in the second it took for me to be sure it wasn't Quinn or Jack, I'd lost my chance. I still fired my gun, but he saw it coming. He ducked and came out shooting.

Two guns. Two shooters. In the Old West, it'd be a simple matter of hammering away at each other until someone went down. But we weren't on a dusty street with six-shooters. In an urban close-quarters firefight, you have two options. Either you duck and weave, while hoping to hell your wild shots hit your opponent. Or you stand still and get a decent shot—while giving your opponent an easy target. I go with the combination platter. Dodge and shoot until I can get to cover and take a real shot. Which works so much better when there is cover. Otherwise? Well, my gun didn't have unlimited ammo.

Shot number three hit his arm. His left arm, unfortunately, meaning he didn't drop his weapon. But he did stumble. I raised my gun and—

"Drop it," said a voice.

I glanced back quickly. It was Roland at the top of the fire escape. He had a gun—pointed at my head. My attacker had recovered, his gun going up—

I hit the roof. Stop, drop, and roll. One of them fired. The bullet whizzed through my jacket. I leapt up and scrambled for the edge.

"Stop her!" Roland said. "Don't shoot—grab her."

My attacker ran at me. I skidded onto my stomach, arms outstretched over my head like I was sliding into home base. If I really had been trying to escape over the edge, I'd have fallen three stories, headfirst. I wasn't suicidal. I had something in my other hand—the radio. I dropped it and then leaped up with a very uncharacteristic roar of rage to cover the sound of it hitting the pavement below.

My opponent hit me. He took me down and wrested

the gun from my hand. I put up a token struggle, but not enough to get the shit kicked out of me. I dropped the radio because I knew I wasn't winning this fight. I had two rounds left, and two gun-wielding attackers, and not enough ego to think I could pull that off. From Roland's orders, he didn't want me dead. Not until he figured out what was going on.

So I let my opponent win while putting up a very noisy fight. Quinn and Jack were both down there. Inside cars. And we'd been shooting with silencers. So I made all the noise I could, until my attacker jammed a beefy hand over my mouth. That's when I got my first really good look at him. In the dark, I'd thought he could be Quinn's size. He wasn't. He had a good two inches and fifty pounds on Quinn. A big bruiser of a thug, with a badly set nose and hair chopped crew-cut short.

Bodyguard. That's why Roland had been getting into the passenger side. It's also why he'd been glancing over his shoulder on his way to the bar. He was old and he was overweight, and he'd had a helluva scare eighteen years ago. Now he had a guy he could call when he went to meet a new client, a bodyguard who'd keep his distance so he didn't call attention to Roland.

Shit.

Which was exactly what Roland said once his thug had my hands bound and he flipped me onto my back.

"Shit. That's . . ."

He shone a penlight on my face and leaned over, his broad face dripping sweat from his three-story climb. He took his phone from his pocket and checked something on it. I knew what he was looking at. Photos. One of the woman his client wanted dead. One of Nadia Stafford.

"Who is it?" the bodyguard asked.

"An explanation," Roland said. "For my missing employee."

The bodyguard's face screwed up. Roland didn't enlighten him. He just turned to peer over the edge of the roof.

"Any sign she wasn't alone?" he asked.

The bodyguard shook his head. "It's just her. She saw you coming out of the bar and went on ahead. She knew where you'd parked. Looks like she was going to take you out from up here."

Take him out? From over a hundred meters with a handgun? Someone didn't know his weapons well enough. Two people, it seemed, as Roland nodded.

"Search her," he said. "Check for any sign she has friends."

That's why I'd tossed the radio. My special Felix phone had another nifty feature—it didn't retain any record of calls or texts. Also, it looks like any other plain-Jane cell. The bodyguard checked it and said, "Burner phone. Seems like she hasn't even used it yet."

"Toss it."

I winced as the bodyguard literally tossed it, sending it thumping across the roof.

"She was definitely watching you," the bodyguard said, pulling out my binoculars. "You think she was the woman who called about the job?"

Roland shook his head, as if he wasn't dignifying such a stupid question with a response. Obviously Mark Lewiston had given me Roland's contact information, and I came here to . . . well, apparently to shoot him, according to their theory, though I'm not sure how that would have helped. Revenge maybe? Or figuring if Roland was dead, his client couldn't send anyone else after me?

Roland leaned over me again and said, "Who are you?"

"You already know."

"I don't think that"—he pointed at my gun—"is the sort of weapon a nature lodge owner uses for vermin."

"Depends on the vermin."

No sneer. No smile, either. His expression remained neutral, brow furrowed as he studied me, far more interested in this mystery than in the fate of his hitman.

"You didn't do your research before you sent Mark Lewiston after me," I said. "You might know what I do for a living these days, but you didn't dig further. You would have if I was a man."

A flicker of disconcertion, followed by a headshake. "In my experience, it's rarely worth the effort to conduct a full background search. That's for the movies, my dear."

"Oh, this wouldn't have required more than ten seconds on the Internet. A cop who shoots an unarmed perp point-blank makes the news."

He winced. The world was changing fast, and old-timers like Roland didn't often keep up.

"She *was* a mark, right?" the bodyguard said. "She killed whoever you sent after her and then came after you?"

Again, Roland deemed this perfectly obvious and only walked to the edge, scanning the surrounding landscape again.

"Okay, so yes," the bodyguard said. "Which means we should finish her off. Collect the payment."

Shit, not a complete idiot. I'd foreseen this, though, as soon as Roland made me. I'd just hoped the cavalry would have shown up by now. Since I wasn't answering my radio, they'd be looking. I only hoped they didn't call my cell. And, while hoping that, it would be even more helpful if I could figure out how to avoid being killed.

"What's a hitman's cut?" the bodyguard asked.

"Less than I'd pay you. Pulling a hit is about more than pulling a trigger, and she's done most of the work for you by showing up . . ."

Yes, let's bicker about money. Perfect. As they hashed it out, I flexed my foot. The bodyguard hadn't found the knife strapped to my calf. I sent up a silent thank-you to Jack for insisting I bring it, but even as I did, I wasn't sure how much good it would do when my hands were bound. I measured the distance to the edge. I could make it. With my hands tied, it could be a nasty landing, but—

They agreed the bodyguard would get 10 percent of the hit price for shooting me. I flexed my hands behind my back, ready to push up, hoping the move would startle him enough—

"You can't do it here," Roland said.

"Why not? No one to see us."

"It's a condition of the contract. She has to disappear."

I'd forgotten that. The client stipulated that it had to look like suicide or I had to disappear. Roland skipped the suicide option for good reason—if I was found hundreds of miles from home, dead of an apparent self-inflicted gunshot wound on a rooftop, that was as suspicious as murder. Of course, they could leave my body here and just hope I wouldn't be found for a long time, but Roland didn't strike me as a gambler. And I sure as hell wasn't suggesting the option.

CHAPTER 25

The bodyguard gagged me with rope. Then he untied my hands to let me climb down the fire escape before he refastened my bonds. They led me to the car and popped the trunk. If I was a civilian, I'd never have gone along with this. Rule one of abduction: don't let them take you to a second location. Do whatever you can to escape or call attention to yourself, even at the risk of death, because once you get to that second—secluded—location, your chance of survival plummets. I still did put up a token resistance so they wouldn't suspect I was playing too nicely.

They dumped me into the trunk and slammed it shut. And I went straight for my knife. A few minutes ago, Roland commented that this wasn't the movies. That was a shame, because in them, I'd have gotten that knife out and had my bonds severed in seconds. Of course, in a movie, the bad guys would have found the knife because viewers wouldn't believe they would actually miss it. If criminals really were as smart as movie audiences expect, my job would be a whole lot tougher. Truth is, I've met very few criminals who strap a weapon to their leg. One reason? It's a bugger to get it off when you need it. Especially if your hands are tied.

It helped that I was in good physical condition,

though after about ten minutes, I started wishing I'd joined my neighbor's yoga classes. I had my legs pulled up behind me as I worked awkwardly at the knife, trying to pull it out without losing a finger. I did get a nick or two when the car bounced.

As we hit a highway, the ride smoothed out. And that's when I started getting worried. I'd been working at the knife for ten minutes. If it didn't come out, and Jack and Quinn had no idea where I was, then there was little chance of escaping this alive.

After ten more minutes on the highway, the car exited onto a quiet road. I heard the distant chug of a train. We clattered over the tracks. Then the car turned again, onto a completely silent, rough back road.

We were getting close to that secondary location. Where they would kill me as soon as they hauled me out of this trunk. Hell, maybe before—to save dealing with my struggles and wordless pleas.

Shit, oh, shit. I should have fought harder. I'd been cocky. I couldn't even stall by pretending I had more information, because my mouth was gagged. The minute the car pulled over—

Just get the goddamned knife out.

I grabbed the cuff of my jeans and yanked my legs up until pain shot through my thighs. I wriggled backward to jam my legs against the rear of the trunk, holding them in that painful position. It helped—I could now wrap my fingers around the knife handle. My grip was still awkward and the blade sliced in, making me gasp against the gag. But at last I got it out.

I took two seconds to catch my breath. Then I wriggled the blade around until I could get at my bindings. Again, the angle was wrong, and when the car hit a pothole, I gashed my wrist deep enough for blood to well up, my fingers and the blade sticky within seconds.

I was bleeding. Really bleeding. Maybe I hadn't missed my artery. Oh, shit.

I struggled not to panic as my hands grew ever slicker with blood. I got the tip of the blade into the binding and sliced it half through. I started pulling, but my hands slid on the blood. Finally it came free.

I wrapped my hand around my cut wrist. I couldn't see a damn thing, but I could feel the blood flowing fast enough to make my heart race. I pulled off my boot, then yanked the strap for the knife over my foot and put it on my wrist, cushioned with my sock, and pulled the strap tight. The whole time the panicked part of my brain shouted for me to just get the hell out of the trunk and bind it later. But the blood was flowing too fast, my heart thumping too hard. Once it was bound, I could focus.

The car was a luxury model. Relatively new. It should have a trunk release. Since I was sure Roland didn't transport a lot of people in his trunk, he wouldn't have tampered with it. Probably wouldn't have known it was there. The problem was finding the damn thing. On some cars, it glows in the dark. I couldn't be so lucky. I had to pat around searching for a button, a handle, a cord, a toggle . . .

The car slowed. Damn it. I wasn't going to have time.

At least I was free. As soon as the trunk opened, I could lunge out.

Except the car didn't stop. It only slowed. Then I caught voices from inside the car.

"Got a tail," the bodyguard said.

"What?"

"Car behind us. Lights off."

"For how long?"

The bodyguard didn't answer.

"We haven't passed any other roads since the damned turnoff," Roland said. "Are you telling me we've been tailed since the highway? You said she was alone."

The bodyguard started to protest.

Roland cut him short. "How far back is it? What kind of car? How many occupants? Oh, never mind."

Roland muttered as he presumably looked for himself. If the lights were off, it must be Jack or Quinn. I breathed a quick sigh of relief but didn't stop searching for that release. I knew what they were driving, and it couldn't keep up with Roland's car. Which is exactly what he said next.

"Some little shit-box," Roland snorted. "Gun it."

The bodyguard hit the gas so hard I rolled onto my injured wrist, hissing in pain. A moment later, I heard the whine of another engine, right behind our car.

"Did I say gun it?" Roland said.

"I'm going as fast as I can on this road. It's practically gravel. I'll wipe out if—"

"Goddamn it!" Roland said. "If you can't outrun—"

"I don't need to. What's he going to do? Run us off the road with that little thing?"

"I don't care! Hit the gas!"

He did. The rental car engine whined as it went full out, but I could hear it falling back slowly. Roland yelled that he knew his car went faster. The bodyguard slammed down the accelerator. My hand joggled and smack into . . . A lever.

I pushed it down. The trunk flew open just in time for me to see—

A gun. I didn't get a good look at the car or the driver, because all I saw was that gun sticking out the open driver's window, aimed squarely at me, as soon as the trunk popped, it fired, and I was sure I was dead. I have no idea who I thought would be shooting at a person in the trunk—or why. I just saw the gun and heard the shot, and I hit the floor of the trunk, flattened there as the lid flew open, and I may have imagined it, but I swear I heard a familiar, "Fuck!"

The rear tire blew. That's what he'd been aiming at, the trigger pulled before the trunk opened, his aim perfect even from the driver's seat of a moving vehicle. Even if I was wrong about hearing the curse, as soon as that tire blew, I knew it was Jack. I also knew I was in deep shit, because the trunk was open and—

The bodyguard hit the brakes. That's what happens when you blow out a tire. It's not so much the damage caused as the reaction to the noise. He hit the brakes, the car started to spin . . . and I was in the trunk with the lid wide open.

As I sailed out, I saw the car spinning toward me and I had a vision of myself splattered on the windshield. But physics was on my side, and I flew clear over the car. I landed on the grass at the side of the road, thankfully. Still, "soft landing" or not, I hit hard, skidding through the long grass before coming to rest without striking more than a few rocks and a small sapling. I'd feel those rocks and sapling in the morning, but for now all I could think was, *Oh, my God, I'm alive!*

That's when Roland's car crashed, so hard that the ground reverberated beneath me. I lifted my head to see it wrapped around a tree. Then I heard pounding footsteps—Jack running toward me, his face . . . I can't even describe the look on his face.

"I'm fine," I croaked, lifting my head so he could see me. "Go." I waved toward the wreck.

He hesitated, slowing. Then a groan came through the smashed windows of the car, and he jogged that way, gun out. I pushed to my feet carefully, not entirely sure that I'd be able to stand. But I did. No spinal damage. No broken leg. It just really, really hurt to move. As I looked around, dazed, I heard the squeal of tires. The flood of headlights followed and, as I blinked against them, something flashed in the long grass. A piece of the car, I was sure, but I stumbled toward it and found my knife.

"Hands up!" Jack was saying. "You reach down, Reggie? I'll put a fucking bullet through your skull."

I could say in the stress of the moment, Jack messed up and called him by his original name. He hadn't. He'd chosen his play.

I staggered over, knife in hand, making my way around the vehicle to the driver's side. I reached the back of the car and stopped. There was nothing in the driver's seat except a deflating airbag. I was about to call a warning to Jack when I saw a pale shape on the ground twenty feet away. I glanced at the shattered windshield, and then started for the heap of the bodyguard's body.

"Gun," Jack called.

I lifted the knife and even from fifteen feet away, in the near dark, I saw his eyes narrow. He'd rather I had a gun. There was no time to find one. Chances were, mine was in the pocket of the man I was limping toward.

"Hey!" a voice called.

It was Quinn, jogging down the embankment.

"Go with her," Jack called, pointing at me. Then, "Hands back up, Reggie. Now!"

I continued to the bodyguard. Quinn called for me to hold up, and I did slow, but I could tell the bodyguard wasn't going to leap up and attack me. He'd gone through the windshield, apparently being enough of a badass not to wear a seat belt. He'd then plowed headfirst into another tree. It seemed that whatever good luck I had during the crash had been siphoned from his reserve.

The impact of skull against tree at a high rate of speed . . . well, let's just say there was no chance this guy was getting up again. Still, I was careful as I dropped beside him, just in case your head could splat like an egg and you could somehow survive. I think that proves I may have been suffering from a tiny bit of shock.

"He's dead," I said.

"Um, yeah . . ." Quinn said.

I straightened—as best I could, which was about 75 percent.

"You okay?" Quinn asked.

"Sure," I lied. "Change of plans here, obviously. Roland knows who I am, so there's no sense in me staying out of the interrogation. I'll help Jack if you can stand guard."

He nodded, then asked again, "Are you okay?" and I knew he didn't mean physically. He was taking my word at that, having not seen what actually happened and presuming, I suppose, that I'd climbed from the trunk postaccident. He meant how shaken up was I over the abduction, the accident, and Roland knowing my real identity. That was harder to lie about.

"I'll be fine," I said. "I should go help Jack."

"Right."

He glanced back at the road and seemed ready to start toward it, then walked to me instead, giving me a one-armed hug, as I bit my lip so I didn't let out a hiss of pain.

"I'm sorry," he said. "We should have been more careful."

"I'm the one who got caught."

"You shouldn't have been alone. Not after what happened." A quick kiss on the top of my head. "We'll make this right. It won't be a problem."

"I know." I also knew that he didn't mean killing Roland. What else can you do to guarantee he'd keep his mouth shut? Nothing, but Quinn would try. Part of me wants to respect him for that and part of me feels, well, it's a little naive. Idealism is a tricky business. It's bright and it's beautiful, and I love that about him and I wish I had more of it but . . . well, that light can be blinding, too. When it comes to my own personal safety, I think I'll take the darker road of realism.

As he turned to go, I kissed his cheek and murmured, "Thanks."

He nodded and left. I found my gun on the bodyguard's body. My binoculars, too. I took a moment to lament the loss of my gadget phone. Then I returned to Jack.

CHAPTER 26

Jack was exactly where I'd left him, with Roland still in the car, hands on the dash, facing forward. I could tell by Roland's expression that he hadn't figured out yet who was holding him at gunpoint. He was thinking about it, though. Thinking hard about who would know him by his old name. And stealing glances, but he couldn't see over the top of the broken window, meaning he was only getting a nice view of a gun and a leather jacket.

Jack didn't ask if I was okay. He knew I wasn't. His gaze traveled over me, his face tight, eyes dark with worry, trying to assess the damage in the darkness.

"He can take you," he whispered, nodding toward Quinn. "Get you help."

"I'll be fine."

Another concerned once-over.

I mouthed, "I'll live," and he could see that was the case—I was up and walking, with no obvious signs of trauma, so he returned to Roland.

"I'm going to open the door," he said. "You're going to get out and then lie on your stomach, hands behind your back."

Roland stiffened. It was the first time Jack wasn't barking orders but speaking in a normal voice. Not *his* normal voice—there was no trace of his accent and his speech patterns had changed—yet it was his usual work voice.

"No," Roland whispered. "Fuck, no."

"Fuck, yes," Jack leaned down to the window. "Now get out of the car, Reggie, or I'll haul your fat ass out and kneecap you for the inconvenience."

Roland seemed to move as if in a trance, and he kept peering at Jack, blinking hard, as if trying to wake from a nightmare. I'm sure that's what he thought this was. He'd taken some ex-cop Canadian lodge owner captive, then gets into a serious accident, and is ordered from the wreck by the hitman who terrorized him almost twenty years ago. Clearly, he was unconscious and dreaming. Or dead and in hell.

Then, as he was lowering himself to the ground, he sucked in breath.

"The bar," he said. "You were at the bar. Sitting by yourself in the corner."

"Yeah."

That's when he realized this was no nightmare. He tried to heave himself up and run. Jack didn't kneecap him. He didn't even move all that fast, probably because Roland wasn't, either—it took him at least five seconds to push his aging bulk off the ground, and Jack waited until he was up. Then he aimed a swift kick at the back of his knee. A crack. Roland yowled and went down.

"I have a question," Jack said. "Since you're the local here. Exactly how busy is this road?"

"What the fuck?" Roland said as he heaved for breath.

"I'm wondering how long it would take someone to find the wreck. Especially if we cleaned it up, got rid of the skid marks and such." He looked around. "It's not thick forest, but the grass is long enough, and the embankment is steep. I haven't heard another car since we got here. I imagine it would be a few days. If I put you back in that car and kneecapped you . . ."

"No." The rage evaporated from Roland's voice, fear seeping in. "No . . ."

"Nah, you're right. Too risky. I'd need to get you farther in. That looks like a field over there. Lots of long, dead grass. I could stake you out, nicely hidden. Sure, the wreck would be seen, but the driver's over there, dead. They'll wonder what's up when they trace the car to you, but they won't put much work into the investigation. Offed by that thug"—he gestured at the bodyguard—"who hid your body and stole your car, then spun out going too fast on a bad road. Not used to the power." Jack hunkered down beside Roland. "Does that sound like a good plan to you, Reggie?"

"You . . . you sick *fuck*. You goddamn . . ." Roland continued raging, but his voice was pitched high, rant fueled by terror.

Jack put his boot on the back of Roland's injured knee and stepped down. Roland screamed. Jack leaned over and said, "Shut up." I don't know how Roland could hear through his own screams, but he clamped his mouth shut fast.

"Here are your options," Jack said. "Either you answer my questions promptly and courteously or I stake you out in that field and come back in three days. And there's no sense calling my bluff." Jack bent, meeting Roland's gaze. "Because you know I'll do it."

Roland swallowed. "What do you want to know?"

"Not me," Jack said. "My client."

Roland's gaze rose to me, standing silently by his shoulder.

"No, she's not the client. Someone hired me on her behalf. She has important friends."

So Jack was going to spin a story. One that didn't connect me directly to a hitman. Which meant either he did intend for Roland to survive . . . or he just wanted Roland to think so. Killing a middleman could be trouble, and if Jack could explain away our connection, I'd remain Nadia Stafford, ordinary citizen. I glanced down at the gun in my right hand and the knife in my left. Well, relatively ordinary.

"You've probably figured out that your hitman is dead," Jack continued. "He made a mistake, taking that job without doing his research. You, however? You made an even bigger mistake by sending him out there, and I'm trying to figure out what you are. Terminally stupid or actually suicidal?"

"What?"

"Should I use smaller words?"

I choked back a laugh.

"Do you know who frequents Ms. Stafford's establishment?" Jack asked. "A certain family from Jersey."

"What family?"

"A nice one with two kids and a dog. What the hell kind of family do you think I mean?"

"I know that. I mean, which one?"

"Do you really expect me to answer? Either you know, which would be the suicidal explanation. Or you had no idea what you were really being hired to do, which would be the stupid explanation. I'd strongly suggest you cop to stupid."

"Look, the job was simple. Find out if this Stafford woman was the one in the photo and if she was, kill her."

"Why?"

"How the fuck—?"

Jack stepped on Roland's shoulder this time, just enough to make him yelp. "I said courteously. That is not courteously. In most cases, a client will provide at least an excuse, true or not. What did this one tell you?"

"Nothing. Only that he wanted her dead."

In other words, he wasn't the usual kind of client who got the middleman's number from a friend of a friend. He understood how the business worked and that you did not need an excuse.

"All right," Jack said. "The question remains. Why target Ms. Stafford? My client believes it has something to do with a get-together planned at her lodge. If your pro didn't know what was really going on, and you don't know what's really going on, then I'll require the name of your client. Along with contact information."

"I don't have it."

Jack set his boot on Roland's back. The big man tensed, but Jack didn't put any weight on it. He just left his foot there.

"Let's try that again," Jack said. "Bear in mind that as you know, I'm not an amateur or a fool. You'd never accept a job without some information on the client."

Which was true. Except, as it turned out, the price Roland was paid directly affected the amount of information he required. For this payday, Roland accepted the bare minimum of client contact. The whole thing was set up with phone calls from a blocked number, followed by a courier package with those photos of me.

"The package came from Philadelphia," Roland said. "There was no return address, but I was curious, so I called with the tracking number. It originated in Philly. But the client didn't sound like he was from there. He had an accent."

"Foreign?"

"No. Nothing strong. I racked my brain trying to figure out what it was, but I couldn't. I just know it wasn't local."

Roland blathered more about the accent and the package, and it was clear that was all he had. Then, just as Jack seemed ready to say "enough," Roland went still. He swore under his breath. Then he looked over his shoulder at me.

"Say something."

"What?"

"Say something. Talk."

"About what?"

Roland snapped his fingers. "That's it. That's the accent. *Oot* and *aboot*. Canadian."

Americans swear this is the surefire way to tell a Canadian from an American—how we say *out* and *about*. I can't quite see—or hear—it.

"The guy's accent wasn't as strong as hers, but that's definitely it. He's Canadian." A pause. "Or he has a speech defect."

Given that Aldrich had been Canadian, I was going with option one. A Canadian possibly living in Philadelphia. That wasn't going to lead me to Aldrich's killer, but it could help narrow down possibilities if we found suspects.

"Okay," Jack said. "If that's all you've got, that's what I'll have to take." Jack hunched over and lowered his voice. "My partner up there"—he waved toward Quinn—"doesn't want me to let you go, so you're going to need to make a run for it. I know you can't exactly run, but do your best. I'll shoot wide. I can't guarantee he won't mow you down, but he's no sniper. Got it?"

What the hell was Jack doing?

"I'm going to count down from five. You run

straight ahead, into those woods. Don't look back. Got it?"

Roland nodded.

"Five . . ."

Jack slid his gun into his holster.

"Four . . ."

He glanced over and motioned for me to turn away.

"Three . . ."

I didn't understand—well, I did understand the gesture, but I couldn't figure out what he was doing, disarming himself before letting Roland run.

"Two . . ."

He mouthed, "Please." I turned away.

"One."

A grunt as Roland heaved his bulk up, exhaling in sudden pain from his injuries. Then, out of the corner of my eye, I saw Jack lunge. I glanced over, startled, as he grabbed Roland by the hair, his foot on his back. A stomp and a yank and a crack. Then Roland sagged, neck broken, as Jack called, "Hey!" and, "Son of a bitch!"

I threw in a "What the hell?" and a "Shit!" as Quinn's footfalls pounded down the embankment. He reached the bottom just as Jack let go of Roland's hair and his body crumpled to the ground.

"He tried to run," I said as Quinn came over.

Jack heaved a deep breath. "My fault. He said the client's number was in the car. I asked Nadia to check. Moment she turns her back? He bolts. Tried to yank him back." Jack shook his head and looked down at Roland. "Son of a bitch."

The story wasn't the most plausible Jack had ever concocted. It wasn't meant to be. It was enough that he'd bothered to give Quinn an excuse that his conscience could accept. I appreciated that, even if Quinn wouldn't.

So Roland was dead. There was a reason Jack broke his neck instead of shooting him—and why he'd kicked him instead of kneecapping. No bullet wounds. Jack and Quinn wrestled Roland's bulk into the passenger seat of his car. I even managed to snake around and get his seat belt on, my hands covered to avoid fingerprints. While Quinn and I moved the rental cars onto the road and erased the tire tracks, Jack pried the bullet from Roland's car tire and found the casing. In the entire hour we'd been there, not a single vehicle had passed. As Jack speculated, it might be a while before they were found.

CHAPTER 27

"Can we swing by that bar again," I asked as we reached the highway on the way back to the hotel.

Jack looked over at me.

"No," I said. "That's not my way of saying I really need a drink ... though I wouldn't turn one down right now. I want to see if my phone survived. Roland's bodyguard chucked it across the roof. It's probably dead, but I'd like to check."

"All right."

I eased back my seat and tried not to wince as I changed position. By morning my body would be one giant bruise.

"Okay," I said. "So we know—"

"Blood," Jack said suddenly.

"Um ..."

He glanced over. "I smell blood."

His gaze flew to the strap peeking from under my jacket sleeve. The edge was dark with blood.

"What the fuck—?" he began.

"You know the problem with strapping a knife on your leg? Getting the knife off without losing fingers—or slicing open your arm."

"Shit!" He veered into the right lane, as if ready to take the next exit.

"I'm fine," I said.

"Not if I can smell the goddamned blood, Nadia. How bad is it?"

"I'm still walking and talking, and not feeling light-headed, so obviously I didn't lose a dangerous amount of—"

"Or it's just bound tight. Fuck. Call Quinn. Tell him to get your phone."

"I—"

He met my gaze. "Call Quinn now."

I did.

Jack didn't take me to the hospital, though he made it clear that would be on the agenda if first aid wasn't enough. He had his kit in the back, with his duffel, but since my arm was adequately bound, he took me to the hotel room, where he could work with clean water and decent lighting.

The cut was worse than I hoped, but not as bad as Jack feared. He had butterfly bandages in his kit—the small strips that could be used in place of stitches for minor cuts. This didn't quite meet his definition of "minor," but the wound had closed and the butterfly bandages did the job.

After that he made me change into my jogging shorts and T-shirt. Then he checked me over, me sitting on the edge of the bed, his hands running down my legs, the adrenaline from the night still pumping, and, yes, I'd be lying if I said I didn't enjoy that, even if he was all business. I seemed to be fine. When he noticed my breathing catching as I inhaled, though, he started checking my ribs again.

"I might have cracked one," I said. "But if so, there's nothing that can be done about it."

"Cracked, okay. Broken? No."

"If it was broken, I'd have noticed."

He ignored me and touched my ribs through my shirt, trying to see which one hurt. It was an imperfect method and when it failed, he fingered the hem of my T-shirt, making a motion to tug it up.

"Okay?" he asked.

I quickly tried to recall which bra I was wearing. Yes, that should be the absolute last thing on my mind, but let's face it, it wasn't. Sadly, the chance that he'd pull up my shirt and catch a glimpse of a really sexy lace number was zero. My collection ranges from new and plain to old and plain. I was just hoping today's was at the newer end of the spectrum.

I tugged my shirt up, being careful to keep it below bra level, just in case. Jack checked my ribs, the usual "poke, does that hurt, inhale" routine. So we were doing that, with me on the edge of the bed, shirt up, Jack on one knee in front of me, feeling my rib cage, when the half-shut bedroom door swung open, and Quinn walked in . . . and stopped dead.

Jack tensed in a split-second pause. Then his jaw set, as if to say "I'm not doing anything wrong, so I won't act as if I am," and he pressed one of my ribs again, saying, "That one?"

"Nope. Pretty sure it's only the one on the left." I glanced up at Quinn. "One cracked rib. Not bad for being thrown from a car."

"You were thrown?" he said, moving into the room now and handing me my phone. "What happened? The trunk popped open?"

"No, I popped it open, thank you very much. I was mere seconds from making my daring escape, rolling onto a deserted highway, armed only with a knife. But my timing sucks. I popped the trunk just as Jack was firing at the rear tire." I grinned at Jack. "I bet that was a shock."

"Yeah."

"You . . ." Quinn turned on Jack. "You *shot* out the tire? With her in the *trunk*?"

"He didn't know I was opening it."

"That doesn't matter. He shot out the goddamn tire with you in the trunk. What the hell were you thinking? You could have killed her!"

"Not in a closed trunk," I said. "Yes, I could have got the crap knocked out of me, but Jack's car couldn't keep up and as far as he knew, I was bound and helpless in the trunk. The second they got away, they'd have pulled over and shot me." I glanced at Jack. "He took a risk, and I'm absolutely fine with it."

"Well, I'm not," Quinn said to Jack. "I don't care if you take idiotic risks yourself, like driving in front of a *train*, but you don't take them for others. That's not your call."

Jack just watched Quinn, his eyes narrowing, a look in them that would have made me shut my mouth. Quinn didn't.

"You could have killed her with a stupid cowboy stunt—" Quinn began.

"And where were you?" Jack said, his voice quiet.

"What?"

"Where the fuck were you, Quinn? So I didn't have to make that choice. So you could cut Roland off instead. Where were you?" He didn't pause for an answer. "Right. Waiting for the fucking train."

"Do you know how close you came to decorating the engine of that train, Jack? Seconds. You were *seconds* from getting cut in half by it."

"Didn't need to cut so close. But had to go around someone else. Who was sitting there. Waiting."

I figured out the scenario. They'd been caught at that crossing where I'd heard the train coming. Quinn had stopped. Jack had gone around him and over the tracks. That's why he'd been so far ahead of Quinn when he shot out Roland's tire.

"Hey, look, my phone's working," I said, pushing off the bed. "You know what I could use? A drink. To celebrate the survival of both me and my cell. If you two want to join me to discuss what Roland said, that'd be great. But if you feel the need to keep snarling at each other, I will be downstairs in the bar."

Quinn backed down first, which was rare. "Sorry. You're right. However it happened, you're fine, and that's all that counts."

He snuck a look at Jack. The comment was as close to an apology as he could manage, but it was a damned sight more than usual. Yet it was like when Jack pretended Roland had tried to escape—they could never see when the other was making an effort.

Jack strode into the front room and started packing his first-aid supplies. I waved Quinn out of the room and got changed. When I walked into the front room, Quinn was standing there, awkwardly, as Jack fussed with his kit.

"Ready?" I asked Jack.

"Nah. Go on."

I stepped closer and lowered my voice. "Jack . . ."

"I'm fine," he murmured. "Just tired. Go. Fill Quinn in about Roland. Get your drink. Relax." A pause. "Have fun."

I glanced at him sharply, seeing if he was being sarcastic.

"Mean it," he said, his voice soft. "Go on. I'm fine."

CHAPTER 28

The hotel lobby bar was closed. According to the desk staff, the nearest open one was a few blocks. Normally, not a problem, but my aches and pains informed me that they did not require alcohol quite that badly. When Quinn suggested the minibar in his room, I was torn. Yes, I kind of did want that drink. No, I didn't think there was any danger in going to his room. But . . .

I texted Jack to tell him what we were doing and ask if he wanted to join us. Was there a test in that? Seeing if he gave a damn whether I had drinks in Quinn's room? Maybe. If he did, he only needed to join us. He texted back one word: *No*.

I should have let it go at that. I couldn't. I texted back saying it was late, and maybe I shouldn't stay, since we had work to do tomorrow . . . Again, he had only to agree. Again, he replied with a single word: *Go*. I did.

Quinn's room wasn't a suite, but it had a comfortable armchair. I settled there. Quinn grabbed beers from the minibar. Then he stretched out on the bed, beside the chair where I'd curled up, and I told him what Roland had said. While it wasn't a complete bust, it would have been nicer to have gotten more, considering the risk and the price.

We discussed that, and as we did, we fell into the old rhythms. When he asked about the problem I'd had pre-Aldrich, I told him about Wilde.

"Damn," he said when I finished. "That's a bitch. A real bitch."

He didn't say I'd done the right thing, not taking a shot that endangered others. With Quinn, that was a given.

"The father was right to hire you to get rid of the bastard," he said. "But he still didn't take the threat seriously enough. No one does. That's the thing with domestic abuse. You tell yourself he'd never kill her . . . until he does. As bad as you're feeling right now, I can guarantee her dad feels worse."

"I know."

Quinn knew that, too, better than most. Before he'd become a hitman, a family friend's daughter had been killed by her abusive ex. When the ex was tried and acquitted, the victim's father asked Quinn to set it right. To kill his daughter's murderer. Quinn said no. The father did it himself and ended up in jail, his life and his family's lives ruined. That's when Quinn took up his second career, focusing on miscarriages of justice, earning himself that nom de guerre, the Boy Scout.

"His biggest mistake, though, was giving her a gun," Quinn said. "Everyone thinks that's the solution to shit like this. But even if she knows how to use it, does she know *when* to use it? How to keep *hold* of it?" Quinn shook his head. "No one thinks about that. They think a gun fixes everything. I had this job once . . ."

He trailed off and glanced at me. Checking to see if I was interested in hearing a story. In the past, I'd always been interested. But things had changed, and I might want to drink my beer and go.

I nodded for him to go on, and he relaxed onto the bed.

"I get a tip, through the grapevine, someone trying to hire me." That's how it worked with Quinn. He didn't have a middleman, but if you asked the right people, they'd tell you how to contact him. "Seventeen-year-old kid dead. Killed by gangbangers. Shot in the head, execution-style, because he took the wrong short-cut in a bad neighborhood. A tragedy, but not really my thing. Still, I checked into it. Turned out the kid was shot with his own gun. After walking into that alley to buy drugs, then pulling it out to avoid paying for them. There was a scuffle. A gangbanger got the gun, and it went off in the fight. Do you know who gave the kid the gun? His grandma. She thought he was living in a bad part of town and needed protection. He did. Against dumbass relatives handing a semiautomatic to a teenage boy."

We talked a bit about that. Gun violence, gun control. Pros, cons. Eventually, though, it circled back to where it started.

"Missing a hit is always tough," Quinn said. "But it happens. It has to, unless you're a psycho who doesn't care if he kills a bystander—or gets caught. And there's always the possibility, if you miss a hit, things will go south. Deep south. I missed one a year ago. Bad situation. The guy had taken out half a family and vowed to kill the rest. They hired me for justice and protection. When I missed my first chance, they changed their mind. Couldn't go through with it. I've spent a year waiting to see them in the news, all dead. I stay awake nights wondering if I should have taken him out any-way. It's an impossible call." A wry smile. "In this busi-ness, most of them are."

As we talked, I began to wonder why I'd let him go so easily. I could blame ego. Or even lack of ego—I figured if he said it was over, I didn't have a chance of winning him back. But here he was, dropping everything to help me. When you're a federal marshal, that's more than a matter of telling the boss you need a few personal days. He'd only managed it because he'd just helped apprehend someone on the FBI's most wanted list, and his overtime was making his superiors nervous.

He came here to help, but also to talk to me. Maybe even to reconcile. We'd been good together. Damned good, and I was a fool if I let him go again. Whatever issues we had, we could work them out. Why the hell was I resisting?

I finished my beer in a gulp.

"If you're getting another, I'll take one," he said.

I laughed. "I wasn't, but I will."

I got up and headed for the minibar. As I passed the bed, he caught my arm and tugged me to him. When I didn't shake him off, he pulled me into a kiss.

If I had any doubts that I still felt something for Quinn, they evaporated the minute his lips touched mine. It felt so good, so damned good, so comfortable and so right.

I kissed him back, moving into his arms, and that loop kept running through my mind, how good he felt, how good we were together, how big a fool I'd be to let him go. But there was a reason I couldn't stop thinking that. I was trying to convince myself. To feel the passion of his kiss and the heat of his hands and the rising heat in me, and tell myself that it proved I should be with him. Only it didn't. It *had* been good. And it could be good again . . . for a while. Until we ended up right back where we'd been a month ago. That was inevitable. He wanted a future that I didn't. There was no reconciling that, however much it hurt not to try. However much I felt like a failure for not trying.

"I can't," I said, pulling away.

"Sure, you can." His grin sparked, eyes shimmering. "I'll remind you how if you've forgotten."

I shook my head. He took in my expression then and let me go, just keeping hold of my hand as I shifted away. He tugged it, turning me to face him.

"I screwed up," he said. "I rushed things."

"It's not a matter of rushing—"

"Yeah, it is. You needed more time. I rushed."

He said the words softly, no defiance in them, no denial, either, and I knew then that it would never work. He wouldn't change his mind, and he'd never be convinced that he couldn't change mine. There was no middle ground here. Not for him. If I cared about him, I should leave. And I only needed to glance at him to feel that flutter, that longing and know that I did care, very much.

"I should—" I glanced at the door.

"Just hear me out, Nadia. I know you consider us over. You have for a month. For me . . . for me it was just a spat. But not for you. I get that now. I can't just pick up and carry on. I need to win you back."

"Quinn, no. I—"

"Not this minute. Though you're welcome to stay the night." The grin glittered again. "Hell, I'd be *very* happy if you did. No strings attached. But otherwise, we'll work this case as colleagues. Then after it's done, we can try again."

"*No*. We can't—"

"Yes, we can."

I met his gaze and shook my head, pulling my hand from his. "You need to find someone who can give you what you want."

"I already have."

"No." I met his gaze. "I'm sorry, but you haven't."

With that, I left.

The last thing I wanted was to go back to my room. Jack was there, and I wasn't in the mood to deal with him. I could go bunk with Evelyn. She'd have a couch. Except I was in no mood to talk to her, either—I was still pissed off with her for bringing in Quinn.

I checked my watch. I'd been gone almost two hours. By now, Jack might have presumed I wasn't coming back and chained the door. Then I'd have an excuse to get my own room.

He hadn't chained the door.

When I slid inside, I caught voices and stopped. Was Evelyn here? No, the voices came from the bedroom . . . and were accompanied by the faint blue glow of a TV. That stopped me in my tracks. I've never seen Jack watch TV. Also, I know from experience that it's a handy way to cover noise during a break-in.

I took out my gun and crept toward the half-open door. I could see Jack's feet on the bed, atop the covers. He was still wearing his boots. I shifted my gun into position, both hands around it as I approached the door, ready to kick it open. With another step, I could see Jack. He was staring at the television. His gaze was unblinking, empty. Ice trickled into my gut. Then he glanced toward the door.

I shoved my gun into my waistband and walked in. He nodded. I looked at the TV. There were zombies.

"What are you watching?" I said.

"No fucking idea. Whatever was on." He flicked it off and swung his feet over the side of the bed. Then he seemed to realize he was still wearing his boots and bent to unlace one.

"You didn't need to wait up," I said.

"Wasn't. Just . . ." He shrugged and stood. "Giving it a while. Before I lock up."

"Well, it's locked now, so you can go to bed. I'm going to stay up and read the journal. I haven't gotten far."

He caught the back of my shirt before I reached the door. When I turned, he let go but stood there, studying my face. I glanced away.

"Didn't go well?" he asked. "With Quinn?"

"I think the fact that I'm here answers that question." I could hear the snap in my voice but couldn't bring myself to regret it.

Jack shrugged and stepped back.

I started for the door again.

"I figured you should find out," he said.

I glanced back. He was still standing in the middle of the room, hands stuffed in his pockets.

"Find out what?" I said.

"If it was over."

"Well, it is."

He nodded. I swung the bedroom door shut behind me. As I made for the couch, I thought I caught the faint murmur of a voice. Had he turned on the TV again? I slumped onto the sofa, stretched out on my back, and stared at the ceiling.

A moment later, Jack came out. He lifted my legs, sat at the end of the couch, and lowered my feet onto his lap. And I wanted to jump up. Tell him to stop doing this. Stop giving signals that weren't signals at all. Stop confusing me.

I did try to pull my feet back, but he only laid his forearms on them, as if he hadn't noticed.

"Did he do something?" Jack said. "Quinn?"

I shook my head.

"What happened?"

I resisted the urge to glare at him. Did he really expect me to share the details? Confide in him? Cry on his shoulder?

Yes, he did. Because he hadn't done anything wrong. Not intentionally. If he'd been sending mixed messages, it was partly because I was open to receiving them and partly because, let's face it, Jack wasn't exactly an expert on relationships. He had contacts and clients. He didn't have friends. Certainly not female ones. So he didn't realize that what he saw as giving me comfort, I might see differently. And he didn't realize that I might feel awkward discussing my relationship woes with my hitman mentor.

If I was pissed at Jack, then that really was my own problem. I might be good at interpreting his speech patterns, but I still had a long way to go before I figured out how to interpret the man himself.

"What happened?" he asked again.

I shrugged. "It didn't work. It's not going to work. And I feel shitty about it."

"Why?"

"Because this wonderful guy that I care about wants to spend his life with me. After all the mistakes I've made in the past, I should count my lucky stars that someone wants to give me a picket fence and babies."

"Bullshit."

I sighed. "I know. It's not the nineteenth century. I'm not sitting on a shelf, anxiously watching my best-before date. I don't feel that way at all. But part of me thinks I should. I like Quinn. I could spend my life with him and be quite content."

"Like? Content?" He snorted. "Those your goals?"

"I don't mean it that way. I . . . I feel as if I'm giving up something valuable, and it should bother me more than it does."

"So it's over?"

I nodded. "I'll keep feeling bad about that, but it won't change anything."

A knock sounded at the door. I scrambled up.

"Just room service," Jack said, rising.

I checked my watch.

"Twenty-four-hour menu," he said as he walked to the door. "Hold on."

So that's what he'd been doing in the bedroom after I stormed out? Thinking, *Huh, you know, I'm kinda hungry,* and ordering food?

I shook my head. Sometimes, it's best to not question.

He signed the bill. Then he brought the tray over and set it on the table beside me. It was a plate of cookies and a glass of milk.

"Bedtime snack?" I said.

"Yeah."

"I didn't figure you for the milk-and-cookies type."

He rolled his eyes. "It's for you." He headed to the minibar, got out a Coke, and popped it. "This is mine."

I looked at the tray.

"It won't bite," he said. "Long night. Didn't eat much at dinner. Sure Quinn didn't feed you. Figured you should have something. Lost a lot of blood."

I took a cookie and held it out for him.

He hesitated.

"I'm not going to eat all six," I said.

He took the cookie and settled onto the sofa with his Coke. "Got something else for you. Possibly. Not much but . . . One of those charges laid against Aldrich? Girl goes to college here. In Pittsburgh."

I straightened. "Really?"

"Happened in New York State. Girl's parents pressed charges. He bolted. Changed his name. That's when he became David Miller."

"It's a recent one then."

"Almost four years ago. Anyway, looked it up in the journal. Trying to cross-reference. Think I found it. Pretty standard. Nothing useful. But then I checked into the case. Through a contact. Girl claimed it wasn't Aldrich who seduced her. Said it was a younger friend of his."

"What?"

"Police didn't buy it. Parents said she was blaming some imaginary partner—"

"Partner?" I turned to face him. "If we're looking for who might have killed him and put out a hit on me, a partner-in-crime tops the list."

"Yeah. I know. Take a trip tomorrow then? Talk to her?"

"Absolutely."

As I drank my milk and ate my cookies, Jack gave me more details on the case. Shannon Broadhurst had been fourteen at the time, eighteen now. He didn't know how she'd met Aldrich or how long the relationship lasted, because she refused to cooperate with the police and give any details. That's not uncommon when the charge is statutory rape. If a girl is willingly having sex with a guy, she's not going to be thrilled when Mom and Dad file charges against him.

The charge was actually second-degree rape. "Statutory rape" is a catchall term used for cases where the charge stems from the age of the girl, not whether she gave consent. The actual charge varies. Most places also allow for the so-called Romeo and Juliet exception, meaning it's only an offense if the guy in question is above a certain age himself, so you don't end up with a fifteen-year-old boy going to jail for having sex with his fifteen-year-old girlfriend. If the guy is over twenty-one, though, and the girl is under fifteen, that's when the charges get serious, like this one. If convicted, Aldrich could have spent seven years in jail.

But he'd bolted and she'd refused to talk, except to insist that her parents were wrong, that it wasn't Aldrich she was sleeping with but a friend he'd introduced her to. Who might be exactly whom we were looking for. A "friend" who knew Aldrich's past and vice versa. A friend who'd panicked at the thought that Aldrich was about to be caught. A friend who'd killed him and was now trying to kill me.

According to Jack—and confirmed by Quinn—the police were still tracing the path through Drew Aldrich's past, connecting the various dots. They had yet to identify him as the same man who'd seduced Shannon Broadhurst and fled New York State ahead of rape charges. That meant she didn't know he was dead. We stood our best chance of getting honest information from her before she found out. We'd pay her a visit as soon as we could.

CHAPTER 29

Quinn had woken to a message from the company that owned the vehicle Aldrich's killer had driven. The car had been rented on a corporate card at the Cleveland airport. The company provided everything they could, thinking they were helping the U.S. Marshal Service.

Speaking of Quinn's real-world career, as I said, getting away from it wasn't easy. Although he was technically on personal leave, he still had paperwork—e-mail, reports, and such. While he phoned with the news about the car right away, he didn't rush up to our room, instead tending to some urgent business while I read the journal and talked to Jack.

An hour later, when Quinn came up, he had coffee for all of us. Evelyn arrived moments later. She didn't get a "good morning" from the guys. She pretended not to notice, just walked to the armchair and waited patiently . . . for about five seconds.

"Well?" she said. "Where are we?"

I told Evelyn about the car rental lead. "The company is a dead end so far. The Internet highway is nothing but roadblocks. The company name is IPP Incorporated."

"A shell company," Quinn said. "That was my guess."

I nodded. "I don't have a lot of experience with things like that, but Quinn says a very generic name combined with no easily accessible information suggests a shell company, which doesn't help us out at all."

"I'll dig some more," Quinn said. "See if I can find it through other sources."

"Evelyn will, too," Jack said.

"Will I?" she said.

"Up to you. Don't feel like helping?" He pointed at the door.

"Of course, I'd be happy to check my sources," Evelyn said. "I would just prefer to be asked."

Jack looked as if he wanted to say something to that, but he brought his coffee over to me instead and we returned to the journal.

As we worked on that, Quinn and Evelyn did research. Quinn's online resources are law-enforcement based; Evelyn's are criminal. The Internet has its share of side roads into the underworld, usually disguised and tightly guarded. Evelyn knew her way into all of them. When she searched for IPP, Inc., though, she ran into a problem: someone, somewhere really didn't like people looking for that information.

The search triggered a computer worm, which set off an alert. She tried another search result link and got the same thing. So did a third.

"This is interesting," she murmured.

"I think the word you want is *scary*," I said. "That's some serious tech power."

"Which makes it interesting." She shut down her computer and reached for her phone. "It seems I'll need to do this the old-fashioned way."

The old-fashioned way was also the slow way, so Jack and I decided to track down Shannon Broadhurst in the meantime. It was her first year at college, so she was staying on campus. I opted for the simple approach—go to her dorm room and knock.

The dorm was in what looked like an apartment building. There was a security desk inside the doors, and no passing it without proper access. I flashed my Department of Intrastate Regulation and Enforcement ID. It's a lovely card really. Even has a photo of me. Very official . . . or it would be, if there was any such agency. The card is from Quinn. It's his standard trick. There are so many damn federal agencies that unless you're dealing with government, no one's going to question the existence of this one, especially if you say it with enough authority. Quinn's got that part down pat. I did a decent enough job to convince a guard who looked barely past college age himself. It helped that I wasn't asking for access to the building. I just wanted to speak to Ms. Broadhurst.

Shannon wasn't in her room. The guard was in the midst of taking a message when he glanced up to see a young, dark-haired woman walking in.

"Oh, that's her now," the guard said.

The girl looked young for her age. Maybe five foot two, barely a hundred pounds. Oversized sweatshirt. Dark hair pulled back. No makeup. When she saw us looking her way, she slowed, and I thought she might take off, but she only steeled herself and walked up to the desk with a casual, "Hey, Billy, what's up?"

"These folks want to speak to you."

I repeated my introduction, quickly adding, "We just need to ask you a few questions about someone you used to know."

"Sure." She waved a thank-you to the desk guard and led us across the lobby. "We can find a quiet place outside. Who's it about?"

"A man you knew as James Emery."

She stiffened and I tensed, ready for her to bolt.

"Did you catch the son of a bitch yet?" she asked finally. "Please tell me that's why you're here."

She looked over and in her eyes I saw something that hit me square in the gut. A rage and a hate so familiar it was like looking in a mirror. I wanted to tell her Aldrich was dead. And I couldn't.

"We aren't at liberty to discuss the exact situation, but a case is being built against him, and he's not . . . at large. I can assure you of that."

"Good. Whatever you need from me to put him behind bars, you have it."

We walked to the road. Jack stayed a half pace behind, but when I glanced at him, he started falling back.

"We don't need two of us to speak to you," I said to Shannon. "My partner's going to head back to the car and do some paperwork."

She only nodded, but relief flickered in her eyes. This conversation would be easier without a man listening in.

Once Jack was gone, I cleared my throat and said, "You weren't quite as willing to help four years ago, Ms. Broadhurst."

"Because I was a kid. A stupid kid who thought she was in love with the sleazeball who took . . ."

She trailed off. She stopped walking, looked around, then led me to sit on a raised platform around an old oak tree. After we sat down, she stayed quiet. I didn't prod. I just waited.

After at least two minutes of silence, she said, "I wasn't a bad kid."

"I'm sure you weren't. That's why he picked you."

She glanced over at me.

"James Emery had very specific targets. Ordinary

girls. Good girls, so to speak. Not into drugs or alcohol or even boys. The shy, quiet ones, which may not have been you—"

"No, it was," she said, bitterness edging the words. "That was exactly me." She tugged her sweatshirt sleeves over her hands. "I found a picture of him in my stuff last year, and I wanted to throw up. He looked different in my memory, you know? It was like . . . like even when I understood what happened, how he used me, how wrong it was, I still had this image of him as this good-looking older guy that I fell for. He wasn't really, and I know that shouldn't matter, but it makes it even worse, as if . . ."

She trailed off and hunched her shoulders, staring out across the campus. "And that's not what you came here to talk to me about at all. I just feel . . ." She inhaled. "Whenever it comes up, *however* it comes up, I feel like I have to defend myself. Explain how that could have happened so I don't come out looking like a total loser."

"He seduced you," I said, my voice soft. "He'd done it many, many times before. He knew exactly what he was doing—taking advantage of girls at a vulnerable time, being what they needed."

She nodded and pulled her hands farther into her sleeves. "So, you had questions?"

"Only one really, but it's important. In the initial police report, you said he had a younger friend. You said—"

"I lied."

"Okay . . ."

She looked over at me. "I was a stupid kid, like I said. I thought I was in love. I had to defend him. Protect him. So I said it was a friend of his who seduced me." She looked away. "There was no friend. I'm sorry.

I know I made things harder for everyone, and maybe if I hadn't, he'd have been caught before he did this to more girls and—"

"Stop."

She glanced over, looking startled.

"Don't do that," I said. "You were one of many girls, over many years. Some of them gave the police everything they wanted. There were lots of charges. Even a trial. The second he knew that the police were coming, he ran. He was very, very good at what he did, and nothing you could have done would have stopped him."

It was the right thing to say, and maybe it helped, but not enough. I could see that in her eyes. Nothing would—or could—help enough, and it was hard for me to even sit there, watching her retreat deeper into that oversized sweatshirt, wondering how much different her life might have been if I'd somehow stopped Drew Aldrich twenty years ago.

"As far as we know, there weren't any girls after you," I said.

"As far as you know," she repeated. "That just means no one else reported him."

She was right. There were entries in the journal past hers. But no charges, so I was giving her that hope. I had to.

"Maybe," I said. "Or maybe it was just the final scare he needed." I waited for a moment, then said, "So when you told the police his friend seduced you, was that completely out of the blue? Or was there anything he'd ever mentioned . . . About a friend who might want to meet you . . ."

She shrugged. "I made it up. I never met any of his friends. He'd talk about people but not very much and only so he'd seem 'real,' you know? Like he'd mention going to his mother's for dinner, when I'm sure now she didn't live anywhere near." She paused, thinking. "Once, when we'd been drinking and toking up, he started going on about how people underestimated teenage girls, how they were just as smart as adult women, just as mature, and how people never saw that and so guys like him had to hide their relationships from the world. He said there were lots of good guys, decent guys who appreciated girls, and he mentioned an old friend as an example. I guess that's what gave me the idea."

"What did he say about this old friend?"

"Nothing really. Or nothing I remember. I was drunk and stoned. We both were. It just seemed to be some guy he met, maybe in an online chat room for people like him. I know they have stuff like that—I did a sociology project on it my senior year. They get together and talk crap and use it to justify what they're doing. If other people do it, then it can't be so wrong, the world is wrong. Which is bullshit." She glanced over. "Sorry."

"No, you're absolutely right. He didn't say anything more about this friend?"

She shook her head.

We talked for another ten minutes, but it was clear that if Aldrich said anything about that "old friend," she didn't remember it.

CHAPTER 30

We were back at the hotel two hours after we left it. Evelyn and Quinn were still in our room. Evelyn had news.

"Dee," she said before I even got my shoes off. "You're the literary expert here."

"Um, no. I've taken a couple of courses—"

"Then let's try a pop quiz." She plunked a hotel notepad in front of me. "What does this mean?"

Three words were written on the paper. Inferno. Purgatorio. Paradiso.

She knew the answer. She was amusing herself. Jack would shove the paper back at her and refuse to play along.

"It's the three books of the *Divine Comedy*," I said. "Is that what IPP stands for? A little obscure for a shell company, isn't it?"

She smiled smugly. "That depends on who sets it up. It was used to hide the rental of a vehicle involved in a murder. Given those intrusion worms, it's a company that's very interested in security. A company presumably involved in criminal activities and quite fond of Dante."

I looked at her and said nothing.

"Really?" she said. "If you can't guess, Dee—"

"Oh, I can guess. But if you're telling me what I think you're telling me, then I'm not sure I trust the source."

Quinn glanced over, confused.

Jack said, "She's right. Helluva coincidence."

"Well, then, it's a helluva coincidence," she said. "Dee's life is in danger, and I would never use that to further my own agenda."

"No?" Jack said.

Evelyn's eyes blazed. "No, Jack. I would not."

"What's going on?" Quinn said.

Evelyn opened her mouth, but I beat her to it. "She's saying that IPP is a shell company for . . ."

I glanced at Jack. He dipped his chin, telling me to go on. There was nothing else to be done, no matter how awkward this was about to get.

"For the Contrapasso Fellowship," I said.

"The what?"

"It's—"

"I know what it is," Quinn said. "But it's not real. Believe me, I've gone looking, like I told you . . ." He studied my expression. "It *is* real. And you knew that. When I told you a few months ago that I checked into it and you said . . ."

Yep, wouldn't it be cool if the Contrapasso Fellowship was real? Too bad it isn't.

"Not her fault," Jack said. "Evelyn's."

"Excuse me?" Evelyn said.

Jack gave her a hard look, one that said, *You owe us and you'll go along with whatever I say to fix this particular mess.*

"Evelyn had a lead on it," Jack said. "Wanted to track it down. For Dee. We didn't believe her. Just wooing a student."

"You mean that Evelyn offered to find the Contrapasso Fellowship for Dee. When Dee wasn't interested, no one"—his gaze met mine—"said *I* might be."

"Dee did," Evelyn said. "And I chose not to pursue it. I won't apologize for that, Quinn. I don't know you as well as I know her, and you aren't—"

"—the one who interests you," he finished.

Which was true, but Evelyn had the grace to soften it by saying, "You aren't in the market for a mentor and even if you were, we'd be a poor fit."

"Dee's not in the market, either," Quinn said. "She's got . . ." A thumb-hook in Jack's direction.

"I believe I could add to her education," Evelyn said.

Jack had a rebuttal to that, and Evelyn had one to his. They argued—diverting Quinn's attention.

What they'd said about the Contrapasso situation was close to the truth. I *had* suggested she take the offer to Quinn, and she'd refused. I'd chosen not to tell Quinn because I knew it was useless—Evelyn wouldn't help him get in the club.

"So you think IPP is a shell company for the Contrapasso Fellowship," I said when Jack and Evelyn finished sparring.

"One of my contacts had heard the rumor, and I followed it up with my Contrapasso contact, who confirmed it. IPP is Contrapasso. The man who killed Drew Aldrich was driving a car rented by them. The hit must have been theirs."

I thought about that. "Presumably, then, they'd been on Aldrich for a while. They set that guy on him, probably pretending he was interested in teenage girls, too. Then Aldrich sees me, calls his new buddy in a panic, and the Fellowship steps up their game. Pulls the hit. Leaves the suicide note to get justice for at least one victim."

"Only to turn around and order a hit on the *other*

girl he kidnapped?" Quinn said. "That doesn't make sense. If you believe in justice, you don't kill *victims*."

"Depends on the victim," Jack said. "What they think she saw."

"You think they might have made me at the scene," I said. "That the killer had backup who spotted me coming or going. Or a cleanup crew that went in later and found something."

"We were careful. Covered our tracks. But didn't know the situation. Anything's possible. These guys? Better equipped. Better connected. Better organized."

"So Aldrich says he thinks he saw me, and they find a sign that someone else was at Aldrich's townhouse. They don't want to handle it themselves because that's not their mandate. They need to distance themselves from the hit. So they hire Roland to send a pro, confirm Aldrich saw me and if so, get rid of the problem."

Quinn shook his head. "I'm not buying it. These guys aren't going to put out a hit on a victim, no matter what she saw."

"No?" Jack said. "If it endangers them? Sure they are."

"Your faith in humanity is overwhelming."

Jack snorted. "Fuck faith. They get caught? Whole system goes down. Won't risk that."

"So if some innocent bystander sees a hit, it's okay to off them, too? Is that how it works in your world, Jack?"

"Not talking about me."

"Why not?"

"Irrelevant."

"I don't think it is. Have you ever done this? Killed an innocent bystander to protect yourself? Because that's not someone—"

"Not someone you want to work with? Bullshit. You already think I would. Think you know what I am.

What I've done. What I'd do. Pretty fucking hard for me to sink lower. Not talking about a pro offing a bystander anyway. This is an organization. Risk is bigger. Stakes are higher."

"I don't know," I said. "The risk seems low. It might be worth it to kill one witness if she endangers the organization, but the fact they hired Roland could suggest it's not the Contrapasso Fellowship ordering the hit. It could be one member whose concern for himself outweighs his concern for victims and innocent bystanders."

"That I'll buy," Quinn said. "Someone orders the hit without group approval. So what's the next step? Evelyn has a contact, right? If she can still get Dee an interview—"

"Yes, that'd be the best plan," Evelyn said. "Let Dee gather information from the inside, while giving her a chance to see if she's interested in what the Fellowship has to offer. Two birds with one stone."

"Um, you're suggesting sending me into a group that might have a bounty on my head?"

"We'll use a disguise. A very good disguise. And, as you and Quinn have reasoned, it's unlikely the group itself—"

"No," Jack said.

Evelyn looked at him.

"Absolutely fucking not," he said.

"I believe Dee is quite capable of making her own decision."

"Yes, she is," I said. "And she says absolutely fucking not. The solution is obvious. You set up the interview for Quinn. He's perfect. He can go in as himself—well, his Quinn self. He's already got the professional reputation for doing exactly the kind of work the society undertakes. Hell, I wouldn't be surprised if they have a file on him as a potential recruit."

"They don't recruit."

"Then I bet they still have that file, in hopes he figures out how to contact them."

"Dee's right," Jack said. "Quinn's a lousy actor. But this isn't acting. He *is* interested. He likes it? He can sign up. He brings us what we need for Dee's problem. We handle it. No connection to him."

Evelyn grumbled, but it was the perfect solution and ultimately she had no choice but to make the call. The Boy Scout was about to apply for membership in the Contrapasso Fellowship.

Evelyn's contact at Contrapasso worked fast—I suspect Evelyn had carried on laying the groundwork for an eventual interview for me. Whatever she'd told them likely fit Quinn, too, since she wouldn't have mentioned my gender. Now that she'd given them the professional name of this potential recruit, she'd gotten a call back within the hour. They wanted to meet Quinn. The interview was set for first thing tomorrow morning in New York.

Quinn left the moment we suspected an interview was forthcoming. He was going to swing by the office in Virginia first, putting in an appearance, which would help if he needed more time off.

Evelyn left as soon as that interview was confirmed. She'd fly to New York, where she'd meet Quinn first thing in the morning and support him through the interview process. And me? Jack and I were going back to the lodge. The Shannon Broadhurst lead had been a dead end, and it looked as if Aldrich's killer came from a whole other direction, unconnected to our "like-minded friend" theory. There was nothing for us to do but wait.

CHAPTER 31

Jack and I weren't in any hurry to leave—we'd already paid for the night. As we were getting ready, I got a call on my regular cell. It was my cousin Neil.

He asked how I was doing, was I enjoying my time off, was I still with my "friend." Not being nosy. Just making conversation and, yes, teasing me a little because that's what cousins do, no matter how old you are.

"I called to see if you had any other questions," Neil said finally. "I wanted to remind you I'm here, if you need to ask something or you just want to talk . . ."

"Thanks. I'm okay right now. Keeping busy, which helps."

"It does." A pause. Then Neil cleared his throat. "I, uh, have . . . I mean, when you were here, we discussed the file. The case file. I know you haven't seen it and I thought you might want to so . . ."

My heart stuttered. "You have it?"

"I do."

"You didn't need to do that."

"It's your dad's copy. He . . . kept one at home. Locked away. When he got sick, he asked my dad to take it. He was worried that when he passed and your mom cleared his things, she might . . . Anyway, I was at my parents' yesterday for dinner and I asked for the file. I didn't tell them why. They just figured I was interested now that Aldrich is dead. But I have it here, if you want to see it."

"No." The word came out fast, sharp even. "I mean . . ." I sucked in breath. "I will. Someday. But right now . . ."

"It's too soon."

"Yes. I'm sorry. I know you got it—"

"Just picked it up while I was already there, like I said. No pressure, Nadia. You never have to see it if you don't want to. I just thought I should have it here, in case you do."

I told him I appreciated that, and we talked for a few more minutes on other subjects, before we hung up. Then I sat on the edge of the bed, thinking. It took a minute to remember that I wasn't alone. Jack stood in the open doorway, bag in hand.

"Right," I said. "Sorry."

I slid off the bed and took my folded jeans from the dresser top.

"Everything okay?" Jack asked as I put the jeans into my bag.

"Fine."

I grabbed my toiletry bag from the washroom. I came out, stuffed it into my duffel, and headed for the door, and nearly crashed into Jack, who hadn't moved. He reached to take my bag.

"Got it," I said.

He took it anyway, prying it from my fingers. Then he nudged me back into the room.

"Sit," he said.

I tried to protest, but he was right in front of me, moving forward, forcing me to step back until I hit the edge of the bed.

"Sit."

I sat. He set the bags aside and pulled a chair in front of me. When I started to rise, he moved his chair so close his legs were against mine.

"Talk," he said.

"I don't want to—"

"Too bad. Talk."

I glowered at him.

"Don't give me that. Really don't want to talk? Fine. But you do. Being polite. Fuck polite. That was your cousin. Don't know what he said. Wasn't eavesdropping. But you're upset. We're not on a schedule. No rush. So talk."

"Yes, it was Neil. He has the case file for Amy's murder. He asked if I wanted it. I said no. I'm not ready."

"Okay. But . . ."

"I feel guilty now."

"Because he got it for you?"

"Maybe guilty isn't the right word. I feel as if I should read it, like I read that journal. Suck it up and get it over with. But I'm not ready, and I feel . . . cowardly, I guess. Like I'm sticking my head in the sand. I'm just so . . ."

"What?" he said when I didn't continue.

"Nothing. We should go. I—"

"Nadia . . ."

"I feel confused," I blurted. "If I seem to be coping, I feel like I'm in denial. If I'm distracting myself with work, I feel like I'm hiding from the truth. If I don't want to read that report, I feel like I'm being a coward. What if I remember things I did wrong? Something I said that made Aldrich—"

"No," Jack's voice was harsh. "No, Nadia. You didn't say—"

"Or maybe I didn't fight hard enough. Maybe if I kicked or bit or—"

"No." Jack gripped my arms, fingers digging in. "You did nothing to make it happen. Nothing you could have done would have stopped it from happening."

I took a deep breath. "And I know that. But it doesn't stop the questions. So many goddamned questions, and I'm handling it all wrong."

"There's no right way to handle this," Jack said. "Just your way. If you *aren't* handling it? Acting out of character? Having nightmares? Losing sleep? I'll notice. I'll call you on it. You know that."

I nodded.

We lapsed into silence. I was still stressing, of course, and trying hard not to show it and failing miserably. So I started making a move to get up, but Jack motioned me back down.

"About what Quinn said . . ." he began.

I looked up.

"Yeah. Change of subject."

"Distraction technique, you mean."

"Yep. So. Let's talk. What Quinn said. What I'd do. What I've done."

It took a moment for me to understand what he was talking about.

"Right," I said. "The innocent bystander issue. I don't know why he was pulling that."

"Fucking obvious why. Doesn't want an answer for himself. Wants it for you. Push me into saying something you won't like."

I shifted. "Obviously Quinn and I still have issues. It's spilling out onto the job. I'm sorry about that."

"Not you. You can keep separate. He can't. He wants you back. You working with me? Rooming with me? Blocking him. He's trying to cause trouble. Between us."

"If so, then he's failing miserably. I don't need you to answer that question because the answer wouldn't change anything. I know you wouldn't kill an innocent bystander if you could avoid it. If you couldn't?" I shrugged. "I'm not going to presume to know how you'd react, but either way, I'm okay with it."

"Don't want an answer? Or you'd rather not know?"

I met his gaze. "No, Jack. Anything you want to tell me, I want to know. But I'm never going to push you for anything. I respect your boundaries and your privacy—"

"Fuck that."

I stared at him.

"Fuck my boundaries. Fuck my privacy. Doesn't apply to you. I don't want to answer? Won't. Won't be pissed at you for asking. Quinn? Hell, yeah. You? Never." He eased back in the chair, legs still against mine. "So I'm gonna answer. You want me to stop? Rather not hear it? Say so."

I nodded.

"Have I intentionally killed a bystander? No. Would I if they witnessed something? Fifteen years ago? Yeah. Today? If the only person at risk is me? No. I fuck up? That's what I get. If it was bigger? Other people at risk? Depends. Gotta weigh all factors. Not saying I would. Not saying I *never* would."

"Fair enough."

"Now the rest. Stuff you've never asked. Stuff you wouldn't ask. But Quinn's not going to drop this. Fact is? I'd rather you knew. Get it out in the open. This is the part where you might want to stop me. What *have* I done? How bad?"

He moved back in his seat, putting a little more distance between us, only our knees brushing now. "Killing children? Fuck, no. But that's the norm. You want a hit with kids? You gotta go deep to find someone who'll do it. Killing family members to send a message? Never, but that's not ethics. That's personal. I went through it. Won't do it to someone else. Other than that . . ."

He paused and reached for his jacket pocket. Then he patted it. "Fuck."

"You left your cigarettes in the car. And you really don't want to smoke in a hotel room. It'll set off the smoke detector."

"Yeah."

"If you don't want to do this . . ."

He looked at me. "You've heard of it? I've done it. Mob hits, yeah. Drug hits, yeah. Plenty of lowlife A wanting lowlife B dead. But there's more, too. Killed people who did nothing to deserve it. Spouse for insurance money. For custody. For screwing around. For freedom to screw around. Business partner. Business rival. Lots of business shit. Lots of bullshit. Innocent people. Couple of bystanders once. Not intentionally. Car bomb. Furious with myself. Fucked up. Only problem . . ."

His hand twitched as if he was ready to reach for a cigarette again. I tried to say something, but he continued before I could.

"The problem? That's *all* I thought. All I felt. That I'd fucked up. I was pissed off at the mistake. Those bystanders? Couple college guys. Never thought about them. Their parents, friends, girlfriends. Just a mistake. Like smashing up my car. That's when I realized how bad it'd gotten. Nothing mattered anymore. Nothing penetrated. Like a fucking robot. So I got my shit together. Still? Not like you and Quinn. Some shit I do? You wouldn't touch. Lowlife A calling a hit on lowlife B. But different scale. Not always 'bastard deserved it.' More like: you wallow in mud, expect to get dirty."

"That might not be what I do, but I don't disagree with it in principle."

"You sure?" He'd shifted as he'd talked, moving his chair back, leaning forward in it, forearms on his legs now. His gaze lifted to mine. "You really okay with that?"

"I—"

"Don't *need* to do that. Got enough money. Could be pickier." His gaze locked with mine. "You want me to be pickier?"

My throat seized up and I could barely squeak out, "Wh-what?"

"I'm asking if you'd like me to be pickier, Nadia."

I wanted to ask what he meant by that, but it was a stupid question. Jack was asking if I wanted him to change the type of work he did. If I wanted him to switch to jobs I'd be more comfortable with. I could tell myself that maybe this was his way of saying he wanted to team up more often. That he was getting older, and he could use a partner. But he was nowhere near the stage where he needed backup.

He was asking if I wanted him to change what he did. To become something else. Something I might prefer. You don't ask that of a student. You don't even ask it of a friend. You only ask it if . . .

I was missing something. Going from friendship to "I'd change my life for you" required a few steps in between, and unless I was doing a lot more than walking in my sleep, we'd skipped all of them.

"I . . ." I steeled myself and looked right at him. "I don't want you to change anything, Jack. I am completely and absolutely fine with what you are and what you do. Nothing you've said, nothing you've done, nothing I could find out is going to change that."

He studied my expression. I kept my gaze on his, letting him look. There was nothing to hide. I meant it.

"I could," he said. "I would."

"And I'd never ask it or expect it. You're not me. I don't want you to be. I want you exactly the way you are."

Was it possible to be any clearer? Short of grabbing him by the jacket and pulling him onto the bed? But he just sat there, his face expressionless. Then, finally, he eased closer, his legs rubbing against mine, leaning over and . . .

And nothing. He stopped there, legs pushed against mine, hands on his knees, leaning forward as if he was going to . . .

Hell, I have no idea what he was going to do. Or if he was going to do anything at all. He was just there, so close I could feel the whisper of his breath, the weight of his gaze, and I had no fucking idea what he was planning to do or what he wanted me to do.

He was waiting for a sign and what I'd said wasn't enough. He needed me to be absolutely clear.

I should do something. Lean forward. Reach out. Do something. Do *anything*.

That was the problem, wasn't it? He wouldn't make a move until he was sure. I couldn't make one until I was. One of us had to take a chance, risk personal humiliation and a very awkward extrication if we'd misinterpreted—

Jack's phone buzzed from his rear pocket.

"Probably Evelyn," he said.

"Probably."

"But maybe not. It's my . . ."

"Your work phone. I know." I paused. "You should check it."

"Right." He pulled the phone out and glanced at the screen. Then he looked at me. "Not Evelyn. Work."

"Okay."

"I should . . ." He glanced down but still made no attempt to answer.

Don't. Just forget it. Return the call later.

He looked at me. The words died in my throat. He glanced away.

"Should get this," he said and answered, rising and taking the call out of the room.

Well, if he'd wanted to distract me, he'd succeeded. I was no longer hopelessly confused over what happened twenty years ago. I was hopelessly confused over what was happening now.

I reached down and picked up my duffel. My laptop was inside. I got it out and started doing research on Aldrich's trial.

I was immersed in an article when I felt a faint draft on my shoulder and looked up to see Jack in the doorway.

"Hey," I said.

He only nodded and stayed there. I tried to read his face. Impossible, of course. If he didn't want to show me anything, I didn't see anything. Which was a big part of the problem, I guess.

"Everything okay?" I asked.

"Yeah. Just work."

"Do you need to take off?"

"Nah. Nothing like that."

"So I should move my ass," I said, closing the laptop. "We have a long drive."

He shook his head. "No rush. Just didn't want to interrupt."

Of course. I'm sitting here wondering what deep and meaningful thoughts you're contemplating, and you were just trying not to interrupt me. Fuck it. I give up.

I closed the laptop and reached for the bag.

"Said no rush." He moved into the room. "Something about Amy's case?"

I nodded. He motioned for me to open the laptop up again and sat beside me on the bed. Sitting with a good foot between us. Keeping his distance. Ah, shit, now I was starting to sound like him, too.

I rubbed my palms over my eyes.

"Nadia?"

I feigned a yawn. "Sorry. Just hitting that midafternoon slump. Reading on-screen doesn't help. We should hit the road—"

He opened the laptop and swiveled it to face me. "You were reading something interesting. Could see it. Keep going. I'll grab coffee."

He took off before I could protest.

CHAPTER 32

"Caffeine and sugar," Jack said ten minutes later, as he set two coffees and a bag of candy on the nightstand beside me.

I smiled and let that last bit of annoyance slide away. The moment had passed. It would come again and maybe we'd do better. For now, if he was bringing me candy, all was fine.

I grabbed my snack, and we went into the other room. I took up position on the sofa. He sat next to me, closer this time, though not as close as earlier. Which I wasn't going to think about.

"I'm not ready for that file yet," I said. "But I thought baby steps might help. I'm looking up references to the case. There's not a lot because it happened pre-Internet. With Aldrich's death and confession, there's some regional media attention, but it doesn't delve very far into Amy's case. For that, what I'm finding is mostly secondary references. So I'm following this trail of bread crumbs, which lead me to . . ." I clicked a link, skimmed the first few lines, and grinned. "A primary source. Thanks to the library system and the power of technology."

It was a series of scanned local articles from the time of the trial. I was still skimming them. There were pieces on Amy's death, on the arrest, on the pretrial hearings, and then, finally, on the trial itself where—

I stopped. Stared.

"Fuck," Jack murmured.

I glanced over. "So I'm not seeing things?"

"If you are? I am, too." He glanced around. "Where's your camera?"

I dug it out of the equipment bag, turned it on, and flipped through until the viewer showed the photo I wanted. The best shot of the guy who'd presumably killed Drew Aldrich. Then I turned back to my laptop. The black-and-white photo was grainy, the scanned resolution less than ideal, but there was little doubt of what we were seeing. A photograph of Aldrich's killer . . . in an article on Aldrich's court case.

It was a group shot. Three men, one woman. Two of the men strode along in front. Older men, in their forties or fifties. The other two—a guy and a woman—looked in their early twenties and hung back. All four were dressed in suits and carried briefcases.

My gaze dropped to the caption under the picture: "The defense team arrives at the courthouse."

Aldrich's killer had been part of his defense team. Did that make any sense? No. Add the fact that the guy had been driving a car rented by the Contrapasso Fellowship, and I was completely flummoxed.

"Makes no fucking sense," Jack said. "Aldrich spots you. Calls his old lawyer. Could see that. Long time, but whatever. Except he's not Drew Aldrich anymore. And this guy? A Canadian lawyer? Shows up within hours. Acts like they're old friends. Kills him. Pins the crime on him. The crime he helped get him *off* of. What the fuck?"

"I can see some logic in the last part," I said. "Maybe

he felt guilty, having played a role in letting a killer walk?"

"Fucking lot to lose if he's caught. Considering he killed him."

"There's the rub. And the Contrapasso connection doesn't fit at all."

"Unless Evelyn's wrong about that."

"Maybe." I saved the photo from the article. "No sense trying to figure it out until we have more information."

I searched for details on Aldrich's defense. Finally, I discovered that he'd been represented by Ellis, Silva, and Webb, which surprised the hell out of me. It was one of the top defense firms in Toronto. How had a guy like Aldrich gotten them? I'd have to ask Neil about that.

Lawrence Webb had been Aldrich's main lawyer—he was one of the older two guys in the photo. So not only had Aldrich hired a top firm, but a founding partner led his team. No wonder he'd gotten off.

I dug deeper for the names of the other attorneys. I got the second older guy—a partner. But even going over the firm's website photos, I found no sign of the mystery man. He could have been an expert witness, a private eye, or just a guy in a suit walking near Aldrich's lawyers.

"I'm going to send this to Neil, see if he remembers who he was."

I e-mailed the photo to Neil and called to explain.

"He *was* part of the defense team," Neil said. "I remember seeing him at their table. Can't recall his name, though. Him and the girl were interns, if I remember right. They took notes and fetched for the big guys."

"And they *were* big guys," I said. "Ellis, Silva, and Webb? Shit."

"You didn't know they represented Aldrich? Strike one against us."

"How did Aldrich get them?"

"Pro bono. Someone apparently convinced them it would be good for PR. Hapless kid railroaded by small-town cops. Big-city firm swoops in to the rescue. It happens. Just our piss-poor luck that it happened here."

"Do you remember anything about the young defense lawyer?"

"Mmm, no. I remember the woman. You didn't see a lot of them in those days. She seemed to be there to handle the parts about Amy. The character attacks. They must have figured they'd seem less hostile and more believable coming from an attractive young woman, rather than a middle-aged lawyer. They also had her dealing with Aldrich."

"Oh?"

"Yeah. Obvious ploy. Get the cute girl to handle the accused, the message being that if she wasn't afraid of him, clearly he wasn't a murdering rapist. The problem was that Aldrich didn't respond. He was polite, but there wasn't any flirtation. He just didn't reciprocate."

"She needed to be about ten years younger for that to work."

Neil gave an awkward laugh. "Yeah, I guess so."

"So when the intern girl didn't work out, did they try the guy? See if Aldrich got along better with him?"

"Nah. It wouldn't have had any impact, and there wasn't friction with the girl, so they left her as his handler. The guy was pretty much a nonentity, from what I remember. But let me make a few calls. Someone's sure to remember him."

The next morning we went for an early jog. Kind of. It was a process of negotiation. I agreed I'd sleep until seven. Jack agreed he'd get up at seven. Then he drove me to the country, let me off, parked down the road, and leaned against the car, waiting until I caught up, before repeating the process.

I was on my last stretch when my cell phone rang. It was Neil.

"I didn't wake you, did I?" he asked when I answered.

"Nope, just out for a run."

A short laugh. "I told myself you wouldn't do that on vacation, but I should have known better. I've got a name on your mystery lawyer. A very interesting name."

Jack was heading toward me at a brisk walk.

"Sebastian Koss," Neil said.

I stopped walking. "*The* Sebastian Koss?"

"The only one I'm aware of. I'm going to guess you know who he is?"

Oh, yes, I knew who he was.

Back at the hotel, I called Emma for a lodge check before doing some research on Koss.

"The guy is Sebastian Koss," I said to Jack once I had what I needed. "A big name in Toronto legal circles. He was a Crown attorney."

"Crown . . . That's prosecution, right?" Jack said.

I nodded. "Americans call them district or state attorneys. I had never even heard that Koss had once been a defense lawyer. Neil hadn't, either, and had no idea Koss worked on the Aldrich case. For a guy who went on to make such a reputation for himself, he got off to a poor start—he was completely forgettable on that case."

"So he's got a rep. Tough on crime?"

"Yes, but here's where it gets interesting. Koss's

'thing' is victim advocacy, particularly in cases involving women and sexual abuse."

"Huh."

"Huh indeed. If you were a defense lawyer with a client accused of rape, you'd do everything in your power to keep it away from Sebastian Koss."

"You admire him."

"I do. Victims' rights. Women's rights. Hard-line justice. Everything I believe in, he did. With a vengeance."

"Sounds like a good guy." He paused. "As long as he stays in Canada. Away from me."

"No shit, huh?" I gave a short laugh. "Actually, though, he hasn't lived in Canada in years. He quit law almost a decade ago and went into full-scale advocacy. Consultant. Lecturer. He started in Ontario, but he's been in Chicago for the last five. That's part of the reason I didn't recognize him at Aldrich's. I'm sure I've seen photos, but it would have been a long time ago. Plus he wasn't exactly dressed like a successful lawyer."

"Never had any contact with him? As a cop?"

"I didn't as a cop, but I did have contact of a sort, after the Wayne Franco shooting. He'd quit law by then, but he sent me a letter, extending his support and offering to help me find an attorney. I called him. We talked for a bit. I wasn't pursuing any legal avenues, but I appreciated the offer. I remember being surprised he contacted me. I guess now I know why."

"Remembered you. Amy, at least. Knew who you were."

"He didn't mention that, but from what I just saw online, that's not surprising. I found an interview where he talked about making the switch from defense to prosecution. He did it very early in his career, apparently after a case that really bothered him and made him decide he'd prefer the other side of the courtroom."

"Aldrich's case."

I nodded. "The timing is right. He saw Aldrich get off, and he didn't like it. He switched sides. Years later, he contacts me to offer his help because he remembers that, maybe feels guilty for being part of the defense team."

"So now he's with Contrapasso."

I looked over as I reached for my coffee.

Jack continued, "Law-and-order guy. Big on justice. Victims' advocate. Former lawyer. Played both sides. Canadian connections. Now consulting. Useful stuff."

"You mean he's someone the Contrapasso Fellowship would find uniquely beneficial to their organization. Which may explain his move to the States. So then . . ." I paused and considered. "Maybe Koss brought Aldrich to them. Aldrich was living under an assumed name, so Koss couldn't just call him up. He probably had to arrange to bump into him, recognize him, and then convince him he's not a threat. He says he's on Aldrich's side. Doesn't blame him for needing to change his name, given the notoriety."

"Possible. Somehow he made contact with Aldrich. We know that. Aldrich thinks he spots you? Calls Koss for advice."

"Thus providing Koss with exactly the opportunity he's been waiting for. The chance to end Drew Aldrich's life. In the meantime, though, he has to tell the Contrapasso Fellowship, including the fact that Aldrich may have spotted me. Someone at Contrapasso decides I need to go. The question is whether Koss knew. I'd like to think he didn't but . . . Roland said whoever took out that hit had an accent like mine, only less noticeable. That fits a guy who lived in the same region and moved to the States five years ago. Sending the package from Philly doesn't fit, if he's in Chicago, but that's a tenuous bit of proof to hold out on."

"Needs investigating." Jack checked his watch. "Quinn's meeting is this morning. Wait for his call. See what he can add. Then we go check out Koss."

When Quinn called, he was hyper-chatty, excited, and flying high. The meeting had been everything he'd hoped for, and I was happy for him.

Did I miss him a little when I heard him that way? I won't deny it. But there was no niggling voice that said I'd made a mistake. I was just happy he was happy, and glad we were able to carry on a normal conversation again. Right now, he was working on gaining their trust. With the information we had on Koss, he could nudge things in that direction. He'd say he did a lot of business in Chicago, and he'd express a particular interest in sexual abuse cases. He'd also ask about recent work they'd done, barring any details, of course, but he'd like to get an idea of the type of cases they handled. Take that and add his professed interests, and he might get us enough to confirm Koss's membership and the Aldrich hit.

It was going to take a while to pan out and longer still to determine who'd put the hit on me . . . and whether the threat had ended. That's why, when Quinn called, Jack and I were already in the car, heading for Chicago to see Sebastian Koss.

CHAPTER 33

Jack hated my plan. I knew this, not because he said, "I hate your plan," but because after I told him what I intended, we spent the next half hour driving in silence. That wasn't unusual. It was the quality of the silence that told me he was pissed.

"I don't like it," he said finally.

"I know."

His mouth tightened as his gaze stayed on the highway. "So that doesn't matter? You're doing it anyway?"

"Did I say that?"

"I fucked up with Aldrich," he said.

When I said nothing, his gaze swung my way. "You hear me?"

"It would be kind of hard not to. We're in the same car."

Another tightening of his lips. "But you're not arguing. Why? Because it doesn't fucking matter. Whatever I say. You'll do what you want. Just like with Wilkes. During the parade."

He was referring to our first "case" together, when I'd intentionally put myself in the killer's path. It had not gone as well as I'd hoped.

"You don't get to bring that up here, Jack," I said, straightening now. "If you want to hash it out again, we can, because I still think I made the right decision, however much it pissed you off—"

"You nearly got killed."

"But I didn't."

Suddenly, Jack veered onto an off-ramp. He drove to the first parking lot he saw and turned in, hitting the speed bump hard enough to make my teeth rattle. He pulled into a spot at the far side, got out, slammed the door, and stalked off.

I watched him go. As I did, I remembered the first time I'd seen Jack lose his temper, after the parade incident. I could hear Evelyn telling me to go after him, to talk to him.

"I know, I know," I murmured.

I waited a minute, in hopes it might give Jack time to cool off. There was a time when I wouldn't have thought Jack even had a temper. Nothing seemed to faze him. But there was a rage there, tamped down so tight that when it exploded, it was like a flash fire, impossible to predict, burning out of control and out of proportion.

I eased the door open and headed in the direction I'd last seen him. I walked across a scrubby field, littered with trash. I found him on the other side of a broken armchair. He had his back to me. I knew he could hear me scrabbling over the rough and rocky land, but he didn't turn.

"Are we going to talk about this?" I called as I approached.

He turned then, his dark eyes blazing. "Why? You've made up your mind."

"Did I say that? No. I believe I told you a potential plan, and you lost your temper."

"I did not—"

"Really?" I waved around us. "You're seriously going with that, Jack? We're in the middle of a field. Something tells me we didn't stop here for a piss break."

He glowered at me.

"Well?" I said.

"You want to discuss it? Fine. You nearly got killed over Aldrich. The guy who set that in motion? Sebastian Koss. Now you want to meet him? No disguise. Just walk up. Say, 'Hi, I'm Nadia Stafford. You may have taken out a hit on me—' "

"That's not—"

"I nearly got you *killed*. Do you understand that?"

I sighed. "Jack, you didn't—"

"Do you understand what that's like?" He started bearing down on me. "For me."

"I'm sor—"

"Do not say you're sorry! Goddamn it, I don't ever want to hear that again. Apologizing to me. Thanking me. Making sure I know you appreciate it. Doesn't matter what it is. Give you a fucking bag of candy? Gotta let me know you appreciate it."

I glared at him. "I'm sorry, Jack—and yes, there's that phrase again. I'm sorry if it bothers you to be thanked and it bothers you when I apologize, but that's how I was raised. It's called being polite—"

"It's not being polite. It's acting like you don't deserve it. Gifts. Time. Attention. Thank me for a gift. Apologize for a so-called inconvenience. Make damned sure you pay me back somehow. I don't want gratitude. I don't want apologies. I don't want payback. You think I do things for you because I'm being *nice*?"

He spun on his heel and stalked off again. Before I could even think to go after him, he wheeled again, facing me now.

"I got cocky," he said. "Arrogant. Fuck caution. I can handle this. I can look after you. You say you don't blame me. Not arguing that. But I've fucked up before. Got cocky. Got arrogant. Lost everything. Were you almost killed by that moron? No. Not even close. Doesn't matter. *I fucked up*. You get that?"

Now I did. I opened my mouth to say so, but nothing came out. I just nodded. When I did, he deflated, the stiffness leaching from his shoulders. I waited a moment, then said, "Tell me what you want to do, Jack."

The problem with nixing my plan? As much as Jack hated it, there wasn't really a viable alternative.

Sebastian Koss was speaking in Chicago late this afternoon. The lecture was open to the public. So I wanted to go. As myself. I'd listen, and then I'd speak to him afterward, in a public place.

Sebastian Koss knew who I was. He knew from the Aldrich case and he knew from the Franco incident. Now the man that initially bound us together—Drew Aldrich—was dead. He'd committed suicide and admitted to the murder. I was understandably shocked and trying to figure things out. I'd spoken to my cousin about the case. I'd discovered Koss had been on the defense, and I remembered him from when he'd reached out after Franco.

If I was "in the area," wasn't it plausible that I'd stop at his lecture in hopes of speaking to him about Aldrich as I tried to deal with this sudden upsurge in painful memories? Koss understood victims. He'd made a career of understanding them. He would know, better than anyone, that my quest for answers was a perfectly normal part of the process. He would not question my motive in coming to see him.

If I went in disguise, I'd lose all that. And I'd lose the chance to see his face when I introduced myself. Were we right that Aldrich had told him that he thought he'd seen me in Newport? Did Koss have anything to do with hiring the man who had tried to kill me? The best way to find that out was for me to appear, unannounced, right in front of him.

Jack knew that. Or he realized it, after two cigarettes and nearly an hour of hashing it out. He still didn't like it, but as long as I was willing to take every possible precaution, he would allow that it was our best chance of inching closer to the truth.

"What time's the lecture?" he asked as we reached Chicago.

"Three this afternoon."

He nodded and switched lanes. "Need to dress up?"

"It's at Northwestern. It'll be mostly students, so my jeans will be fine."

A minute of silence, as he tapped the steering wheel. Then he cleared his throat. "Reason I'm asking . . . Made dinner plans. Or Evelyn did. Found us a place. Says it has the best steak in Chicago. Only problem? There's a dress code. Which is bullshit. You want something more casual? I'll switch. I just . . ." Another throat-clearing, his gaze still on the road. "Thought we'd go someplace nice. Seems that means a dress code. If you needed to buy something for this lecture . . ."

"Then I could buy something that would also be suitable for this evening. No, if we're going fancy, I'm not wearing business clothes. It's nice to dress up every now and then and, believe me, I don't get many chances to do it. Let's hit a mall, and I'll go shopping."

"I'll buy."

"You don't need to—"

"Yeah. I know. Bit awkward, though. Taking you out. But you gotta spring for a new outfit."

I smiled. "I'll survive."

"I'd like to pay—"

"No, Jack. Really. That's *my* definition of awkward."

Jack did not help me get my pretty frock. He had to do some shopping of his own, because his working wardrobe looked a whole lot like mine—jeans and casual shirts. He tried to argue that we had time for him to accompany me. While I'm sure he had absolutely no interest in helping me pick a dress, I suspect he was planning to slap down cash, in spite of my protests. So I told him I'd meet him in an hour and took off before he could follow.

It wasn't just about paying for my outfit. I didn't want to buy it in front of him because I had decided I wasn't just dashing into the nearest department store and grabbing something vaguely suitable off the sales rack. I was going to buy a date dress—the kind where I'm willing to flaunt the fact that I'm in good shape. It doesn't happen very often. I'm not comfortable being that woman. Maybe that means something, in light of my newly discovered past, but I think it's just the way I've always been. I'm not completely inept, though. I know how to wear heels and put on makeup and do my hair and even pick out a sexy dress . . . with a little help from the sales staff.

At four, I was in a huge lecture hall at Northwestern, listening to Sebastian Koss. Seeing him on the stage—and projected on several screens—there was no doubt this was the man we'd spotted at Drew Aldrich's townhouse.

Koss had gone to visit Aldrich last week. Aldrich had been alive when he arrived and dead when he left, and while it was always possible that an accomplice had snuck in to do the deed, it seemed a fair bet that Koss had killed his former client.

That day, Koss was speaking on privacy rights for deceased victims. It's a contentious issue and an increasingly important one. The age of cheap video recorders has given sadistic killers the perfect way to relive their crimes. They tape themselves raping, torturing, and murdering their victims. If found, those tapes are invaluable to the prosecution. But does it violate the rights of the deceased to show them in an open courtroom? Not only do all the jury members and journalists and courtroom observers see it, but there's the risk it will end up on the Internet, where anyone can view the horrific last moments of a life.

For myself, I wouldn't care if it meant my killer was punished. But what if there was a tape of Amy's rape and murder? Would I want anyone to see her that way? To remember her that way? Every time someone watched that tape, I'd feel as if she'd been victimized again.

I sat riveted by Koss's talk, even as students around me shifted and whispered, probably only here because they'd been assigned a paper on the subject. The audience was mostly students, but there were enough older adults that I didn't look out of place. Nor did Jack, sitting across the hall, near the back. I'd glanced at him once, before the talk began, to orient myself, but now I kept my gaze forward.

When the lecture ended, most of the students bolted for the door, but there were enough who'd been truly interested in Koss's talk that it wasn't easy getting near him. At least twenty crowded down at the front, either to ask a question or to simply listen to him a little longer. I'd been near the back of the hall, which meant I was now at the rear of that crowd, unable to even wriggle forward.

Koss answered questions politely, with a charming

smile, but his gaze kept sliding to the side, looking for an escape route. When he announced that he'd be speaking locally again next week, I knew he was ready to bolt. And I was still a half dozen layers of students away from him.

"Please do come out and see me," he was saying. "Admission is free and if you sign up now, there's an informal meet-and-greet afterward, where we may continue the conversation. Today, however, I have a pressing appointment."

"Mr. Koss!" I called the moment he broke for breath, raising my hand to get his attention.

For a moment, as his gaze lit on me, his expression was blank. Then there was a flicker of "where do I know that face?" followed by what looked like a genuine smile. Koss motioned for me to wait and leaned over to the young man who'd accompanied him onstage to whisper something. As Koss took his leave of the group, the young man beckoned me to a side door.

"Mr. Koss would like to speak to you," he said. "I'll take you to the green room."

The "green room" was a small lounge with snacks and beverages. There was a security guard at the door, but he said nothing as the young man ushered me past. Koss stood inside, guzzling bottled water. He turned as we came in.

"Ms. Stafford," he said, setting the bottle down and extending a hand.

"Nadia, please. I'm surprised you recognized me."

"It took a minute, but I have an eye for faces."

"I know you're rushing off to another engagement . . ."

"Not really 'rushing.'" He smiled. "I have dinner plans, but they were only an excuse. Otherwise, it seemed I'd be there awhile. So I'm free for a chat. I presume that's what you wanted?"

I nodded. "It's about Drew Aldrich."

There was a flicker of surprise. Again, it seemed genuine enough. The problem was figuring out *why* he was surprised, and what it said about his involvement in my predicament.

"I'd heard of his death," Koss said. "An old colleague contacted me. I won't say I was sorry to hear of it. That was . . ." A brief tightening of his lips. "Not my proudest moment as an attorney. I presume you've learned that I was on his defense team."

"I have."

"Let's talk then. There's a place nearby where we can grab a drink."

CHAPTER 34

I'd like to think Koss's warm greeting meant he wasn't responsible for the hit on me, but I wasn't foolish enough to follow him into any empty buildings or down any dark alleys. Fortunately, he didn't try to lead me to any. He took me just off campus to a small pub, where we sat in a spot private enough to talk, but not so private that he could shoot me under the table and escape undetected.

I caught a glimpse of Jack on the way to the bar, only because he let me see him, so I'd know he was nearby. If he came into the pub with us, he stayed out of sight.

After we ordered a drink, Koss said, "When I first contacted you, I didn't get the impression you knew I'd helped represent Aldrich."

"I just found out a couple of days ago. His death brought it back and I wanted to know more about the trial, to better understand what happened. I saw your picture. I was already taking a few days off work, and I have friends in Chicago, so I decided to see if you might speak to me. You seemed sympathetic before about Wayne Franco, so I thought . . ." I shrugged. "I don't know what I thought. I'm not laying blame. I know where that lies—on Drew Aldrich. It's just that . . . I never knew much about the trial. I was too young. I heard plenty, all from my family's side. I just . . . I want to understand."

"And I'm happy to help with that," Koss said. "Though I fear nothing I have to say will make you feel any better about the matter. Aldrich was guilty. We all knew it. But as a former officer of the law, you know that it's the defense's job to give their client his best shot, however uncomfortable that may be sometimes. Even for those who *don't* see it as a game, who *are* interested in justice, we tell ourselves that by offering the best defense possible, a guilty man will go to jail, that justice will be served, with little room left for appeal."

"I'm aware of that."

"Even so, I couldn't handle being on that side of a courtroom. Aldrich's case was instrumental in making me see that."

He took a sip of his whiskey before continuing. "You may hope I'll tell you he got an unfair trial. To say that there was evidence tampering or underhanded legal maneuvers. There wasn't. It was, in my opinion, worse than that, because this case shows a basic failing of the legal system. What Aldrich got was a world-class defense pitted against a small-town prosecution team. My firm saw the opportunity for an easy pro bono win, one that would bolster their reputation as both lawyers and humanitarians. They seized it. Your family paid the price, and I'm sorry about that."

"That's what I figured when I found out who took the case. Can you talk a little about it? If you have time?"

"I do, and I will."

He said little I hadn't already gleaned from news reports. As for getting a read on Koss, I failed on that, too. All I could tell was that he still seemed troubled by his involvement with Aldrich's case.

Did I find myself questioning whether he'd killed Aldrich? Not really. Whether he pulled the trigger or not, he was guilty, and I didn't have a problem reconciling that with the thoughtful man sitting before me. If you believe in something strongly enough, you'll kill for it. I know that better than anyone.

Did I think it was possible for him to sit here, being so patient and considerate, if he'd put out a hit on me? I doubted it. As good an actor as I was, I couldn't have pulled that one off myself. But I couldn't rule it out, either.

So we talked. He answered all my questions with no sign that he had better places to be. In the end, even when I was worrying that I was holding him up, he made sure I had everything I needed, and offering to facilitate discussions with others involved in the case. He sat with me for over an hour before he finally made his excuses and said good-bye.

Though I may have failed to come to any conclusions about Koss's role in my hit, that was certainly not the only reason we'd taken the risk of meeting him. We wanted to see what he'd do after I made contact.

I let him leave the pub first, as I made a pit stop in the restroom. Then I followed him at enough of a distance that if he glanced back and saw me, I'd seem merely to be heading in the same direction. There were enough people on the sidewalk that it was unlikely he'd even spot me. I watched to see if he made a call or texted anyone. He didn't. He headed straight to a campus parking lot, which happened to be the same lot where Jack had parked. I managed to get his car's make, license number, and the direction he was headed before Jack whipped up and I climbed into the backseat.

I changed my clothes and added a wig and glasses. I

had no intention of getting close to Koss. The disguise was simply in case he glimpsed me in the car.

We followed him through the city. It was late rush hour, which meant the streets were busy enough to make tailing simple. As we drove, I kept the binoculars trained on Koss to see if he made any phone calls. He didn't seem to. He drove straight to a shopping plaza in the suburbs and pulled up to a park outside a restaurant.

"His dinner engagement," I said as we watched from a distance.

Koss hopped out and hurried over to where a woman waited just outside the restaurant doors.

"And that would be his wife," I said.

"You sure?"

"Yep. I saw her photo online."

They went into the restaurant. We didn't follow. Koss wasn't about to place a panicked call to his Contrapasso colleagues while dining with his wife. Which would seem to imply that he wasn't placing a panicked call at all.

Still, we weren't done checking out Sebastian Koss. Our next step would have been to break into his office, except he didn't have one. Or he did, but it was at home. Which was convenient, actually, giving us the chance to search his personal and business life at once. Except that when Jack called to check, a girl answered, presumably Koss's teenage daughter. No way were we breaking in with kids at home.

"What do you think?" I asked as we sat in the parking lot, car idling.

"Not going to assume anything," Jack said. "But he seems clean. Of wanting you dead, at least. Dig more tomorrow. For now?" He checked his watch. "Reservation's in just over an hour. You still up for it?"

I smiled. "Absolutely."

━◦◦◦━

We hadn't gotten a chance to check into our hotel yet. Now we did.

"This is nice," I said as I gaped around the elevator, all polished brass and shimmering marble.

Jack mumbled something I didn't quite catch, but that told me I shouldn't comment on the fancy hotel. Just accept it.

The "not commenting" part got harder when I walked into our room. The door opened into a living room with sofas, a full bar, and a massive window overlooking the gorgeous Chicago skyline. There was no way I couldn't *not* say something, so I settled for, "This is *really* nice," while walking to the window, giving him the chance to opt out of a reply, which he did.

"Got two bathrooms," he said after a moment. "Figured that would make things easy. Take the bedroom one. Probably bigger."

"All right."

I headed that way, and I was almost to the door when Jack got in front of me, so fast he startled me.

"Um, about the bedroom," he said. "Only one bed. Got a sofa bed, too. I'll take that. Wasn't a two-bed option. Just . . . wanted to let you know."

"Sounds good. I'll get ready then."

"Right," he said and stepped out of my path.

It took me a while. I might know how to do the dress-up thing, but I'm rusty. After thirty minutes, I realized I was putting our reservation in jeopardy and opened the door to tell Jack I was almost ready. The room was silent.

"Jack?"

No answer.

I slid from the bathroom to peek around the bedroom door. Yes, I was decent, but I wasn't quite done yet and didn't want to ruin that first impression.

"Jack?"

The room was empty. The other bathroom door was open and the inside light was off. I was looking around when I noticed a note on the table. I scampered over to it.

Bringing the car around. Just come down. Don't rush.

Of course I did rush. I took this as a subtle message that I was indeed late. So I finished getting ready and then hurried down.

Was I a little disappointed with the arrangement? Yes, I'll admit it. I'd taken some serious effort to make an impression, and his first sight of me was going to be as I dashed out the hotel front door while he waited in the car. Worse yet, when I got down to the lobby the car wasn't even there. Two vehicles idled out front—a BMW and a Jag.

Then the driver's door on the BMW opened and Jack stepped out. He started to come around. As he turned toward me, getting a full look for the first time, he stopped. He stared. Then he caught himself and continued striding over to meet me.

I was trying not to stare myself. I've seen Jack dressed up. He'd worn a tux for the opera during a stakeout. At the time, I'd wondered how he'd carry off the look—it didn't seem right for him. I'd been wrong. Jack looked as comfortable in a suit as he did in a biker outfit. It just brought out another side to that dangerous edge, making him look like he was ready to throw down in the boardroom rather than in a bar. Tonight he wore a sports coat and tie, but the effect was the same. Freshly shaven. Black hair gleaming. Wearing that suit like it came from his closet, not straight off a store rack. He looked good. Damned good.

"Something happened to our car," I said as he reached me. "It must have been sitting in that parking garage too long. The other vehicles rubbed off on it."

He smiled. He didn't say anything, though, just put a hand on the small of my back and guided me toward the car as he leaned over to open the door. He didn't say anything about my outfit, either. I didn't expect him to. Before the opera, it'd been Quinn who'd told me how good I looked—multiple times. With Jack, I hadn't even been sure he'd noticed. Now, he noticed. I could feel his gaze on me as I got into the car, and that was more flattering than anything he could have said.

When we reached the restaurant, I could see why he'd switched cars. If we'd driven our economy rental up to the valet, they'd probably have refused to park it. As it was, we fit right in. As we walked inside and through the restaurant, Jack's hand still resting at my back, we caught some glances. Mostly women, checking him out, as discreetly as possible, given the venue. I earned some looks, too, and held my head a little higher. Most of the time, I'm happy to blend. I want to blend. Every now and then, though, under the right circumstances, a little attention is nice.

I'd been worried dinner might be awkward with both of us out of our comfort zone, but as soon as we were seated, we started talking as we would over any other meal. Except it wasn't "any other meal." We both knew that. The car, the restaurant, the dress, the suit . . . it all said that this wasn't just dinner between friends.

We stayed at the restaurant until there was only one other table of diners left. When we finally stepped outside, the cool night air was as refreshing as any country breeze, and I paused a moment, drinking it in.

"Nice night," Jack said as the valet hurried over.

I smiled. "It is."

Jack motioned for the valet to wait. "You want to walk?" He shrugged off his jacket. "Saw a park over . . ." He glanced down at my shoes. "Something tells me those weren't made for strolling."

"Actually, on the scale of heels, these are as stroll-worthy as they come. I know my limits. I'd love a walk."

Jack gave me his coat. I didn't argue. As I put it over my shoulders, he spoke to the valet. He got the keys back and directions to the parking garage for later. Then he slipped the young man a tip and led me down the restaurant steps. When we reached the bottom, his hand brushed mine. I took it, and we headed out.

CHAPTER 35

W e talked a little as we walked, but mostly we just enjoyed the quiet and the empty streets. The park was only a block over. As we entered, I could see Jack's gaze flickering about. We might be pretending we were just ordinary people out for an ordinary night under ordinary circumstances, but I still had a price on my head and I had just made contact with the guy who might have put it there.

It seemed safe enough, though. This end of the park was so quiet we'd hear footsteps if anyone approached. The thick trees made sniping from nearby buildings impossible. I hated having to even think about that tonight, but I had to.

Jack steered me down the most wooded path, where we'd be best hidden.

"So," I said as we walked. "Am I allowed to thank you for dinner?"

A soft chuckle. "Yeah."

"But I'm not allowed to show my appreciation in any way. Correct?"

I glanced at him as I said it. My voice was light, teasing. My look was not. Jack caught it, and I heard a faint intake of breath. His grip loosened on my hand and for a moment, I thought he was going to let go. But he only adjusted his hold, pulling me to a stop and turning me to face him.

"Depends," he said. "You know that appreciation isn't necessary?"

"I do."

"And nothing was expected?"

"I do."

"Then, if you wanted to—"

"I do," I said, and I lifted onto my tiptoes and kissed him.

I was sure he'd known how I planned to show my appreciation, but he just stood there, not reciprocating. I saw the jolt of surprise in his eyes and I thought, *Oh, shit!* I'd screwed up. I'd been so sure, so damned sure. The dinner, the car, the hotel . . . How the hell did that not mean what I thought it meant?

I pulled back fast. "Sorry. I-I thought—"

He cut me off, arms going around me, pulling me into a kiss that took any doubt, shredded it, and set the leftover bits on fire. The last time I was kissed like that— Oh, hell, I don't know if I'd ever been kissed like that. When it finally broke, I was gasping.

"Okay?" he said.

"Oh, yeah."

He chuckled and kissed me again, softer this time, his hands moving to my face, holding it in a long, sweet kiss.

When we parted for breath, I said, "I thought I surprised you there."

"You did."

"What did you think I was going to give you? A back rub?"

A light laugh. "No. Hoped you meant this. Didn't expect. Sorry if I—"

"It's okay," I said.

I tugged him toward me until my back was against a tree. As my arms went around his neck, his dropped to my waist and then slid down as the kiss deepened, coming to rest on my ass, pulling me to him. Heat shot through me as I arched against the tree, lifting up to straddle him. His hands dropped lower then and pushed my skirt up. I felt a tickling whisper of cold air, disappearing as his hands cupped my ass.

I wanted him. Right there, and I didn't care if it wasn't anything I'd done before, if it was something I'd feel guilty about in the morning. The park was empty, and even if I hadn't been certain of that, I'm not sure it would have changed my mind. All I could feel was the hunger of his kiss and the heat of his hands and the hardness of his body and I didn't give a damn where we were.

When the kiss broke, I reached for a button on his shirt and murmured, "Yes?"

He hesitated.

I stopped. "Or no . . ."

"Yes," he murmured, his voice thick. "Hell, yes." He buried his face in my hair, kissing my neck as his hands gripped my ass, pulling me close. "Just don't want to fuck up. You want a bed—"

"Next time."

I undid his shirt as he kept kissing my neck. I couldn't manage the tie, so I just shoved it aside, then slid my hands under his open shirt, his hard muscles moving under my fingers as he shifted, his lips moving to mine again. His hands shifted, too, tugging my panties down over my hips.

I reached down and pulled at his belt as my panties dropped to the ground, but his fingers moved across my thighs, which completely distracted me from my mission. I paused, realized I was pausing, and cursed as I reached for his belt again.

Jack laughed and broke the kiss. "Let me get—"

A light flickered, somewhere in the trees. We both saw it. And we both heard the click that followed.

"Down!" Jack said, grabbing me by the shoulders.

He pushed me down before I could get there myself. He dropped, too, covering me in a half crouch, his gun already out.

When we heard that click, I'm sure we both thought the same thing: gun. There was no accompanying shot, though. The park had gone silent. Jack stayed over me, scanning the trees. Then it came, the faint crackle of a dead leaf underfoot. Jack trained his weapon in that direction. We could see nothing except black trees against the night. Standing, we'd caught light from the path. Down here, it was completely dark.

When I started to move, Jack stopped me, hand on my shoulder.

"Gun," I whispered. "In my bag."

He paused, as if just realizing there'd been no way for me to conceal a gun under my dress. Hell, I think a tube of lipstick would have been noticeable.

"Got it," he whispered. "Stay."

He passed me his gun. I bit my lip to keep from arguing. I did, however, grab his jacket, which was lying beside me, and hand it to him, to put over his white shirt. He tugged it on and crept hunched over to where I'd let my purse fall.

I covered Jack as I continued scanning the landscape, still seeing nothing. The leaf crackle had come about twenty degrees away from the light flash and the click. If it was the same person, he was on the move. I listened for footsteps, but the ground here was too soft. I glanced at Jack. He was trying to find my purse—black against the dark ground.

Another crackle. A shape moved from behind the trees, less than fifteen feet away. An arm swung up. I caught the faintest glint of the lamplight against metal.

"Jack!" I said.

I fired. I had no idea if I'd seen a gun. It didn't matter. I saw that arm raise. I saw a glint of something in a hand—twenty feet from Jack, pointing right at him, and I didn't care if it was an assassin with a gun or a kid with a knife. I just didn't.

Jack hit the ground as soon as I said his name. Two shots, mine a split second before the other. A soft grunt, my bullet hitting flesh. Then, almost in echo, a crack as the other bullet struck a tree.

Jack's would-be attacker swung on me, gun going up. I saw a flash of a pale face under a dark hood. I fired again. My bullet hit him square in the chest. He stumbled back, grunting again.

A grunt and a stumble. Not the proper reaction to getting a bullet in the chest. The gunman was wearing a bulletproof vest.

Jack lunged at him as I shot a third time, aiming for his head, but he saw Jack coming and veered out of the way. He swung his gun around to shoot. I fired and hit him in the shoulder. There was a different sound now, a gasping hiss of pain. The man fired two rounds in quick succession. Jack hit the ground. The man took off running.

I started after him, but Jack leapt to his feet and caught the back of my dress.

"Hold up," he said.

"But—"

"Let him run. Lots of room here. Got time."

I nodded and scanned the ground. I caught sight of the chrome clasp on my purse and picked it up. I noticed something else, too—my panties. I grabbed them. Then I gave Jack back his gun after he finished buttoning his shirt.

"The guy's wearing a vest," I said.

"Yeah. Figured."

"In other words, this wasn't a random mugging."

Jack gave me a look.

"I know. The chances of that were slim to none. I was being optimistic."

"Yeah. Wish it was. Could just let him go." He hefted his gun and checked to make sure I had mine out. "Ready?"

I nodded.

CHAPTER 36

O ur attacker may have been quiet when he ambushed us, but he wasn't nearly as silent as he
made his escape. Like the pro Roland sent to kill me at
the lodge, clearly this guy had expected an easy mark. It
probably even seemed as if he had one, when we
strolled off from a romantic dinner to take an equally
romantic walk through an empty park followed by a
much more strenuous—and distracting—form of romantic activity.

Even when we hit the ground, he probably only
thought we'd moved into a more gravity-friendly position. God only knows what he figured Jack was doing,
fumbling around on the ground.

And when that bullet hit him? Well, I wouldn't
blame the guy if his shorts weren't entirely dry after
that shock. He'd recovered nicely, his hitman instincts
kicking in. But now another instinct had taken over—
the one that told him to get the hell out of that park
before we put more bullets in his ass.

Jack was right to stop me from tearing after our
attacker. When we didn't follow, he slowed down. I
could imagine what he was thinking. Despite what he'd
been told, the woman obviously realized she was a target and had armed herself. He wasn't unprepared for

this, having worn the vest. Yet right now we'd be doing what any normal couple would do after a gunfight in the park—get to safety.

So as we tracked him, his pounding footsteps turned to walking ones and then to slow, measured steps as he likely considered whether the hit was still salvageable. When the guy neared the edge of the park, he stopped to consider some more.

"Time to split up and circle around," I whispered.

Jack kept his gaze forward. "I can do this. Just stay—"

"No." I got in front of him and forced his gaze to mine. "I don't stay on the sidelines, and if you think that has changed—"

"Circumstances. You're the target."

"You're the one he actually shot at. He'll take you out to get at me. If you keep arguing, we'll lose him."

I tugged off my heels. I was going to leave them behind, but Jack shoved one in each jacket pocket. Then he pointed at my bare feet. "Be careful."

I figured stepping in dog shit—or even on broken glass—was the least of my worries, but I nodded, and we split up. I went south, into the trees, picking my way past windblown piles of dead leaves as I hurried to flank our target. He was on the move again, slow now, as if still undecided about searching for us on the streets. I hoped he wouldn't. The park was far more conducive to a takedown and interrogation.

I was less than thirty feet away when he moved under a path light. Just a guy dressed in black—black jeans, black sneakers, black hoodie pulled up. From what I could make out of his face, he was a little old for the hoodie look, maybe forty. Otherwise, average height, average size, average looking. I studied his face, trying to impress it on my memory in case we lost him.

He tucked his gun into the pocket of his hoodie. Getting ready to head out. Shit.

I glanced around for Jack. Maybe we could still do this. Get me to lure—

A crash sounded in the woods on Jack's side. I heard a muffled oath, followed by an angry whisper. Jack's voice.

Our target bought the fake out. He gave a low chuckle as he pulled out his gun and went after the stupid marks hiding in the woods.

As he slipped along the path, I followed from the woods. Jack had gone quiet now—he wouldn't overdo it. But the guy had already pinpointed the location of the sounds and when he drew close, he stopped and listened again, wondering if we could see him on the lit path. If we did, we'd make some noise, a small exclamation of fear or the rustle of a retreat. The woods stayed quiet.

The man eased toward the trees, rolling his footsteps, moving slowly as he watched and listened. When he passed the tree line, I started toward the path. Now came the tricky part. I had to cross that path, and the smallest noise would cause him to turn and see me, a lit target. I paused at the edge, calculating the best route and waiting until he was a little deeper in—

A rustle deep in the patch of woods. The man stiffened as he pinpointed the sound, intent on that. A second rustle. His strides lengthened as he hurried toward his target, off to his left now. I smiled and mentally thanked Jack for the diversion as I dashed across the path.

I darted into the forest on the other side. I could see the man ahead. He'd stopped now and was looking around. He was in deep enough that it must have been pitch-dark, and he was trying to pick up another sound.

One came, conveniently enough, the soft snap of a twig. He started in that direction. I slid into his wake.

Maybe it's because I've spent plenty of time in dark forests, but I could see decently enough. Better than our target, who kept stopping, head rotating. The crackle of a leaf put him on the move again. Jack was drawing him in deeper. Perfect.

I got as close as I dared, following maybe five feet behind him, my gun poised should he turn. He didn't. He kept going until he stepped past a massive oak and . . .

"Stop."

It was Jack, standing right in the man's path, gun drawn. I closed the gap quickly as the two faced off.

"Lower the gun," I said.

The man started at the sound of my voice, right behind him. He began to turn and then thought better of it and just stood there, gun still trained on Jack.

"Lower the gun now," I said. "Or I put a bullet in the base of your brain."

I pressed my gun barrel to his neck. He flinched and tried to cover the reaction by pulling himself straighter. He still didn't lower his gun. He did, however, make the small concession of aiming slightly away from Jack.

"You've been duped," I said. "As you might have figured out, we're not your typical marks. You're the second pro they've sent after us. Do you want to guess what happened to the first?"

The man said nothing.

"We tried to extend him professional courtesy," I continued. "All he had to do was answer a few questions about who sent him. He wouldn't. Are you going to be smarter?"

Still no answer. Which proved, sadly, that the guy probably *was* smarter—smart enough to guess I was bullshitting and that nothing he said was going to get him out of this situation alive.

Jack motioned that he'd take over. The moment either of us moved from our position, we provided an escape route, so I kicked the guy in the back of the knee to send him down. He anticipated that and feigned a fall. Then he spun on me, gun going up. Jack kicked him so hard the guy almost took me down as he fell. Jack was dropping on him when someone called, "Over here!"

Jack pinned the guy as another voice called, "Hold up!" A drunken giggle. "Where'd you go?"

"Over here! Come on!"

A third voice said something, the words too slurred to make out. Drunk kids. Three young men from the sounds of it. They were on the path heading into the park.

"Hey!" our target called, the cry cut short as Jack slammed his face into the ground.

"Shut the fuck up," Jack whispered.

"Did you hear something?" one of the boys said.

"Nah. Come on. You have to see this!"

Our guy tried to yell again. Jack ground his face into the dirt, but he kept trying, his muffled cries as loud as shouts in the quiet night.

"I heard something," a boy said. "Seriously, man. It sounded like someone in trouble."

"And what are you? The Caped Crusader?"

"No," another giggled. "He's Brother Power the Geek."

"Hey, I've heard of that one. Didn't—"

"I mean it. I hear something. In the woods over there."

The whole time they were talking, Jack struggled with our captive, trying to shut him up. The guy wasn't listening. His nose was broken, blood streaming into the dirt. When Jack yanked the guy's head back, his lips were bleeding, too, one front tooth broken. Still he managed a stifled cry. Jack got his hands around the guy's throat, knees pinning him as I crouched in front, gun at the guy's forehead, whispering for him to shut up, shut the fuck up, knowing he wouldn't because I wouldn't, because this was his only chance.

Even with Jack's hands around his throat, the guy kept gurgling. Jack squeezed harder. Then harder. The guy's eyes bulged and I wanted to tell Jack to stop, that we needed him alive, but no matter what Jack did, the guy made all the noise he could, thrashing now, arms and legs beating the ground.

Pass out. Please just pass out.

It seemed to take forever, but finally, his eyes closed, and his arms and legs went still. I moved to check his pulse, but Jack stopped me and motioned toward the drunk kids. He was right, of course—that was the priority. They were crashing about in the woods now. And I do mean crashing, moving with so much noise that it was impossible not to know exactly where they were.

"It's stopped," one of the boys was saying. It was the one who'd noticed the noise first—the one who seemed the least incapacitated.

"Yeah, because whoever it was heard us coming," another said. "Probably some poor guy trying to get lucky and now you've fucked it up for him. Way to go."

I kept my gaze straight ahead, not daring to look over at Jack. Adrenaline had knocked my hormones back in check, but there was a little part of me still going, *Shit, of all the lousy timing* . . . And I didn't mean the boys coming into the park and disturbing our interrogation, either.

The boys traveled east for a couple of minutes, arguing, and then decided to give up the hunt. It took them a while to find the path again, and more than once they seemed to be stumbling our way. I'd glance at Jack, to see if we should bolt, but he held steady. Eventually, they found the path and decided what they really needed was more booze. Maybe even some dope. One of them "knew a guy," and they all trudged out of the park to find him.

I bent beside our would-be attacker and felt his neck for a pulse.

"He's gone," I said.

"Fuck."

"He knew his choices. Either bring those boys over or win himself a quick death." I looked down at the body. "He got option two."

"And we got shit."

"I know."

I checked the man's pockets. There was a wallet with a few hundred in cash and the bare minimum of ID, out of state and probably fake. Unlike our first attacker, though, this one had a cell phone.

I turned it on and got a password screen.

"Fuck," Jack said, leaning over.

"Yep. I'm sure Evelyn can crack it. In the meantime, we have a body. Do we drag it farther into the woods?"

"Nah. There's a pond."

"I missed that."

"Didn't pass it."

"Ah, meaning you know from experience. All right then. Let's get this guy to water."

I started to turn.

"Hey," Jack said.

I glanced over. He was poised there, watching me, his gaze shuttered.

"Hmmm?" I said.

"Lousy timing, huh?"

"No kidding."

He relaxed a little, but his face was still tight as he said, "You okay?" and I knew he wasn't asking if I'd been hurt or if I was shaken up.

Before I could answer, he said, "Earlier . . . We okay?"

"We're fine, Jack. I had one glass of wine. I knew what I was doing."

"Yeah, I know. Just . . ."

"I knew what I was doing and I wasn't doing anything I didn't want to do. Everything is fine." I glanced down at the corpse. "Except for the dead body that needs to be taken care of. Very inconveniently."

"Yeah."

CHAPTER 37

Jack made me put my heels back on to move the body. Because, apparently, tetanus was a serious concern. He did most of the heavy lifting, but we did need to carry the guy, not just drag him across the park. And it was a bit of a hike. Still we managed it.

We weighed the body down and tossed it into the pond. That makes it sound easy. It wasn't. There's no sense hiding a corpse if you're going to be careless about it. By the time we finished, it was nearly two in the morning. And the night wasn't over yet.

We had to get back to the car. Then we had to make damned sure that it hadn't been tampered with—particularly that it wasn't going to blow up when Jack turned the ignition. He knew how to check and showed me.

Then, having ascertained that the BMW was indeed safe to drive, we had to get rid of it. Or at least leave it at the rental company lot and pick up our less conspicuous car.

The rental place was closed. That was fine. Jack had rented the BMW under a different alias and left our previous car in a public parking lot two blocks away.

After that, we still couldn't return to our hotel until

we were sure we hadn't been followed from there to the restaurant.

So who did we think called in the hired gun? The answer seemed obvious: the guy who knew I was in town. Sebastian Koss. Yes, we hadn't seen him make a call or anything after our meeting, but that didn't mean he hadn't contacted someone, maybe a text under the table as we'd talked, getting my would-be assassin over to the pub to follow me.

Earlier, I'd said I thought it entirely possible for Koss to have a drink with someone he'd hired a hit on. He was, after all, a killer, however justified his cause. And yet to hire a hitman *after* talking to me? That took a level of cold that I couldn't fathom. As we drove, I asked Jack's opinion.

"Talk to a mark? Yeah. Done it."

"So have I," I said. "A few words at most. I've never had a full-length conversation, though. Have you done that?"

"Conversation?" A snort. "Fuck, no. Worse than killing. More painful."

I smiled. "Okay, for you, maybe. But it feels like . . . I don't know. Maybe that's my ego. I don't like to think someone could talk to me for an hour and still want to kill me."

"I wouldn't."

I laughed softly. "Thank you."

"Mean it, though. Even the first time. When Evelyn sent me. I was worried you'd be a risk. Even if you were? Don't think I could have done it. For someone else, though? Talked to them, then had to kill them? Could manage. If I had to. Rather not. Probably easier if you're not the one pulling the trigger, though."

"True. So we're certain Koss hired him."

"Never certain. But . . ."

"It almost definitely is because, well, who else could it be?"

"Yeah." He glanced over. "Sorry. Know you liked him. His reputation anyway. Respected him."

I nodded. "I did. But that's not going to stop me from putting the bastard down before he can do the same to me."

"Good."

We were standing outside Koss's house. It was a typical upper-middle-class home in a typical upper-middle-class suburban neighborhood. I'd been hoping for a more ostentatious show of wealth, as if it might prove Sebastian Koss was indeed evil. I know it doesn't work that way, but it would have helped.

The place was dark. We had no way of telling whether Koss was home, but we presumed he was. There's no sense hiring a killer if you aren't going to make sure you have an alibi for the time of death. So when Jack said, "I'm going in," I turned and stared at him.

"There's a family in there," I said.

A slight narrowing of the eyes, relaying an offended "no shit."

"There's no need to go in," I said. "We're ninety-five percent sure he's sleeping beside his wife, establishing his alibi."

"And I'm gonna check. Also getting a better look. Security, layout, whatever. In case."

I didn't ask "in case of what." I knew. In case we decided to kill Sebastian Koss.

"What else?" I said.

A wordless shrug told me it was a valid question.

"You're going to leave a message, aren't you?"

A moment's pause as he glanced away. Then, "Yeah."

"Jack . . ."

He turned his gaze back on me. "You really think I'd let this slide? Fuck, no. I was sure it was him? I'd put a bullet in his brain while he slept beside his wife. Wouldn't take the chance he'd call another hit first thing tomorrow. As it is . . ." Another shrug. "Just leaving a message."

"What?"

He pulled a pair of sunglasses from his pocket. I presumed they were the hitman's, though I hadn't seen him take them.

"Don't worry," he said. "Gonna wipe them down. Before I leave them."

"I'm not concerned about that. It's a house with four people in it, plus security, maybe a dog . . ."

"I won't kill the dog."

I gave him a look.

"Yeah. I know. Not easy. I can do it. Done worse. Brought tools. Not a problem."

There was little I could say to that. As pissed off as Jack was, he wouldn't take an unnecessary risk with me standing watch outside.

Jack got in and out without incident. Koss was in bed. Jack had done a little searching in Koss's office, too, but found nothing.

In the car, we both got quiet. Now that the rush of the last few hours had passed, I realized what had happened. Someone tried to kill me. And that assassination attempt killed my romantic evening with Jack.

I know the two things shouldn't weigh equally on the scale. Yet people have shot at me before. I'd like to say I'm used to it, but afterward, there's always that "holy fucking shit" moment when I realize I could have died. Still, it's not much different from avoiding a car accident. I could have died; I didn't; I'd be more careful now.

As for Jack, I'd spent the past year wanting to be with a guy who didn't seem the least bit interested. Then he gives me the most perfect date I could imagine. The dress, the hotel, the car, the restaurant, and then the park with that moment of complete, unbridled—and, yes, unexpected—passion.

The night should have ended back in our penthouse hotel suite, where I'd watch the sun come up from the king-size bed. Instead, I was watching it rise through the window of our tiny rental car, my dress dirty, my hair bedraggled, makeup smeared, even my shoes on the backseat because one of the heels was nearly broken off. We were looking for a hotel, any hotel, not to finish what we'd started, just to sleep. Shower off the filth of the night and collapse, probably into separate beds, as if it was any other hard night of work. I thought of that and I wanted to cry.

"There's a Holiday Inn," I said, pointing at the sign ahead.

Jack glanced over. It was indeed a Holiday Inn, and not even a particularly nice one. His lips tightened.

"Gotta be more up here," he said. "Better."

I sighed. "We haven't passed anything else since we left the suburbs. Let's just take it."

He glowered at the hotel, as if it had committed some unspeakable offense by existing. Then he turned in.

CHAPTER 38

I hovered by the elevators while Jack got the room. The lobby was, thankfully, empty. When I saw Jack coming, I hit the button, got on, and held it for him as I hid out of view.

He stepped on, shaking his head at me. "You look fine."

"No, I look chewed up and spit out."

"You look fine *to me*."

I smiled. "Thank you." The doors closed. "And thank you for tonight. It was memorable."

A low chuckle. "Yeah, that's one way to put it."

He stepped toward me tentatively, his gaze sharp, evaluating my reaction. When I smiled, he eased a little closer.

"Did I tell you I liked your dress?" he said. "I'm not good at that. Saying the right thing."

"I got the impression you liked it."

"You looked good. But to me? You always look good. Then. Now."

"I could wear dirt and smeared makeup more often if you'd like."

He laughed softly. "Can if you want." He sobered. "I just meant I know you dressed up. For tonight. Should comment." He paused. "That doesn't sound right. Fuck. I'm no good at—"

I grabbed him by the shirtfront and pulled him into a kiss, and this time there was no surprise, no hesitation. Hell, there wasn't even a moment of transition. I kissed him and it was as if we'd only pushed *pause* in the park. Two seconds later, I was up against the side of the elevator, his hands under my ass, mine in his hair.

In the rare times that I'd dared let myself imagine what it would be like to be with Jack, I'd had a pretty clear idea of what to expect. Sex with Jack would be like Jack himself. Slow, measured, cautious. Hell, no. It was like driving a pipeline straight into that intensity boiling under the surface.

"How far's our room?" I gasped when we broke for air.

"Too far."

I glanced over his shoulder and grinned. "There *is* a stop button."

"Yeah?"

"Yeah."

He reached over and hit it. I laughed, and as we kissed again, my fingers slid between us, and I started to unbutton his shirt as he hiked my skirt up—

The elevator phone began to ring.

"God-fucking-damn-it."

"Agreed," I said.

Jack swung toward the phone like he was ready to shoot it. I reached over and hit the button to restart the elevator.

"Two minutes," I said. "In two minutes, we'll be locked in a room where no one can interrupt us."

When the doors began to open, Jack gave them a hand. There was a moment at the room door when the key card didn't want to cooperate—Jack took advantage of the pause to slide his hand under my skirt—and I began to wonder if we were going to make it into the room after all. But the door thankfully opened and we stumbled in.

As I flipped on the light, I realized Jack had managed to get us a suite again, which meant there was a separate bedroom, which was lovely . . . and much too far away at the moment.

Jack swung me up against the armchair, and I eased up onto the low back, legs wrapped around him. It was a bit of a balancing act, but hey, all that exercise does pay off.

We managed to kiss for about five seconds less than the last time before he had my skirt up and I was undressing him. Foreplay—like the bed—could wait for next time. Even the simple act of undressing seemed like too much work. I popped two buttons on Jack's shirt and the one on his trousers was left hanging by a thread. The ripping sound I heard as he pulled off my dress suggested I might not be wearing it again. And while I'd taken great care in picking out a matching bra and panty set, I don't think Jack noticed. The bra was off in seconds—after some cursing with the clasp—and the panties where about to follow when he stopped.

"Shit!" His eyes widened. "I didn't bring . . ."

"Let me guess . . . You weren't expecting the evening to end this way."

"Fuck, no."

I laughed, pulled up my panties, and crossed to where I'd dropped my purse. "Luckily, I know this guy who's taught me that I need to be prepared for every contingency . . . even if he apparently isn't."

He exhaled a deep sigh of relief as I pulled out a condom. I laughed. As I did, he stopped, as if just seeing me. His gaze traveled over me.

"Fuck."

I nodded at the bra on the floor. "Yep, a matching set. Like I said, I was prepared for every contingency."

"Didn't mean the underwear," he said, and crossed the space between us, swooping me down onto the floor.

We did make it to the bed. After we were done. Better late than never. As we lay there, Jack on his back, me curled up against him, his arm under me, I looked over and said, "There's something I need to tell you. I know you aren't going to like it."

His head whipped my way, and the expression in his eyes was almost enough to make me regret it. Almost.

I took a deep breath. "I really appreciated that."

He sputtered a laugh. "Yeah, deserved that. I was being an ass. Didn't mean it. No fucking good at this."

I grinned. "Oh, you seem plenty good at it."

Another laugh. "Got a good partner. Makes a difference. You know what I mean, though. Relationships. Fucking clueless." He stopped laughing and rubbed his mouth with his free hand. Then he looked over at me. "That's what this is for me. You know that, right? Not one night."

"I sure as hell hope not."

He relaxed, shifting to rub my back. "Good. Not trying to jump the gun. Make demands. I just know . . . Expectations . . . Not understanding them . . . That was a problem. Don't want that."

"Neither do I."

"Don't have any expectations except one. That I want to make this work." He met my gaze. "I really want to make this work."

"So do I."

"You're gonna need to be patient with me."

I smiled. "I have plenty of experience with that."

He laughed softly and pulled me on top of him.

———

I slept until nearly noon, probably because it'd taken us a while to get to sleep. Round one had been feverishly swift; round two deliciously slow. While part of me just wanted to lie there, curled up against Jack as he slept, once I'm awake, I'm awake, and I was only going to disturb him if I stayed.

He was sleeping on his stomach, leg over mine. I eased out. He was too far gone to even notice. I crept from the bedroom and into the bath, quietly shut the door, and climbed into the shower.

I was finishing washing my hair when I had the sensation of being watched and turned to see Jack just inside the door. He'd closed it behind him and was standing there, watching me. When I looked over, his expression changed, open admiration vanishing in a hesitant look, as if I might still have changed my mind.

"Hey," I said, smiling as I opened the shower door. "If you need a shower, I can hurry. Or . . ." I stepped back, leaving the door open.

"Don't need a shower," he said and stepped in with me.

I was lying in the living room, dressed in a robe that I hadn't bothered to fasten, stretched on the sofa, blissed out like a kitty on catnip, staring into nothing, mind empty. Jack had stepped out to get coffee. Also, more condoms. Not that I expected sex this afternoon. Jack wasn't my age, and three times set a personal record for me. But, well, I wouldn't turn down the chance to make it four.

Yes, we did have other things to do. Important things. Life-preserving things, even. But Jack had called Evelyn, and we were going to courier her the locked cell phone. So I was lying there, naked on my open robe, happy to stay that way for a while longer, when a knock came at the door. I scrambled up. I vaguely recalled putting out the Do Not Disturb sign, and I couldn't imagine Jack would take it down, but the cleaning staff might have decided that two in the afternoon was as late as they were waiting.

"The room's fine," I called as I walked to the door, fumbling for the robe belt, which I'd apparently left elsewhere.

"That's good," came the reply. "Because I'm not going to clean it for you."

Even through the door, I recognized that voice and I stopped midstep.

"Quinn?"

"Bearing coffee and muffins, which I'm going to eat myself if you make me stand here much longer."

No. It couldn't be. He was in New York, and there was no way he could know which hotel we were in. I must have dozed off on the sofa and fallen into a dream.

More like a nightmare.

"Dee?"

I carefully slid the chain, trying not to make any noise as I fastened it. Then, cinching my robe, I cracked the door open the two inches the chain would allow. Quinn stood there, holding a coffee tray and bag, his brows arched, a smile playing on his lips. The smile grew as his gaze traveled down me.

"May I come in?" he asked.

"Sorry. I was getting into the shower. Just . . . Let me take the chain off and give me five seconds to get into the bathroom."

"Um, even if you weren't wearing the robe, it's nothing I haven't seen before." His grin grew, eyes glinting. "And nothing I'd complain about seeing again."

Wonderful. Quinn wasn't just here at the worst possible time. He was here in the worst possible mood.

"Right. Sorry. I'm just . . ."

"Rough night? I heard. Which is why I'm here, though I'd prefer to be inside . . ."

"Right. Just a sec."

I closed the door and counted to five, getting my thoughts in order. Call Jack. That's what I had to do. Before he walked in with breakfast and a box of condoms. My phone was in my purse, on the floor, half spilled from last night.

Last night . . .

Ah, hell. Hell, hell, hell. Really, Quinn? Now?

"Dee?"

I snatched up my cell phone. Then I unfastened the door. I was backing away to let him in when I caught a glimpse of green lace by the chair. I managed to kick my panties underneath with a punt that would make a footballer proud.

Quinn walked in. His gaze traveled over me again. "Nice robe."

"Um, thanks. I'm going to take that shower."

"You want company?"

My cheeks flared.

"Sorry," Quinn said. "I'll behave. Go on."

I was starting to leave when I remembered that half of my undergarments were still unaccounted for. I looked over and saw a bit of my bra strap on the armchair. As Quinn put down coffee, I tossed the throw pillow back onto the armchair, covering my bra. Then I scampered into the bathroom.

I locked the door, started the shower, and called Jack.

"Quinn's here," I said when he answered.

Silence.

"Not a joke," I whispered. "I wouldn't do that."

Another moment of silence. "Fuck."

"Exactly. I have no idea what's going on. I'm holed up in the bathroom pretending to shower to explain why I answered the door in a robe."

"Fuck."

"Right. So just . . ."

"On my way."

"Thanks."

CHAPTER 39

I stuck my head into the shower and towel-dried my hair. Then I prepared to dress and . . . realized I had nothing to wear except, well, the dress. Which had a rip down the seam. Even my undergarments were in the next room. So I put on the dress and then I put the robe over it.

I walked out of the bathroom just as Jack was coming in. We made eye contact. I mouthed, "Fuck," and his lips twitched in a smile. He fired a look across the room, one that suggested he was wondering how much I'd complain if he accidentally shot Quinn.

I walked out and cleared my throat. Quinn was on the sofa—having thankfully not chosen the armchair, a possibility I hadn't considered. He glanced up and said a quick hello to Jack, who emptied his expression and grunted a return greeting.

"I, uh, I'm a little short of clothing," I said to Quinn, waving at the robe as I walked to take a coffee from Jack. "We had some trouble last night, as you heard, and we had to switch hotel rooms. So all I have is what I was wearing, uh, on the job last night."

Quinn looked at my bare legs and grinned. "Which appears to be a dress."

"Yeah."

"It looks like a *short* dress." His grin grew. "Can I see?"

Jack's look said he was no longer contemplating murder; he was now trying to figure out where to hide the body.

"Um, actually," I said, "I know you just got here, but could you do me a huge favor? I saw a gift shop downstairs. Could you see if they have something—anything—I can wear? My dress got ripped while we were running around last night."

"Sure, I can do that."

I headed for my wallet, but he held up a hand. "I've got it. Jack? I'll get you a shirt. Looks like you're missing a button or two." Quinn reached into his pocket and pulled out a bag of candy. "Dee? I grabbed this for you, too. In case the muffin wasn't enough." He tossed the candy onto the table and headed out.

When he was gone, I latched the door and turned to Jack. "I have absolutely no idea how he got here or how he found out where we were staying."

"That was me."

"What?"

Jack set his coffee down. "Right after I left. Quinn calls. Says he needs our hotel address. Room number. Sending something over. Didn't expect it to be *him*."

"Well, I still don't know what he's doing here."

"Saving you. Because I obviously can't."

"I don't think—"

"He is. I called Evelyn about the cell phone." He took a coffee and waved me to the sofa. We sat down. "Last night? She notified Quinn. About the botched hit. Didn't want him complaining about being out of the loop. He was pissed. He thinks I'm not handling this. Don't have what it takes. Obviously you need him."

"So she let him come without warning us?"

"Nah. Thought she'd talked him down. Never knew he took off."

I swore under my breath. "Okay, but if he seriously thinks you're to blame for that near miss, then we're going to have a talk, because I'm not exactly sitting around waiting to be rescued. You and I are both working this, as hard as we can, and he was doing a lot more good in New York."

"He can't impress you in New York. Can't buy you fucking candy in New York. He got his second wind. Bouncing back. Flirting. Now he's gonna fix this. Because I can't."

"I'll convince him that he's more help to us in New York."

Jack exhaled. "No. I'm being an idiot. Just pissed off. In a way? He's right. Evelyn says New York is stalled while Contrapasso considers him. We could use him. His skills. Crack that cell phone. Investigate Koss. Get his phone records. Track the dead guy's aliases from his fake ID."

"Evelyn can do all of that, too."

"But she's in New York. Stepping in with Contrapasso. Talked about that last night. Infiltrating Quinn? Too slow. She can move faster. Quinn's better off here."

"Um, that's kind of . . . awkward. Once I tell him, I'm not sure he'll stay."

"Not telling him. No reason to."

"But I can't—"

"We'll put it on hold. You're not sure he'd stay? I'm sure he wouldn't. To fix this? Use every resource I've got. Even Quinn."

"So I'm supposed to let him help us, thinking it means we have a chance of getting back together? I can't do that, Jack. I won't."

"Don't have to. Just keep telling him it's over."

"Jack, I can't—"

"You think he'd want to know? Now? No. Tell him later. Like it took time for us. Make it easier on him."

While Jack was right, I knew he didn't give a rat's ass about Quinn's feelings. He'd use whatever he could to convince me to keep quiet about us, if it might cost us Quinn's help.

I sat there, looking toward the window. A half hour ago, I'd been lying on this sofa, happy, so damned happy.

"Nadia . . ." Jack's voice softened and I could see him leaning over, trying to get my attention, but I just kept staring at the window.

"Nadia . . ." He reached for me.

I stood up. "You're right. I hate it. I absolutely hate it, but . . ."

I trailed off and just stood there, frozen again, ensnared in my thoughts, feeling . . . Feeling like shit. Like I was a shitty person doing a shitty thing to someone who really didn't deserve it.

"No," Jack said, pushing up. "*You're* right. We'll send him back to New York. He can work from there."

"That doesn't solve the problem, Jack. He still thinks we can work things out, when I'm already with someone else—"

"His problem. You told him it's over. Didn't do anything wrong."

"I feel—"

Jack stepped in front of me, hands on my arms. "I know you feel guilty. But you've got no reason to. It was over. Completely over. I wasn't making a move until you were sure of it and I was sure of it."

I inhaled. "I know. I just . . ."

"Still feel guilty."

I forced a smile. "I'm good at it."

"I know."

His hands slid around my waist. He leaned in and kissed me.

Quinn rapped at the door. I pulled away and answered while Jack headed back to the sofa.

"You know what would make this much easier?" Quinn said as I opened the door. "If you got me my own key card."

I sidestepped to block the look Jack shot him. Then I took the gift shop bag. "Let me get dressed and we'll talk."

I brought Quinn up to date on the night's attack.

As Jack expected, there was a lot Quinn could do. He took the cell phone first and tried it out.

"Yep, that's a password. A lot of times these are simpler to crack than you'd think. Once this is cracked, I'll run Koss's home number and cell against this phone's call list. I'll also run Koss's number separately and see if he placed a call during or after your meeting. And I'll see if that fake ID pops anything."

"Thank you." I glanced at Jack. "Do we want—?"

My cell phone rang. My personal one. I glanced down at the number.

"It's Koss," I said.

Quinn motioned for me to answer but hold it away from my ear. I was sitting on the chair. He moved over, perching on the arm. Jack stayed where he was.

I answered.

"Nadia?" Koss said.

I said it was me, and we exchanged pleasantries. It seemed civil enough, but after having spent some time with the man, I could pick up strain in his voice. Maybe it was getting harder, pretending to be nice to someone you were trying to kill. Or maybe finding those sunglasses had him stressed.

Finally, Koss said, "There's a reason I'm calling." He paused. "Are you in any kind of trouble?"

It was hard to answer that straight. It really was. I managed a surprised, "No. Why?"

"Because someone called about you. Last night and again this morning."

"What?"

"Well, I'm presuming it's the same person, though the number came up blocked. He called my home office last night. I wasn't here, and he didn't leave a message. Another call came this morning, and I answered. It was a man asking how I was acquainted with you. The question threw me. I could only presume it was someone who knew you and perhaps got my number from you. I said simply that you had an interest in an old case of mine and why was he asking. He hung up."

Was this some trick? Koss lying about a call as an excuse to contact me? It was a very odd excuse.

Quinn mouthed, "Play along."

"I . . . don't understand," I said. "I didn't give your number to anyone. I didn't even tell anyone I was going to see you."

"Then it makes even less sense. I'll ask again. Are you in any kind of trouble, Nadia?"

"Not that I know of. But I guess . . . I guess I should be careful."

He agreed that I should. He promised to notify me if he heard from the mysterious caller again, and we signed off.

"That was . . ." I began.

"Weird?" Quinn said. "Oh, yeah."

"No," Jack said. "Not weird at all. Guy's covering his ass. Diverting attention. Setting up a story."

Quinn looked doubtful, but I had to agree it was the only thing that made sense, though it still seemed strange.

"All right then," I said. "Back to what I was saying before Koss called. Where are we otherwise? ID'ing the hitman and tracking his middleman?"

"Not sure they're using one," Jack said. "Probably going direct. Got lots of contacts."

"You mean Contrapasso," Quinn said. "You still think they're behind this."

I cut in. "I know you're impressed by them, Quinn, and you don't want to think they'd do this. I don't, either, but it seems clear that I was targeted last night because I met with Sebastian Koss."

"I completely agree. I'm just not as sure that the logical connections fall where you're putting them. Would Contrapasso kill a bystander to protect themselves? I have no idea. Would they hire an outside hitman to do it when they have their own? That's even less clear. If you or I felt we absolutely had to kill a bystander, would we hire someone else to do it? Or would we see that as moral cowardice?" Quinn eased back. "Hell, even you, Jack. Would you hire another pro to clean up your mess?"

I bristled at Quinn's tone, but Jack only shrugged. "Wouldn't hire anyone. I wouldn't trust it'd be done right."

"I'm not saying it's impossible," Quinn said. "I'm going by impressions after a few meetings, which could be wrong. But I think it's *more* likely that Koss hired these guys himself. Aldrich was his hit and something made him think you were on to him. He screwed up; he's protecting his own ass. There's also a third possibility. That someone else followed you from that meeting with Koss. Someone who was tailing him because both of you are targets after Aldrich's death."

"You mean whoever is targeting me is also targeting him? I meet with Koss. The killer switches his focus to me."

"Right."

"But if Koss is a target, why's he still walking around? There would have been plenty of opportunities to kill him since Aldrich. He's right where he should be—at home. Unlike me."

"But he's a public figure who's particularly popular with law enforcement. And his tough-on-crime rep means he's bound to have enemies. If he dies, it stirs up a shitload of attention. The hit has to be done with extreme caution."

I glanced at Jack.

He shrugged. "Possible. Would explain the phone call."

"Exactly," Quinn said. "I'm not ruling out Contrapasso or Koss, but let's start by seeing if this mystery call actually came to Koss. Between Evelyn and me, we should be able to get Koss's phone records."

Getting those records wasn't easy, but it wasn't as hard as it probably should be. Evelyn said she'd handle it and called back an hour later. She spoke to Jack, as she usually did.

The problem with Jack taking the call? It was nearly impossible to eavesdrop. I couldn't hear Evelyn's side and from Jack all I got were grunts and single-word answers. He did, however, make notes, which would have been a lot more helpful if his note-taking was any more loquacious than his speech. There were numbers. That's it.

When he got off the phone, though, he was quick to explain. Koss hadn't been lying about receiving two calls to his home office, one last night and one this morning, both from the same number. The one at 7:30 last evening had connected just long enough to suggest the answering machine picked up and the caller listened to the message but didn't leave one. The second call, at 11:45 this morning, lasted nearly two minutes, which confirmed Koss's story that they had spoken briefly.

Evelyn had also pulled Koss's cell record. He hadn't made any calls or texted anyone from the time his lecture started until after he left the restaurant with his wife. Which gave some serious weight to the theory that someone else hired last night's hitman.

Evelyn had even gone one step further, running the number that called Koss. It had placed a call around five, then received two from the same number later in the evening—one at nine, one just before midnight.

I took out my phone.

"Whoa," Quinn said. "Hold on. You don't want to call that number just yet."

"Not the one that called Koss," I said. "The one *that* caller phoned and received two calls from."

Quinn looked confused. "Okay, but still, you don't want to use your phone for that. Even a burner."

"It can scramble the outgoing calls. The number won't match anything I've used before."

"Shit. I've heard of that but where—? Ah. Felix."

I nodded.

"I partnered with the guy for a week last year and *you* get the toys."

"Not me." I hooked a finger at Jack.

"You want one?" Jack said. "Just ask. It'll cost, though. Not cheap."

I dialed the number while they talked. It took a moment to connect. Then it started to ring . . . from the end table beside Quinn. He picked up the locked phone.

"Shit," he said. "You saw that coming, didn't you?"

"Playing a hunch," I said. "So whoever phoned Koss also called our hitman. Presumably, he's the client."

"We really need to learn who's at the other end of that phone," Quinn said.

"Yep."

There was no pressing need now to crack the hitman's phone. We still would, but having his number meant we could track his calls. Evelyn would do that. She'd also tried phoning the number that called Koss. It had gone straight to "customer not available." We tried and got the same, suggesting it was either off or he'd replaced the SIM card.

"The question is," Quinn said as we settled in again, "who would put out a hit on both you and Koss? I could guess Contrapasso covering a bad hit, but the Aldrich hit wasn't bad. I've been monitoring the case through law-enforcement contacts. Nobody suspects this was anything except a remorseful killer who offed himself. To them, it's a good-news story. They have no interest in looking closer."

"Agreed," I said. "So there's no reason for Contrapasso to panic and take out one of their own, especially someone as valuable as Koss. Which means we're back to our original theory that Aldrich had friends. Nasty friends."

"Right," Quinn said. "We know a fellow scumbag didn't kill *him*, but that could be who's after you."

I nodded. "Koss might not have been the only person Aldrich called after he saw me." I looked at Quinn. "Can we get Aldrich's phone records?"

He nodded. "So the theory would be that this guy is worried either Koss or you know something—or will find something—that will bring *him* down. Which suggests not just some scumbag friend but . . ."

I glanced at Jack.

"Partner," he said. "Aldrich had a partner."

CHAPTER 40

Aldrich did not have a partner when he raped me and then raped and murdered Amy. My memories of that night might have shattered, but I'd retained enough pieces to be sure I hadn't seen or heard anyone else at that cabin. What I suspected, instead, was that we were reverting back to an older theory, one supported by what Shannon Broadhurst had said about Aldrich having met "like-minded friends" later in life. Except, it seemed, more than just friends. A true partner-in-crime, who was worried that Koss or I had found something.

Found what? The journal, of course.

"Is it in the car?" I asked. "Shit. Our stuff. We left our bags at the other hotel."

"Called," Jack said. "Paid an extra night. Get it later. Journal's in the car. With my tools."

"I could go and grab your things," Quinn said. "That might be better, so no one sees you guys showing up again."

I remembered the fancy hotel . . . with the single bed. We could explain it away, of course, but it wouldn't be easy.

"Nah," Jack was already saying. "You show up? Ties you to us. Better not. I'll grab it later."

"Thanks for offering, though," I said.

Jack was gracious enough to second that, if only with a grunt. Then he headed out for the journal. Quinn called Evelyn to get her working on the hitman's cell phone records. There was something I could do, too. Something I should do, as much as I'd been avoiding it. I was still thinking of that when Jack slipped back in, journal in hand.

Quinn was on the phone. I was sitting in the corner of the sofa, deep in thought, and barely noticed Jack until he said he'd be reading in the bedroom. I led him to the other end of the room to not interrupt Quinn's call.

"I was thinking that I should really get that case file from Neil. I should read it."

"I can."

Another smile, a little more genuine. "You finish the journal. I'll handle the file. Since Neil said there's nothing on my rape in it, Quinn can read it, too, and help me look at it objectively."

Neil was at work, which proved that on a case I lose all sense of time. I said I'd call back but he was doing paperwork and happy for the interruption.

"I can e-mail it to you," Neil said. "I scanned it all a couple of days ago. And, yes, I expect you to be very proud of me for knowing how to *use* a scanner. I actually have one on my new printer but hadn't gotten around to figuring it out. This gave me the perfect excuse. I've now officially entered the twenty-first century."

"Congratulations. You're a couple of steps ahead of me. I think the lodge printer still uses a ribbon."

He laughed. "Then you'll be even more impressed to hear that I have the file on a thumb drive, so I can e-mail it to you right now." I could hear him pecking on the keyboard. "And there it goes. One case file, sent electronically."

"I owe you."

"You do. And I'll take a weekend at the lodge with the kids this winter. They want to learn cross-country skiing."

"You've got the weekend and private lessons."

"Great. I'll expect a call later, to talk about the file."

Reading Amy's case file was as hard as I thought it would be. Maybe harder. When we first found the journal, I'd expected to read details on Amy's murder that I'd never wash from my mind. Yet I'd been ready to do it. The case file, with its cold, documented facts, should have been easier to digest. It wasn't. Because those facts weren't written by anonymous professionals.

I'd read a summary of the case years ago, but it had been just that—a typed summary. This was very different. I recognized the handwriting of Dr. Foster on the autopsy—the same Dr. Foster who'd been our family physician most of my young life. I read the report and I heard his voice and I imagined him there, working on Amy, his former patient. The notations about the crime-scene photos were all in Neil's writing. I read a badly spelled typewritten report and didn't even need to check the signature to know it was Myron Young, who'd gone on to replace my father as chief. Other reports had curt notes in the margins, the pen pushed so deep I could still feel rage emanating off the page. Uncle Eddie—Amy's father.

My father and uncle hadn't been allowed to work the case—it was bad enough they'd been first on the scene. But while other police had assisted the prosecution in gathering evidence, it was clear Dad and Uncle

Eddie had kept abreast of the investigation, making their own notes and keeping track of the evidence.

There were the pages and pages of meticulous notes written in my father's hand. I read those, and I was back at my kitchen table, sipping hot chocolate, watching him work as my mother and brother slept. Those were some of my most cherished memories and now, seeing his notes here, detailing some of my worst memories . . . It was almost more than I could take.

I think having Quinn there made it harder. I'd rather have read them alone. No, I can be honest now—I'd rather have read them with Jack. Quinn tried to distract me by keeping it professional, hashing it out, trying to help me distance myself from these pages, but I couldn't distance myself. I didn't want to.

That's how it had always been with Quinn. We could talk for hours, and they could be deep conversations and heated debates that got to the core of our beliefs, but . . . Evelyn once said that for Quinn, it was all about the head. Cerebral. She'd been referring to his vigilantism, but the same could be said for the connection I had with him. I told Quinn what I thought, not what I felt.

Jack came to the door a few times, standing in the opening, where Quinn couldn't see from his angle. I'd feel him watching me and look up to see him there.

The file contained both the police work and trial papers. There wasn't much in the police part that I didn't already know, especially the early events my father and uncle had been involved in. I'd heard the story so many times I sometimes felt that I'd been there.

When my father and uncle left the station, they took two cars. There was no need for that, but neither could bear to be the one in the passenger seat, helplessly urging the other to go faster, Jesus Christ, can't you drive *faster*? They even took separate routes, each certain they knew a quicker way. They raced through town and barreled down the rutted back road so fast that my uncle nearly ripped off his muffler. The road didn't go the entire way to the cabin. But my dad continued past the end of it, driving the car in so far it needed a paint job afterward. Only when it would be faster to run did he and my cousin Pete leap out with my uncle and Myron Young right behind them.

As they ran, they saw a figure through the trees, fleeing the cabin. Dad told Myron to stay with Uncle Eddie, while he and Pete went after the fleeing figure. It wasn't much of a chase. Aldrich was already at his truck, parked down a side trail. My father saw it speeding away. That's when, according to the file, he heard Uncle Eddie "call out" from the cabin. He didn't "call out." I remembered overhearing Pete say Uncle Eddie's screaming was the worst thing he'd ever heard.

Dad called the station to get an APB out on Aldrich's truck, then ran to the cabin. He went inside and found his brother with Amy. She was dead. Strangled. Raped and strangled.

Dad wanted to stay, but Uncle Eddie begged him to go after Aldrich. There was nothing more to be done for Amy except get her justice. Dad caught Aldrich packing to flee town. There was a standoff at the house where he'd rented a room. Shots were fired when Aldrich came out with a hunting rifle. Aldrich was hit in the shoulder and taken into custody.

I'd known about Aldrich being shot. I'd known who shot him, too. My father. Now, though, reading the file, I thought instead of Wayne Franco. Of how I'd shot him when he'd reached into his pocket, giving me an excuse. Had the same thing happened here? I'd never know. Did it matter? Maybe not.

We were getting ready to start the trial pages when Jack came out of the bedroom.

"Dee?"

I looked up.

"Need a coffee. Want a stretch?"

"I would love both," I said, getting up. "Thank you."

"I'll join you," Quinn said.

Quinn closed the laptop and was pushing his chair back when his cell phone rang. He answered. It was Evelyn. Jack murmured that we'd bring him something and prodded me to the door. Behind us, I could hear Quinn saying, "Can I get back to you with that? Ten minutes?" Then, "All right. I'm looking it up."

Jack ushered me out.

"Lucky timing," I said as we headed to the elevator.

"Not really luck."

"You asked Evelyn to call him?"

"Sounded like you needed a break. From the file. From Quinn." He paused. "Reading the file *with* Quinn, I mean. He's behaving."

"He is on his *best* behavior."

"And you kinda wish he was being an ass."

"Yes, I kinda do."

There was a coffee shop two doors down. Jack took me the other way instead and we walked until we found one a couple of kilometers away. We discussed the file as we walked and he knew exactly what to ask to make me open up. I told him how I felt about what I had read, the memories it was bringing back, the issues and the conflicts. Jack didn't say much, but he said all the right things, and by the time we returned I was ready to tackle the next part.

CHAPTER 41

On to the trial transcript, annotated in my father's hand. And this was where I began to see the case break down. The job of the police is to accumulate enough evidence to make a case against the accused. It's only when the case goes to trial that the holes begin to show. And here, they were bigger than I'd ever imagined.

According to the version I grew up with, my father and uncle had seen Drew Aldrich fleeing the scene. In truth they had seen the figure only from the back and noted build, clothing, hair color. At trial, three witnesses testified to seeing Aldrich earlier that evening. He'd been wearing a light T-shirt, jeans, and sneakers—as he was when he was arrested. The man running from the scene had been wearing a dark shirt.

"Why was it an issue at all?" I asked Quinn. "Aldrich confessed to killing Amy—he said it was an accident. Why *not* admit he was the one running?"

"The discrepancy bolstered the case against your family's reliability."

The next problem followed immediately after, with the standoff at his apartment. Witnesses said Aldrich did indeed threaten that he had a rifle. He even came to the door holding it . . . but he was holding it out, showing that he was surrendering. That's when my father shot him.

Again, the prosecution could argue that it was night. The door was not well lit. All my father saw was a gun. But it still added to the defense's story. My father over-reacted, which was very uncharacteristic of him and therefore supported the idea that he was responding as a grieving uncle.

I knew from the journal that Amy had prearranged our meeting with Aldrich that night, but I'd never real-ized that had come out in the trial. There was even ev-idence of a phone call from Amy's house to Aldrich's apartment the day before, when apparently she'd given him the train number and arrival time; he'd jotted down the info on a piece of paper that had been found in his wallet. From there, it became much easier to say Amy willingly had sex with Aldrich.

Memory is a strange thing. I guess I should know that better than anyone. But now, reading the trial tran-scripts, I realized just how many holes my mind had filled in. Maybe that makes sense. My brain had inten-tionally *made* those gaps as it ripped apart my recollec-tion of that night. To deal with that, I filled in the blanks and came to believe them as fact.

One of those false memories was right here, in my own statement. I said that I'd caught a glimpse of Al-drich strangling Amy and that's why I ran. Except I hadn't. I knew that now, from the nightmares and the fresh memories. Aldrich had raped me. When he left me, I'd gotten free of my bindings. I'd heard Amy. I'd known she was being hurt. I'd believed she was also being raped. So I'd run for help. But I'd never looked in that room because I knew if I had, Aldrich would real-ize I'd escaped and I'd never be able to get help for Amy.

Yet apparently, I said I'd peeked in. I'd identified Drew Aldrich as the man with his hands around my cousin's throat. Had I believed it at the time? Or had I simply believed I had to say it to put him in jail? I don't know.

Now I had to admit that to Quinn, without letting him know about the rape. Maybe I should have. But I couldn't tell him and just move on. It would slam down a stop sign on the investigation while we dealt with that—he'd want to know how I found out, how was I coping, what he could do to help. For now I could only tell him that I *hadn't* seen Aldrich killing Amy.

"I was tied up in the next room," I said. "I got free, and I could hear her in trouble, so I ran for help. I don't know why I said I looked in."

"Because you wanted him caught and punished."

"I guess so."

"No." He caught my gaze. "I know so, and I'd have done the same. Hell, there have been times I've wanted to lie under oath to put a bastard away. If I don't, it's only because, as you've told me many times, I can't pull off an act." A wry smile. "But that doesn't mean I've never fudged the truth, when I knew I could get away with it. You said what you thought needed to be said. Unfortunately, it didn't work, and I can see why."

I bristled a little at that, and he laughed.

"No," he said. "I'm not insulting your acting ability."

"That's not—"

"Oh, yes, it is." He shot a smile my way. "You might ethically worry about having told the lie, but you'd be insulted if I said you didn't do it well enough. You're a web of contradictions, Nadia, and that's what I—" He stopped and the smile vanished. "Dee, I meant. There was nothing wrong with your statement. It's just that it . . . Well, again, it only added fuel to their theory. The defense painted you as the good girl. The police chief's daughter. A straight arrow. Fiercely loyal. Loves her family and worries about her cousin. Smart and sensible but sheltered, too. The kind of girl people want thirteen-year-olds to be."

"The kind of girl Amy wasn't."

"Exactly. So your much more worldly cousin tricks you and you end up at some cabin with a guy, and there are drugs and booze and you're completely out of your element. Confused and terrified. You don't understand what's going on, because you'd never think of willingly doing drugs or having sex, so you presume your cousin wouldn't, either. You certainly wouldn't understand anything about breath-control play. When you saw him seeming to strangle her during sex, you drew the obvious conclusion and panicked."

"And by saying I saw Aldrich, that gave the defense the excuse to say that *Amy* panicked. That she spotted me and fought, and, in trying to defend himself, Aldrich accidentally killed her."

That's where both theories hit a rough patch, one that only made sense to me now. Aldrich had scratches, which he used as proof that Amy attacked him. Except there was no skin under her nails, so the prosecution claimed he'd been scratched by branches while fleeing the scene. He hadn't. I'd attacked Aldrich during my rape. That's how he got the scratches and I got the knife cut.

But the biggest shock in the file? There was absolutely no forensic evidence that Drew Aldrich raped and killed Amy. No skin under her nails. No fingerprints. No traces of semen. No blood, either, despite proof that Amy had coughed blood at some point. As I read that I began to wonder if there may have been a valid reason

Aldrich left nothing behind at Amy's murder scene: if he wasn't the one who raped and killed her.

When I even thought that, my stomach lurched and my brain threw on the brakes. Of course he'd killed her. I'd been there. No one else was in that cabin. I was sure . . .

Or was I? *How* was I sure if I'd never looked in the other room as Amy was being attacked?

What if Aldrich did have a partner? And that partner killed Amy? It would explain the lack of evidence. It would explain the dark-shirted man seen fleeing the scene. It would explain, too, why there was nothing about her murder in the journal, why Aldrich had seemed to dismiss her and focus on me. And it would explain one last piece of evidence, something both the prosecution and defense had ignored.

A small note on the autopsy report said the pressure of the marks was consistent with a right-handed attacker. Aldrich was left-handed. That was in the file, too. Yet in regards to the strangulation report, neither side made anything of it.

"Because they weren't arguing whether or not Aldrich killed Amy," Quinn said. "Also left-handedness doesn't always mean you do *everything* left-handed. If one side argued, the other would bring in experts, and it just wasn't worth it if Aldrich had confessed to strangling her."

"But it does mean . . ."

"Yeah. Someone else might have killed Amy."

Quinn pushed the laptop away. Then he reached over and tugged my chair to face him. He leaned forward, gaze on mine, his eyes dark with concern and I felt . . . I felt terrible. A spark of grief for what we'd had, and a full-blown flame of guilt over Jack and because I hadn't been what Quinn wanted.

"You okay?" Quinn asked.

I nodded.

"Aldrich was still involved," Quinn said. "He still lured you girls there and he probably did more than that."

Oh, he did. And even if he didn't kill Amy, I don't regret the fact that he's dead. I was ready to kill him, not for what he did to me but for luring her to her death and for all the other girls he raped. Whether he killed Amy doesn't change that.

But it did change everything I thought I knew. Everything I'd been damned sure of, for twenty years, one of the few constants in my life, that kernel of rage blaming Aldrich for killing my cousin. And maybe more important that confusion and internal struggle over him being set free, not wanting to blame my family but, in a little way, doing exactly that.

Now that I saw the file, I knew Neil and Koss were both right. It was a fair trial. Even if Aldrich did do it, it was hard to convict him of murder based on this. Statutory rape? Definitely. Manslaughter? Probably. If they'd bargained down, he'd have gone to jail. But the prosecution must have thought their murder case was sound and Aldrich hadn't tried to bargain. If he didn't do it, that gave him all the more reason to be sure he'd be acquitted. So why say he'd accidentally killed her? That I didn't know.

At a noise beside me, I turned to see Jack.

"You got something?" he asked.

"We do," I said. "And you?"

"Yeah."

"Tell me."

CHAPTER 42

Jack had found a reference in one of the more recent entries in which Aldrich wrote that he had "shared" a fifteen-year-old conquest with another man. The details of how that came about weren't in the journal, just an allusion to the fact that alcohol and drugs had been involved. Aldrich was always careful to avoid details. I suppose he figured if the journal was found, he could claim it was just fantasies. Without details, investigators might be unable to find his victims and prove otherwise. So there was nothing there except a description of the encounter itself. We skimmed that. Like everything else in the journal, this was where Aldrich put his detail in, and no one needed to read that.

Here, he'd written that he'd forgotten how good it could be to "share," and that he'd missed it, not just the sex but having someone to share the entire experience with, someone who can open you up to things you'd never dare try on your own. "This wasn't the same," he wrote. "There was none of that this time. It was just sex. But it made me long for the old days. I got scared off back then. We both did. I know more now, though, and sometimes I wonder if it's not too late to go back."

"Damn," Quinn said as we finished reading. "It really sounds like he's referring to Amy. Being tried for murder would definitely scare anyone off, even if he was acquitted."

"What'd you find?" Jack asked.

I told him, and when I finished, we agreed that while it still wasn't solid proof that Aldrich had a partner it was enough to proceed in that direction. But how the hell would we find his partner? There sure weren't any clues in the journal. I'd gotten all I could from Shannon Broadhurst, and there was no way of knowing this partner was even the "old friend" he'd mentioned to her. We could start interviewing his other known victims, see if he'd said more, but that was time consuming, risky, and a long shot.

Quinn was quiet for a minute. Then he leaned forward, elbows on his knees, looking over at me. "We know Aldrich was being investigated under other names. Jack has all that. I'm going to suggest that I start looking into it officially. Obviously, it's not my area, so I'm not *investigating* officially. But I'd be looking as myself. As a marshal. That will make it a lot easier."

I straightened. "I don't want you taking any risks—"

"I'm not, and here's the part you might not like. You know I didn't keep our relationship a secret. I couldn't. Friends, family, they knew I was seeing someone. A few even got a name. You and I agreed that was okay. While I wouldn't announce that I'm looking into Aldrich or why, if it came up, I have an excuse. You had questions after his death. I agreed to dig."

"Yeah," Jack said. "Do that."

"I was asking Dee."

"Who is gonna ask me if it's safe. I say it is. You're okay with it? Go ahead."

I kept my mouth shut. Jack was answering because

I could not in good conscience tell Quinn to do anything that would even slightly risk damaging his professional reputation.

"Good," Quinn said. "I'll get on that. Jack, if there's anything—anything at all—you can give me from the journal that will help me . . ."

"Few things. Other attacks. Got a list."

"Thanks." Quinn looked at me. "This is going to be the proverbial needle-in-a-haystack search, but I think it's the best we can do for now."

"I have some feelers out, too," Jack said. "Got our pro's fake ID. Got his burner phone. Seeing if that leads anywhere."

"Great," Quinn said. "Every potential lead is going to count here."

Jack nodded, but I could tell I wasn't the only one who kind of wished Quinn was being his testy, confrontational self instead.

Night comes fast when your day starts past noon, and it was almost nine when we ordered pizza and eleven by the time we finished. Jack called it a day then, though I suspect he was just hinting for Quinn to go to his room.

Except Quinn didn't have a room yet, and when he went to the desk, they were fully booked for a convention. So he had to crash on our sofa bed, which added a whole new level of awkward.

"I'll take the sofa," I said quickly. "You have one of the beds."

"Nah," Jack said. "I'll sleep on the—"

He stopped before offering, as if realizing that meant Quinn and I would share a bedroom. Yep, more awkward.

Quinn insisted on the sofa, being gallant. We agreed

and I scampered off to our room at the earliest possible opportunity.

Jack went out after that. I heard the door close, and for a moment I thought maybe Quinn had left for a walk, but I knew by the soft click that it was Jack. A few seconds later, my phone buzzed with a text. *Stepped out. Making some calls. Be in soon.* Then, before I could finish reading it, a second one. *Sleep tight.*

I smiled and put the phone aside. I was halfway between waking and sleep when he came in later. I could still hear Quinn moving around in the other room, so I kept my eyes closed. Resist temptation.

Jack left the light off. His footsteps crossed to the top of my bed, and I felt him pausing there. He bent, his lips brushing my forehead, and then he climbed into the other bed.

I hadn't had a nightmare since I found Drew Aldrich dead. Even discovering that he'd raped me hadn't brought on the midnight screaming fits. It was as if when he left this world he took that baggage with him. Or enough that I was able to cope with the rest. Except now I had to face the real possibility that Amy hadn't been avenged by Aldrich's death.

After reading the file, I finally realized that testifying wouldn't have helped. Admitting I'd been raped wouldn't have been enough. Even if he'd been convicted of that, he'd have been out after five years, and from his journal, that's about as long as he'd been "scared straight" anyway. He'd have left Ontario, changed his name, and gone right back to victimizing young girls. I wouldn't have saved them.

But I still might have saved Amy if I'd stayed instead of running. I can argue against that during the daytime.

At night, though, I was certain if only I'd stayed, she'd be alive. At least if I'd peeked into that room, I'd be sure of who really killed her. But I'd run.

That night the nightmare returned from a fresh angle. Aldrich was walking away, and I was lying on the floor, hurting so bad, hurting everywhere, from the rape and from the knife wound on my neck. I didn't really know what happened. I did and yet I didn't. He'd told me to lie still, and I'd thought I could do that, but when he'd pulled my legs apart, I just . . . I just couldn't. I'd gone crazy with fear and panic and rage and there was no way I was letting him do *that*—I just wasn't.

I'd fought, and he'd held me down, and I'd kept fighting, and the rest was a blur of pain and terror, and when it finished, I wasn't sure if he'd done it or he'd only tried to do it or what exactly happened, only that I hurt inside and I was bleeding and I thought maybe that meant that he hadn't done "it," because Amy said "it" wasn't supposed to hurt and maybe the pain meant he'd only injured me trying.

I was lying there, confused and numb and aching and trying very, very hard not to cry. I had to stay quiet and get away. I managed to get up and find my underwear, and it seemed to take forever to figure out how to get them on, and even then there was a part of my brain screaming that it didn't matter, forget my underwear, but I couldn't.

I was struggling to get my jeans on when I heard a voice. A man's voice. Not *his* voice. I stopped. The voice did, too. Then I heard Amy, saying she'd do what he wanted, whatever he wanted, just don't hurt her and don't hurt me. A voice answered and this time it was *him*. Aldrich. I strained to listen, but part of my brain was shouting, louder now, telling me to go, just go. Amy was smart. She wouldn't fight and get hurt like I had. She'd stall. She was good at that with boys. She'd stall and I'd get help and she'd be okay. I could still hear them talking, and it was only Aldrich and Amy. No one else. It must have been Aldrich the first time. It must have, because we were the only ones here.

In real life, I'd run then. In the dream, I kept trying to hear that other voice. It was important. I had to hear it. Better yet, I had to see. Look around the corner and see who it is. I slipped to the doorway, took a deep breath, peeked and—

And I saw Amy, on the floor, being held down by Aldrich as another man climbed on top of her. The other man turned, but his face was blank, no eyes, no mouth, just a horrible, blank face and—

Hands caught my arms. I tried to wrench away, my heart pounding in panic, but the hands held me fast. I heard a voice—one that scattered the nightmare.

"Shhh, shhh. It's okay, Nadia. Wake up. It's okay."

My eyelids fluttered, and I saw Jack's face bent over mine. I felt the bed under me, the sheets wound around me.

He gingerly laid a hand on my arm. "Okay?"

I nodded, and I could feel my cheeks now, hot and wet with tears. I swiped at them. "Sorry, I—"

"Shhh."

He squeezed my arm and then disentangled the sheets and crawled in. I was moving back to give him room when I remembered Quinn and glanced at the door.

"Locked," he whispered.

I still pushed up. "Did he hear . . . ?"

"Nothing to hear."

Jack stretched out beside me and put his arms around me, and I curled up to him, head on his chest, his arms tight around me, and it felt so good, so damned good, the warmth of him, the reassuring beat of his heart. He smelled faintly of sweat, more strongly of soap, comforting smells that chased away the last bits of the dream. He rubbed my back and whispered, nothing that needed a response, just words, quieting the ones in my head until, finally, I drifted back to sleep.

I woke up a few more times. No nightmares. Just waking, perhaps roused by the unfamiliar feeling of someone in my bed. Jack woke, too, enough to tighten his arms around me or whisper something I couldn't quite catch. I thought of saying I was all right and he could go back to the other bed, but I didn't want to disturb him. No, I didn't want him to leave. So I relaxed against him and slept.

Quinn was pounding on the door. Okay, in retrospect, it was just a rap, but it seemed like pounding, Jack and I both jumping up so fast—and looking so guilty—that you'd think Quinn had walked in on us having sex. Jack motioned for me to be still and mouthed a reminder that the door was locked.

Quinn rapped again as Jack slid from the bed. Then he whispered, "Dee?"

Jack gestured for me to hold off answering. He crept to the door. Then he nodded and I said, "Yes?" loudly, in hopes of covering the click as Jack unlocked the door.

"Did I wake you?" Quinn's muffled voice asked as Jack crawled into his bed. "I didn't mean—"

"Open the damned door," Jack said. "Don't talk through it. Seven in the fucking morning."

Quinn opened the door. Jack was braced on one arm. I was sitting, rubbing my face.

"Sorry," Quinn said. "I was just trying to see if Dee was up yet and if she wanted to go for a run. If you're still sleeping . . ."

"Up now," Jack grunted. He looked at me. "You want a run? Gonna drive you. Keep an eye on you."

He made it sound like a warning, but I knew it was a reassurance, telling me I could have my morning run without being alone with Quinn.

"I don't think I have anything to wear . . ." I began.

My gaze snagged on my bag, across the room on a chair.

"Grabbed it last night," Jack said.

"You should have taken someone with you," I said.

He shrugged. I gave him a look. He nodded, acknowledging the point. While I'm sure he could take care of himself, he *had* been shot at and I didn't want him walking around without backup, either—especially not going to a place we'd been spotted.

"Was everything okay?" I asked.

"Yeah. No sign of anyone in our room. Watched my back leaving. Wasn't followed."

"So are we going?" Quinn said.

I nodded and he backed out of the room to let us get ready.

CHAPTER 43

W e ran. We ate. In between the two, Jack got a call that confirmed the identity of our dead hitman and his regular middleman. Jack knew the guy—the middleman, not the pro. He was convinced our guy hadn't bypassed his middleman for this job. It was a big name, not a rookie who'd forgive his pro for stepping out.

We discussed it over breakfast. The diner was busy and noisy, both of which meant that no one was going to overhear our conversation and call the cops.

"So you know this guy, Duncan," Quinn said after we placed our order.

"Yeah. Been around a long time. Knows Evelyn." He paused. "Knows Evelyn well."

"Doesn't everyone?" I said. "I swear every pro and middleman over a certain age 'knows Evelyn well,' or did at some point, at least for a night."

Quinn chuckled and Jack gave a short laugh.

"Yeah," Jack said. "Pretty much. She blames it on the times. Sixties. Seventies. I think it's just her."

"Oh, I don't doubt it. So is this one of those guys that looks back fondly on the affair? Or one of the others? Because they seem about evenly split."

"This was a serial thing. They were tight." He

paused, looking thoughtful. "Don't even think she ever double-crossed him."

"Sounds like love," I said. "Or at least a strong case of like."

"Yeah. All good last I heard. Did some work for him years back. Went fine. Haven't seen him in . . ." Another pause. "Five years? Six? Point is, I can talk to him. Friendly chat. Maybe meet him at a bar. Have a drink."

Quinn laughed. Then he realized Jack wasn't kidding.

"Um, I get that this guy is a colleague," Quinn said, "but Dee's in serious trouble here. It's no time for silk gloves."

"Not just a colleague. *Respected* colleague. Important friend of Evelyn's."

"Okay," Quinn said. "I see the problem. So I'll handle this. Yes, I know it's not my thing, but I can manage it. The guy's got to be at least, what, sixty? It won't require working him over. Just a little intimidation."

Jack shook his head. "No intimidation. Straight-up talk."

"Not good enough," Quinn said. "We have to—"

"Damn," I said. "I need more coffee. I must be drifting off, because I could swear Quinn's arguing to interrogate a guy, while Jack wants to just talk to him. Did I miss the Freaky Friday switch? Oh, no, wait. Jack's sentences aren't getting any longer."

He gave me a look. I made a face in return.

"I'm going with Jack on this," I said. "I have no problem with stronger persuasion, but I'm not feeling threatened enough right now to beat answers out of an old man who might be perfectly willing to part with them. If it fails . . ."

"I'll go harder," Jack said. "No question." He looked at Quinn. "I want answers as much as you do."

Quinn's gaze dipped. "I know."

"I'll do what it takes to get them. But Duncan? He's reasonable. He finds out I'm friends with his mark? Evelyn is, too? And we're both pissed? He'll turn on his client in a heartbeat. We're more valuable."

"All right then," I said. "Let's set this up."

Getting in touch with Duncan proved even more complicated than deciding how to handle him. Jack had Evelyn call first. She couldn't get an answer at Duncan's and was heading off to breakfast with someone from Contrapasso. So Jack tried and had no better luck. Neither was worried. Apparently, Duncan didn't have a cell phone or an e-mail address. He didn't even have an answering machine. Jack and Evelyn had his home number. Clients had to use an answering service. Jack and Evelyn had tried both and left a message with the service, which only promised he'd respond in the next forty-eight hours.

Jack decided a personal visit was in order. While I wasn't going to meet Duncan face-to-face—too risky—I didn't want Jack going alone. We decided I'd accompany him while staying in the background, as Quinn returned to the hotel to work.

Jack may roll his eyes over Felix's tech toys, but that didn't mean there weren't any in his kit. I think he sees them the same way I see all the gadgets and gizmos to aid distance shooters—as a crutch. Skill is a lot more reliable. But some things you can't manage with skill alone. Like letting your partner listen in on a conversation you're having on the other side of several walls. Jack wore a miked earpiece, though I think he was more interested in the connected piece I was wearing, which would let him hear if *I* was in any trouble.

All that hassle was for nothing. We got the pieces on and tested them out and found me a safe place to hole up in Duncan's condo building . . . only to discover that the guy wasn't home.

"He's away," Jack said.

"You broke in?" I asked as we left the building.

"Nah. Saw a neighbor taking his mail. Got a good idea where he is, though. Duncan isn't a traveler. He's not home? He's at his cabin. Over in Wisconsin."

"Wisconsin?" I swore. "How far is that?"

"Little over an hour. Easy drive."

"Ah. I need to brush up on my American geography, don't I?"

"Never hurts."

I laughed, and we headed out.

Duncan's cabin was near Lake Geneva, which was, as Jack said, just over an hour from his condo in north Chicago. We arrived at a nice piece of forested property that reminded me of the lodge.

"He's here," Jack said.

Before I asked how he could tell, I squinted down the long drive. Through the trees, I could just barely make out a car a hundred meters away.

"I'll jump out here," I said.

"Thought you could stay in the car. Safer."

I waved behind us. "We've just driven two miles down a dirt road. There was no one behind us the whole way. If I stay in the car and he looks out, he's going to at least be able to tell I'm female and not Evelyn. And if you're here to talk about a hit on a woman . . ."

"Yeah. You're right. Hop out. Stay close."

Jack waited until I'd ducked into the forest before he drove up the lane. I watched as he parked, got out, double-checked the other car, and murmured, "Yeah. His." Then he went to the front door.

I circled through the forest to get to a better spot. I heard Jack knock. Then he knocked again. A grunt.

"Hold position," he said. "Might be outside."

I waited as Jack circled the cabin. It was a nice place. Not large but clearly the property of a man with money and good taste. I could see the edge of a huge back deck, and I listened as Jack's footsteps tapped across the wood. They paused. A rap on glass, presumably at a patio door.

"Fuck."

"What's wrong?"

"Nothing. Just not answering."

"Ah, so that was the exasperated 'fuck,' not the dismayed 'fuck' or the concerned 'fuck' or even the annoyed 'fuck.' Normally, I can tell the difference, but the mike isn't good for conveying tone."

A short laugh. "Yeah." He rapped again. A moment. He sighed. "Ah, fuck."

"Now that one I know. That one says, 'Damn it, he's not answering' and now I'm going to need to break in to see if he's there, which is not just risky, but if he's on the toilet it's really not going to get this meeting off to a good start.'"

"See? Two words. Didn't need all the rest."

I laughed.

Another sigh rustled over the mike. "Gonna try the front again. Peek in some windows. Probably in there. Don't want to piss him off."

"Can I take a look around out here if I'm careful?" I asked. "I'll stay in the woods and just see if he's out for a walk or something."

"Doubt it. But yeah. Stick close, though. He won't go far. Bad knees."

The forest around Duncan's cabin looked so much like the landscape at home that I half expected Scout to race through the trees to greet me. I could even smell water. The place wasn't on Lake Geneva itself, but was a short walk from a smaller lake, similar to mine at the lodge. Being off-season, the woods were empty. I could see a cabin on the neighboring lot, the windows dark, no sign of life. The only signs I did see were animals—a scampering mouse, a darting rabbit, a grouse making a last-second escape from a clump of ferns, startling me as it took to the air.

When I heard rustling in the undergrowth a minute later, I thought it was another bird or small animal and continued on. Then I heard the growl. I stopped. I peered toward the sound and made out a light brown flank. Then the sound of nails scrabbling in dirt as it decided I'd been sufficiently warned off.

I could have just moved on. But, well, maybe human predators aren't that far removed from the animal variety. I knew better than to turn my back on a potential threat.

I took out my gun. Then I carefully bent and picked up a rock. I pitched it into the thicket where I could see the flank. I wasn't trying to hit the beast, just get its attention. The rock cracked against a tree and a blur of brown fur leaped from the bushes. Seeing me, it planted its forepaws and growled. It was a canine, maybe two feet at the shoulder. A coyote—or a coydog—it gets harder to tell the full-bloods from the hybrids as the populations intermingle.

Coyotes are pack animals like dogs and wolves, but they're more likely to be found alone, and this guy was.

I took out my earpiece and covered it so Jack wouldn't come running. Then I said, "Go on. Get out of here."

The coyote growled, a little less certain now. Ears flattened at the side of its head, tail stiff and horizontal. I took a deliberate step forward. Then another, my gaze locked with its.

"Go," I said, injecting a little growl in my voice as I waved my gun. Then, louder, "Go! Scram!"

I lunged. The coyote took off. They usually will. I have to deal with them and stray dogs at the lodge, and while I wouldn't suggest confronting one for fun, I can read the dominance and submission signals well enough. This guy had been uncertain, and belligerence from a larger predator was all it took to help it decide.

I pushed aside long grass to get into the thicket. It was bigger than it had seemed. Bigger than it should be, really, in the natural landscape of the forest. A large empty space blanketed by dead leaves . . . when most of the overhanging trees were evergreens.

"Jack?" I said.

There was silence at first, and my heart started to pound. I said it louder and he came on, his voice tinny and distant, as if we'd neared the end of our range.

"I'm in," he said. "No sign of him."

"I . . . think you need to come out here."

CHAPTER 44

By the time Jack arrived, I'd pushed aside the leaves where the coyote had been digging. I could see its nail marks in the dirt. Dark dirt. Overturned—and not just where it'd been digging.

I heard Jack and twisted, still crouching, careful to keep my shoes on the leaf carpet so I couldn't leave prints. Jack stared down at the clearing floor.

"Fuck."

I nodded.

"You okay?" he said.

"Me? Sure. I startled a coyote in here, which is how I found it, but the coyote took right off."

"Don't mean that. This . . ."

He waved at the clearing and he didn't say "looks like where we found Sammi." He wouldn't, just in case I wasn't thinking that. I was. I wouldn't have mentioned it because this wasn't about me or my murdered teen employee.

"Yes, it looks like where we found her," I said. "But I'm okay." I glanced around the clearing. "You'll want to be sure, I suppose."

"Yeah. You can stand guard. I'll—"

"No, I'll help."

We didn't discuss what we thought we'd stumbled

on, because we didn't need to. We'd seen enough shallow graves to recognize one. A hidden spot. The undergrowth cleared. The body buried. Leaves dumped on to cover the site. The coyote smelling spilled blood and digging in hopes of scavenging a meal.

The coyote would have had to work for that meal, but it could have gotten to it. Duncan was buried under only a foot of soil. We uncovered enough for Jack to identify him and see the cause of death. Duncan's throat had been slit. There was also blood on the back of his head, from a gash and a huge bump.

"Hit him from behind," Jack said. "Dazed him. Led him out here. Slit his throat. Blood on the dirt. Brought the coyote." His voice hardened. "Guy was eighty. Still need to bash him from behind? Fucking coward." He paused. "No, not a coward. Sadist. Bring Duncan here? Sees this place? He knows what's coming. Can't shoot him? Show some mercy? Slit an old man's throat. Watch him bleed out." He shook his head. "Fucking sadist."

"I'm sorry," I said.

I moved closer and leaned against Jack. He put his arm around my waist and squeezed.

"Thanks. He wasn't a nice guy. Wasn't a good guy. Still didn't deserve this."

"I know, and we'll find who did it."

A moment's pause. Then he patted my back and said, "Should go. Cover him up. Check the house."

I nodded and we set to work.

Duncan didn't have a phone in the cabin, so we couldn't see if his killer had contacted him. We'd check his regular line, but that wouldn't likely help, as the killer probably only had his messaging service. It was starting to feel like, without telephones and phone records, we didn't have an investigation at all, which was hellishly frustrating. It was as if our case existed in some invisible cyber-realm, and Jack and I were stuck here on earth, spinning our wheels, waiting for the miracle of technology to present us with an actual suspect.

Who killed Duncan? Presumably whomever we were chasing. Whoever had put a mark on my head. When two hits fail and the first middleman dies, our suspect starts severing all connections between himself and his hired killers. Why kill Duncan and not Roland? We had vague theories—Duncan knew something or our suspect knew we were closing in—but no actual good ideas. Spinning our wheels. It was better than standing still, though. Just keep spinning, and eventually we had to gain traction.

Jack was grieving. Even if he was quick to point out that he hadn't known Duncan well, he had been a well-liked colleague, which was pretty much as close to a friend as Jack got. So he grieved.

The call to Evelyn hadn't been easy. I'd tried to step away to give him privacy, but he'd kept me there, and I'd heard her, on the other end, raging and spitting fury. That, for Evelyn, was grief, and I knew that was hard on Jack, too.

I would have liked to offer more comfort. Find a place where we could be alone. Even going for a drink would have been something. But Quinn was waiting and the case was waiting and when I suggested we call and tell Quinn we'd be a while, I could see Jack considering it. I could see him wanting it. But he said, "Nah. Gotta get back," and he meant it.

I'd left Quinn my key card, so at our door I waited while Jack got his out.

"I'll tell him," I said. "You can just go work in the bedroom or whatever."

"I'm good."

I touched his wrist before he could put the card in. "You don't have to be."

He looked over. "Yeah. I know. But it's okay. Just keep moving. Feel bad. Mostly for Evelyn. And like I said, he didn't deserve that. Also . . . ?" He rolled his shoulders. "Frustrated. Feel like I'm slipping. Target's there. Right there. Can't hit it. Can't fucking see it."

"I know how you feel," I said. I lifted up to kiss him and then stopped myself. A wry smile. "And the current situation doesn't help. Frustration all around."

"Fuck, yeah."

He opened the door and held it for me. I walked in. Quinn was sitting in the armchair, with his back to us, and even when we walked in, me saying, "Hey," he didn't move and for one second, my heart rammed into my throat, thinking of Duncan's lifeless eyes . . .

Quinn rose. He moved stiffly, not turning.

"Hey," I said again as I walked around to the sitting area. "Everything okay?"

He turned and the look on his face . . . My heart jammed up again, certain he'd heard us at the door, brain whirring to remember what we'd said, what he could have heard, but there was nothing. Still that look . . .

"Cracked the password," he said.

"Hmmm?"

He lifted a cell phone and it took a moment to recognize it as the one we'd taken from the hitman.

"Broke the code," he said. "I was sitting around, waiting for some calls, and I decided to take a shot at it. I got it."

"Oh? That's good. Did you find anything?"

He met my eyes. He had blue contacts in, from earlier, and his gaze was ice cold. I opened my mouth to say something—I don't know what—but he stepped forward, phone out. I could see the tiny screen. There was a photo on it. At first, all I saw were trees, but that was enough. I knew what else was in that picture. Then I saw it. Jack and me, in the park, my arms around his neck as I kissed him.

"You like that one?" Quinn said. "How about this one?"

He flicked to a second picture. I didn't see it as Jack stepped between us.

"Okay," Jack said. "That's—"

"Enough? No, I don't think it's enough at all. We haven't even gotten to my personal favorite."

He sidestepped Jack and shoved the phone in my face before Jack could stop him. On the screen was a shot of me, with my back against the tree, legs wrapped around Jack, his hands on my ass, skirt pushed up. Jack grabbed the phone.

"You like that one, Jack? I bet you do. I bet—"

"Was a mistake," Jack said. "My fault. Went out for dinner. Nadia was upset. About Koss. Seeing him. Remembering the trial. We drank too much. I took advantage."

I tried to cut in, but Jack slid in front of me, his heel stepping on my toes, warning me to keep quiet.

"You took advantage?" Quinn said. "Huh. I don't see *any* resistance here."

"Because she was drunk. Drunk and hurting. Then the shooting started. After that? Apologized. We worked it out. Nothing else happened."

"And that was that. You guys worked it out, and nothing else happened."

"Right."

They locked gazes. My gut was roiling so hard I thought I was going to be sick. I don't know what was worse—letting Jack take the blame or pretending nothing happened. Both crossed an ethical boundary that wasn't fair to either of them.

"I—" I began.

"Nothing happened," Jack said. "It was all a mistake."

"Is that right, Nadia? You got drunk, Jack took advantage, and nothing else happened?"

"Isn't that what I said?" Jack cut in before I could answer.

"I'm not asking you. And you know what? I don't even need to ask her. All I need to do is look at those photos, Jack. There are a few before it, too. Of you two, going out for dinner. A nice, thoughtful dinner, to make poor Nadia feel better. Dressed to the nines, driving a fancy car, walking into an expensive restaurant . . . Yes, that's *exactly* how I treat my friends when they need a pick-me-up."

"We were taking a break," Jack said. "Having a nice meal. Getting dressed up."

"Right, and let's talk about that. Dressing up. It was a nice suit, Jack, but that dress, Nadia? Hell, that was a dress. Didn't leave much to the imagination."

"Stop," Jack said.

"That's the kind of dress you normally wear for dinner with your mentor, isn't it, Nadia? It must be, because you sure as hell never wore one for me. Tight little black dress barely long enough to cover your—"

"Stop."

"No, Jack, I won't stop. But you can. In fact, you can get the hell right out of this conversation because it doesn't concern you. This is exactly what I expected from you. So we don't have anything to discuss. But Nadia? I expected a little more from her. A little more—"

"Stop right there." Jack moved forward, his voice lowering, gaze fixed on Quinn.

"Why? Because I'm overreacting? Hell, it's not a big deal. I just found out my girlfriend is screwing—"

"She is not your girlfriend," Jack enunciated carefully. "She has not been your girlfriend for a month. She has told you that it's over. Told you again and again. You won't accept it. So she's supposed to wait until you do?"

"No, she's supposed to wait a goddamned decent amount of time before she jumps the first lowlife in sight, like a bitch in heat—"

Jack hit him. I didn't see it coming. I was frozen there, unable to believe what Quinn was saying, when I heard the thwack of Jack's fist hitting his jaw and saw Quinn stagger back. Quinn started to take a swing, but Jack hit him again, hard enough to send him to the floor. Then he grabbed Quinn by the shirtfront and hauled him up.

"Leave now," he said.

"You don't like that, Jack? You don't like being called a—"

"Don't give a fuck what you call me. But you don't call her that. Ever."

"I'll call her whatever—"

"No, you won't. You'll leave. If I thought you meant it? You wouldn't be walking out. But you don't. You blow up. Say things you don't mean. Regret it later. Doesn't make it right. Just too fucking immature—"

"Immature? Oh, that's it. Obviously. I'm immature to be pissed that my girlfriend—"

"*She is not your girlfriend,* you thickheaded ass.

You fucked up and yet somehow, that's her fault, and you're gonna make her suffer because she didn't want to stay in whatever fucking little box you wanted to stuff her in. You lost her, and now you're pissed because you're willing to *let* her come back, and she doesn't want to. She's moved on—"

Quinn took a swing. Jack managed to duck fast enough to avoid more than a glancing blow, and he tried to back off, but Quinn kept coming at him. Two more dodged blows, and then Jack stopped trying to back him off. He hit Quinn, and the fight began in earnest. And me? I walked away.

They weren't fighting about me. Too much had built up over the past year for it to be just that. And even if it was partly about me, I sure as hell wasn't going to watch them fight, like a princess at a joust. I wasn't going to stop them, either. They were big boys—they'd work it out. So I walked into the bedroom and closed the door.

The fight didn't last long. I heard a few blows. I heard a few words, mostly from Quinn. Jack was right. Quinn didn't mean what he was saying now. He was hurt, and he had a right to be. But that didn't make it okay.

The hotel door slammed. The bedroom door clicked open.

"I'm so sorry."

I glanced over to see Jack. His lip was bleeding. There was more blood spattered on his shirt. He stood there, one hand on the doorframe.

"It's okay," I said.

"No. No, it's not." He dropped his gaze and let out a shuddering sigh. "Fuck."

I got to my feet. He took a step but didn't release the doorframe, arm tightening as he stopped himself there.

His gaze lifted. "Shouldn't have happened. Any of it."

"If you're saying what happened between us was a mistake—"

"No. Fuck, no." A growl in his throat. "Didn't mean that. Just . . ."

He started forward again and stopped again, and I realized he was holding himself there, in the doorway, as if he didn't dare come past, as if I'd retreated to my own space and he'd lost the right to enter it.

"Meant the rest," he said. "Making you keep it a secret. Lying to him. You're pissed. Got a right to be."

"I'm not *pissed*, Jack." I walked over. "If I'm upset, it's not with anything you did. I'm upset because Quinn had to find out that way, and I wish I'd handled it better, so you didn't have to."

"You shouldn't have had to handle it. He was so far out of line—" Jack bit off the sentence with an angry shake of his head. "I shouldn't have hit him."

"Mmm, not going to blame you for that. If I'd been less shocked, I think I'd have done it myself. He deserved hitting, and not just for what he called *me*."

Jack shrugged. "Under the circumstances? Don't expect him to call me anything nice."

"I guess not." I stopped in front of him. "Are you okay?"

"Hell, yeah. Just a fight." He glanced down. "Might need a new shirt."

"I think so. But otherwise you're okay?"

"I am."

I moved until we were almost touching. "That lip looks sore."

"It's not."

"Are you sure? Because it seems to be split and if it is, this is going to hurt."

He leaned forward, closing the gap between us. "Don't care."

"And the door . . . ?"

"Locked and bolted."

I put my arms around his neck and kissed him.

CHAPTER 45

Yesterday afternoon I'd been lying on the sofa, staring blissfully out the window, waiting for Jack to run an errand. Now, just a day later, I was back there again. Under the circumstances, it wasn't quite the same level of blissful oblivion. But it was still sweet enough.

I was feeling reflective, thinking of what had happened, wishing Quinn hadn't found out that way, but the guilt and recriminations had passed. For now. I enjoyed the mental peace and quiet. Then my cell phone rang.

For a second, I froze, thinking it was Quinn calling to tell me what he thought of me in greater detail. Then I recognized the number.

"Jack stepped out," I said in greeting.

"Yes, I know," Evelyn said. "He just called me. So we've lost Quinn."

I exhaled. "Yes."

"Well, I suppose that's to be expected," she said. "Eventually he was going to find out about you two, and when he did, he wasn't sticking around. It's just inconvenient timing."

I hesitated.

"Did I say I just spoke to Jack, Dee? He told me everything."

"Right. Sorry. Yes, we should have seen it coming, but we were careful."

"I'm sure you were."

She didn't say anything else, but there was a note in her voice that started me cursing.

"Jack didn't tell you about us, did he?" I said.

"He said only that you and Quinn had a falling out. Not the actual cause."

I cursed some more.

"Oh, stop, Dee. If you two were really trying to keep things a secret, you were doing a damn poor job of it. I could tell the minute I walked in on you two giggling on the sofa."

"We hadn't actually—"

"But you were heading there. At warp speed. Until I brought Quinn along. Which I will admit was a mistake. I was trying to goose Jack into making a move by applying a little competitive pressure, only to discover he was already on that path and instead had to throw on the brakes. Which, as I've told him, I will not apologize for. You two have been circling each other so long I was getting dizzy watching."

"Uh-huh."

"But that's not what I called about. Quinn's gone, and he's not coming back."

"I think so."

"That's a statement, not a question. He's gone until this investigation is over. That's how he'll punish you." She paused. "And I sincerely hope you don't think you deserve that punishment."

"No. I feel bad, but it was over. I'd made that clear."

"I'm sure you did. I've never slept with a man and didn't make it damned clear he was renting, and there could be other tenants. He'd say he was fine with that. Then he'd find out someone else was sharing my bed, and you'd think I'd screwed around on our honeymoon. When I said we weren't exclusive, what he heard was me giving *him* permission to sleep with others. God forbid I should. I suppose not all men are like that, but the ones we hang around with, Dee? Alpha dogs who won't stand for trespass—real or imagined. Quinn's not coming back until you don't need his help anymore. Which means we have a problem."

"I know."

"I may be able to circumvent it, but I need your permission."

I sat up. "My permission?"

"We have little hope of finding Aldrich's partner without Quinn, and I'm not sure we would have found him anyway. The other route is through Contrapasso. I've been laying the groundwork to the point where I can ask about Aldrich. That's too slow now. I need to talk straight with them. Ask about Cleveland and Drew Aldrich and Sebastian Koss."

When I didn't reply, she said, "Dee?"

"I'm here."

"And being quiet because you know what that means, don't you?"

"I do."

"I will do everything in my power to avoid linking you to me. And by 'you,' I mean *you*, not Dee."

That was the problem. It was fine for Evelyn to go to the Contrapasso Fellowship and ask blunt questions to protect a student. Except the person with a price on her head wasn't Dee. It was Nadia Stafford.

She continued, "There is a chance that to get the answers we need and get this mark off your head, I might have to reveal who you are." Tell them that Dee was me. That their mark was a hitman. That Nadia Stafford was a hitman. "And if I do that . . ."

"I can't be me. Not anymore."

"I wouldn't go that far. This isn't an incompetent gang of thugs who would blackmail you for pocket change. However, if they did know, you would no longer be as secure in your normal life. You would need to be on alert and ready to leave at the first sign of trouble."

"Leave my home, you mean. Leave my life. Which, I know, you don't really understand the appeal of anyway . . ."

"I don't. You could make a very handsome living off your second career, and I completely fail to see the point of struggling at something else instead. But you want it. And, God help me, Jack wants it. He wants it for you, and he wants to share it with you."

I thought I heard a faint intake of breath, as if she'd spoken too quickly, too bluntly, which was never usually a problem for Evelyn.

After a moment, she said, "You understand that, don't you? What Jack wants?"

No, not really. It wasn't anything we'd discussed, but if he wanted what she said he did, I'd give it to him. Happily. So I said, "Yes, I understand."

A soft exhale, as if in relief. "Good. So you have your outside life, and I know you want to keep it, and if Jack knew I was even considering doing anything to ruin that, he'd kill me . . . possibly literally."

"Which is why we're having this conversation without him."

"Yes. You're probably wondering why he isn't back from changing the key card. I managed to persuade him that given the hour and the fact you two skipped lunch, you must be hungry. Normally, he'd see right through that, but he's a little distracted right now."

"Is he *too* distracted?" I said. "I mean, we both are, a little, but . . ."

"Jack's fine. Distracted is the wrong word. He doesn't lose his focus. But, even before this, the mere suggestion that you might need something would be enough to send him scrambling to get it for you. It's nauseating, actually. You may want to work on that."

I managed a faint smile. Then I sobered. "But you mean he left the building? I didn't want him going out, not when he's already been shot at—"

"He's been shot at many, many times, Dee, and there is no one more capable of looking after himself. Your concern is very sweet, though, also in a nauseating way. At least you two are equally infatuated, which I suppose helps, if you like that sort of thing."

"But Jack won't be out long, which means we need to settle this. You're asking permission to blow my cover, if necessary."

"Yes. It's not Jack's decision to make, and he shouldn't have to make it."

"You're right. I wouldn't put that on him."

"So your answer is . . . ?"

Was I willing to risk the lodge, risk my identity, risk the world I'd built, the world I loved? The gut answer was no. Absolutely not. But the stakes . . . that was the problem. What was at stake if I said no? My life. My actual life.

There was a time, not that long ago, when I'd have taken the risk. When the lodge *was* my life. It still was a huge part of it. But even if that identity—Nadia Stafford, lodge owner—was stripped away, I was still me, and that was worth holding on to.

I was also worried about Jack's involvement in this. But I had to put that aside and make the decision for myself. That wasn't an easy place for me to be in—it's so much easier for me to think of others. Yet I can't live like that. It's a bottomless morass of guilt and denial.

"Yes," I said finally. "If you have to, do it."

"I won't unless I have to." A pause. Then, "I know you don't believe that. You don't trust me. I've given you reason not to, and I won't apologize for that. But . . ." She trailed off and there was a long silence. Then she came back, her voice strong. "I'm going to say this once and only once, and if you ever remind me of it or—God help me, tell Jack—you will wish you hadn't. You have done something for someone I care about very much, Dee. You make Jack something I didn't ever think he could be. You make him happy. I want that for him, and as long as you're doing that, you can trust me. Jack wants you to keep that other life, so I will do everything in my power to make sure you keep it."

"Thank you. And I'm sorry about Duncan."

"He was old," she said, sounding more like herself. "Shitty way to go, though, and I hope that whoever did this will suffer just as much, but mostly, I just want the bastard dead. Get this whole goddamned mess solved, and let everyone get back to their regularly scheduled lives."

"I'm sorry about all this."

"Why? You're not the idiot who had to make the grand romantic gesture of finding Drew Aldrich." She snorted. "There's one you don't see in the movies. Nothing says 'I love you' like 'I tracked down this guy for you to kill.'"

A knock sounded, saving me from a reply.

"Jack's at the door," I said. "Or, at least, I hope it's Jack."

"If it's not, leave it locked."

"Oh, I plan to."

It was indeed Jack. With food.

"Don't worry," he said as he walked in. "Just went two doors down. Got ambushed. He missed. Had to hide the body, though. Took a while."

"I know you're joking, but given our recent history, I wouldn't be shocked if you weren't."

"Yeah." He brought the food to the table and, without even looking over, said, "Everything okay?"

"If I say yes, are you going to call bullshit?"

"Yep." He paused, his hand still on a sandwich wrapper. He looked over. "Quinn call?"

"No, Evelyn."

"Ev—" He looked at the food. "Ah, fuck. I fell for it."

"Don't feel bad. She tricked me, too . . . into admitting that we're together by pretending you'd already told her."

"She could have asked *me*."

"Oh, but that would be no fun at all." I pulled out a chair, sat, and punched a straw into my drink. "That's not what she was calling about. I'd like to think she wouldn't send you out into the street, following assassination attempts, just to find out the status of our relationship. There was something else she needed to speak to me about."

"Supposed to come through me."

"Yes, except that in this case, she was right to do an end run around you."

I told him what Evelyn had said. I wasn't starting a relationship with Jack by keeping secrets. But by the time I'd finished, he looked stunned and a little queasy.

"Maybe I shouldn't have mentioned—" I began.

"No." He shook it off. "Course not. Just . . . Didn't think . . . Fuck. I didn't *think*."

"Let's face it—this is a risk I accepted when I took Paul Tomassini's first job offer. There was always the chance that I'd be caught and I'd have two choices. Run or accept my punishment."

He looked over sharply. "Hope there's no question which you'd choose."

"In the beginning, honestly, I think I would have given myself up. Gone to jail, because that's what I would have felt I deserved. Now, though, there's no question. I'd run."

"Good." He paused. "You probably don't want to talk about it. The possibility."

"No, actually I do. I'll feel better knowing I have a plan. If Evelyn tells Contrapasso who I am, and, for whatever reason, they turn me in or threaten to, I'd give the lodge to the Waldens. Then I'd take Scout and leave. You have most of my money in safekeeping, so I'd be okay."

He nodded. "Got your money. Would get you out. Set you up. New identity. New lodge."

"A new lodge?" I shook my head. "I don't think I'd ever be able to do that again."

"Yeah, you could. *Would*. I'd make sure of it. Buy it for you."

"Jack, I'd never let you—"

"Too bad. I would." He leaned over the table. "I'd do it because I want to and because I can. Got enough money to buy you ten lodges, Nadia, and not a fucking thing I want to spend it on." He straightened. "Not going to discuss this now. You'll just argue. Any luck? Never have to discuss it at all. But it happens? You'll be okay."

I smiled. "I know I will."

He squeezed my hand and then gathered the trash from our meal as he stood. "Was thinking while I was out. Few things we can follow up on. Leave Chicago. Head to New York. Couple stops on the way. Safer out of Chicago anyway."

"Agreed," I said. "I'll go pack my stuff."

CHAPTER 46

We left Chicago. I was driving, but it quickly became apparent that Jack wasn't going to take advantage of the chance to rest. I pulled over and let him take the wheel. He was stressed and anxious, and it gave him something to do.

Jack had contacted a private-investigator associate—the man he'd used to help him find Drew Aldrich. He was having him dig for any clues on the mystery partner, and we were going to meet up with him in Detroit. Our final destination was New York. Our best lead was there, with the Contrapasso Fellowship.

I napped after that. When I woke, it was after six, and I suggested Jack might want a coffee if he planned to keep the wheel all the way to Detroit.

"Wouldn't mind a walk," he said. "Stretch my legs."

"Absolutely."

"Saw a sign for a park. 'Bout five miles."

"We'll stop there."

A couple minutes of silence. "Want to talk, too. Some stuff. That okay?"

I smiled. "I am always up for talking."

"More like listening."

"I can do that, too."

We pulled in at the park. It was a small one, unmanned, with signs warning it was closed at night. Dusk was still a couple of hours away, but the tiny lot was already empty.

We parked and headed in.

"Don't really need the walk," Jack said as we reached the path. "Just wanted to talk. Not in the car."

"Okay."

He lapsed into silence. We walked about half a kilometer before he continued.

"Was thinking. About our talk earlier. Your lodge. Me having money. Got me thinking. I know about you. Where you live. How you live. You don't know that about me."

"Not for lack of interest, Jack. If you wanted to tell me, I figured you would, and if you didn't, I sure as hell wasn't going to pry."

"Ask then."

I hesitated, but I could tell he seriously wanted me to ask. "Okay, where do you live when you're not on the road? You've got a house somewhere, I presume. A condo or something."

"Nope. Got mailing addresses. Couple post boxes, here and there. Otherwise? Nothing. No house. No apartment. Not even a fucking car. Between jobs? Find a place to stay. Motel usually. Sublet sometimes."

"How long have you been doing that?"

"Always. Never saw the point of owning. Leaves a paper trail. I travel too much anyway. No reason to stay in one place."

"So you've never been married, I take it?"

He gave me a look.

"Hey, it's a perfectly valid question. I take it that's a no. Any kids?"

Another look. "I would have mentioned that."

I met his gaze. "There were times when, for all I knew, you had a wife, kids, a house in the suburbs and a day job in Connecticut. Yes, I was pretty sure you didn't, but it wasn't outside the realm of possibility."

He nodded. "Should have said more."

"No, I understood the need for privacy. Now, though, I *will* ask, and if there's anything you don't want to share, just say so."

"There's nothing. You want to know? I'll tell you." A few more steps in silence. "So, don't have a house. Or car. Got a few storage lockers. Mostly equipment. Clothing? Buy it as I go. Don't really have *things*. Just money. No bad habits to spend it on. Don't gamble. Don't use drugs. Don't drink much. Worst habit? Damn cigarettes. Maybe a pack a week. Doesn't exactly make a dent in my savings."

"No, I imagine it doesn't. And I don't think I've seen you smoke one in a few days."

"Yeah. Might be wishing for one in a minute." He cleared his throat. "Asked if I've ever been married. Fuck no. Said before about relationships. Don't do 'em. Should explain better. Don't really want to."

"Then don't."

"No. Get it out. Make sure you understand. However awkward this is."

We rounded the next curve in the path before he continued, "Don't do relationships. Don't date. One night? Yeah." He paused. "Even that? Been a while. Getting older. Too much hassle."

He steered me around a patch of mud. "Probably more than you want to know. More than I should say. Just proof that I don't know shit about doing this right. Point is, I'm going to fuck up." He paused. "Don't mean screw around. Wouldn't do that. Mean in general. Last time I dated? High school. And, as I've said, I dropped out after two years. So . . ." A sigh. "Fuck. That's embarrassing."

I laughed. "I didn't expect you'd have a string of girlfriends across the country. Too much work and too much risk. I'm not exactly an expert in the field myself, as my disaster with Quinn might suggest. I've been engaged, as you know. When that ended and the Wayne Franco thing blew up—at the same time—I backed out of the dating scene. So I have no expectations, Jack. I wouldn't anyway. That's not how I am."

"I know. Just wanted you to understand. Don't have to worry you'll find out. Which brings up something else. About Quinn."

I must have stiffened, because he looked over quickly. "Not that. Not even Quinn really. About you two." He paused. "No, not you two. Like that. Just . . . Fuck."

"Tell me what you want to say, Jack."

"You mentioned expectations. Want to talk about that. Different expectations. Awkward conversation, though. We just get together and I say, here's what I expect? Like I've got a right to expect anything."

"You do," I said, looking over at him. "It's not as if we just met, and you're right—even if it seems early to be laying out expectations, it doesn't take long before it's too late, and both parties are headed down very different paths."

"Yeah."

We reached a fork in the trail. I thought that's what stopped Jack from continuing, but even after we started down one, he said nothing.

"Do you want me to go first?" I asked.

"No. Got this. What do I expect? No, not expect. Want. Anything you don't—"

"Jack, stop qualifying. You're only going to make the conversation longer and I'm sure you've had enough of it already."

A short laugh. "Yeah. All right. I want a relationship. A committed relationship. Marriage? Can't offer that. Legally? The guy I was? John Daly? Long gone. Presumed dead. Can't come back. Ever. Otherwise? Got three surnames. Don't consider any of them mine. None are legal. It's just Jack. Can't marry like that. Kids? Never considered it. No real opinion on it. You wanted one? We could figure something out. Wouldn't be easy, though. My past. My identity. Makes everything tough."

"I don't want children, Jack. And I don't need a wedding band to be in a committed relationship."

"All right. Good. Not that I expect . . . Fuck. Been two days. I'm already talking about that."

"You're talking about long-term possibilities and laying out the issues, which I'm absolutely fine with." I glanced at him. "Just as I'm fine with a scenario where someday those would be questions we had to consider."

"Good. All right. So that's what I can't do. What I want to do?" Three more steps. Then he turned, his hands going to my hips, stopping me and holding me there as he looked me in the eye. "You know I'm tired of the job, Nadia. Not ready to get out. But ready to start moving that way. I want something else. Something more. Something with you."

I pressed my lips to his and murmured, "Good."

He exhaled and kissed me back, and I could taste the relief in his kiss. He was right. This was difficult, putting ourselves out there for rejection, admitting what we wanted. Hell, after three years of not even daring to say that I expected to *see* him again, there was a part of me that was terrified of even admitting I wanted more than a fling. But he did. And that was, as I said, good.

"So you're fine with that?" Jack said as he pulled back. "Me spending more time at the lodge? Maybe staying? Between jobs?"

"I am absolutely fine with it. I'll just need to strike the right balance between taking advantage of having an extra pair of hands around the place and not giving you so much work that you're scouring the papers, looking for someone to kill, so you can get a break."

He laughed. "Wouldn't happen. I like keeping busy. I just . . . I want to be sure it's all right. That's your place. Your personal place. And I know you never brought . . ."

He trailed off before saying Quinn's name.

I nodded. "I kept telling myself that I was just waiting for the right time to introduce him, but I don't think that was it. It was . . . it was different. You've been honest, so I'm going to take the same chance, even if it doesn't exactly reflect well on me." I looked up at him. "I was with Quinn because there was no reason not to be. We got along. I liked him as a friend. The guy I really wanted to be with wasn't showing any signs that he felt the same. So I settled for what I could get."

"I'm sorry."

"You don't need to be sor—"

"Yeah, I do. You know how long I've been wanting this? Since the third time I came to see you. Hell, maybe from the first time. I just didn't realize it until the third. I was driving to see you. Had no reason to. Made an excuse. So I'm driving there. Got stuck at the border. Customs backup. Impatient as hell. Worried I'd get there too late. You'd be tired. Wouldn't want to talk. That's when I realized it. How I felt. Turned around. Pulled into the nearest pay phone. Called and said I couldn't make it."

"I remember that."

"Yeah. Turned tail and ran. Month later? Talked myself down. You needed help. I could give it. Shouldn't turn my back on you. Keep it what it was. Good enough. So I went back. Three fucking years of that. Run away. Come back. Try to be what you needed. What I thought you wanted. Even if I'd thought you wanted more? Not sure it would have changed anything. Getting involved with me? Fucking stupid. No point. Got nothing to offer. You deserve better."

I tried to cut in, but he wouldn't let me.

"If I cared about you?" he continued. "I'd want what's best for you. Which is not me. Quinn comes along? Start thinking maybe that's it. Much as it hurt. Seemed good for you. Tried to rise above it. Couldn't fucking do it. Ran again. Left you hanging."

"Egypt," I murmured. When Jack had begun staring the possibility of retirement in the face, we'd discussed things he might want to do. There wasn't much on his list, but he did want to see Egypt. Just not alone. So I'd offered to go, and it seemed like a plan and then . . . and then it wasn't.

"Yeah. I knew if we went? The two of us? On vacation? I'd let you know. So I stayed away. Hurt you more. Confused you and hurt you. Eventually, decided I couldn't do it. Couldn't pretend. If I saw any sign you weren't happy with Quinn? I was going to move. Stop whining that you deserved better. Take the risk. *Be* what you deserve. Make you happy."

"You have always made me happy, Jack. You have always been what I deserve." I put my arms around his neck as he lowered his mouth to mine. "And you have always been what I want."

We lay on the forest floor, clothing scattered around us. It was getting cool, the sun dropping, but Jack hadn't made a move to dress yet, so I wasn't, either. I stretched out against him and enjoyed the moment. When he finally did stir, I rolled onto my side, but he reached out and tugged me back.

"Cold?" he said.

"Nope."

"Few more minutes. No rush. Meeting my contact in the morning. So . . ." He stifled a yawn. "No rush."

"Good." I curled up against him. Something crackled under me. The condom wrapper. I pulled it out and lifted it. "May I suggest that after all this is over, we get a clean bill of health and I get myself on birth control? Otherwise, we may need to start buying in bulk."

A chuckle. Then he sobered. "You want me to slow down? Just say so."

"Yes, yes, I do, because I am very clearly not enjoying it. Can't you tell by the way I just lay there, quietly. Very quietly."

Another chuckle.

"If I want you to slow down, Jack, I will tell you to slow down. Admittedly, we are going through these"—I flicked the condom wrapper—"a little fast, but we're both anxious and stressed and frustrated over this hit business. I don't know about you, but it definitely helps for me."

"Yeah."

"It's stress relief. That's my excuse and it's a damned good one, so I'm sticking to it."

He laughed and pulled me into a kiss. When we separated, he looked up at the darkening sky. "Could stay here. Quiet. No hitmen."

"Always a bonus."

"It is. I—"

My cell phone rang, the sound muffled. I glanced toward my jeans, a few feet away.

"So much for quiet."

Jack rose and snagged my jeans and tugged out the still-ringing phone.

"If it's the guy who's trying to kill me, take a message," I said.

"Nah. Almost as bad. Evelyn." He lifted the phone. "You want me . . . ?"

"No, I'll take it."

He handed it over, and I answered.

"It's me," she said. "I tried calling Jack, but he's not answering his phone."

"I think he left it in the car."

"You're not in the car?"

"Nope."

"Where are you?"

I looked around. "A park. We went for a walk."

She grumbled at the preposterousness of that. Hit-men apparently did not take walks, unless they were stalking someone.

"Okay, then, where is this park? How far are you?"

"Mmm, I dunno. Few hours from Chicago?"

"Either I just woke you up from a lovely nap or . . ." She paused. "A walk, was it? Well, I did tell you to make him happy. That's one way."

"It is." I stifled a yawn. "We're on schedule. I know that much. Do you want to talk to Jack?"

"Actually, I need to speak to both of you. Does that thing have a speaker?"

"Mmm, huh. Apparently, it does."

"Then use it and try to wake up. Give Jack a shake, too. I'm sure he's not in much better shape."

I put her on speakerphone. I expected her to make some comment to Jack about what we'd been doing.

When she led with, "We have a problem," instead, I sat up quickly, drowsiness falling away.

"I need you to head back to the car," she said. "Now."

"Um . . ." I looked at our scattered clothing. "Right."

I tugged my jeans over as Jack grabbed his. We tried to be quiet about it, but the sound must have carried.

Evelyn sighed. "Get *dressed* and then head back to the car. Quickly, please."

"Keep talking," Jack said. "We're moving."

"I got our answers from the Contrapasso guys," Evelyn said.

"What cost?" Jack asked.

"We'll discuss that later. For now, what's far more important—"

"*That's* important," Jack said. "What did you—?"

"It's okay," I said as I pushed to my feet. "Evelyn's right. We can get that later."

Jack and I started walking, quickly, back along the darkening path as I asked Evelyn, "What's wrong?"

"The Contrapasso Fellowship did not order a hit on Drew Aldrich."

"Wh-what? Sorry. I heard you. I just . . . They didn't order the hit? But I'm sure Koss killed him. Are they saying he didn't?" I paused. "No, they're saying Koss isn't one of them. That's where we made the wrong connection."

"No, the connection was correct. Sebastian Koss is a part of Contrapasso. They confirmed he's been a high-level member for years, and his primary role is bringing them cases exactly like Aldrich."

"So they rejected Aldrich, and Koss took matters into his own hands."

"No. Drew Aldrich's name isn't in their files. No one there has ever heard of him. Koss acted completely on his own."

I swore. "So what does *that* mean?"

"I have no idea, and it's not important right now. The point is that to get this information from them I had to tell them about Aldrich, obviously. And about Sebastian Koss and the fact that he used a car rented by their fleet. Now they want answers. From Koss. They're going after him and once they get to him, we lose him. He disappears into their custody until they sort this out, and they won't give a rat's ass about you, Dee. Anything Koss knows is about to disappear with him."

CHAPTER 47

"Koss was Aldrich's partner," I said as Jack peeled from the parking lot. "He had to be. Koss . . ." My stomach lurched. "Amy . . ."

"Don't know that."

Jack drove as fast as he dared. As urgent as the situation was, getting pulled over for speeding would consume any extra time we gained.

"I never even considered the possibility," I murmured after a few minutes. "Why the hell didn't I consider it?"

"Because it didn't fit. We knew Koss was Contrapasso. That answer made sense. He killed Aldrich for them."

Jack's gaze was fixed on the road, his face expressionless. I knew that face. It said he was keeping it blank on purpose, so I didn't read something in it.

"You *did* consider the possibility, didn't you?" I asked.

No answer.

"Jack . . ."

"Considered. Only to be thorough." He paused. "That PI we were meeting? Asked him to look into Koss. Any connection between Koss and Aldrich. Other than Amy's trial. Honestly? Didn't expect anything. Would have told you otherwise."

"Does Evelyn know you suspected him?"

"Nah. Wasn't really suspecting. Covering all bases." He paused. "I mentioned it to Quinn."

"Quinn?"

"Yeah. Before the fight. Wanted him to look into Koss. Said he doubted any connection. Koss is one of the good guys. Quinn didn't even like me suggesting he might not be. So I called the PI."

Another few minutes of silent driving. Then, "Maybe I should have told you. Didn't think so. Not without proof."

"Because I would have reacted just like Quinn did."

"Nah. Not exactly."

"But close enough. I know Koss's reputation and I admire it. Even after meeting him and suspecting he could be the one trying to kill me, my opinion didn't change. I'd have thought you suspected him because, in your world, guys like Koss are never as good as they seem."

He shrugged. "Tough call. Long shot, too. Even now? Koss as Aldrich's partner? Amy's killer? Huge leap."

"It is if I keep looking at him as Sebastian Koss, defender of justice, protector of women. But if I strip that away, and he's just any other guy? I can imagine what happened."

"Tell me."

Did Jack really need me to lay it out? Probably not. He would have come up with his own theory when he considered Koss for the role of partner. But he wanted to hear mine, untainted by his own conjecture.

"Koss and Aldrich knew each other somehow, before Amy's death. I don't remember exactly how old Koss is, but if he'd just passed the bar before the trial, he's within a year or two of Aldrich. So same rough age, same rough geographic area. I'd theorize that they knew each other. Aldrich was already preying on young girls. Koss . . . I couldn't speculate how he got involved, because it's not like having a friend who likes to race motocross and thinking that sounds like fun. Somehow, though, they hatched the plan. Aldrich gets me; Koss gets Amy. Maybe Aldrich convinced Koss that Amy would be into it."

I paused, considering before I continued. "Yes, that fits. Koss thinks Amy will be a willing partner, except she isn't, and he panics and kills her. Koss flees the scene and is spotted, but Aldrich is the one who's caught. He doesn't roll on his buddy because Koss has a plan. He's just been hired by a big Toronto firm. He'll convince them to take Aldrich's case, and Aldrich will get off, because he wasn't the killer anyway. It works. Aldrich is free. Koss helps set him up with a new identity and tries to wash his hands of the business. Driven by guilt, he makes crimes against women his life's work. But he stays in touch with Aldrich. Or, more likely, Aldrich stays in touch with him—blackmailing him into helping him change identities, maybe hitting him up for cash. Koss goes along with it until Aldrich calls to say I'm following him, and Koss has had enough. He knows how to kill Aldrich from his work with Contrapasso, so he does. Then he sends a hitman to the lodge to kill me if I was there. I show up in Chicago . . ."

"And he knows he's right. Aldrich's photo *was* of you. Hitman's missing. Middleman, too. Koss gets spooked. Sets a new pro on you."

"That's the theory, then. Now we need to test it by confronting Koss, and we need to do it fast, before Contrapasso gets hold of him."

Silence.

After a couple of kilometers, Jack said, "You gonna suggest a way?"

"Nope."

"You have an idea."

"Yep, and it's the same idea you have, which is the only way of doing this fast. I'm just not going to be the one to suggest it. That ball is in your court."

"Fuck."

"Uh-huh."

The solution was, of course, the very one that set Jack off in a temper two days ago. I needed to meet with Koss.

I called and told him someone was trying to kill me. Hey, nothing works like the truth. Of course, if you are under threat of death, it's probably best not to run to your probable assassin for help. That may have explained the awkward pause after I finished explaining the situation. Koss recovered quickly, though, and offered to help.

Okay, I didn't actually *say* someone was trying to kill me. That would be crazy. I just said that I thought someone was following me and I knew it was silly, and it was probably only because he'd told me about getting that call warning him away from me, but I didn't know where else to turn and . . .

He understood my predicament. He also feared that I had gotten unknowingly involved in something, and, while he wasn't jumping to any conclusions, we really should speak, in person.

"While I don't think you're in any immediate danger, Nadia, I would suggest we not meet in a public place."

Of course not. It would be so much harder to kill me in a public place.

I agreed and he continued, "I have an idea. I've been looking at alternate office space. My kids are teenagers now and some days I feel like I'm running a youth shelter here. A very loud youth shelter." He laughed and I obligingly joined in.

"There's a place I've been considering," he said. "It's an old building that a developer is remodeling. He's given me access while I make my decision. It's mostly vacant and at this hour, I suspect we won't find anyone else there."

Meet you in a vacant building at night? What an awesome idea. Apparently, Koss didn't think much of my intelligence level. Which would be insulting if I wasn't already plenty insulted over the fact he was trying to kill me.

After I hung up, I joked about it to Jack, but he knew I was actually hurt. Not about Koss's assumptions regarding my intelligence. Not even so much that he was trying to kill me. I was hurt because, as Jack had said, I'd respected the man. A lot. Part of me had still hoped he'd do or say something to convince me he was innocent. Instead, he was inviting me to meet him in a vacant building.

Jack kept me from dwelling on that by keeping me planning. We discussed how I'd get Koss talking and the various contingencies if that failed. Meanwhile, Jack would take his place in the shadows.

I dropped Jack off a kilometer away. Then I took a circuitous route. The streets were almost empty, but even if Koss saw me driving around, it was easy enough to explain that I'd made some wrong turns looking for the place in the dark. Once Jack said he was at the building and had Koss in his sights, I parked. Koss had given me very specific instructions for that, citing concerns "in case" I was being followed. Or, you know, in case he decided to kill me and needed to find my car in order to move it . . . with my body in the trunk. As I expected, the spot he'd chosen was tucked away where it was unlikely to be noticed, lending further credence to the theory that Koss had no intention of letting me walk out of here alive.

I noticed Koss approaching, but I pretended I didn't, getting out of the car and fussing with the lock as I watched his reflection in the car window, ready to pull my gun if he made any move toward a weapon of his own. He didn't. Nor, however, did he make any noise on his approach. I turned and feigned jumping.

"I'm sorry," he said. "I didn't mean to startle you." He looked around. "It's quieter than I expected." He smiled. "Which I will appreciate if I get an office here."

"Are you sure this is an okay place to leave my car?" I asked. "It's kind of . . . secluded."

"It's fine. There are better break-in pickings two blocks over. A very trendy nightclub. Or so my kids tell me, despite the fact neither of them is old enough to visit a nightclub."

"Right, you said you had teens. How old?"

"Shane is eighteen and Meg is fif— No, she just turned sixteen. As you can tell, I'm trying to forget the fact that my baby is now old enough to drive."

He steered me toward the back of the building, murmuring there was a door there. What he didn't say was that going around the front would have taken us past a bank with a street-front ATM, complete with camera.

As we walked, he continued chatting about his kids. I wasn't sure how to take that. Obviously, having children does not make you a good person. But this guy was trying to kill me and willing to talk about his kids to throw me off guard. It was a depth of disturbing that I couldn't reconcile with what I thought I knew about Sebastian Koss.

Unless there was something else happening here. I tried to sneak looks at Koss. Did he seem nervous? Any sign that he was acting under duress? That there was someone else in the building, waiting for us?

I couldn't tell. He just kept talking. Or maybe that was the tipoff. Nervous chatter.

I wanted to ask Jack for his take on it, but there was no way to do that. If he was concerned by Koss's chattering, he gave no sign of it.

We reached the back door. Koss took out his keys and pretended to unlock it. I could tell he was faking. He'd opened it earlier. Broken in, I presumed. If I was right about what he planned to do here, he would have no actual connection with this building.

He swung the door open and waved me in. I obeyed, but now I was the one talking, asking about his son's college plans, which gave me the excuse to be looking over my shoulder at him. Then I stopped inside and waited, facing him. He held the door open, as he reached for a wall switch. He flicked it. Or he pretended to. Nothing happened.

I managed a laugh, a little tight, as if I might be getting nervous. "That could be a problem."

"No kidding. They must be working on the electrical. Luckily . . ." He lifted his keychain and flicked on a tiny flashlight.

"Handy."

"It is. Some promotional gewgaw I got at a conference last month. Yet another gadget to make women feel safe in a deserted parking garage at night, when the truth is that the only thing that will make them truly safe is not going in that parking garage, as unpopular as that opinion is."

"Because it shouldn't be that way. We should be able to get to our cars at night, without lights and panic buttons and handguns, but the fact that we *should* be able to doesn't mean we are. Unfortunately."

"Exactly."

As he ushered me down the hall, that feeling of unease congealed in my gut. First reminding me he was a dad. Now reminding me of his life's work, fighting violence against women.

Was he trying to communicate a message? A plea even? Warning me that something was about to happen and it wasn't his fault, and for me to remember that he was, at heart, a decent guy, a man with a family, a man with a reputation.

Jack, are you there? Damn it, I really hope you're there.

Koss opened the door to the stairwell.

"No elevator, I guess," I said with a short laugh.

"Not yet. But we're only going to the third floor. There's a model suite there we can talk in."

"Got it," Jack said through the earpiece, and I breathed a sigh of relief.

As we reached the second flight, Jack whispered that he was in the other stairwell. Koss took me down the hall and opened a door. When we walked in, I said, "Oh, this is nice," even before I got a look around. Jack grunted a thanks, knowing my comment really meant "we're in the room now and it's clear."

Light seeped in through the windows, making the flashlight unnecessary. I went over to the window and looked out . . . at the wall of the neighboring building.

"Well, I hope they aren't charging you for the view," I said.

I expected a laugh and a comment. But Koss said nothing. I turned to see him standing there, in a shard of light, watching me.

"Everything okay?" I asked after a moment of awkward silence.

"Oh, yes. I'm just trying to figure out what Drew saw in you."

"Wh-what?"

"Drew Aldrich. I never understood why he wanted to fuck you so badly."

My brain stopped. I swear it did. I couldn't seem to process what he'd said. I stood there, gaping, certain that I'd heard him wrong. It wasn't just what he said; it was how he said it. Completely calm, conversational even.

"Emotionally stunted," Koss said. "That's what I'm sure a psychiatrist would say. Drew liked little girls because he wanted them to like him back. He couldn't face women his own age. He liked sweet little girls, and he was always hoping if he fucked them just right, they'd fall in love with him. Did you fall in love with him, Nadia?"

"Uh-uh," he said, as soon as I made a move. "If you go for your gun, I'll go for mine and this will not end well."

"Not for you."

A humorless smile. "I doubt that, but I also doubt you're going to shoot me. Not until you have some answers. So we are going to raise our hands together, Nadia. Then we are going to sit down at that table, our hands on it where we can see them, and we'll have a little talk."

CHAPTER 48

Jack's curse whispered through the earpiece.

"You need me?" Jack asked.

"I've got it," I said. Then I paused, so Jack would know I was really answering him, before continuing with, "My hands are going up, and I'll walk to the table as long as you do the same."

My heart was hammering, but there was no need for Jack to jump in. Not as long as Koss was willing to talk. I just needed a moment to get my mental footing. Get him talking. Give me time to regroup and refocus.

"I was wrong," I said as we sat.

"Oh, I'm sure you were wrong about a lot of things. I presume you mean about who killed Amy."

"I knew you did. I just misunderstood the circumstances. I thought you were pulled into it by Aldrich, partying with a couple of teenage girls, things went wrong, and it was all a terrible mistake."

"I don't make mistakes." He leaned forward. "Who are you, Nadia? Who are you really? Not just some screw-up ex-cop hiding in the forest. That's clear. *What* are you?"

"Is that why we're having a conversation? Because I'm not the only one with questions?"

"I'm curious. As an expert in double lives, yours

seems fascinating. Admittedly, I still haven't confirmed what that double life is, but I have an idea. Am I correct in believing you're armed?"

"I am."

"With what?"

I said nothing. His eyes narrowed slightly, as if annoyed. Here he was, so clearly willing to communicate, and I was being difficult. My brain was still trying to reconcile this man with the Sebastian Koss I knew. I might lead a double life, and there might be sides of me that I hide from the world, but nothing like this.

"You came here to kill me," he continued. "But there are so many easier ways to do it. Safer ways. You're taking this risk because you can't kill me until you have your answers. That's rather pathetic, don't you think?"

"This coming from someone who wants answers himself?"

He shrugged. "Mine is pure curiosity, and the moment I feel an honest threat, I'll kill you, regardless of whether I have my answers. You won't, because you need a reason. Once you have it, you'll put a bullet in my brain." He paused. "That's what you do, isn't it?

"I've never denied I killed Wayne Franco."

"That's not what I mean. What happened to the man you met last weekend, Nadia?"

"I met a few men last weekend. I was at my lodge."

"This wasn't a guest. It was a man sent to kill you. I don't know exactly when you met him. Or under what conditions. Or the outcome. I only know that he went to see you and was never heard from again."

"It's beautiful country up there. Maybe he decided to stay."

"I'm sure he did. I'm sure he'll stay until he rots and becomes part of that beautiful country. And then there's the matter of the man who hired him. A fellow named Roland. He's missing, too. Do you know anything about that?"

"Nope."

"Do you see the pages beside you, Nadia?"

I looked over. There were sheets on the table.

"Turn the top one over."

I did. It was a blown-up photograph of one of the shots from the park. Jack and me, making out. My heart started to thump, but I told myself not to panic. I should have known there was a chance the hitman passed these along to his client before his death. And it was just a blurry shot of me kissing someone with his back to the camera.

"It's a photo of me kissing a guy," I said, so Jack would know what was happening.

"Do you recognize him?" Koss asked.

"Vaguely. I had a few drinks the other night. I picked him up in a bar. He was hot."

I expected a reaction from Jack, maybe a chuckle. The earpiece was silent. Not really the time for jokes, I guess.

Koss flipped over the next picture. It was Jack and me walking into the park. A close up. Of Jack's face. Without any disguise.

I tried not to react. Oh, God, I tried not to. I know I did. I could tell by Koss's satisfied smirk.

It was all right. Sebastian Koss wasn't walking out of this room alive, so it didn't matter if he knew who Jack was, no more than it mattered if he knew what I was. He'd killed Amy. I was ready to put a bullet in him at the first chance I got.

Except I couldn't. Not now. Because I had to make damned sure he was the only one who knew about Jack and me.

"Jack," Koss mused. "A boring name, don't you think? Particularly for a hitman." He turned to the next shot, the one of me straddling Jack. "You don't seem to find him boring, though, do you, Nadia?"

How do I play this? Dear God, how do I play it?

I treat it like an interrogation. I exercise my right to remain silent.

He shoved the picture in front of me. "Seeing this, I have to think maybe Drew's dream wasn't as crazy as I thought. It seems he did leave a lasting impression. You've developed a taste for . . . I would say 'bad boys,' but that sounds like punks who screw around and toke up a little on the weekend. This is a whole other class of bad, isn't it, Nadia?"

I swore I could feel him tensed there, watching me hungrily, waiting for a reaction, for any flinch. I didn't give it. If anything, I had to fight the impulse to laugh at the very thought that I'd see a link between Jack and Drew Aldrich.

"So how did it happen, Nadia?" he continued. "Did he come to take a break at your lodge? Needed a little R&R after blowing up innocent people? It's a stressful job. But you know that, don't you?"

He paused only a split second now, as if he wouldn't wait long enough to give me any satisfaction.

"It wasn't easy finding out who your friend was," he said. "When you managed to outwit two hitmen and disappear a middleman, I started suspecting you had some experience in the field. It was a long shot, but it paid off . . . after employing all of my extensive resources and a good deal of money. I tracked down a rumor about a hitman and a woman he'd taken under his wing." Koss glanced down at the photos. "Or maybe that's not the right phrase."

He looked over at me. "Is that what happened, Nadia? Your new boyfriend shows you a way to make some extra cash? You're an ex-cop. You're a champion distance shooter. You already had the skills. And you already had the experience, with Wayne Franco."

I just sat there, letting him talk.

"I caught a lucky break the other night." He paused. "Well, not so lucky, given that you're still alive. And, I'm sure, not so lucky for that poor sap you killed. But before he disappeared, he sent me those photos. And after he disappeared, I passed them to my contact to confirm that this did seem to be the Jack he'd heard the rumor about. He also very helpfully told me where I could go for more information. Another middleman. The same one, it turned out, that I'd hired here in Chicago."

Duncan.

He continued, "I tracked the old boy down, but he really wasn't feeling chatty. Fled to his cabin. I followed. We had a talk. He didn't give quite as much as I'd hoped for. A tough old bastard. Loyal to his friends. You don't see a lot of that with these criminal types. Admirable, even if it didn't help him, in the end."

He fingered the photos again. "So I know who your friend is, Nadia. And I'm pretty sure I know who you are. Dee, that's your professional name, isn't it? Nadia—Dee—not terribly imaginative."

A rap at the door made me jump. Koss only smiled.

"It seems we have guests. Should we invite them in?"

CHAPTER 49

The door opened as he was talking. The first thing I saw was Jack and my brain stuttered. There were people I could imagine sauntering into a standoff. Evelyn, for sure. She'd stroll into the room and throw her opponent for a loop and shoot him before he recovered.

But Jack didn't have the ego to take such an unnecessary risk.

That's when I saw the man behind him, with a gun pointed at the back of his head, and my brain didn't just stutter—it seemed to shut down altogether.

Not possible. Not fucking possible.

Wasn't it? Jack's been distracted. Off his game. Was it impossible to believe he was so caught up in worrying about you that he forgot to pay attention?

Yes. It was.

Koss laughed and I glanced over to see him watching me. Watching me react to Jack being brought in. Watching *Jack* react, his gaze down, ashamed.

"That's what happens when you're fucking your partner, Nadia," Koss said. "He's not a world-class hitman anymore. He's just a guy worried about his girlfriend."

The man holding a gun on Jack smiled. I looked at

him. He was in his late thirties. Former military. The short dark hair didn't give that away—his bearing did, and the way he moved from the door as quickly as possible, getting his back from it.

"This is Henry," Koss said. "Henry, you've already met Jack. This is Dee, the hitwoman who's been the cause of my current dilemma."

Henry turned his cool gaze on me in a contemptuous once-over.

"Jack? Go stand by your girlfriend," Koss said. Then to Henry, "He's been disarmed, I presume?"

"Yes," Henry said. "I found two guns and a knife."

As Jack came over to me, I shifted, letting my jacket fall open. His gaze caught mine and he nodded, almost imperceptibly. I had a gun, but couldn't get to it, not without taking my hands off the table. He'd been disarmed, so they weren't paying attention to *his* hands. As he passed, though, he murmured, "Wait."

Jack took up position behind my chair. I glanced back at him, but he kept his gaze up, over my head, fixed on Koss.

I looked at Henry, standing beside Koss, hands behind his back, feet apart.

"So, Henry," I said. "You work for Contrapasso, too. It seems their screening process isn't quite up to snuff."

Henry's chin lifted, just a fraction, enough to know I'd surprised him with my guess . . . and enough to tell me I'd guessed right. Behind me, Jack grunted. Confirming it?

Damn it, I really needed more information here. Time for me to get chatty. If nothing else, it might distract them enough for Jack to do . . . whatever Jack planned to do, because I was certain he planned something.

"Your mistake was renting that car under their name," I said to Koss. "Oh, I'm sure you rent them all the time. The group wouldn't have thought twice when it came up on the monthly billing, and if someone else tried to trace it, it would lead to a dead end. Unless the person tracing it knows what the Contrapasso Fellowship is and has a way to get in touch with them."

"True, it was an oversight. But we weren't the only ones who didn't consider all the possibilities."

I nodded. "Like the one where you aren't the only scumbag hiding in Contrapasso."

Henry stiffened. Koss only smiled, bemused.

I continued. "Henry heard that you'd been made. That Contrapasso was coming for your ass. He tipped you off, so you were ready for them. And ready for me to make a hasty play to get to you before they did."

"Not bad for someone who barely got her high school diploma," Koss said.

He smiled at me, as if he'd repaid me for the scumbag comment with the worst insult he could imagine. And there I saw his weakness. Sebastian Koss was a twisted, sadistic son of a bitch. And he was damn pleased with himself for pulling off his double life—for having the intelligence to pull it off. That's what put him above mere thugs like me and Jack.

And Henry? Ah, poor Henry. He might consider himself an equal partner, but Koss had no equals. No partners.

"Do you think he's such a good idea?" I said, jerking my chin at Henry.

Koss lifted his eyebrows. I paused, waiting for some sign from Jack that this was not an avenue I should pursue. But he stayed motionless behind me.

"You said earlier that sleeping with my partner isn't a good idea," I continued. "But it does have its advantages. We'll fight for each other. Without that, well, it's every man for himself eventually. Now, in the military, you're taught to protect the guy beside you, to trust the guy leading you. Henry isn't in the military anymore. Those rules don't apply. He's on the other side of the law, where no one gives a shit about loyalty." I looked at Koss. "As you yourself just said about Duncan, it's a rare trait. And yet, apparently, you trust Henry."

"He's like a feral dog. Intensely loyal, as long as I keep feeding him. And I feed you very well, don't I, Henry?"

The man's eyes narrowed.

"It's true," Koss said, conversationally, as if he had no idea how much he was insulting his partner. Or he just didn't give a damn. "As you guessed, I joined Contrapasso for the same reason I made my living fighting for justice for women. It's not just a smoke screen but an unbelievably rich source of information and opportunity. Henry's more like you. He has ethics, damn it. And morals. Unfortunately, those ethics and morals don't play nicely with his compulsions and obsessions, do they, Henry?"

A faint tightening of Henry's lips. Still, he said nothing. Koss had something on him—a lot of things, I presume, making this partnership more like a hostage situation.

"So you feed those compulsions and obsessions," I said. "Poor Henry here goes to Contrapasso for redemption, and you drag him deeper into the pit with you."

Henry finally spoke. "I don't see how this is any—"

"Oh, relax," Koss said. "We're all just getting to know each other better. We can't expect Nadia and her friend to listen to our proposal if they don't know us."

"Proposal?" Jack said.

"The man speaks, his tongue loosened by the potential for profit. That's the trick with your kind, isn't it? Anything for money."

I glanced back as Jack shrugged. "Willing to listen."

A smug smile. "Of course you are. But it seems your girlfriend has some compunctions about Henry here. She doesn't quite trust him."

"Do *you*?" I asked. "I thought you'd have learned a lesson from Drew Aldrich. That particular partnership was more trouble than it was worth, wasn't it? An albatross around your neck, having Aldrich out there, knowing your secrets. I bet it feels good to have finally gotten rid of him."

Henry shifted. He was thinking of Aldrich. Thinking of Koss's obvious contempt for him.

Keep thinking, Henry. Of how much you'd like to be free of him. Free of what he offers. Free of temptation. Free of blackmail. Do you really want to trust—?

Koss turned and shot Henry. Right through the heart. And I sat there, gaping like an idiot.

Before Henry even hit the floor, Jack lunged and yanked the gun from my holster. Koss spun and there was a brief flash of surprise on his face as he realized he'd left his flank open. Surely the very shock of his action should have stunned us into immobility. And it did—for me, at least.

Jack shot Koss in the right shoulder. The blow sent him spinning, gun flying from his hand. I dove for that gun and grabbed it before it hit the floor, then twisted and managed to land on my ass, gun pointed at Koss, before he recovered from his stumble. It was a sweet move, and Jack nodded his approval, which was nice, though I would have preferred to have been the one who'd actually had the presence of mind to shoot Koss. Moves, I've got. Nerves of steel? Aluminum more like.

Once Jack trained his gun on Koss, I disarmed Henry. He was still alive. Dying, though, lying on his back, staring at the ceiling, mouth working. I watched him in his final moments, and all I thought was, *What has he done? What crimes has he committed?* That shouldn't matter. A man was dying. If I could comfort him, even briefly, I should. But I couldn't.

So I took his gun and patted him down, and I found Jack's weapons, and took them, too.

"Four guns and a knife," I said, holding them up. "We have an arsenal."

"Got another gun under my pant leg."

I grinned. "Of course you do." I looked at Koss. "You *winged* him? Seriously?"

As I joked, Koss's scowl grew. Clearly he did not appreciate the casual response to the situation. Too bad.

"He winged me because he won't kill me," Koss said, struggling to find his smirk. "He knows you want me alive, and he wouldn't do anything that might cut him off. That's how you emasculate a hitman, Nadia. You fuck him and then—"

"He likes to talk," I said to Jack.

"Noticed."

"So I'm guessing there's a real reason why you kept him alive. Something to do with why you let yourself be captured?"

"Let himself?" Koss snorted. "You're as moonstruck as he is. He screwed up and got caught; he just managed to reverse the situation. A half-assed reversal because he needs to keep me alive so you—"

"Are we keeping him alive for someone else?" I said. "Because if not, I'd like him to stop talking now."

"So would I," said a voice from the doorway. "Unfortunately, we need him alive."

I turned and got my umpteenth shock of the night when I saw who was standing there. Quinn.

CHAPTER 50

Quinn walked in, followed by two men I didn't recognize. Both were armed, but they trained their guns on Henry and Koss. One lifted a radio.

"Bryant is still alive," the man said, meaning Henry, presumably. "Get Hayes up here and we might be able to keep him that way."

"Are you sure you want to?" I asked.

The man looked up at me and for a second I thought he wasn't going to answer. Then he dipped his chin and said, "I'm afraid we do. At least long enough to find out what he knows. And what he's done."

I nodded back and turned to Quinn and Jack. "Contrapasso?"

"Yeah," Jack said. "Cut a deal."

"They get to question Koss," Quinn said. He moved closer to me, lowering his voice so Koss wouldn't hear. "They want to know what he's done, so they can investigate any other partners. And so they can give the families closure if possible. We'll interrogate him together. Then they'll hand him back to you." He looked me in the eye. "Is that okay?"

"That's fine," I said.

He nodded, pulling away, any softness in his face vanishing as he straightened. A woman arrived then, with a medical kit, and hurried over to Henry. I looked at Koss, standing there, his shoulder bleeding, his gaze fixed on the wall. Figuring out how to spin this. How to use that keen brain to get himself out of this mess.

The Contrapasso team hadn't asked us to put away our weapons, but theirs were holstered, so Jack and I did the same.

"So how do we do this?" I said. "The interrogation?"

"We'll take Sebastian," one of the men said. "His injuries aren't life threatening. We'll patch him up at our destination."

"We aren't doing it here? The building is empty."

"It won't be in a few hours. This could take a while."

The other man took Koss by the arm. "You have a car, don't you?"

I nodded.

"Meet us around front. We're in a dark van. You can follow us."

"Actually, I'd rather go with you."

"I'll take the car," Jack said.

A look passed between the two men.

"Sure," the first one said. "Bring her down right after us. We'll do this in stages."

I thought he was talking to his partner. Then I noticed two other men right outside the door. They came in as the first two led Koss out.

I stepped toward the door. "I'm not letting him out of my—"

The men blocked the exit. I wheeled just in time to see Jack going for his gun. Quinn went for his, too, spinning on Jack. It should have been an easy victory for Jack. He had the jump on Quinn. He was a faster draw than anyone I knew. But he fumbled, just for a brief second, as Quinn pulled his gun and I pulled mine and—

And then Quinn's gun was pointed at Jack's head.

"Hands up," Quinn said. "Dee? Gun on the table."

When I didn't move, Quinn's finger twitched. "You really think I won't do it?"

I put my gun down.

"You set us up," Jack said.

Quinn gave a short laugh. "And you're shocked? Really?"

Jack lifted his gaze to Quinn's. "Thought you cared about her. No matter what happened. That doesn't change. Not that fast."

"That depends on whether there's anything to change," Quinn said. "Your mistake was thinking I gave a shit in the first place. I just thought she was a really good lay."

Jack dove at Quinn. There was, once again, that split second of "what the hell?" confusion. Jumping a guy holding a gun on you? An amateur move.

Like getting caught by your target's partner.

Or fumbling while drawing your gun.

Jack and Quinn were up to something. It seemed we were still in the middle of a grand performance. And I had yet to be given my script. Luckily, I've taken a few classes in improv.

The two Contrapasso guards gaped at each other, as if to say "What are we supposed to do about this?"

I helped them answer the question by pulling my gun on the unarmed woman tending to Henry. She stared at the gun, then up at me, eyes wide.

The moment I distracted the guards, Jack and Quinn each tackled one.

There was a scuffle. My part was easy—the medic just sat there, terrified. Only when the guys had their targets pinned did I lower my gun.

"Is he dead?" I said, nodding at Henry.

She stared at me. Maybe it was my conversational tone. Maybe it was the fact that I was using that tone while my partners grappled with the two guards.

I repeated the question. She finally nodded. Henry was dead. I don't know what else they expected, sending someone with a medical kit to tend to a guy shot through the heart. I suppose they felt they had to make the effort.

Across the room, the two guards were now trussed with zip ties. Jack and Quinn were patting them down for weapons. Neither had been shot or even badly injured. Quinn tossed me a zip tie for the medic. I asked her to turn around and put her hands behind her back. She did without argument. I put them on.

"You're okay," I said. "They're okay. But this would have gone a whole lot easier if your team hadn't double-crossed us. Remember that. We acted in good faith."

She nodded mutely.

I rose. "And talk to them about getting you a gun. Just because you're the medic doesn't mean you shouldn't know how to defend yourself."

A snorted laugh behind me. I turned to see Quinn shaking his head.

"What?" I said.

He started to reply, but Jack cut him off with an impatient "let's move" wave. We took off.

Jack led us along the empty hallway toward the stairwell. Quinn whispered to me as we went, telling me that the Contrapasso team consisted of five people. We'd left three in the model suite. Two had taken Koss, which meant we wouldn't encounter any guards lingering in the hall.

"So is anyone going to tell me what's going on?" I whispered.

"They took Koss," Jack said. "We're getting him back."

I glowered at him.

Quinn laughed softly, then said, "It's a long story. The short version is that Evelyn called me, and I got myself in on the Contrapasso operation. Jack made us coming in."

"Which you knew he would."

Jack waved for silence as he checked the stairwell. He held up a hand for us to stay there as he went in. Quinn held the door cracked open, making sure Jack didn't get jumped, and it was such an automatic response that I felt a pang of . . . regret, I guess, that it couldn't always be like this. Throw them into a situation together and they watched each other's back, anticipated each other's moves.

Jack waved us into the stairwell. We stayed silent there, the empty space too prone to echoes, but once we were on the first floor, I resumed talking as if we hadn't been interrupted.

"You knew the Contrapasso folks didn't intend to let us interrogate Koss," I said.

Quinn looked uncomfortable, and I knew that whatever Contrapasso had done here, he wasn't ready to frame them as the bad guys. "They couldn't. You and Jack, you're clearly doing the right thing, but . . ."

"We're still hitmen. We can't be trusted."

"But they *would* have interrogated him," Quinn said. "And he'd have disappeared afterward. This wasn't about cutting one of their own loose. When they got here and realized Henry Bryant was in on it, too? I thought Diaz—the guy who took Koss away—was going to be sick. He worked with Bryant for years."

"We done?" Jack said as he stopped us at the front door.

"Yes," I said. "The situation has been explained."

At least as well as it could be explained right now.

Jack checked outside as I held the door. I peered out. The street was empty.

"They're long gone," I whispered as Jack motioned us out. "How are we going to find them?"

Quinn lifted a portable device. "We can track Koss with this. I volunteered to man it. We just need to hurry before Contrapasso find out I went rogue and they shut down access."

"They track their agents?" I said. "How the hell do they do that?"

The same look of discomfort passed over Quinn's face, obviously reluctant to give away their secrets.

I held up my hand and said, "It doesn't matter. So where is he?"

"Not far," Quinn said as Jack waved us toward our car. "It took them a while to get him in the vehicle. We should be able to catch up."

Jack looked over his shoulder at us.

"Or we will," I said. "If we shut up and move faster. Right?"

Jack didn't reply, only waved for me to lead the way to the car.

Jack and I went ahead to get the car, while Quinn stood guard near the road.

"You okay?" Jack asked when we were out of Quinn's earshot.

I nodded.

"Sorry about all that. Could have told you. With the earpiece. But . . ."

"You needed a genuine reaction from me, which you wouldn't get if I knew what was going on. I know. It's fine. I figured it out. Eventually."

He took the keys from me as I held them out. "And the rest? Koss?"

I started to say that was fine, too, but I could feel his gaze on me. I shrugged. "That's harder to take. I was so certain, if I was right about Amy, that there was an explanation. Not that you can ever explain something like that, not really, but that it was a one-time thing, he regretted it, he suffered for it, and he tried to make amends. Obviously not."

"We'll get him."

CHAPTER 51

Jack drove. Quinn navigated. I got the backseat. I tried to help, leaning over the seat and watching the darkened road for Jack while checking the GPS over Quinn's shoulder.

"Sit," Jack said. "Butt down. Seat belt on."

"Before we swerve and you go through the windshield," Quinn said.

"Seriously? I'm not twelve, guys. I can—"

"Next right," Quinn cut in.

Jack took the corner sharp and fast, and I went flying back in the seat.

"Got that belt on?" Jack said as I recovered.

I flipped him the finger as he checked in the rearview mirror. I did, however, fasten my belt. There wasn't really much to do anyway. They didn't need the third pair of eyes. I felt helpless, imagining Koss getting away. Chicago wasn't a quiet city, even at night. Eventually, we'd hit traffic and once we did, we were screwed. There was no way of forcing the other car off the road with onlookers.

Luckily, the Contrapasso guys seemed to be sticking to the least-traveled roads. And Jack was a good driver—a fast one when he wanted to be. It was probably a wise idea for me to have my belt on.

"Got him," Quinn said. "One block up and one block over. Sticking to the speed limit."

"That thing have a map?" Jack asked.

"It does. They seem to be heading . . ."

"Roughly the same way we went to Duncan's cottage," I said.

They both glanced back at me, straining to see over the seat.

"I have my belt on," I said. "It's just not tightened. They're heading north of the city, presumably to find a quiet place to interrogate Koss and bury his body. They might take the highway or they might stick to regional roads. Either way, they'll be going straight for at least another four blocks."

Jack grunted.

"Your best bet . . ." I began.

I wriggled a little closer. Quinn sighed, then obliged by lifting the screen.

"Get ahead of them," I said. "Two blocks up, then make a left and another left. You'd cut them off while they're on a long stretch of narrow road. No easy way to get past or turn around." I glanced at Quinn. "Right?"

"Looks good to me. Now sit down and let me—"

A crash sounded in the distance, loud enough to reverberate through the closed windows. I jumped. Quinn fumbled the GPS, nearly dropping it. Jack made a left, so sharp I was grabbing the seat backs for support.

"Right here?" he asked.

When no one answered, he glanced at Quinn. "Turn right here?"

"Uh, yes. Sorry. Turn—"

Jack was already careening around the corner. Ahead we saw a dark, midsize car plowed into a parked truck. Billowing white airbags filled the car's interior. I could make out two heads in the front seat. One of the rear doors was open.

"That's theirs," Quinn said.

Jack grunted as he steered to the curb and braked hard enough for me to wish I'd tightened my seat belt. I'd have a bruise for sure.

Quinn was out of the car, gun pulled, as soon as it stopped. I followed, exiting on his side. He started for the crash. I grabbed the back of his jacket.

"Wait."

He stopped. Jack had, too, over on the sidewalk. When they did, the scuffle of their footsteps stopped, and I could hear another set of running feet, growing more distant by the second.

Quinn's chin jerked up, catching the same sound. He cursed. Koss was on the move, having presumably caused the crash.

Quinn's gaze went to the crash. I raced past him.

I turned, hands out. "GPS?"

He hesitated. Jack was loping over, waving for me to go on, that he'd get the GPS and follow. I ran while they figured it out. Quinn would be torn between wanting to check the men in the car and not wanting to lose his prey. I knew which he'd choose, but I wasn't waiting around until he figured it out.

I could still hear Koss ahead, loafers slapping the pavement, too intent on escape to hear us. When his footfalls did stop, I ducked into an entryway and got my first good look at the playing field. Offices mostly, dark windows shooting into the sky, the occasional light left on, the workers gone. There were shops down here, too, but all closed. I couldn't rule out the possibility that people lived over some of those shops. No one had come out to see the crash, though. The street was still and silent.

Jack caught up. He pressed the GPS into my hand. The screen showed a blip for Koss, who seemed to be moving around an intersection, likely catching his breath and figuring out his next move. I told Jack.

"Quinn coming?" I whispered.

"Yeah. Checking them out. Calling it in. Joining up."

I caught the faint pounding of footfalls. A moment later, Quinn rounded the corner. I waved him over as I checked the GPS.

"Koss is taking a breather," I said. "The Contrapasso guys?"

"One dead. One wounded. I'm guessing Koss got free and caused the crash, but the wounded guy is in no shape to talk. I called my contact. He'll deal with it. Nothing I can do."

I nodded, and we came up with a plan, quickly, before Koss got his second wind.

Koss had stopped prowling the intersection and set out again. He wasn't running now, presumably having decided no one was coming after him. We kept as quiet as possible, speeding up only when the roar of a distant car would mask our footfalls. We had split up, too, with Quinn across the road and Jack fifty feet behind me.

We'd reached a slightly busier area. As the occasional car passed, we'd all hear it and take cover momentarily. Each time, I'd tense, fearing I'd see a taxi. If Koss spotted one, he'd grab it. But they were just cars and he continued on, heading east toward a four-lane road that *would* promise public transit. We needed to get to him before he reached it.

I glanced back at Jack. That's all it took for him to break into a lope and catch up as I continued walking. Across the road, Quinn glanced over. I motioned for him to keep an eye out. Jack checked the GPS and quickly calculated how long we had. Not long enough.

Not at this speed. Any faster, though, and our footsteps would echo through the silent streets.

He handed me back the GPS, then I took off my shoes and broke into a run. That fixed the problem, even if I couldn't go quite as fast as I would otherwise. The sidewalk was old, crumbling in spots, gravel-covered in others, and it was like running on marbles. Across the road, Quinn had taken off his sneakers and he soon caught up. Jack was hanging back to cover us.

I kept checking the GPS as I ran. We were closing the gap fast. Then Koss halted. I thought he'd just paused and I went another half block before realizing he'd stopped altogether. I put on the brakes and waved Quinn over.

"He's stopped," I whispered, pointing at the GPS. "Right around the next corner."

"You think he heard us?"

I shook my head. Jack was less than a block back, but I couldn't hear his footsteps.

"He see us?"

We were all dressed for a night mission—head to foot dark colors. It took a moment, but I could make out Jack's figure, even as he stuck close to the buildings. The streetlights were too bright to hide him.

"Maybe," I whispered. I checked the GPS. Still no movement.

"Got some alleys and service lanes here," Quinn said. "I'll take— No, whoever's got the GPS should take the back way. I'll stick to the sidewalk."

I backtracked to the nearest alley. By then, Jack was close enough to jog over. I put my shoes on as I explained the plan.

As we walked, I kept checking the GPS. Koss was still just around the corner.

"In the building," Jack murmured.

I glanced over at him.

He pointed to the screen. "Not on the sidewalk. He's inside."

Jack was right. We were within a hundred feet of the transmitter now, and Koss was too far from the street to be on the sidewalk.

I looked up. From the back, it was near impossible to tell what the building housed. I just saw brick and windows. Barred windows, all too high to peek through.

"Seems empty," Jack said.

I looked at him.

"Saw a real estate sign," he said. "Construction, too."

He'd taken a closer look at the building, which is what I should have done before ducking behind it.

"Can't be certain," Jack said.

But it made sense. We'd just left a building under renovations. If Koss wanted a place to hole up, and he saw lease and construction signs, he'd slip in there.

"Do you think he made us?" I whispered.

"Presume he did. Safer."

I nodded and texted Quinn. A moment later he replied confirming the building was indeed empty and in the early stages of reconstruction.

We crept down a service lane beside the building, picking our way past bins filled with ripped-out material.

We reached the road. I checked the GPS. Koss seemed to be still in the building, but it was a little less clear now, his "dot" closer to the road. Which could mean he was hiding in an alcove or doorway.

I peered out. It was a straight, flat wall with no alcove or doorway at this end. I could see Quinn waiting by the door. I waved him in, and he disappeared.

Jack took my wrist, tilting the GPS screen so he could see it.

"Hug the wall," he said. "Go slow if you have to. Just stick right to it."

"Because he could be watching through a window."

He nodded. We headed out, me in front, Jack behind. It was about fifty feet to the door. A very long fifty feet at this rate. When I checked the screen again, Koss had moved farther the other way. Had he heard Quinn come in? Or was Quinn letting himself be heard to distract Koss? Impossible to say. I knew only that I'd feel a lot better if that GPS blip moved farther into the building. It didn't.

We were about fifteen feet from the door when I heard the faintest squeak. My brain was still processing the sound when Jack shoved me, saying, "Down!"

I heard the shot. I twisted, weapon up, in time to see a gun pointing from an open second-story window. I fired as it shot again. As we tumbled into the shelter of the entrance, Jack muttered, "Fuck!" and I thought he was referring to the situation in general, until he said it again, the word coming between gritted teeth, sharp with pain. I wheeled to see his hand pressed to his chest.

His hand to his chest. Blood staining his fingers. My heart stopped.

"In," he said, through his teeth.

"You—"

"Inside."

He reached past me with his free hand. The door opened. Quinn got us inside. He saw Jack and whispered, "Oh, hell."

I was on Jack as soon as he got through the doorway, getting him seated, peeling his jacket back and his shirt up, my fingers trembling. Above me, I could vaguely hear Quinn asking what happened, and Jack telling him to stand guard. Jack kept saying it was fine, just fine.

He'd been shot in the chest. He was not fine. He knew that. I knew that.

I finally got his shirt up enough to see the wound. It was off to the side, as far as it could go and still pass through. Still, he'd been shot in the chest.

"Small caliber," Quinn murmured at my ear and I realized he was crouching there, right beside me. "Clean track. Through and through?"

"Seems so," Jack said. "Might have nicked a rib."

"How's your breathing?" Quinn asked.

"Little short. Just impact. Missed the lungs." He inhaled and winced. "Yeah. Hurts like hell. But I can breathe."

Quinn asked another question and Jack answered, but I barely heard. They were both so calm, as if assessing the damage to a mark. I wanted to shout at them. Shake them. Jack had been *shot*. In the *chest*.

"We need—" I could barely get the words out, breath short, as if I'd taken a bullet to *my* lungs. "Doctor. Need to get him—"

"No," Jack said. "That's what Koss wants. I'm fine. Go on."

"You're not—"

"I'm fine. For now. You know that." He leaned in, hand gripping mine, voice lowering. "Nadia . . ."

I wanted to tell myself that I wasn't overreacting. That Jack's calm was just shock. But Quinn was equally calm, on his feet now, waiting to go after Koss.

I was panicking, which was what Koss was hoping for. Earlier, he'd scoffed at my relationship with Jack, how it made us weak. I was doing exactly what he expected. Freaking out at my wounded lover's side while he escaped.

"Go on," he said. "Longer you wait . . ."

I glanced around. We were in a hall. I only realized that now, which proved, maybe, that if anyone was in shock, it was me.

"Go," Jack said. "Got my gun. Hell, got two. And a knife. I'll be fine."

When I still hesitated, he said, "Koss is trapped. Barred windows. One rear exit. But he's gotta find it. You make sure he doesn't? You got him. He comes this way?" Jack lifted his gun. "I got him."

I nodded and turned to Quinn. "Can you stay with him? Please?"

"Go with her," Jack said. "I'm fine."

I would like to think that my request held more weight with Quinn, but he didn't even hesitate. He nodded and motioned for me to take backup position as he started down the hall. I took one last look at Jack. Then I followed.

CHAPTER 52

There was, as Jack said, no place for Koss to go except that back door, which he had to find first. I knew exactly where it was, and I could tell from the GPS that Koss was nowhere close.

Before I presumed anything, I asked Quinn if there was any way for Koss to "lose" the GPS transmitter. Presumably, he hadn't known he had one, but he may have figured it out by now. Quinn said no, which I guessed meant they implanted them, unbeknownst to the agents. Kind of scary, though Quinn didn't seem bothered by it.

That GPS signal meant that what could have been a long game of hide-and-seek was not. The only thing we had to do was be careful. I couldn't think of Jack. I couldn't rush. I had to plot out a trajectory that would keep Koss away from Jack, should he bolt, and keep us between Koss and the rear exit.

We also had to stay quiet. That was the harder part. Walking softly was easier indoors, on wood and old carpet, but it was still tough going. For one thing, it was dark. For another, the building construction meant trip hazards everywhere. We both had penlights but, to avoid Koss seeing the glow, we had to block the beams, so they gave off a diffuse light instead.

Koss hadn't moved since we started our trek. He was holed up. Waiting for us to drag our wounded comrade off to get medical attention.

The building was three stories, which could be a problem—the GPS only showed Koss's horizontal location. But Quinn pointed out a strength meter on the signal. When we found the stairwell and ascended to the second story, the signal decreased. Koss was on the main floor.

When we finally neared the area where Koss was hiding, we hit a snag. The building was absolutely silent. Which meant that even the scuff of a shoe was going to be heard. Taking off our shoes wouldn't help creaks and whispering fabric.

On the plus side, we were in an area where the walls still stood. So Koss was in an enclosed room. And the door to the room where he seemed to be was closed.

We stopped and conferred. The number of ways of doing this were limited to one, really, given that there was only a single entrance. We had to employ standard procedure for entering a door with an armed fugitive on the other side.

Guns out, we moved as quietly as we could to the door, each taking a side. If Koss heard us, he gave no sign of it. When we were in position, Quinn banged on the door, as hard as he could.

"Sebastian Koss?"

That's all he said. That's all he needed to say, because the noise had the desired effect. It startled Koss, and he scrambled to the left back corner of the room. Staying to the side, Quinn reached over and twisted the door handle. As expected, it was locked or otherwise barricaded.

Quinn kicked it open, one swift kick before twisting out of the way—a split-second ahead of the bullet that responded. Another followed. Completely unnecessary—Quinn and I were both plastered to the wall, out of the doorway.

"Koss?" I said. "You're trapped in there. You know you are."

Two more bullets in quick succession. The wall behind me reverberated.

"Seriously?" I said. "You're trying to shoot through the wall with a twenty-two? Word of advice, Koss? Next time? Pack a real gun."

"Ask your lover if he thinks it's real enough. He's not with you, is he?"

"No, but I'm not sobbing over his dead body either, am I? A twenty-two is for pros. People who know what they're doing. You're an amateur. And a piss-poor marksman."

Another shot, this one through the door, angled my way.

"Not even close," I said.

I expected him to fire again. He didn't, meaning he was keeping track of his ammo. Damn it.

"You know how you could shoot me?" I said. "Come on out of there."

Koss laughed. Down the hall, a floorboard creaked and I swung my gun that way just as Jack's hand waved around a corner. He moved into the hall. He'd bound his chest by ripping up his shirt into strips. His face was pale and he was moving slowly, but he was moving.

He motioned he'd stay out of the way. He wasn't here to help; just to let me know he was fine so I could relax.

"Thinking up a new strategy?" Koss said. "Hard work, isn't it. Thinking, I mean. Not your natural state. I suspect it's not your partner's, either. Another hitman, I presume?"

"How about a game?" I said.

"A game?"

"You like them. At least, you'll like this one. It's called 'give Sebastian Koss a fighting chance.' You were right earlier. I can't kill you while I have questions. Not while I know you had other victims. Their families deserve to know the truth."

"How touching." His voice dripped scorn.

"So here's the deal. You give us all the details, and we let you leave."

"Oh, I'm sure you will. I'm afraid I have to decline that offer, as would anyone whose IQ reaches triple digits."

"Let me explain how it will work. As you spill your guts, my partner and I will begin backing away from the door. We'll go down the side hall here. When you finish, we'll step into another room. You'll hear the door close. You'll hear us call to you from inside. That's when you run."

He didn't answer. He was thinking it through.

"It's not flawless," I said. "Whether you get away depends on how fast you are—and how fast we are. Clearly, I'm betting we'll be faster. And even if you escape tonight, I have every intention of hunting you down and killing you later. But I really do want that information. So I'll give you a fighting chance. The only one you'll get."

Koss stayed silent. Working through all the angles we could screw him over. Because he knew we planned to. It had to be a dangerous proposal. He'd see through anything else.

He made his demands next. He wanted us to test the doors along the side hall, and he'd tell us which to go in—presumably the one with the nosiest hinges. Also he wanted us both in the same room. Minor concessions. None would really improve his chances much.

He knew that. He just needed to make demands to feel as if he was in control.

Finally, he agreed. He'd tell us about his crimes. I'd lead the conversation while Quinn took notes. We didn't tell Koss about the note-taking. I'm sure he figured we were stupid enough to rely on our memories.

So Koss began to talk. After every "confession," Quinn and I would retreat farther down the hall. Before we started, I'd closed Koss's door partway so we wouldn't move into his line of sight. That had pissed him off—I'm sure he'd been counting on getting a better shot—and it had temporarily delayed the interrogation, but he'd recovered and kept talking.

He could have made things up. Changed names and dates and places. But I was listening for any hesitation and there was none. He was too arrogant for that. And, maybe, too desperate.

He'd killed Amy, as I knew. But she wasn't the last. She wasn't even the first. He'd been a teen when he took his first victim, just a girl, no connection to him. He raped and murdered her, and he got away with it. In the next three decades, he'd killed six more girls, including Amy.

He would go years between them, pacing himself and plotting each one meticulously—no more partners after the failed experiment with Drew Aldrich. He constructed his entire life around those murders, building his reputation as a lawyer and an activist and joining the Contrapasso Fellowship, all to conceal his crimes and teach himself how to avoid detection. Or so he said. I suspect part of it was pure ego. He got off on playing the role, laughing behind everyone's back, feeling superior.

By the time he finished his story, we were at the adjoining hall.

"Now, Ms. Stafford," he called, before Quinn and I started down it. "I've conveyed my crimes, and we'll be parting soon, but before we do, I'd like you to give some serious thought to your plan. Do you really want to tell the world what I am?"

"Absolutely."

"Really? Think about it. You know my reputation. You know what I've done for victims' rights, a subject which seems very important to you. Do you want the world knowing that the man who made those inroads was actually a killer? What impact would that have? Not a positive one, I'm sure."

"True. There will be fallout. But none of the advances you lobbied for will be reversed simply because you're exactly the kind of monster they were meant to thwart. In the end, you may have even done one last great service for victims' rights. You are living proof that not all monsters appear monstrous. That decent-seeming people can be as dangerous as any thug lurking in a dark alley. That's an important message, don't you think?"

He only laughed. "It's a pointless one. Think on it some more, Ms. Stafford. And think on this too: no one will reward you for unmasking me. No one wants to see a hero fall. The families of those girls don't need to know who killed them. Now, let's finish this."

Quinn and I did exactly as promised. We retreated into the office Koss had selected. We closed the door. Koss heard it shut and asked us both to recite the first few lines of our respective national anthems, just so he could be sure our voices sounded suitably distant and muffled.

Then we heard his feet pounding and the door of his room fly open. We heard him skid into the hall, sliding on something in his haste. I could picture him there, eyes wild, heart thumping, gun raised, sprinting down the hall, knowing we'd burst out of our room and come after him.

Except we didn't. We simply stepped out and—

One shot. Koss gasped in pain and shock. A second shot. A thud as he hit the floor.

I broke into a jog and wheeled around the end of the hall to see Jack kicking Koss's gun out of the way.

"Huh," I said as I walked over to Koss. "Seems you forgot someone."

I crouched beside Koss. His face was pale with shock. Blood gushed from his thigh. The femoral artery, I was guessing. More blood seeped out around him from a shot to the back. Neither was immediately fatal.

It took a moment before he realized that. He wasn't dead. He'd been shot by a professional killer, at point-blank range, and he was still alive. Hope flashed in his eyes. Then they narrowed, as his brain whirred. We'd kept him alive. We still wanted something. He could use that.

"Quinn?" Jack said. "Could you guard the front?"

Quinn nodded and headed off. I waited until he was gone. Then I flipped Koss onto his back. He let out a squeal of agony as fresh blood surged.

"Hurts, huh?" I said.

I crouched beside him, staying out of the blood.

"The crime-scene report from Amy's murder said she was found on her back," I said. "Just like this. Is that right?"

Koss's eyes rolled with pain. "I need—"

"You *need* to answer the question. Was she like this?"

"Yes. Is that what you want? An apology?" He gritted his teeth. "Fine. I'm very, very sorry—"

"Don't bother. I was just checking." I put my hands around his neck. "This is how you did it. right?"

His eyes widened then, panic sparking. "N-no."

He tried to buck me off, but he'd lost too much blood, was too far into shock, too far into death, his body shutting down.

"This is how you killed her," I said. "And this is how you'll die."

CHAPTER 53

We spent Friday in Chicago. Not much choice there. Jack was in no shape to leave, and we had the mess with Contrapasso to clean up.

The latter wasn't nearly as big a deal as I'd feared. They'd screwed us over, and we'd retaliated. They were shockingly fair about the whole thing. We hadn't injured their people. We hadn't caused the car accident. They might have wanted to interrogate Koss, but they'd lost that right when they double-crossed us.

They even offered medical care for Jack. He refused. He had someone in the area so that's where we took him. The bullet hadn't done any serious damage. One nicked rib and torn tissue. He wouldn't be work-ready for weeks, but he'd be fine.

As for Koss, we let Contrapasso handle that—both the immediate cleanup and the long-term repercussions. They'd make sure the families of his victims got closure and that their daughters' remains would be found wherever possible. Investigations would be re-opened. Koss would be fingered as the culprit, apparently having left his confession and fled for parts unknown.

Would those investigations find him guilty? Or would people say his enemies framed and murdered him? Impossible to predict. He was dead. The families would know their daughters' fates. That was all that mattered to me.

We left Chicago Saturday morning. Though Emma and Owen didn't expect me back for the weekend, Jack knew it was best if I missed as little of it as possible. I'd drive us while he rested. Or that was my plan, though I knew sedation might be required to actually get him to rest.

Quinn was still with us, dealing with Contrapasso. What happened hadn't soured him on them—or vice versa. If anything, his loyalty to his comrades seemed to solidify their initial interest and they'd moved from flirting to making plans for a first date.

Contrapasso was also interested in Jack and me. While I knew Jack was a "hell no," he wasn't actually saying that. They knew more about us than we liked. It behooved us to play coy, rather than reject their overtures outright.

When Quinn came to see me before we left, it was the first time we'd talked since Koss's death. He helped me carry the bags to the rental car while Jack rested in the hotel room.

"I want to thank you again," I said. "For coming back."

"I shouldn't have left," he said as we got on the elevator. "Jack was right. I lost my temper. I said things I didn't mean. I stormed out when you needed me."

"You shouldn't have found out like that. I should have told you."

He leaned against the elevator wall. "Nah. I only would have stormed off sooner." He shifted my duffel, looking uncomfortable. "It was over. You'd made that clear. You had a right to move on. I just . . ." He exhaled. "If it was anyone else, I'd still have been hurt, but Jack . . . I don't get it, Nadia. I really don't."

The elevator stopped in the parking garage. We got off and headed for the car.

He continued, "I think he made his move when you were vulnerable."

"Quinn . . ."

"I'm not blaming him. I've known he was interested in you since the day we met. But you weren't interested back, so he kept his distance. He didn't interfere with you and me. I respect that. We broke up, though, and he brought you Aldrich, and you were grateful and he misread that. You care about him. So when he made a move and you were in a bad place—with our breakup and this Aldrich business—you gave in."

"It wasn't—"

"It was." His voice was firm. "You just don't see it. You will. You're making a mistake, and you're going to realize that, and I just hope he doesn't hurt you too much in the meantime."

Quinn unlocked the trunk. I looked over at him, and I knew there was nothing I could say. He'd come up with an explanation he could live with, an explanation he needed. I had to let him have that.

When he bent to put the duffel bag in, I kissed his cheek. "I'll be fine."

He put one arm around me, a quick squeeze. "I know you will."

CHAPTER 54

I stood on the edge of a small bluff overlooking my lake. Ice crept in along the edges, the shore blanketed with a foot of pristine early December snow. I turned at the soft crunch of snow underfoot.

"This one?" Jack said.

"I think so." I hunkered down for a look through the thin line of trees. "We'd need to build back from the bluff, though, for stability. It might be too far to see the lake from the porch."

"Second story."

I glanced over at him.

"Add another story. Bedroom loft. Balcony."

When I hesitated, he walked over beside me and looked out as I straightened. "Nice view. Wouldn't want to lose it."

I smiled and shook my head. When I'd first considered building a separate cabin for myself, I'd envisioned a tiny cottage, little more than a bedroom and bath. The plan kept growing, though, at Jack's prodding. We hadn't even decided on a site yet, and we were already up to a full-blown cottage, complete with small kitchen, sitting area, and office. Now this.

Jack squinted into the rising sun. "Yeah. Don't want

to lose the view. Full-length balcony. Bedroom loft. Fireplace."

"We're already putting a fireplace on the first floor."

"Have two." When I opened my mouth to protest, he said, "I'm paying."

"Part. A *small* part. I'm not going to let you—" I stopped. "No, I'm not falling for that again. Every time you add something and I argue, you bring up who's paying because you know it'll distract me and the next thing I know, there's two fireplaces on the plan."

" 'Cause I'm paying."

I made a face at him. He pulled me over for distraction technique number two, one that invariably worked. Thirty seconds later, I was up against a tree kissing him, cabin construction forgotten, my hands in his hair, his under my jacket and under my shirt, fingers deliciously cool against my skin. His hands moved up my back, unhooking my bra, then sliding around to cup my breasts—

"Stop!" a voice shouted.

I jumped about a foot. Jack only shook his head as the voice came again. "Don't go near the ice!"

I nudged Jack away and glanced down the bluff to see a family of guests out by the lake. They caught sight of me. I waved and called down to second the warning against the kids getting too close to the ice. Jack sighed.

"I swear," I said. "We could be in the high Arctic and still get interrupted. In this case, though, it's probably for the best. You have a flight to catch. You wanted to leave at noon and it's . . ." I checked my watch. "Ten past."

"Yeah."

He looked out over the lake, and I could see the wistfulness in his eyes. He didn't want to go. It would pass, though, once he got out and in the field again. Then he'd return and he'd be glad to be back, and we'd have our time together.

It'd been almost two months since Chicago. I will admit, in the beginning, I'd been worried Jack might realize this life wasn't for him. That I'd wake one morning and he'd have left a note. *Emergency job,* it'd say, but I'd know the truth—that he was restless and there wasn't enough here to hold him.

That didn't happen. Once he'd recuperated, he'd taken off a couple of times. Not on jobs, but managing his business. Easing out of it, too. He wouldn't retire. Not for years. But he was cutting ties, telling lesser clients that he wouldn't be working for them much longer. Each time he left, it was with reluctance. And each time he returned . . . I smiled to myself. Returning was good.

As for the rest, the Contrapasso Fellowship was still trying to woo us, through both Evelyn and Quinn. While I wasn't interested now, could I foresee a day when I might be? Maybe. If I ever was, Jack said he'd come along. Not because he'd developed a sudden interest in justice, but for me.

I wasn't giving up the life. Finding Amy's killer hadn't "fixed" me. There was, I'd realized, nothing to fix. This was who I was. It wouldn't change. It didn't need to.

Quinn and I still talked. It wasn't what it used to be. I didn't know if it ever would be, but we talked, and that was something.

"I want to be back by Christmas," Jack said.

"I know." I also knew he couldn't guarantee that with an overseas job, but I played along.

"Where's Scout?" Jack asked, looking around.

"Right there."

I pointed about twenty feet off, where she was digging out the snow around a fallen log. Jack squinted before seeing her.

"Remember what you said when you bought her for me?" I said. "That a white dog would be easier to spot? And I said, 'Not in the snow.' Case in point."

"Huh." He peered over at her as she started toward us, a black nose and dark eyes bounding through the snow. "Could get another shepherd. Black-and-tan. That'd help."

"How?"

"They'd stick together. Like Evelyn's dogs. Always be able to find them. Scout in the summer. The black-and-tan in the winter."

I laughed. "I am not getting a second dog so I don't temporarily misplace the first."

"Get one for Scout then. Dogs are pack animals. Not easy for her. Having me here. Taking your attention. She gets jealous."

I whistled. Scout bounded over and leaped on Jack, nearly knocking him down, as if she hadn't seen him in days, dancing and nudging his hand as we walked.

"Yes, she obviously *hates* you."

"She's good at hiding it. Gonna get you another dog. Safer with two. Never know what's on those roads. Bear. Coyotes. Hitmen."

I gave him a look. "If you want another dog, fine. I will buy one—for you."

He glanced over, blinking in surprise. "No. Didn't mean—"

"Yep. I am totally buying you a dog. Did you hear that, Scout? Jack's getting a dog, and you're getting a friend."

He protested, of course. It didn't matter. I might act like I was kidding, but I now knew what I was getting him for Christmas. He'd never admit to wanting one—no more than I did before he bought Scout—but I knew it would please him. He'd had a dog once, when he was a boy, and getting one now would be a symbol of a new home. Of a life where he could have a pet again.

Jack was already looking to buy a car. I could say it was because he was uncomfortable borrowing my pickup to run errands, but I know it's a step he wants to take, like helping with the cabin. I've never been big on personal possessions, but I can't imagine living with none. That was changing and he seemed glad of it.

For this trip, he'd picked up a rental in Peterborough last night, which he'd drive to the Toronto airport. I'd offered to take him, but he insisted—it was a Saturday and the lodge was filled to capacity.

"I'll be back for Christmas," he said again as we reached the rental, his bag already in the backseat. "I mean it. If the job takes longer? I'll come back anyway. Few days off won't hurt."

I started to protest, but he stopped me. "Know you don't really celebrate. But I want to be here."

"Okay."

He paused, as if he'd expected me to argue.

"If you can be here, I'd love that," I said.

I leaned in and gave him one last kiss. He climbed into the car. I stood there, watching him drive off, knowing he'd be back as soon as he could. When he was gone, I whistled for Scout and headed back to the lodge.

Also by #1 *New York Times* bestselling author
Kelley Armstrong

The Otherworld Series

THIRTEEN

978-0-14-219674-8

THE HUNTER AND THE HUNTED

TWO STORIES OF THE OTHERWORLD

eSpecial

978-1-101-59342-4
**Available exclusively
for your e-reader from
Dutton**

SPELL BOUND

978-0-452-29799-9

WAKING THE WITCH

978-0-452-29722-7

BITTEN

978-0-452-29664-0

STOLEN

978-0-452-29666-4

www.kelleyarmstrong.com

Also by #1 *New York Times* bestselling author
Kelley Armstrong

Introducing Cainsville

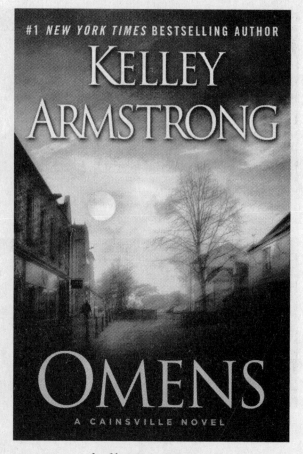

www.kelleyarmstrong.com